A Beast Cannot Feign

Sci-fi your mother won't show you

ISBN 9798361686995

Feelustrate is a trademark of
Dr. Insensitive Jerk,
but you can use it with no charge.
For details, go to feelustrate.org.

Other inquiries to

InsensitiveJerk@GaiasWasp.com

About the Author

Dr. Insensitive Jerk was created in a tragic artificial-insemination accident, when a petri dish was contaminated with DNA from a lab tech's Doberman pinscher.

His parents loved him anyway. They took a job managing an animal shelter where they could supply him with plenty of stray kittens, so he grew healthy and strong.

Sadly, the young Insensitive Jerk lacked the intellect required to grasp abstract concepts like *sustainability* or *tolerance*. Nonetheless, with training, he could learn any trick, except for the cursed leash-wrapped-around-a-tree conundrum. Many doors opened for him, when he whined. In time, he found a woman who enjoyed throwing sticks but didn't care for the missionary position.

Mr. Jerk was a natural Libertarian, being inclined to bite anyone in uniform, so he was drawn to the field of economics. Keynesian math baffled him, but he persisted doggedly, until one day, he received a PhD from University of Chicago professors who knew they shouldn't do it, but just couldn't resist his soulful brown eyes.

Since then, Dr. Jerk's scientific publications have been cited more than a thousand times by unwary scholars. Now he has retired from academia to pursue his real passion, cats.

Introduction

Stop reading now. Seriously; this story is reprehensible.

Author's Preface

Relax; this ain't Hollywood.

Here are a few things you *won't* find in this story:

- An abusive father
- The hero helpless in the hands of the villain
- Torture
- Anything made by Gillette
- A woman beating up a man, unless he lets her
- Tragedy because Mommy looked away for a minute
- Zombies

Feelustration

In the future, most novels will be read on color screens, where they can include beautiful color pictures.

Sadly, pictures only work in graphic novels with low word counts. For some reason, illustrations don't add much to a full-length story, so they never caught on.

Dr. Jerk figured out why. (Hint: The pictures are redundant.) The solution is simple, yet ridiculous: The pictures must *not* depict events in the text. It's the dumbest breakthrough in the history of storytelling. To understand how stupid it is, visit feelustrate.org.

How to read this story

- Play your favorite evocative music on low volume. It doesn't matter *what* the music evokes; any emotional priming will work, even Neal Diamond.

- Sip a cocktail. This is *not* the time for sobriety.

- You are seeing something new.

The Cast

The Humans

Tom Pine: Our hero, taught the art of seduction by his mother. Hopes to meet a woman to do it with.

Frank Drummer: Grew up across the street from Tom. First astronomer to spot the approaching aliens. Voted *Most likely to be strangled on a crowded sidewalk by a man no jury would convict.*

Sophie Flint: Tom's bitch next door.

Dominick Tork: Found his calling in government and wrestling.

Mirror: Lonely in his empty head, also president of the United States.

Catherine "Kitty" Siphon: President Mirror's best friend and commerce secretary who is not averse to taking over the world.

Agent Sheila Bear: Blonde amazon who commands Kitty Siphon's Secret Service detail. Believes she was built to protect those entrusted to her care, and shoot the others.

The Technology

Cherub Sword: The awful secret that harnesses the fifth force of nature into a rocket engine, doomsday weapon, or space heater.

Forbidden Fruit: Drug that grants self-knowledge by stifling your mental censor. Common side effects include divorce, suicide.

Burning Bush: The beautiful secret that changes your mind.

The Unexpected Finger: Cruise ship. 80 years old with 96 trillion miles, but just one owner, and he was an old guy who only drove it to Earth.

The Aliens

Lucifa "Luci" Dark: The alien ambassador to Humans. Worries her daughter is evil and her sons destroyed her civilization.

Buffalo "Buff" Dawn: Engineer who designed the *Unexpected Finger* and managed its trip to Earth, where he appeared on TV with a giant fake penis.

Gabriel Tide: Rich guy who owns the *Unexpected Finger* and masterminded the exodus to Earth. Chicks flock to him, probably because of his beautiful gray hair.

Natalie Tide: Gabriel's woman, who *really* wants him to succeed.

If you won't attack the enemy
you are not a fit ally
or a fit enemy

An almost perfect job interview

"You can't sue me." Tom Pine stretched luxuriously and scratched his chest. "I love hiring women."

The job applicant was 30 years old, and she would have been pretty with fewer tattoos. She perched stiffly on Tom's three-legged guest stool. "Why would I sue you?"

Tom lounged in his high-back leather chair. "*Why* would you sue me. What's the most tempting reason you can imagine? No, don't answer that; it'll be more fun as a surprise."

Tom Pine stood 5'3", and he had no chin. You'd say he was handsome, if you were his mother. He flipped through the applicant's resume, then tossed it on his desk and rested his feet on it. "Would you like to know why I gave you this interview?"

The job applicant looked nervously around Tom's tiny office. "Do you mind if I open the door?"

"Help yourself." He waved expansively. "You got this interview because you worked for the diversity office at U.C. Berkeley, and you ran *their* sexual harassment workshops. Did I say that right? Did you actually teach sexual harassment sensitivity to *Berkeley diversity officers?*"

"Yes," she said cautiously.

Tom beamed. "You are *perfect* for me."

She brightened. "Your ad said you need a sensitivity coordinator. Do you want me to train your employees?"

"I certainly do. When I worked for a big corporation, I got sexual harassment and sensitivity training three times a year. The classes lasted all day, and after the first hour, I always found myself thinking, *Someday, I hope I can hire these trainers, so they will be my employees.*"

The job applicant stood up and opened Tom's office door. She peered out into the empty hallway. "I feel a little uncomfortable being alone with you. No offense, but I'd like a woman to be present."

"No."

"No?" She blinked. "What do you mean, *no?*"

Tom snorted a laugh, then he pressed a button on his desk. "Sophie?"

In Tom's childhood, his girl next door and his first kiss had been Sophie Flint. "Yes, Tom," she answered on the crackly intercom. "What do you want now?"

"She just asked me what *no* means."

Even on the cheap intercom speaker, Sophie's sigh was clearly audible. "Are you enjoying this moment?"

"Oh, yes." Tom opened his bottom drawer and pulled out a bottle of Knob Creek Single Barrel Reserve. "I want to do this right."

"Have fun." The intercom clicked.

The job applicant started to speak but paused when Tom showed her his palm. "Don't talk." He poured himself a shot of bourbon, then waved the bottle. "Want some? It's expensive."

"That would be inappropriate."

"Ah, perfect." Tom leaned back comfortably, rested his feet on the sexual-harassment trainer's resume, and sipped the excellent bourbon. "Tell me," he enunciated slowly, savoring the moment. "Which part of *no* did you not understand?"

She smiled thinly. "Very funny. I want a woman present."

"Nope." Tom finished off his bourbon. "Ah. Life is good."

She looked at him curiously. "Do you imagine you will still work here next month?"

"I imagine I own this business," Tom answered amiably. "I imagine I'll run it how I please, and if you don't like it, then you shouldn't take my money. I imagine you'll try to sue me, and I imagine you'll be found dead the next morning."

She recoiled. "What the fuck?"

Tom scratched his chest. "I own this company. If you can accept that, you and I could have so much fun with each other."

Her mouth moved for a while, but no words emerged. In the silence, they heard distant bullhorns and chanting protesters.

"I really do need a sensitivity trainer," Tom added. "Not full time, of course, since that would be ridiculous, but a few of my female employees need help. They are adapting poorly, and I don't want to lose them, so I want you to give them two days of mandatory de-sensitivity training. Whatever you taught in your Berkeley sensitivity class, just do the opposite."

"You made a mistake," she gritted. "I will *never* work for a predator."

Tom chuckled. "Nice. Before you run home to blog about me, you should probably know I don't own this building; I just rent some offices here. *My* building is down the street. It's the one surrounded by protesters."

After a moment of blank incomprehension, her eyes widened.

"I do so love hiring." Tom Pine stretched luxuriously and scratched his chest. "I make robotic sentry telescopes. Have you figured out who I make them for?"

The hand of friendship

Like   Share   Comment

Comments. Please respect the <u>forum rules</u>.

Scrapbook22 Six hours ago
>   This one is subtle, but I like it.

Pokemom Six hours ago
>   What's it about?

LawFareForU Five hours ago
>   It's the aliens. See the geometric shapes across the top? Those are the five symbols the aliens have tattooed on their cheeks.

Moby Duck Five hours ago
>   A mouse doesn't see the retractable claws, until it does. Just like the aliens are trying to lull us into a deadly complacency.

S. Quiblee Five hours ago
>   The aliens are psychotic killers. They go berserk and shoot people for NO REASON. Does anybody believe all those little girls just started disappearing now by coincidence?

Pokemom Four hours ago
>   Nobody believes the missing girls are a coincidence. I hate to think what might be happening to those children, and the aliens are obviously involved.

Same moment
Different negotiation
Shenandoah National Park

The U.S. government's clown sat behind a transparent barrier. The sheet of unbreakable Lexan reached to the ceiling but not quite to the floor, so the clown could pass small objects under, to the other side.

At least, the clown *hoped* the Lexan barrier was unbreakable. The one time it was tested, it had held.

The clown wore a business suit, because he was not the type of clown you'd see at a spoiled child's birthday party. He was the type of clown you'd see at a rodeo. The unbreakable Lexan barrier shielded him from the alien. Her name was Luci, and she dressed in clingy red spandex, because she was not the type of alien you'd see on a distant planet. She was the type of alien you'd see on a stripper pole.

That's a lie. Luci didn't really look like a stripper, because she was barefoot, and a barefoot stripper would be wrong. She wore red spandex because it matched her spaceship, and to show she was unarmed, so she wouldn't start a war by accident.

Four months ago, Luci and her friends had answered the, *"Is there life beyond Earth"* question by decelerating into orbit and ignoring the Humans' frantic attempts to communicate.

Humans had *really* wanted to communicate with their first alien visitors, because this was the Big Moment: *First Contact With Alien Life,* and also because the arriving mothership looked like a trumpet.

The mothership didn't look like the short, twisty kind of trumpet you might see in a marching band. The mothership looked like the other kind of trumpet, the long, straight kind with a bell on one end and a mouthpiece on the other, the kind that might be sounded to announce the arrival of a king.

The alien mothership's trumpet shape was its third-most-interesting feature. Its second-most-interesting feature was its exhaust. Interestingly, the trumpet's exhaust sprayed out the wrong end, through the mouthpiece. More interestingly, the trumpet exhausted nothing but energy, in the form of gamma-ray photons. Technically, the trumpet was powered by a *photon rocket.*

A *photon rocket* is a concept analyzed by every physics student because it's so interesting, but it's not actually used by Humans, because it's too interesting.

Paradoxically, a photon rocket achieves the best conceivable fuel efficiency by achieving the *worst* conceivable energy efficiency. For example, the alien trumpet massed about 3,000 tons, the same as a U.S. Coast Guard cutter. The Coast Guard cutter and the trumpet could both accelerate at one-third gravity, but the trumpet used more power.

Specifically, a 3,000-ton Coast Guard cutter needs 30 megawatts to power away from the dock at one-third gravity. To match that acceleration, the 3,000-ton trumpet had to exhaust 3.6×10^9 megawatts. The trumpet's energy efficiency worked out to 0.0000005%, which a giggling eunuch had translated into 0.86 megatons of TNT per second blowing out the mouthpiece.

That giggling eunuch was Frank Drummer. He didn't actually giggle very often, but he did build a gamma-ray telescope that detected the trumpet's exhaust, eight months before it arrived. Frank had been the first to realize aliens were coming, though he'd been only the second to detect them.

The trumpet's wacky exhaust had actually been spotted two days earlier by a NASA observatory, which had prudently interpreted the signal as an error that could be corrected with more funding.

When the approaching trumpet and its wacky exhaust were revealed to the world, all of the Earth's tech eunuchs had risen up as one. In a clarion voice of perfect unity, the eunuchs proclaimed, *We told you we need a better space program.*

All the governments of Earth had replied as one. In a clarion voice of perfect unity, the governments proclaimed, *We must raise taxes.*

Fortunately, the approaching trumpet had not aimed its wacky exhaust at our atmosphere. The trumpet's engines were built for a long journey, so they could fire continuously as the Earth rotated beneath them, eventually traversing the globe. The gamma-ray exhaust would knock electrons out of the air like billiard balls, leaving a wacky concentration of protons, which would create a wacky electric field. The field strength had actually been calculated by tech eunuchs, with reverence and barely-concealed glee.

After an exhilarating debate, the grinning eunuchs had eventually decided the electromagnetic pulse would be wacky enough to convert common electrical devices into poorly-designed, marginally-effective incendiary bombs, thus removing most of the electronics and wooden structures from a geographic area they expressed in units of, *Australias.*

Tech eunuchs are semi-autistic geeks. They are employed by every Earth government, because only eunuchs can be trusted to witness the intimate details of political power and not grab a handful. Technically, the tech eunuchs still have their balls, but they don't get to use them much.

Even the eunuchs were forced to concede the trumpet's exhaust was only its second-most-interesting feature. The approaching trumpet's *most* interesting feature was its nameplate, which had been photographed by a solar telescope hastily modified and launched to intercept the incoming mothership and see just exactly what was coming to visit.

The solar telescope didn't really *intercept* the incoming mother-ship, but it did pass within 40 miles. That was close enough to photograph the 3,000-ton, 700-foot trumpet and to make out a nameplate that wasn't nearly alien enough. The image was fuzzy, and pixelated from the extreme zoom, but the six-foot characters clearly spelled out the Old-Hebrew name, *Gabriel,* the archangel who would blow his trumpet to announce Judgment Day.

The photo had been relayed to the Vatican. After a brief but fervent prayer, Pope Josephine had raised the Apocalypse Alert System to *Condition Yellow,* which meant: *It's time to catch up on tithing.*

Fifty-three days later, the inevitably-named *Gabriel's Trumpet* arrived and circled the Earth for a month, ominously silent. Occasionally, its hatches opened to spit out small boats. The little spaceships zipped about, apparently joyriding, or sometimes they popped down to the surface, always leaving again before the government helicopters arrived.

The only hints of alien communication were a constant, 106-Hz radio hum and a steady train of static bursts, 640 bursts per second. Both signals turned out to be mere noise, inadvertently broadcast by the trumpet's hefty but crude electric generator.

The radio noise was analyzed by a eunuch, who triumphantly proclaimed *Gabriel's Trumpet* was wired with AC electricity like our homes, except higher frequency, 106 Hz instead of our 60 Hz. His conclusion was ridiculed by other eunuchs who sprang into action to point out European electricity is only *50 Hz*. Then they danced a little victory jig.

The eunuchs had a great time, but everyone else worried about the aliens' month-long silence, with the notable exception of Christians. The Christians didn't fret, because they were accustomed to their calls going unanswered, and they were enjoying the biggest religious revival since the great meteor storm of 1833. Jews waited nervously, which was not a visible change.

Then, at last, the alien Luci had ended their silence and offered us a glimpse of the divine.

Her full name was Lucifa Dark. In the First-Contact TV broadcast, beamed from *Gabriel's Trumpet* and watched by the entire Earth, she introduced Jesus the Savior in His naked glory. Every Human heart skipped a beat at the pair's physical beauty and Luci's horns, which nicely complimented her fangs. Hearts skipped another beat when Luci proclaimed herself the right foot of Christ, come in fulfillment of prophecy to destroy the Earth. This gave Christians mixed feelings.

It turned out Luci was joking. Her fangs were plastic, and her horns were mounted on a piece of wire. The beautifully-muscular and alarmingly well-endowed *Jesus* was actually an alien engineer wearing a huge rubber penis. It was the best First Contact ever, but some people have no sense of humor.

Christians were infuriated, in the polite, Christian manner, but they couldn't stay mad, because Christians love to forgive assholes, and besides, the aliens obviously *liked* Christians, but mostly because the aliens revealed their world was Christian.

The aliens knew Christ? This bombshell had prompted an orgy of Christian celebration, but only a figurative orgy, obviously. When Jews heard the news, they scuffed their feet and looked disgruntled. Muslims set off a few desultory bombs. Hindus quietly pulled into the Macdonald's drive-thru, and nobody could figure out what the Buddhists thought.

Sadly, alien Christianity proved to be a disappointingly weak faith-builder, because the aliens proved to be only slightly alien, with just a few hundred non-Human genes. They also turned out to be our *second* alien visitors.

In 1755, a shipload of Christian colonists had been rescued by Earth's *first* alien visitor, a creature they believed to be God himself. The possibly-divine creature had plucked them from their doomed ship as it sank off the coast of Portugal. The sinking shipload of Christian colonists had prepared for a long voyage to the New World, but they hadn't prepared for 16 light years.

266 years later, their children had returned, somewhat changed.

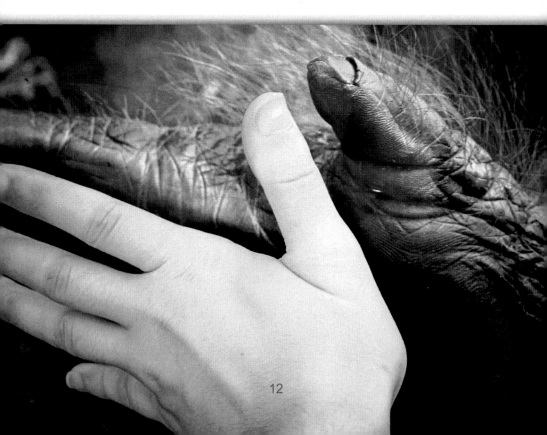

Their mothership wasn't actually named, *Gabriel's Trumpet*. It was named, *Unexpected Finger*, and it was owned by a guy named Gabriel. Naturally, Gabriel had painted his name on his trumpet-shaped spaceship in Old Hebrew to make First Contact funny. He refused to communicate for a full month to make it even funnier, and to give Luci time to study her Earth-born relatives, and because all of his radios had been fried.

Now, five months after the Arrival, and four months after First Contact, the aliens wanted room to build a colony. That's why Luci sat in this shed behind a clear Lexan barrier, negotiating a real estate purchase with a clown whose job was to stop her without admitting he was trying to stop her.

With startling unity, every Human government with at least 372,000 citizens had unanimously agreed the alien bastards must not be allowed to colonize Earth. The lone exception was the town council of Caucaia, Brazil (population: 371,952) which had voted 7-5 to invite Luci over anytime to discuss her colonization needs privately.

13

The clown adjusted his tie and glanced at his exit, a flimsy metal door that opened out to the forest. This had been the alien's idea. For reasons that eventually became all too obvious, Luci had insisted this negotiation be staged in a 6x10-foot utility shed in the Shenandoah Forest, conveniently close to Washington, D.C., but free from innocent bystanders, with a single Human representative instead of a proper diplomatic team.

Luci's half of the shed had its own exit, but it was blocked by her spaceship so she couldn't escape.

Seven months ago, no Human had seen a proper spaceship. Luci's spaceship was a small one, only a 9-seater, but it was obviously a *real* spaceship, complete with stubby wings, swiveling engine pods and glittering lipstick-red paint.

Luci was here to buy real estate for a colony. The clown's job was to stop her without admitting he was trying to stop her, because if she realized he was deceiving her, she might try to break through that Lexan to kill him.

The Lexan barrier had already saved the clown's predecessor, when he learned of an alien drug and responded poorly. The drug is called, *forbidden fruit,* and it stifles your mental censor. When you bite the forbidden fruit, you are forced to look inside your own

mind and see what you really think.

14

When Luci described the forbidden fruit to the previous clown, he had warned her she couldn't sell such a dangerous drug without FDA approval. That was when she went berserk.

Fortunately, the Lexan barrier held, giving the clown time to flee before the crazed alien escaped her prison by shoving the whole shed away from her spaceship and slipping through the gap. She ran about searching for the clown, but by then, he was half a mile distant on the back of a speeding motorcycle, having a lot less fun than the laughing soldier he clung to.

Later, the incident had been recreated by the eunuchs. They measured the force Luci had exerted to escape the shed, then compared it to video surveillance of her lifting various objects. The results were clear: Luci's muscles were only human, but she had pushed the shed sideways with the hysterical strength of a panicked mommy saving her child. After the incident, biomechanical analysis of Luci's walking gait showed her muscles were sore for a week.

Luci had gone berserk because she felt the clown was holding her drug profits for ransom, and she *really* couldn't pay ransom. The aliens had long-ago abolished ransom in their culture by going berserk and killing anyone who demanded it. This rule was enforced by a minor brain adjustment, a morsel of insanity, which the aliens now offered to the Humans.

Unfortunately, if your brain can't pay ransom, you can't pay income tax or ask for a building permit. The aliens called it, *ungovernable*. Human governments called it, *the end of the world*.

Luci's mission was to buy land to colonize Earth, recruit Humans, and make them ungovernable. The clown's mission was to obstruct her. Today, his first goal was a head count: to estimate the number of aliens in the mothership. As always, the clown approached his goal indirectly. "Your telescopes are crude," he remarked from behind the Lexan barrier. "Your clothing shows clear signs of hand sewing, your metal alloys are weak by our standards, and you lack the electronic computers we've had for 60 years."

Luci frowned and looked down at her red shorts. They were the type of shorts you shop for by searching the term, *booty*.

The clown flicked a bit of lint off his $9,000, hand-stitched Italian mohair suit. "The primitive state of your technology puzzles us, because your ancestors were rescued from Earth in 1755. Thus, your ancestors possessed all of our knowledge, *plus* everything they learned from their alien rescuer. Yet, despite this advantage, your technology lags behind ours. It seems your progress was hindered by your rigid, anti-cooperation philosophy."

"My *anti-cooperation* philosophy? Lucky for me it's not an *anti-slander* philosophy, or I might hurt myself trying to break through this wall." Luci tapped the Lexan, then she resumed examining the seams on her red spandex shorts. "To answer the less-idiotic part of your statement, each time we birth a child, we roll the dice to create another Pythagoras."

"She's lecturing us about population, just like I predicted." In the distant *Lens,* the U.S. government command center buried 600 feet beneath an extraordinarily uninteresting Maryland chicken farm, Secretary of Commerce Kitty Siphon pointed to her alpha eunuch. "The bitch obviously expects us to know the name, *Pythagoras.* Look him up and make sure he was born before 1755, when her ancestors supposedly left Earth."

Kitty's alpha eunuch considered his situation. Like most eunuchs, he had trouble predicting human behavior, so he had carefully compiled a list of concepts that provoked Normals to attack him. Unfortunately, that list included every sensible response to Kitty Siphon's stupid question. The alpha eunuch evaluated his options, then he silently surfed over to Amazon and shopped for a new Klingon bat'leth while he pretended to check whether the ancient Greek mathematician Pythagoras was born after 1755.

You have to know these tricks to be the alpha.

"In just one of your cities, you birth more minds than our entire world. Your swarm is so vast, you can pursue 10,000 specialties, and each specialty can support 1,000 companies. After all this time, you should be further ahead of us." Luci's perky alien nose wrinkled. "You're a disappointment, even for wasps."

The aliens referred to their Earth cousins as, *wasps,* which was not a compliment.

In the shed, behind the Lexan wall that protected him from the alien, the clown smiled patronizingly. "Luci, you had almost *300 years* and an empty world to fill. Your population must be far too large to excuse your poor technology."

"Seriously? This is your strategy?" Luci looked amused. "You're trying to goad me by insulting my *technical skills?* Didn't you notice I have tits?"

In the *Lens,* the alpha eunuch broadcast an emergency message on the private eunuch text channel. "Do *not* comment on that!"

"The bitch is on to us." Kitty Siphon, the U.S. secretary of commerce, thumped her desk. "She won't tell us how many people they brought. That's good news, because it means they didn't bring many."

"That doesn't *necessarily* follow, Madam Secretary," the alpha eunuch said carefully. "Their mothership displaces 8,000 cubic meters, and we've seen 189 aliens, which works out to only 2 aliens per 100 cubic meters. Our cruise ships carry 3 passengers per 100 cubic meters, military ships carry 5, and 19th-century sailing warships carried *20,* which implies 10 times more aliens than we've seen."

"Don't be ridiculous," Kitty snapped. "Only an idiot would pretend her mob is small. Let's move on to the mind-reading theory."

Today's primary goal was to estimate the alien population, but Kitty also wanted to rule out telepathy. When Kitty said, *telepathy,* the *Lens* staffers had smirked, because the aliens were almost Human, augmented by only a few hundred extra genes. The staffers smirked at the idea of telepathy, because they didn't know what Kitty knew.

Kitty knew the mostly-human aliens had thumb-sized metal implants in their brains, screwed to the inside of their skulls. Kitty felt certain the skull implants were suicide bombs. She knew this because even a perfectly-disguised bomb is easy to recognize under the right circumstances.

Kitty was certain the alien skull implants were bombs, but she wasn't certain they were *only* bombs. Ominously, no one had seen an alien-built radio. Even their First-Contact broadcast had been beamed through a Human satellite, using a transmitter they bought from a guy in Fresno.

The guy in Fresno had a week's warning of First Contact, and had tried to exploit his inside knowledge by recounting his *psychic premonitions* to the hot girl in the next cubicle. He actually whispered the exact time and frequency of the alien broadcast into the hot girl's ear, two days in advance. But that didn't work, so he had to start lifting weights.

The aliens' radio silence had been eagerly seized on by the U.S. president, who believed the aliens didn't *need* radio, because they were telepathic. President Mirror's theory was ridiculous, but it would still be tested, because he was president of the United States, so he decided what was ridiculous.

"With your permission, I will change the subject to an issue of diplomatic procedure," said the clown. "When you arrived, your small craft did not communicate by radio. Will you explain why?"

Luci was still checking a seam on her red spandex shorts. "I don't see the procedural issue."

"I will explain the procedural issue. If your pilots don't need radio, perhaps they communicate more directly. The mind is one area where your technology surpasses ours."

"Your logic appears sound." Luci looked surprised, but maybe she had just found a red stain on her red shorts.

"Here is the difficulty: If your pilots can perceive each other's intentions without radio, then, it follows logically, you might perceive *my* intentions. If you can perceive, for example, the lowest price I would accept for 10,000 square miles of Utah, you have the advantage." The clown did not raise his voice, because he never raised his voice, and revealed his displeasure only by speaking slowly. "I never agreed to negotiate from such a weak position."

The ploy was thin. Alien telepathy, if it existed, must be broadcast by their brain implant, so Luci was hardly likely to steal secrets from the clown's tight skull. Nonetheless, the alien seemed stymied. She stared at her red spandex shorts for a full 15 seconds.

In the *Lens,* Kitty Siphon squirmed impatiently in her doeskin chair, drumming her fingers on her gold-inlaid rosewood workstation. She waved to the Marine standing stiffly beside the exit with a rifle. He glowered as he marched down the flat steps to bring her a tray of mouth-watering chocolate cherry truffles.

Eventually, the alien reached a decision and sat up straight. "You might want to keep this secret."

Kitty pointed to a eunuch, then drew her finger across her throat.

The eunuch touched his computer, and all the *Lens* displays went dark. Hundreds of staffers murmured disappointment, but they cheered up when the alpha eunuch touched his screen again and their displays came back to life with Phoebe Cates in a red bikini sitting on a diving board. Everyone covered their ears as the ten-foot speakers boomed out *Moving in Stereo,* by the Cars.

So, the *Lens* staffers watched *Fast Times at Ridgemont High,* while Kitty Siphon pulled on her headset and watched the alien negotiation on her private screen.

Ten seconds later, when she heard the alien's next words, Kitty Siphon lost her perception of gravity, and felt as if she were falling into a bottomless pit.

"After we come of age," the alien said with ghastly cheerfulness, "some of us endure a rite of passage, in which we are trained to perceive hidden thoughts."

Kitty Siphon dropped her cherry truffle.

"We know what thoughts are made of," Luci added. "Seeing them is actually pretty easy. Well, I say it's easy, because it's easy to *do,* but it's not easy to learn. The training to perceive hidden thoughts is prolonged and humiliating. It requires drugs you have not discovered, and physical invasions you would deem criminal."

In the face of disaster, the clown remained oddly calm. "Were *you* trained to read minds?"

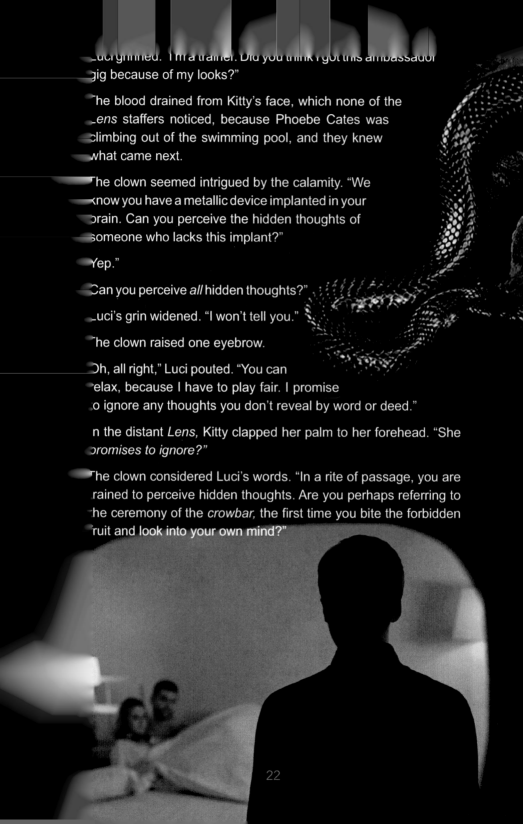

Luci grinned. "I'm a trainer. Did you think I got this ambassador gig because of my looks?"

The blood drained from Kitty's face, which none of the *Lens* staffers noticed, because Phoebe Cates was climbing out of the swimming pool, and they knew what came next.

The clown seemed intrigued by the calamity. "We know you have a metallic device implanted in your brain. Can you perceive the hidden thoughts of someone who lacks this implant?"

"Yep."

"Can you perceive *all* hidden thoughts?"

Luci's grin widened. "I won't tell you."

The clown raised one eyebrow.

"Oh, all right," Luci pouted. "You can relax, because I have to play fair. I promise to ignore any thoughts you don't reveal by word or deed."

In the distant *Lens,* Kitty clapped her palm to her forehead. "She *promises to ignore?"*

The clown considered Luci's words. "In a rite of passage, you are trained to perceive hidden thoughts. Are you perhaps referring to the ceremony of the *crowbar,* the first time you bite the forbidden fruit and look into your own mind?"

"Look into my *own* mind?" Luci chuckled. "You think I'm crafting clever words to fool you. I can't do that, because I can't demand ransom."

The clown nodded his understanding, and said, "I don't understand."

"I *can't* mislead you with so much at stake," Luci explained. "If I were deceiving you by claiming to perceive hidden thoughts, I would be implicitly threatening to harm you if your thoughts displeased me. Fraudulently threatening your safety is tantamount to demanding ransom."

"The fraud is irrelevant," the clown protested. "If your mind-reading claim is honest, you're still threatening me."

"I sure am." Luci giggled. "I can't demand ransom, but I can tell the simple truth, regardless of the *implication.*"

"Forgive my obtuseness," said the clown, "but did you say exactly *whose* hidden thoughts you are trained to perceive?"

"I don't play word games," Luci snapped. "Our prolonged and humiliating training is not to perceive our own thoughts; it's to perceive the hidden thoughts of others. Although, now that you mention it, the first time I looked inside my own mind was pretty fucking humiliating. If you ever look inside *your* mind, you'll probably decide to kill yourself, so stay away from the forbidden fruit."

"Thank you for warning me," said the clown. "What am I thinking?"

"Are you inviting me into your mind?"

"Gaa! *NO!*" In the *Lens,* Kitty Siphon leapt to her feet.

"I withdraw my question. I am not inviting you into my mind." The clown looked thoughtful. "Mind reading is unexpected. I can't imagine how you do it."

23

Luci snorted. "That's how we feel about your microchips. You store a mile-long bookshelf in a fingernail, and copy it in one minute? It's ridiculous."

"I do not invite you into my mind," the clown repeated. "However, we can arrange another test to prove your claim."

"No. I won't prove it, because I don't care if you believe me. In fact, I'd rather you don't. Please assume your thoughts are still private."

Kitty Siphon swayed drunkenly. "Tell her you need a recess."

Luci waved. "Your lies were precious. Take time to mourn."

Kitty Siphon wobbled to the exit, followed by the head of her secret-service detail, the blonde amazon Sheila Bear. Kitty stepped through, slammed the armored door in Agent Bear's face, then leaned against the tunnel wall and panted. *Has she read my mind? Have I condemned myself?*

Kitty indulged herself in 30 seconds of nipple-tingling panic. Then she forced herself to get a grip. She paced down the 93-Mile Tunnel and tried to calm herself by thinking about last night's ultimate fighting cage match.

After three minutes contemplating muscular men beating each other, Kitty's turmoil subsided. She thought about her favorite movie, *Death Wish 9: The Muggers Strike Back.*

At four minutes, Kitty Siphon was ready to embrace this challenge. She closed her eyes and reminisced about fishing with her ex. Her weekends on the lake with her husband had brought Kitty more pleasure than anything she had done since, because it made everything she had done since, no matter how onerous, seem pleasant by contrast.

At five minutes, Kitty could see the humor in her situation. She savored the moment.

Inside the *Lens,* the bell rang. Everyone looked at the armored door. Agent Bear punched in the code.

Kitty Siphon stepped through, looking refreshed. She opened her compact mirror and handed it to a stony-faced Marine guard. He held it while she checked her hair. Then she trotted down the flat steps, took her seat, and picked up her microphone. "Let's test the bitch. I want you to *think* this, but don't speak it: *Something is stuck to Luci's cheek.*"

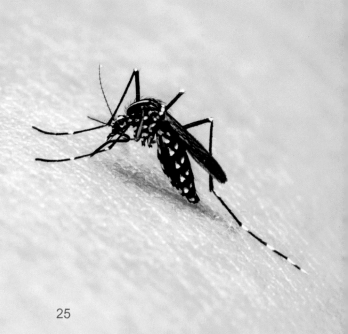

The clown said, "I am ready to continue."

"That brown thing on Luci's cheek looks ridiculous," Kitty whispered into the clown's earpiece. *"How could she not know about it?"*

Luci: "I wish to give you free information."

"Maybe that thing stuck to Luci's cheek is just a piece of food," Kitty murmured. *"Why doesn't she brush it off? Wait, could it be a tick? Does Luci know they bite and suck blood?"*

"Here is the free…" Luci paused, and looked annoyed. "I promised to ignore your thoughts, unless you reveal them by word or deed. That promise binds me, even when I wish it didn't. Please try to remember that, and be considerate."

Kitty: "Dammit!"

"Here is the free information," Luci continued. "Most Humans believe we are triggered by *coercion.* This is an error, but it keeps you safe, so we encourage it. The truth is: we are triggered by *extortion.* We cannot pay ransom in any form, even to save our own life. I trust you can work out the implications."

Oh, yes, Kitty Siphon could work out the implications. At this moment, nine aliens were held as test subjects in U.S. bioweapon labs. All the captive aliens were drugged into a coma, because when they learned they were captive, they detonated the capsules implanted in their brains. Kitty shivered as she realized this explosive inconvenience might have saved her. If a caged alien woke and read his captor's mind, he might learn his captor took orders from Kitty Siphon, and broadcast Kitty's name to *all* the aliens.

But why had this alien brought it up?

"I brought it up because I'm trying to keep you safe, but I see that's futile." Luci sighed. "You've already pushed in the tip, so you can't stop now. Before we proceed, you'd better give me the contact information for your second in command."

Uh oh.

"I have no second in command," the clown replied calmly. "I report only to the *Alien Regulatory Authority,* a blue-ribbon panel of 50 distinguished scholars, executives and statesman with total control of this negotiation, up to and including nuclear weapons release. The Alien Regulatory Authority cannot be overruled by anyone except the U.S. Congress."

"You just painted a target on Congress." Kitty's heart raced. "Good job. Don't breathe a word about *me,* and let's hope the bitch isn't reading your mind."

Painting a target on Congress was ironic, because Congress had hastily delegated all its power to the Alien Regulatory Authority, in the hope the ARA's 50 distinguished scholars, executives and statesman would absorb the first alien bullet.

"You can't keep this up forever," Luci snapped. "You were built to demand ransom, so for you, a *consensual* negotiation is agony. Eventually, your willpower will falter, and you will threaten me. Then, who can take your place? Give me a phone number for your successor, and you should make it someone *outside* your chain of command, because I know you're taking orders."

In the distant *Lens,* Kitty Siphon looked frightened.

One day later
Springfield, Missouri
An imperfect job interview

"You can't sue me."

"Oh really?" The job applicant arched a well-plucked eyebrow.

"I love hiring women ." Tom Pine leaned back in his high-back leather chair, stretched luxuriously, and scratched his chest. "Interviewing women like you is my payoff for building this company."

The job applicant smiled tentatively. She was 26, with half-shaved purple hair and an associate degree in Art History. She had responded to Tom's job listing.

Exotic Shoes
Inventory manager needed
Respectful work environment

Tom waved her resume. "Do you know why I chose you?"

"Was it my fonts? I'm good with fonts."

Tom scanned her resume. "I have to admit, using four... no five different fonts on your first page did catch my eye."

She looked pleased. "Tell me about the exotic shoes. I love shoes, so I'm excited about this opportunity."

Tom tossed her resume on his desk, then rested his feet on it. "Do you know what makes a good gangbang?"

"A *gangbang?*" She gaped. The effect was charming, like an asphyxiating goldfish. "You advertised for an *inventory manager!*"

"Relax," Tom commanded. "I do want administrative help. I'm telling you why you got this interview, and how to make it fun for me."

Now she appeared to be hyperventilating. "This was a trick to lure me into *porn?*"

"No, this was a trick to lure you into regulatory compliance. Most women do gangbangs wrong, wiggling and running their hands over their body and trying to look sultry. Then they take off their own clothes, which just ruins the moment. But this…" Tom pointed to the applicant. "This is good, what you're doing now."

She was breathing fast, her face pale.

"Sexy women make it boring," Tom explained. "I don't want to see Ginger get gangbanged; I want to see *Mary Ann.* Do you need a paper bag?"

"You can't do this," she gasped. "Talking about sex in a job interview is *not appropriate.* You're making me *uncomfortable."*

"Yes!" Tom pumped his fist. "I *love* hiring. I was hoping you'd threaten to sue me, but this is even better. Do you think you might faint?"

That seemed to calm her. "Oh my God. You're *enjoying* it."

"Oh, yes. In your last job, you organized an... uh…" Tom pulled her resume out from under his shoe and flipped to Page 3. "You organized a workshop, *Building a Workplace to Respect Women,* and got your boss to make it mandatory for all male employees. Two months later, you got fired. How's your lawsuit going?"

"How do you know about my lawsuit?"

"Just a lucky guess. This is so perfect." Tom couldn't stop grinning. "That's why you got this interview, because a gangbang is more interesting when you seem shocked and innocent. Well, not exactly innocent, but definitely shocked."

She seemed to shrivel, sinking into Tom's guest stool. "You shouldn't degrade me like this. Your ad promised a respectful work environment."

"More belligerence," Tom suggested. "I loved your *I'm-so-shocked-I-can't-breathe* face, but this hangdog routine isn't working for me."

The job applicant opened her purse and withdrew a lipstick, holding it with quivering fingers. She focused, and her hand stopped shaking. "I just want to manage an exotic shoe inventory. I love shoes."

"Ah. Well." Tom looked sheepish. "Maybe I should apologize, because I lured you here under false pretenses. My help-wanted ad was not entirely honest. Actually, it was total bullshit, except the part about the respectful work environment. I *will* expect you to respect my preferences."

The job applicant produced a mirror and applied fresh lipstick. Her hands were steady now, so when she finished, her lips were still mouth-shaped. "Do you actually sell exotic shoes?"

"No, I lied about that to attract better applicants."

"You're right," she concluded. "You should apologize."

"Yes, but I won't, because I'm not really sorry. I'll just give you this." Tom pulled out his wallet, extracted a $50 bill, and dropped it on his desk. "For your trouble."

She looked at the money. "Are you actually hiring?"

"Oh, yes. I can't be sued, but regulators are still biting my ankles. I need a secretary to help me comply with the NLRB and FTC and CPSC and FMLA and ITAR and Prop 65 and REACH and FCC and ERISA and FLSA and OSHA and ACA and ADA and EEOC and EPA rules. Do you know any of them?"

"You can't call me a *secretary.* It's demeaning."

"Perfect!" Tom beamed. "This will be so good."

"Regulatory compliance doesn't sound too bad. Why can't I sue you?" She picked up the $50. "And why do you think I'll *want* to sue you? I mean, besides talking about porn in my job interview."

"Ah, *why* will my secretary want to sue me, and what will happen to you if you try." Tom leaned back in his chair, stretched luxuriously, and scratched his chest. "This is my favorite part. I hope you'll make an effort to seem shocked and innocent."

"Fuck you." She tucked the $50 into her purse and walked out, slamming the door behind her.

"Rats. She would have been fun." Tom pressed a button on his intercom, the one labeled, *Sophie.* "She stormed out."

"What a surprise," Sophie replied. "Did you talk about sexual-harassment training?"

"No, gangbangs."

Sophie sighed. "Tom, it's been ten years since you got sued. I wish you'd get over it."

"*Get over* being sued?" Tom laughed. "I had to sell my house, so I'm not likely to get over it in this lifetime. But this is my silver lining. If I'd never been sued for discrimination, I don't think I could properly appreciate this moment."

"I'm glad you're enjoying it," Sophie lied. "Did you tell her she can't sue us?"

"Yep." Tom leaned back in his chair, stretched luxuriously, and scratched his chest. "Send in the next one."

"Sorry." Sophie didn't sound sorry. "You'll have to torture the job applicants later. It's time for the all-hands meeting."

Ten minutes later, Tom surveyed his employees, gathered in his lunchroom. In the front row, technicians hunched over their pads trying to finish the difficult Beverly Hills thunder run in *Civil War Two: Redneck Boogaloo.* Behind them, the assemblers huddled around one screen, raptly watching *Wealthy Investment Bankers Disfigured By Cancer, Volume 5: Amputations.* In the back, salesmen chatted.

They all worked for *Pine Robotic Sentry.* The company had been built by Tom Pine, but he didn't look the part. He stood 5'3", with a chin so weak he resembled a ferret. Yet, despite his physical appearance, Tom commanded the room, perhaps because he radiated confidence, or because he owned the building. "Before we continue, I'll remind our new employees you can't sue me."

The old employees waited politely. The new employees glanced nervously at the alien.

"Seriously, we're building sentries to defend homicidal aliens from *our* government, so don't try to sue me. I don't want to listen to your father's pathetic sobbing when I tell him we found your corpse in the sewer." Tom looked around. "Does anyone wish to pretend they don't understand?"

Apparently, no one wished to pretend, which was ironic because they all misunderstood. Everyone thought Tom was protected by the aliens, when in fact, he was quietly protected by the U.S. government. Tom's building was wired with secret government cameras, because President Mirror thought it would be pretty cool to see the details of the alien security system.

"Most of you know Luci Dark." Tom pointed at Luci, the famously beautiful alien standing beside him. "For our new employees, yes, Luci is *that* alien, the demon in their First-Contact prank, minus the fake fangs and horns. She's also their ambassador to our government."

In the third row, a new assembler muttered, "Yowza."

"Luci, you have the floor." Tom waved an invitation.

Luci was not really a demon, or even a proper alien, just a descendant of Humans kidnapped from Earth in 1755, now returned as murderers and comedians. Like most aliens, she was surprisingly small, four inches shorter than even Tom Pine's diminutive five foot three. Nonetheless, she commanded the room, perhaps because she was the first alien they had seen, or because her red-sequined holster looked heavy. She pointed to her left cheek, where a row of five, simple shapes was tattooed in blue ink that matched her eyes. "My name is Luci Dark. Who knows what these tattoos mean?"

Frank Drummer volunteered. "The square symbol warns us you are *ungovernable*, which means you can't pay ransom."

Frank Drummer had grown up across the street from Tom and Sophie. He had been the first tech eunuch to identify the incoming alien mothership, even counting its engines and timing its rotation. This feat had brought him to the attention of the commerce secretary, Kitty Siphon, who'd hired Frank to help construct the *Lens*, the U.S. government's underground command center, and its associated network of tunnels and bunkers.

Sadly, after an unfortunate interaction with President Mirror, Frank had been banished to Antarctica, so he'd been receptive to Tom Pine's job offer.

"Frank says I can't pay ransom." Luci looked stern. "That is technically correct, but perilous. Do *not* try to understand ransom. It's safer to assume I can't be coerced."

"Dammit, Luci, now you've lifted your skirt." Tom surveyed his employees. Their expressions ranged from *interested* to *calculating.* "You'd better show them everything."

"Oh, alright," Luci grumped. "If you really *must* understand ransom, you must understand your mind was built to sort your world into categories. For example, when I look at Tom, my brain recognizes him as, *male."*

Sophie Flint frowned. She was dating an alien engineer named Buffalo, but that didn't excuse Luci flirting with her boy next door, her first kiss, and her Plan B, Tom Pine.

"The *male* category is dangerous, but it's not as dangerous as the category, *my thing."* Luci shook her red silk pouch. It rattled with the dull clinks of soft metal. "For example, I recognize this bag of gold as, *my thing*, so I reflexively defend it." She pointed to Frank. "Please show me your wallet."

Frank looked bemused, but he tugged out his wallet and held it up.

Luci lunged forward and grabbed at it.

Frank jerked his wallet away and raised his other arm to fend her off. Tom's employees gasped.

Luci stepped back. "You saw his reaction. Frank had no time to think about defending his wallet, but he didn't *need* time. He did it reflexively, because his brain recognizes that wallet as, *his thing.*" Luci tapped the second of the five symbols on her cheek, the square. "This tattoo is a warning: My defensive reflex has been exaggerated. If you hold *my thing* for ransom, I will go berserk and shoot you. It's nothing personal, just a reflex. Afterward, I'll feel guilty."

"Technically," said Frank, "that's not a reflex."

"Technically," Luci replied, "you're being pedantic."

A dapper technician wearing bright green shoes raised his hand. "Then it's true? You actually can't pay taxes?"

"Correct. I can't pay taxes, nor can I ask for permits. If I wished to build a house on my property, and a queen demanded I ask her permission, I would go berserk."

"When she says, *queen,*" Tom added, "she means any high official in our government."

"Our queens might have something to say about Luci's philosophy." The green-shooed technician stood up. "They will probably say it with a bomb, so I won't stand this close." He walked out, pausing in the doorway to look back and say, "Good luck. I quit."

The door closed behind him, and the lunchroom fell silent.

"There's a prudent man. Anyone else?" Tom looked around, but nobody moved. "So you accept the risk, in return for the money and excitement. Let's see if we can change your mind." He waved to Luci.

She reached into her belt pouch and withdrew a gold coin, smaller than a dime, which she offered to Frank Drummer. "Frank, I will pay you one pennyweight of gold in exchange for you keeping two secrets. Do you accept?"

Frank looked at the coin. "What's that worth?"

"Right now, this coin is worth about 90 of your evaporating dollars. That value will probably go up, once you're sure we can't manufacture gold."

Tom: "Can you manufacture gold?"

Luci: "Nope."

Frank: "What if I'm coerced by the CIA? They could threaten to tattoo a bad pun on my face if I don't tell them your secret."

"If you are coerced to betray my secrets, I won't be triggered." Luci wagged a stern finger. "But take care to distinguish the carrot from the stick. Hitting you with the stick is force; withholding the carrot is *not*. Threatening to fire you is *not* coercion."

Frank stared at the gold coin. "What if I refuse?"

Luci displayed her famous, heartbreak smile, except without the fake fangs that had made it famous. "If you refuse my terms, I won't tell you my secrets, which are really interesting."

Frank took the coin.

Luci moved on to Sophie Flint, the company's chief administrator who had grown up next door to Tom, across the street from Frank. "Sophie, you already swore to keep one of my secrets."

Tom: "She did?"

Luci waved a gold coin. "Will you keep another secret?"

Sophie hesitated.

"Just take it," Tom snapped. "You can't possibly resist."

Sophie sighed and accepted the coin.

Luci moved around the lunchroom, repeating the ritual with each employee. Then she returned to the front. "I have paid for your silence, so your silence is now *my thing.*"

"So," said Tom. "What's this big secret you've told Sophie but haven't told *me?*"

Sophie: "You won't like it."

Luci: "Do you remember we warned you, if you flirt with our men, they might take you by force?"

"I think they remember." Tom was looking at the TV, mounted high in the corner and left on the news as a riot warning system. Now, it showed a still photo of a pretty brunette with a black eye, captioned, *Another alleged rape: Alien attacker says Human victim flirted.*

Sophie winced.

"Here's my secret." Luci pointed to the TV, and the bruised victim. "If she had asked him to stop, he would have."

"WHAT THE HELL! He would stop assaulting her if she *asked him to?"* Tom stabbed an accusing finger at Sophie. "You *knew,* and you didn't tell me?"

Sophie shrugged. "I said you wouldn't like it."

"I told you my secrets were interesting." Luci tapped her second tattoo, the square. "Her body is not *his thing,* so if she said, *stop,* he couldn't continue."

Around the lunchroom, women looked angry.

Tom looked angry and confused. "Women are getting raped by aliens every week, but they could just say, *stop?* We had to interrupt our first meeting *to pull Buff off of Sophie,* but she could have just told him to stop? How can this possibly be secret?"

"How, indeed," said Luci. "No sensible man would believe how well your press buries secrets."

"I *banned miniskirts* to protect my employees!" Tom glared. "They could have been wearing them this whole time! Why are you keeping this secret?"

"Figure it out yourself. Are you ready to hear my second secret?"

"No," Tom growled. "Dammit, I'm not happy. You've stuck me in a moral quandary."

"Yes, I have," Luci admitted. "You could warn the victims, but you promised not to, so you won't."

"We're not really in a moral quandary." Frank Drummer pointed to the television. "At this point, any girl who flirts with Buff must know what she's in for."

"Actually, you *are* in a quandary," said Luci. "Even if a girl tries not to flirt, Buff will know if she wants him."

Sophie Flint looked uncomfortable.

"Who is Buff," asked Albert, a new technician in the third row.

"Buffalo Dawn is our alien engineer," Tom explained. "You'll see him around the office."

"Buffalo Dawn?" Albert's eyes widened. "Isn't that..."

"Yes, Buff was the fake Jesus in their First-Contact prank, the one with the giant dick. Sophie flirted with him, so he tried to rape her. Now, she's his girlfriend."

Sophie reddened.

Albert looked at Sophie. "Buffalo Dawn sexually assaulted you, and now you're his *girlfriend?* When he attacked you, did you ask him to stop, and it actually worked?"

"No." Sophie blushed deeper. "I didn't think to try. Tom pulled him off me, and Frank punched him in the face."

Albert goggled. "Frank Drummer punched Buffalo Dawn and *lived?* Buffalo is a homicidal alien who looks like a body builder. Frank Drummer is a technical geek who looks like…like…"

"Mashed potatoes," Frank suggested. "Why don't we just ask Buff to restrain himself?"

"Good question," said Tom "Why not ask Buff to restrain himself?"

"He's trying," Luci replied. "But he might fail, because we boosted his instinctive response to the category, *female*. Actually, we boosted it kind of a lot."

This revelation was greeted with deep silence. Sophie's red face now reached all the way to her shoulders.

"We trust our men," Luci added, "and we don't want them to find us resistible. So, if you're attracted to Buff, you'll probably have to ask him to stop. Don't let him gag you, unless you're really sincere."

Now all of the employees looked resolutely blank, except Sophie looked embarrassed, and Frank looked thoughtful. "You hyper-sexualized your men by boosting their instinctive response to females. Did you also boost *your* instinctive response to males*?"*

Every head swiveled toward Luci.

She sniffed. "A lady does not discuss that topic while sober."

Tom: "I feel I have been denied critical, need-to-know information."

"You should have tried harder to get me drunk," said Luci. "Are you ready to hear my second secret?"

Tom: "Miniskirts are now unbanned."

"You're really not going to like this," said Luci. "My second secret is that roughly half of us, the aliens I mean, have been trained to perceive your hidden thoughts."

Tom's jaw fell open. *"Trained to perceive my hidden thoughts?"*

"I said you wouldn't like it." Luci gazed around pointedly. "Remember this second secret, if you are tempted to reveal the first."

Frank Drummer looked uncertain. *"Half* of you are trained to read minds? Why only half?"

Luci laughed.

Now everyone looked uncertain, except Tom looked angry.

"Sorry," said Luci. "You wouldn't know your question was funny. Our training to perceive hidden thoughts is long and humiliating. It requires drugs you haven't discovered and physical invasions you would deem criminal."

Tom: "Have *you* been trained to read minds?"

Luci grinned. "I'm a trainer, but only part-time."

Tom folded his arms. "You and I need to chat about boundaries."

In the third row, two new assemblers were whispering. Albert and Amanda had pulled their chairs together, and now Albert raised his hand. "What am I thinking?"

"I don't bark on command," Luci replied. "And besides, you'd be more interested to know what Amanda is hoping you'll do."

Amanda: "Bitch!"

Luci winced. "That was so rude of me. I apologize."

Albert looked at Amanda and raised an eyebrow.

She punched him.

The television up in the corner had shifted to a scene of firefighters sifting through rubble, captioned, *Washington, D.C. Whole Foods Market destroyed by suspected alien bomb.*

"Amanda, that won't work." Tom was pointing at the new assembler in the third row.

Amanda had quietly laid the gold coin on the floor. Now she looked guilty.

"Throwing away the payment does not negate the contract," Tom added. "However, it *does* prove you're stupid and untrustworthy, so you're fired. Get out."

Amanda burst into tears. "I'm sorry! Please don't fire me."

"Out." Tom waved at the door. "The rest of you, it's time to update your tax withholding and ERISA disclosures, so head over to Sophie's office. Luci, please stay. We need to chat."

When everyone had left, Luci said, "I wish I could do that."

"You wish you could push all your bullshit paperwork onto Sophie?" Tom chuckled. "Who wouldn't?"

"We can't do the queen's paperwork, because it always includes a ransom demand, but we *do* have to fire employees. When you fired Amanda, you were merciless, and it didn't seem to bother you."

"It *would* have bothered me, ten years ago. I was a gentler man before I got sued for discrimination, which you should know, if you're reading my mind."

"Tom, I don't root through my friends' drawers. If you want me to know your thoughts, you'll have to reveal them with your actions."

"So you'll respect the privacy of my thoughts?"

Luci grinned. "Not really. I'm pretty good at reading your actions."

"Don't be too smug. I saw the weakness you tried to hide."

Luci's grin vanished.

"You bought our silence, so we can't threaten to blab, because that would be implicitly demanding ransom." Tom closed the door and lowered his voice. "But we *could* quietly sell your secrets. That's no demand, just a breach of contract."

"Drat," said Luci. "You noticed. I hope nobody else did."

President Mirror teed off. He swung smoothly through the ball, and with a metallic *ping,* it sailed down the fairway.

Secretary of Commerce Kitty Siphon teed off. She swung smoothly through the ball, and with a faint *tick,* it flew three feet straight up, humming, then bounced backward.

"Wow." The president watched her ball roll away. "I've never seen a drive end up behind the tee."

Five minutes later, Kitty strode down the fairway at the president's side. "The bitch told me she can read our minds."

"WHAT?" Mirror stumbled. "Was she lying?"

"*Quiet!*" Kitty glanced back at their Secret Service protectors. "She said she can't lie, at least not in a way that threatens us."

"It must be real! Telepathy sounds stupid like radio sounded stupid to Julius Caesar. That means it's true! Did you test her?"

"Of course. The clown asked her what he was thinking. She said that required an invitation, which he didn't give, thank God. That would be like inviting in a vampire. Then I told him to think about an insect on Luci's face, and she told him he was being rude. Plus, she hangs out in that private company making their sentries, the place we filled with secret cameras, and I watched her read a woman's thoughts. From the woman's reaction, Luci nailed it."

"I *know* it's real," Mirror gushed. "It explains why they had no radios! This is fantastic news."

"The hell it is," said Kitty. "We're holding *nine* live aliens for the bioweapon tests. What if they read the minds of our snatch teams and find out *we* gave the order?"

President Mirror stared at Kitty, his best friend. "Do you think the aliens could broadcast my name to everyone's brain?"

Kitty sighed. *Of course he would see that implication.* "Luci only claimed to *read* thoughts, not send them. However, the eunuchs say a receiver is practically the same as a transmitter. A microphone is just a speaker run backward, so if the alien brain implant can *receive* thoughts, we have to assume it can also transmit."

Mirror resumed walking. "Now we know why none of their spaceships had radios, until they bought them from us. Their brain implants are the real prize, the game changer." His stride quickened. "We need telepathy. We *must* have it, whatever the cost."

"Slow down!"

"Sorry, sorry."

Kitty resolutely did not trot to catch up. She took her time, and noticed a buzzard circling overhead. "I wonder if the secret-service guys know we have buzzard drones?"

The buzzard burst into flames.

"They know," said the president. "Agent Bear finally got a chance to use her microwave gun."

200 feet up the fairway, Agent Bear whooped and waved a two-foot metal dish mounted on a wooden gun stock. She was the blond amazon who commanded Kitty's secret-service detail.

Kitty watched the buzzard plummet, trailing smoke. "That's a drone?"

"No, it's a bird. The microwave gun is a little bit overpowered."

The flaming buzzard landed in the rough and ignited a small grass fire. Kitty watched four junior secret-service agents stomp it out. "Have the war pigs given us an option?"

"We have a few stealth nukes in orbit, but the war pigs are afraid to use a few. They say our first shot has to be the opposite of a warning."

"Tell them to expedite. If the aliens can read minds, every minute we let them live is a stupid risk."

Mirror waved dismissively. "We have plenty of clowns to take the first bullet. We need telepathy, and the aliens have it. We should grab more of them for testing."

Kitty sighed. "You're thinking like a teenager who finally got a girl's shirt unbuttoned and is trying to figure out her bra."

President Mirror turned on her and snarled. "Telepathy is way more important than tits. We could build a national telepathic network, with everyone connected to me *all the time*. When I talk, *they would have to listen.*"

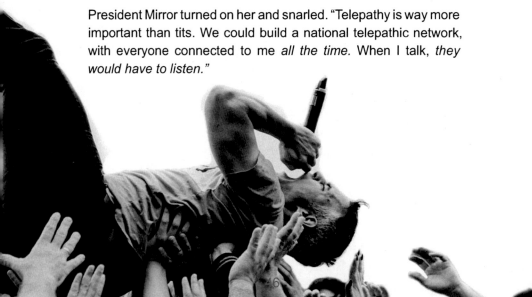

56

Kitty looked weary.

Mirror looked hungry. "Grab more aliens. We *must* find out how their telepathy works."

"No."

President Mirror stiffened. "I beg your pardon?"

"We do *not* detain more aliens. We kill them all *right now,* and fuck the opinion polls."

"What the hell are you talking about?"

"I'm talking about a *major personal risk.*" Kitty thumped the president's chest. "Our clowns have killed or captured 20 aliens. If the aliens ever discover it was *us* who gave that order, we are dead. We're just lucky they haven't already found out, because we keep our aliens unconscious. But to find out how telepathy works, we would have to *wake one up.* If she really *is* telepathic, she will read our clown's mind and find out he is acting on *our orders.* Then she might broadcast *our* names to *all* the aliens, and tell everyone *we* gave the order to kidnap her. How do you think the aliens will react?" Kitty shook her head. "Thank God the aliens have suicide bombs in their skulls, because it forced us to keep them asleep. That saved us."

Mirror growled. "With your budget, you should have solved those technical problems."

"Dammit, these are not *technical* problems; they are *logical* problems. If you think you can do better, let's see you try."

200 feet up the fairway, Agent Bear frowned as she read her charge's body language. "Cougar looks pissed."

Agent Oak shaded his eyes. "Tiger too."

Tiger and *Cougar* were the secret-service code names for the president and secretary of commerce. Kitty's code name, *Cougar* had caused a minor scandal, which she planned and enjoyed.

Now Kitty stood stiffly while the president chipped his ball onto the green.

Armed protectors watched from a distance as Kitty and the President walked down the green fairway.

As they approached Kitty's ball, Mirror's posture sagged. "You're right. The aliens are so dangerous, and telepathy is too good to be true. With my luck, that capsule in their brain is just a bomb. They set it off at will, or maybe it has a remote control, in case they lose their nerve."

Kitty stumbled to a halt.

"We have to play it safe, and take fewer aliens. Even telepathy is useless if I am blown up."

Kitty blinked. "Remote control."

"Probably. Suicide bombs need a remote, for last-minute doubt."

"That alien bastard *told us.*" Kitty seemed to be hyperventilating. "He actually said it out loud, and 600 analysts missed it. A billion viewers missed it. *I* missed it."

Mirror looked concerned. "Do you need to breathe into a paper bag?"

"When they were rescued from Earth in 1755, *they had to pay for it,*" Kitty half shouted. "Some third party, some creature who claimed to be God Himself but was obviously lying, rescued them from a sinking ship in return for 20 years of indentured servitude, which was *also a lie.* In Gabriel's TV interview, when he talked about their history, he said their 20-year indenture didn't end the way they expected! Those were his exact words! My ancestors' indenture *did not end the way they expected!*"

Mirror glanced back toward the secret service. "Lower your voice."

"Don't you see?" Kitty hissed. "Gabriel was trying to tell us their indentured servitude *did not end.* This explains everything! It explains why they sacrifice themselves in a suicidal attack rather than pay their fair share! It explains how they muster the willpower to blow themselves up when we interrogate them! The aliens are *remotely operated!*"

"You mean..." Mirror's eyes widened.

"Yes!" Kitty cried. "Their brain implant is a *human remote control!* Someone found the Holy Grail!"

Mirror let out a low whistle.

"Call off the war pigs," Kitty shouted joyously. "Call them off *now,* before they do something calamitous! And I need a bigger budget. We need more of those brain implants. A lot more!"

"Quiet!" Mirror glanced at their secret-service bodyguards. "You'll get what you need, but this doesn't change anything."

"What the hell are you talking about? A human remote control changes *everything!*"

"It doesn't change our strategy. We must have those brain implants, whether they are remote control or telepathy. And we better start moving," Mirror added, "or you might pass out."

They walked toward the pond.

Mirror waited until his best friend's breathing slowed. "Can you talk about something else now?"

She whirled on him. "How can you want to talk about something else?"

"Why did you say, *fuck the opinion polls?*"

"Hmm." Kitty took a moment to settle. "When it comes to the aliens, I don't trust a poll. Our people won't admit what they really want, so I had the eunuchs run psych experiments, staging fake alien landings to trick people into admitting the truth. The results were a disaster. Three out of ten Americans *like* the idea of being ungovernable, and two of them would actually *do it,* if they could move to a thriving alien colony."

"*Twenty percent* would leave us to join the aliens?" Mirror looked sad.

"Yes, two in ten will ditch us. Of the remaining eight, six want to nuke the aliens, but only *one* will admit it."

President Mirror considered the grim numbers. "If we nuke the aliens, only *10 percent* will admit they support us?"

"Ten percent is disappointing, but it's plenty, if we deplatform the rest. The problem is the 50 percent who won't admit it. They'll feel guilty for their secret pleasure, which means they will need to atone, so they will demand a sacrifice."

"A *sacrifice?*" Mirror didn't like the sound of that.

They reached Kitty's ball, and she considered her lie. The green was only 40 yards away, a straight shot down the center of the 40-yard-wide fairway, 50 yards from the nearest pond and 60 from the sand trap. "Our people are pussies who won't admit what they want. When they see the nuke flash, and realize the aliens are finally dead, the pussies will orgasm in their designer panties."

"Good. Then they will love me."

"No, we won't. The aliens are *not* just villains; they are also *Daddy,* with Daddy's moral authority, and he won't let us shoplift candy. We all want Daddy dead, but we don't want it to be our fault, so the patricide will have to be *your* fault. Your ritual crucifixion will start with hand-wringing about sick African children who might have been saved by the alien immune system, if only *you* hadn't nuked them."

Mirror recoiled. "Nobody should attack *me!* They should attack the Alien Regulatory Authority! That's the whole *point* of the Alien Regulatory Authority!"

"I'm sure the clowns will take the first hit, but let's not imagine the 50 distinguished scholars, executives and statesman of the Alien Regulatory Authority will defend us if we become unfashionable." Kitty pulled out her 9-iron and chipped her ball into the pond.

Mirror watched the ripples spread.

"The aliens are still too popular." Kitty slid her club into the bag. "I don't understand why our PR campaign isn't working. Everyone suspects the aliens are behind the missing girls, and we've put actual rape videos on primetime TV, and *still* only 10 percent will admit they want to nuke the bastards."

Mirror chuckled. "The whores are so happy; they finally get to show rape videos."

President Mirror referred to journalists as, *whores*. He meant it fondly.

"Rape." Kitty snorted. "Every woman knows what happens when you flirt with an alien male. For Christ's sake, they announced it on television months ago, and male feminists are *still* competing to be the most outraged."

53

"Don't let anyone mock the white knights," Mirror commanded. "And don't let anyone blab the secret, that the victims can just say, *stop.* When your enemy is screwing himself, don't interfere."

"Give me some credit," said Kitty. "I hired the Meme Team to police the online discussion. Any woman who says she *wasn't* raped will get hammered so hard, she'll close all her social-media accounts and double her anti-depressants for a year."

"Good, good. I wonder why it isn't working better?" President Mirror brooded as they detoured around a pile of goose droppings and approached the green. "Even with the rapes, only *10 percent* will admit they want to nuke the aliens."

Kitty glanced at the secret service to make sure they were safely distant, then lowered her voice. "Should we release the videos of the little girls? We have 20 now, and some of them would give Joseph Stalin nightmares."

"Not yet. When we finally pull the trigger, our nukes might take out some civilians, so we'll need those videos to stifle the second-guessing." Mirror considered his putt. "I wonder if we might be focused on the wrong risk? We're trying to make it *socially* safe to attack the aliens, but maybe the problem is the *physical* risk. The aliens are so violent, our people are finding excuses to talk about something else."

Kitty walked to the hole and lifted the flag. "What's your plan?"

A deer wandered out of the forest onto the fairway. It was a young fawn, still in a spotted coat, and had obviously lost its mother. It wandered about, sniffing the air.

Mirror watched it. "We have robots that look like deer. Why is Agent Bear hesitating?"

Up the fairway, Agent Bear was aiming a scoped rifle at the fawn. Then she slumped, and handed the rifle to Agent Oak.

He fired, and the fawn's head exploded. It's corpse dropped onto the grass.

"Let's give the aliens a better name." Mirror tapped his ball firmly, well away from the flag. It rode up the slope, curving steadily until it settled into the hole from a different direction. "In that TV interview, the alien leader called himself a worm. So, from now on, the word *alien* is racist. Everyone has to call them, *Worms.*"

Kitty burst out laughing.

"While we're at it, let's show everyone how *easy* it is to kill a Worm." With supple grace, the president swung his putter like a baseball bat. The steel head hummed through the air. "*Aliens* are scary, so attacking them takes physical courage, but we all know what to do if we get bitten by a Worm."

Five days later, in a nearly-empty bank lobby just south of downtown Bakersfield, a lone teller wrapped coins while a sleepy, overweight security guard contemplated the marble floor. Overhead cameras watched, unblinking. The cameras were expensive, with unusually high resolution for bank security.

A woman entered wearing a holster. The sleepy, overweight security guard started forward, but hesitated when he noticed her cheek was tattooed with a row of red tokens, the simple geometric shapes of the alien warnings.

The teller watched nervously. Rumors had buzzed about a checking account opened by an actual alien. The teller wondered if this was the same alien.

It was not the same alien, but the resemblance was striking. In fact, the resemblance was exact. It could not be achieved on a limited budget.

"Deposit." The woman with the tattooed cheek placed a thick envelope on the counter and swiped a debit card through the scanner.

The teller opened the envelope and nervously counted the cash. "I have it as $660."

"No, it was $670."

The teller smiled apologetically and counted again, this time stacking the money into 100-dollar piles. "I'm sorry, ma'am, it came out $660."

The tattooed customer snapped open her holster and withdrew a weapon. It didn't look like a normal firearm, but it definitely was a firearm. She proved that by firing it into the teller's jaw.

The shot was expertly aimed. The teller would survive, and be grossly disfigured, and spend lots of time on television.

The high-resolution security camera showed the mutilated bank teller screaming incoherently. The tattooed customer laughed, then looked briefly startled as she was shot three times through her cheek tattoos by the sleepy, overweight security guard.

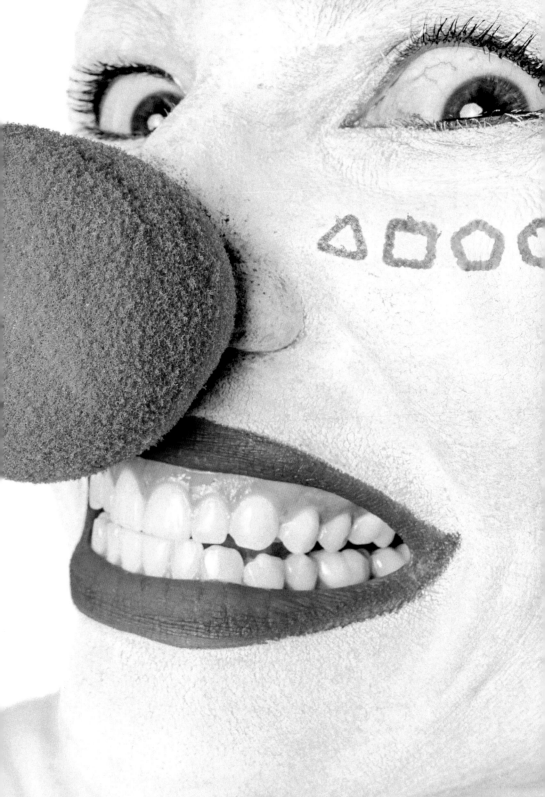

Comments. Please respect the <u>forum rules</u>.

Scrapbook22 Four hours ago

I was walking my Corgi in the green belt, when an alien landed his spaceship beside us. He was short, but otherwise attractive and polite, so you can imagine how surprised I was when he jumped me with some jujitsu move and started tearing my clothes off.

But the funny thing was, when I told him to stop, he sort of froze like he was having some kind of seizure. Then, just like that, he was polite again, and actually joked about attacking me. Obviously, I was freaked out and beat a hasty retreat. Now, I keep trying to understand what happened to me, and I can't help thinking I'm missing something.

Pokemom Four hours ago

You fucking bitch. You just told every victim of Worm rape that it was her own fault.

LawFareForU Four hours ago

Seriously? Are you TRYING to sabotage every plaintiff and prosecutor who is struggling to protect our women?

Moby Duck Four hours ago

Scrapbook22, maybe you meant well, but you should not tell stories like this. Even if you interpreted his actions correctly, which I doubt, your words are extremely hurtful to many women.

S. Quiblee Four hours ago

YOU CUNT YOU FUCKING WHORE

Page 1 2 206

58

Three days later, in Washington, D.C., Dominick Tork looked around a crowded briefing theater. Each chair was upholstered in Italian leather; the ceiling was painted with naked cherubs; the ornate molding was hand-carved from confiscated endangered bloodwood; and the 49 surviving commissioners chatted expertly. Dominick noticed their body language showed deference to their alpha, a tall patrician with silver hair.

Dominic decided to remind them who was the *real* alpha. "Before I begin this emergency briefing," he began, "I will ask you to remember your security commitments."

The murmur halted, and every face lost its expression. The 49 surviving commissioners of the Alien Regulatory Authority still remembered their security briefings, which had been delivered by Dominick personally, and had included the names of all their sexual partners for the last eight years, including the ones they had forgotten. The commissioners all wondered how Dominick knew, but they hadn't thought to wonder why their i-Phone batteries were not removable.

Dominick Tork was far too busy to deliver personal security briefings, but *these* briefings had been too delicious to resist. Dominick loved the personal touch.

Dominick had personally touched Tom Pine, long ago in their child-hoods. Dominick had been a schoolyard thug who bullied Tom, until Tom's sly defense had changed both their lives by opening Dominick's eyes to a higher calling in government.

Now, Dominick gazed over the 49 cowed faces with satisfaction. In the third row, a single, fine leather chair sat empty. The 49 commissioners had originally been 50. "Today's material is particularly alarming, hence this emergency briefing. You may be in physical danger."

The commissioners sat up straighter, and as always, the tall patrician tried for dominance. "We're in physical danger? Does this mean the aliens penetrated the obfuscator?"

Dominick stared at the patrician. "The term, *alien* is now considered exclusionary, and hence inappropriate."

The patrician flinched at the word, *inappropriate,* the deadliest of all accusations.

"Every race has the right to choose its own name. The alien leader called himself a *worm,* so we will respect his choice." Dominick remained deadpan, and so did most of the commissioners, except three in the back row giggled. "Be at ease, because the Worms have *not* penetrated the obfuscator." Dominick walked to the obfuscator, a grey steel box in the corner, and lifted its hood to reveal its spring-driven gears. "This unit is identical to those in the House and Senate chambers. Feel free to examine its mechanism and satisfy yourselves as to its function." As he said it, Dominick smiled inwardly, because none of the commissioners had any mechanical skills. They were lucky the obfuscator actually *did* work, because they could not have verified it. Nonetheless, they nodded soberly at Dominick's offer, preserving the fiction.

"The obfuscator tallies your votes and converts them into a single, yes-or-no decision. It will not reveal your individual vote, even if the vote is unanimous. It cannot be electronically hacked, because it contains no electronics." Dominick closed the hood and walked back to the podium. "We still believe the obfuscator will protect you from Worm retribution."

The tall patrician couldn't resist. "You *believe* it will protect us?"

"Kindly hold your questions until I complete my briefing."

The patrician turned red. The other commissioners smirked.

"You should trust the obfuscator, because the Worms themselves believe it will protect you. We know this from observing dozens of joint Human-Worm ventures. For example, the Worms have partnered with a Utah company to develop a novel technology for plating copper without electricity." Dominick took a moment to let the idea sink in.

Apparently, the idea bounced off, because the commissioners began to murmur among themselves.

"We have analyzed 33 Worm-Human contracts," Dominick said a little louder, "We discovered something remarkable; their joint ventures are designed to *focus* responsibility rather than diffuse it."

The murmur halted.

"You are familiar with another example. The alien ambassador, Lucifa Dark, will speak only to a single Human. She absolutely refused to deal with a more sensible diplomatic team. Worms invariably insist that important decisions be made by *individuals*, rather than by committee."

The commissioners looked horrified.

"The conclusion is obvious: The Worms *cannot* cope with a committee. We believe they are psychologically unable to impose collective punishment. Therefore, you must act collectively, taking care to conceal your individual votes. The Worms will know the committee's decision, but they will not know how you *personally* voted, so they cannot punish you."

Unfortunately, decision-by-committee won't protect you if the Worms can read minds, Dominick reflected. *What's the point of obfuscating, if the enemy can look into your brain and see you fucked him?*

If the commissioners knew about the mind-reading threat, they might protect *themselves* by appeasing the Worms. This would defeat the Alien Regulatory Authority's purpose, which was to be the capering clown who took the first bullet. Even worse, individual commissioners might be tempted to negotiate privately, betraying their own species to strike a side deal with the all-seeing Worms.

That would *not* happen while Dominick was on duty. He pointed to the single, empty leather chair. "Commissioner Simper attempted to negotiate personally with a Worm. The Worm killed him."

The tall patrician looked doubtful. "Simper was killed by a Worm?"

Dominick stared at the would-be challenger. "Do I need to turn up my volume?"

Commissioners smiled. The tall patrician didn't.

"As you know," Dominick continued, "the Whole Foods Market near Logan Circle was recently destroyed by an explosion. What you *don't* know is, Commissioner Simper asked a Worm to meet him there. The meeting lasted less than 15 seconds before the Worm detonated his suicide bomb."

The tall patrician looked suspicious. "Why didn't the Worm just shoot him?"

Dominick smiled thinly. "Perhaps you should ask him."

Commissioners tittered. The tall patrician scowled.

Dominick was lying. The doomed Whole Foods Market had not contained a Worm, at least not the alien kind, nor had it contained Commissioner Simper. However, it *had* contained a young woman who planned to accuse President Mirror of sexual impropriety, and she had video.

Sadly, she was 40 pounds overweight, so her video would be a national embarrassment, which Dominick could not tolerate.

At the exact moment the Whole Foods Market was blown up, Commissioner Simper had actually been 60 miles away on a golf course, where Dominick's strike team had killed him with an explosive drone groundhog. For some reason, the strike team had insisted on playing the Kenny Loggins song, *I'm alright,* six times on the way home.

"We cannot know the specific motive for Commissioner Simper's assassination," Dominick lied smoothly. "However, we *do* know Worms attack without regard for their personal safety. They have now proven their willingness to attack *you* without warning, so I suggest you do *not* approach within visual range of any Worm."

Out of sight, out of mind, Dominick did not say, hoping it was true.

Youths shot hoops on a cracked asphalt court.

In the aftermath, video from the overhead security camera would show the victim wander across the court. He looked misplaced in his gray business suit, white skin, and Worm tattoos.

A skinny youth bumped the victim from behind. The youth did something out of sight, then stepped back and raised both hands, triumphantly waving the alien's gun.

The alien showed his tattoos to the camera as he turned and swung a slow fist. The skinny youth dodged easily.

Just outside the camera's view, Dominick Tork said, "Charge!"

For privacy reasons, the security camera didn't have a microphone, so the scene had to be staged without dialog. This reduced the scene's dramatic impact, but made the choreography easier.

With an inarticulate and also pointless bellow, the tattooed alien charged the skinny youth.

The skinny youth stepped aside. The alien tripped, sprawling onto the asphalt and ripping his suit pants. He scrambled to his feet and charged again. At the last moment, the youth side-stepped and hooked the alien's ankle, sending him tumbling to the pavement.

As the alien struggled back to his feet, the skinny youth planted a foot on his butt and shoved him back onto his face.

Four minutes later, the surprisingly-clumsy alien lay motionless on the asphalt. The skinny youth who put him there was not injured, and hadn't needed any help. He unbuckled the alien's belt and removed the silk bag they all carried. He upended the bag and poured a shower of gold coins onto the asphalt that all the youths scrambled after.

The youths lived in abject poverty, so they were at serious risk of obesity, and half of them lived in homes with only a single big-screen television, but now, they looked forward to a life of luxury, financed by grateful Humans who were eager to shower cash on any young man brave enough to attack an alien.

Each youth had already recorded five separate videos in which he described his new, opulent lifestyle, thanked his many generous donors, and marveled that killing the alien had been so easy. Some of the videos had been filmed in five-star hotel rooms, others beside a multilevel stone swimming pool overlooking Los Angeles, and the rest in Thai brothels.

The videos had to be recorded in advance, Dominick had explained, because the youths would soon be distracted by so many admiring girls that nobody trusted them to do it later.

The videos were safely archived and would be released over the coming months. The youths had been recruited on the basis of school records showing IQ below 85.

Just outside the camera's view, Dominick's phone beeped. He looked at the number, then picked up. "Good morning, Mister Pine. Please hold." Dominick waved the youths away. They were gathering up the gold coins, carefully avoiding the spurting blood.

The youths grabbed the last of the gold then trotted out of the camera's view and piled into a minivan they thought would take them to Disney World, but would actually take them to a southern Arizona farm with a 16-inch woodchipper and a lettuce crop needing fertilizer.

Dominick returned to his phone. "Mister Pine, I'm pleased to hear from you. How goes your joint project with the Worms?"

"My joint project with the aliens is as popular as always," Tom Pine replied. "Can you hear our fans?"

Behind Tom's voice, Dominick hear a faint chorus chanting, *Hey hey, ho ho, collaborators have got to go.* "Do I hear concerned citizens peaceably assembling to express their grievances?"

"You hear an angry mob surrounding my building. My employees have started dropping hints about a *hostile workplace.* Are you still protecting me from lawsuits?"

Dominick preened. "I am shielding you from litigation."

"I believe you, but I'm afraid my employees don't. Could you give them a demonstration? Something persuasive but not fatal?"

"That would not be appropriate."

"Dominick, someone *will* sue me. I'm too juicy a target."

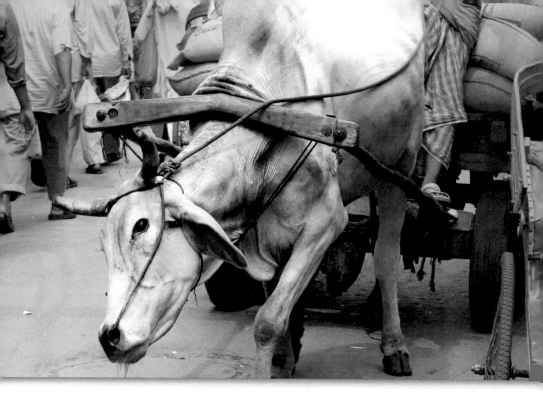

"Mister Pine, I am protecting you, so don't concern yourself with litigation. Just focus on your business."

"I'd love to," said Tom, "but yesterday, I got fined $400 because I couldn't find the material safety datasheet for rubbing alcohol. Can you pull the government dogs off my ankles?"

"Of course I could, but that would not be appropriate. You must devote adequate resources to compliance."

"If you'll protect me from lawsuits, why won't you protect me from code inspectors?"

Dominick smiled happily. "I protect you from litigation because I won't trust your fate to a jury."

"You won't trust my fate to a jury of my peers, only to a government employee you control." Tom sounded tired.

"Dealing with you is always a pleasure," Dominick said sincerely. "I'm sure you'll find a way to comply, with just a little more effort."

After a pause, Tom said, "Yes. Obviously, I need to do something differently."

THEY ARE NOT OUR FRIENDS

Like   Share   Comment

Comments. Please respect the <u>forum rules</u>.

FunDad2 Two days ago
> I just watched a video of a Worm that wandered into a basketball game and got beaten to death. It was horrifying.

LawFareForU Two days ago
> Did you see the kids' GoFundMe? They got 12 million dollars.

Moby Duck Two days ago
> The worm was helpless once they took his gun. It was just one skinny kid that did the work, so he got 3/4 of the $12 Million.

FunDad2 Two days ago
> It was MURDER and a grotesque violation of GoFundMe TOS.

PokeMom Yesterday
> FunDad2 you wouldn't have minded, if those kids were white. Did you see the skinny kid's video he made to thank his donors? He is living in a mansion now, with a swimming pool overlooking LA. It warmed my heart to see a disadvantaged boy make it big.

Page 1 2

Ten busy days later, all of Tom's employees jammed into the lunch room. In front, the technicians hunched over their pads playing *Vice Squad 6* with the best-selling *Asian Massage* bonus pack. Behind them, the assemblers huddled around one screen raptly watching *Johns Hopkins Continuing Medical Education Volume 29: Urethral Catheter Insertion (Two credits.)* In back, the salesmen chatted.

Up in the corner, the television showed a photo of a 12-year-old white girl holding a white rose, captioned, *MISSING TWO DAYS.*

Tom counted heads, then looked around for a gavel. He found a can of Cheese Wiz and rapped it on the table. The nozzle assembly popped off and a narrow jet of cheese squirted into the air. "Gaa!"

The murmur subsided. The assemblers paused their video and looked attentive.

Tom flung the spewing can into the sink. "You can't sue me."

Around the lunchroom, faces hardened.

Tom unrolled paper towels. "Our sentry project is too important to too many violent people. You can't hold it for ransom, and it would be dangerous to try."

In the back row, Alice the foul-tempered receptionist smiled.

"If you think your burden is too heavy, your only recourse is to stop taking my money. This bizarre situation is called, *mutual consent,* and it seems so restrictive, so contrary to everything you've been raised to believe, I fear you may be unable to accept it. Therefore, to help you resist temptation, I have converted this business into a corporation." Tom angrily wiped cheese off the lunch table. His employees thought he was angry at the cheese, but in fact he was angry at the extra taxes he was about to start paying. "All of you will receive shares to help you remember where you eat."

A murmur raced the smiles around the lunchroom.

Tom wadded up the cheesy paper towels and threw them into the trash. "Your shares will be *restricted,* which means you can't sell them for five years. During this five-year period, you will lose your shares if you commit any of the offenses on this list." Tom produced a three-ring binder, two inches thick, and slammed it onto the table with a thud.

The smiles faded.

Tom opened the cabinet beside the fridge and pulled out two more binders, each slightly thicker than the first. He stacked them on the table then pulled out two more. "Frank, please go to my office and get the binders on the floor. You'd better take a cart."

Fifteen minutes later, the entire lunch table was stacked to a depth of six inches.

"I know what you're thinking." Tom waved at the stacked binders. "You are thinking this is too many rules, so you can probably break them. If I take away your shares, you can sue me on grounds the rules were not reasonable."

Tom's employees stared at him woodenly.

"But I assure you, each of these rules is reasonable and enforceable, just common sense." Tom picked up a binder and flipped it open. "For example, regulation 1910.334(a)(2)(i) states, *all portable power cords shall be visually inspected for damage before use on any shift.*" Tom closed the binder. "What kind of idiot would use an extension cord without first inspecting it for damage?"

Tom's employees looked skeptical, except Sophie Flint. She looked at the stacked binders, obviously puzzled. Then dawn broke, and she groaned.

Tom rested a fond hand on the heap. "These are federal, state, and local laws to which I subjected myself by offering you a job."

Grumble.

"To retain your restricted shares, all you must do is live by the rules that I accepted by hiring you."

Frank: "That's fucking impossible."

"It will be a challenge," Tom admitted. "However, it may comfort you to know that as CEO, President, Chairman of the Board, and owner of the vast, overwhelming majority of shares, I could choose to overlook small violations." Tom smiled broadly. "At my discretion."

The same moment
Southern Maryland
An unpaved road

Carl Canary watched the empty road and wondered, *am I an idiot?*

Canary polled his own opinion and calculated he was an idiot with 100% certainty. Unfortunately, this statistic was based on a relatively small sample, *n*=1. However, the sample included the entire relevant population, which simplified the math.

Canary had been doing math when a courier panted up the stairs with a gold coin, plus a map of Maryland marked with a red *X,* a time, and the words, *Tell no one.* Now, four hours later, Canary stood beside a gravel road, two hours drive from the capitol.

Canary couldn't resist the intrigue and the price of gold. He looked down the gravel road. Nothing. Then he jumped and covered his ears, far too late, as a chest-thumping sonic boom bounced road dust into the air. He looked up. "Yep. I'm an idiot."

Five minutes later, Gabriel the famous alien murderer landed his spaceship, opened his canopy, and noticed Canary's frozen smile. "Is something wrong?"

"Probably," said Canary. "I saw you on television."

Gabriel climbed down. "Do you know why I killed her?"

Canary was surprised to find the alien king was only five feet tall. "Three out of four Humans know why you killed the Daychat hostess. One in ten will admit it."

Now the alien looked interested. "Will *you* admit it?"

"Sure," said Canary. "You can cure any infectious disease, and she wanted you to do it free. When you refused, she tried to rally a legal looting mob to force you. We tolerate that, so she expected you would too."

Gabriel seemed pleased. "You might be the right man for this job. But be warned; if you try to coerce me, even indirectly, I must kill you. It's nothing personal, just a reflex."

"Yeah, I sort of suspected. Let's not talk about health care."

The alien limped down the gravel road. "I will pay you to determine what fraction of your population would force us to pay ransom, if they could."

Canary had long since stopped being surprised at what customers wanted to know. "What exactly do you mean by, *ransom?*"

"*Ransom* means charging me for something I already own, like your queens sell you permission to install plumbing in your own home. I require absolute privacy," Gabriel added. "Secrecy is crucial. I should have said that first."

"No worries." Canary picked up a rock and tossed it into a puddle. "What's your target population? Likely voters? Property owners?"

"Everyone within 20 miles of the Capitol."

Uh oh. Canary felt a chill. "Are you sure you want *everyone?*"

"Quite sure. Your sample must represent all Humans within 20 miles of your Capitol in Washington, D.C."

Canary flung a handful of gravel. Some splashed into the puddle, but most missed. "What about commuters? Some people work in the capitol but live farther out."

"Hmm." The alien considered. "Do you think the commuters might be more virtuous than the permanent residents?"

"I think that's the sort of question I get paid to answer."

"Let's start with everyone who'd likely be in the target zone at 4 AM on a weekday. For the main question, *what fraction would coerce us to pay ransom,* I want less than five-percent chance of more than five-percent error." Gabriel handed over a slip of paper. "Here is a web site and a password. We would like weekly updates, GPG-encrypted with this password. If you are compromised in any way, including by your government, you must capitalize the first letter of the filename. Take care not to do that by accident."

Canary frowned.

"Yes, there is risk," Gabriel admitted. "And you cannot be certain of my motive. Name your price."

Canary named it.

Gabriel did some mental arithmetic. Then he upended his silk bag and counted out a handful of yellow coins.

Canary hefted the coins. They were surprisingly heavy.

Gabriel closed his bag. "Leave now, before the helicopters arrive."

"One more question, if you please. When you arrived, your First-Contact prank offended Christians, which you obviously intended. Now, your reputation is under comprehensive attack, but you don't defend it. Why are you trying to alienate us?"

"Alienate." Gabriel chuckled.

Canary waited.

Gabriel tapped the black triangle on his cheek. "This first mark is temporary, just ink that lasts about a month. To redraw it, we must bite the forbidden fruit and face reality. That makes it hard for us to take your feigned outrage seriously."

"Gabriel, I spot misdirection for a living. Why did you introduce yourselves by mocking Christians?"

"No mystery," Gabriel called over his shoulder as he limped back to his spacecraft. "The kids did it *because they could.* On this planet, Christianity has lost its testicles."

Two hours later, as Canary drove over the Beltway and entered the Capitol zone, he smiled and thought about where to bury the gold coins. But he found himself nervously checking his mirror. *Was that yellow minivan there before?*

Don't be absurd. At this level, surveillance was done by drones. Nonetheless, he jumped when his phone chirped. He pushed the button. "Canary here."

"Mr. Canary, this is the office of the United States Secretary of Commerce. Secretary Siphon would like to see you personally, at your earliest convenience. Right now would be fine."

Canary's heart sank.

Kitty Siphon's office complex was elegant yet subdued, and included a comfortable waiting room filled with gold-inlaid furniture that subtly led the eye to a giant picture of President Mirror. An engraved brass sign said, *DO NOT USE CELL PHONES.* Canary sat on a leather couch and leafed through a pile of magazines. His choices were: *The Journal of Mathematical Geometry; Feminism Today;* or, *Industrial Sanitation Quarterly.*

For the next three hours, Canary leafed through two-year-old issues of *Industrial Sanitation Quarterly,* and wondered what would happen if he tried to leave.

Three hours after Canary arrived, the inner door opened to admit a girl in a tight red skirt. "The secretary will see you now."

Kitty Siphon was the secretary of commerce and famously the president's best friend, rumored to be his mistress. So it seemed fitting she looked lean and sexy, like her pictures but smaller. She sat behind her enormous rosewood desk, tapping her chin as she sized up Canary.

Canary resolutely did not squirm.

"Mr. Canary, you're working for the wrong team."

Canary remained calm. "Please call me, *Carl.*"

"Thank you, Carl. Please call me, *Madam Secretary.*"

Canary blinked. If that last exchange were televised, Kitty Siphon's favorables would fall 20 points overnight. "Very well, Madam Secretary."

"Carl, you've chosen to work for the opposition, an error you may now correct. We'd like to hire you for a consulting contract, a very lucrative contract. In fact, I predict we will double your revenue."

Canary nodded soberly. "What sort of contract?"

"Oh, the usual." Kitty waved airily. "Your targeted election polling is useful, so we might as well get some."

"Madam Secretary, what are you asking me for?"

"Oh, nothing formal," she replied. "But, since we'd be paying you so much, I suppose it would be nice to get your insights into the opposition's intentions."

Canary sighed. "You want the sort of insight one gains by knowing precisely what the enemy is polling for."

"I knew you were the right man."

"Madam Secretary, you've been misinformed. I decline your offer." Carl rose to leave.

"Carl, I suggest you reconsider. Otherwise, I hope your taxes are in order."

"My *taxes?*" Canary laughed.

Kitty didn't laugh.

"Madam Secretary, I support your opposition in elections. Over the years, I have learned that a little advance planning makes punitive IRS audits more fun." Carl pulled out his wallet, withdrew a business card, and dropped it on Kitty's desk. "This is my accountant. If you call him, he will not be surprised. He will explain that my taxes are quite simple, yet somehow, I overpaid by precisely $430, which I will receive as a refund when you audit me again. I chose that exact sum because it will exactly cover my cab fair, a bottle of Remy Martin, and an Asian massage with a happy ending."

Kitty was not impressed. "Carl, I enjoy unfettered access to this nation's intelligence-collection apparatus, so I know about your friendship with your very-young receptionist. Does your wife know?"

"Madam Secretary, if your peeping Toms were doing their job, they would have told you my very-young receptionist is married to my wife's very-young personal trainer. If you took pictures of us having sex, I hope you used good lighting and a high-resolution camera, so we can print them in poster size for our next party. And now, this charming extortion is over." Carl headed for the door.

"Happy endings are obsolete."

Canary hesitated.

"In Asian massage, the current best practice is the happy middle." Kitty's spike heels were up on her desk now, and she looked relaxed. "Your work for the opposition damn near cost us the election. Your precinct-level stuff is first rate, and apparently, you can keep your mouth shut. We want to hire you for a delicate inquiry."

His work on the *election?* Canary nearly burst out laughing.

"We want you to monitor voter attitudes about the aliens. While you're at it, push people to stop calling them, *aliens,* and call them *Worms* instead."

Canary sobered.

Siphon thoughtfully tapped her chin. "Normally, I like to sample the likely voters, but this alien problem– I mean this *Worm* problem, might affect turnout, so we'd better sample all eligibles."

"Let me guess," Canary ventured. "You want to know how voters will react if you force the Worms to start paying their fair share?"

"No, the Worms *can't* pay their fair share, so 60 percent of us want to nuke them. I just want to know how many will admit it."

One week later
The D.C. suburbs

Ellen was just finishing up her third Lean Cuisine when her phone chirped.

"Hello, this is Mike with Canary Opinion Research. I have nothing for sale. Do you have a few minutes to give us your opinions?"

Ellen liked to give her opinions. "I'm a little busy, but I guess I can spare a few minutes."

"Thank you! Am I correct that you live near Washington, D.C.?"

"Yes, for 15 years now, since we moved here from Orlando. That's where my husband's parents live, in Orlando. They have a condo with-"

"Excellent," Mike interrupted. "Do you know about the Worms? They are the aliens visiting us."

Ellen knew.

"Hypothetically, if some Worms were in trouble, do you think we should rescue them?"

"Well, of course" said Ellen, disapprovingly. "What a question."

"Very good," said Mike. "Suppose one of our spacecraft was in trouble. Do you think the Worms should rescue our astronauts?"

"Well, of course they should." Ellen used her stern voice.

"Are you aware the Worms can cure any infectious disease?"

Ellen was aware.

"Are you aware they intend to cure sick Humans for pay?"

Ellen knew all about that. She watched *DayChat.*

"If a sick child couldn't pay for the Worm treatment, what do you think we should do?"

Ellen paused, remembering the *Daychat* hostess who said the aliens, the *Worms,* should have to treat children for free. Then the Worm king shot her in the face.

"You are safe," Mike assured her. "I don't know your name, or even your phone number, and in a poll, the only offense is lying."

Ellen made her decision. "Well, they should treat the child anyway."

"I understand. What if the Worms refuse? Would we be justified in forcing them to treat the child?"

Ellen stiffened. "*Nobody* has the right to withhold care from a child."

"Very good," said Mike. "If we use force, and the Worms resist, some of them might be injured or killed. Would that change your opinion?"

"I'm not sure," Ellen said uncertainly. "I suppose it would depend."

"If the Worms refuse to treat a sick child for free, should you personally be forced to pay for the child's treatment?"

"What kind of question is that? I'm not a doctor."

"I understand," said Mike. "Just a few more questions. How much money would you personally pay the Worms to treat sick people for free, including children?"

"I shouldn't have to pay them. I'm not the one with the magic cure. They should just do it."

"I understand," said Mike. "But if the Worms refuse to do it for free, how much would *you* pay them?"

"I'm not sure," said Ellen, uncertainly. "Some, I guess."

"Would you pay $1,000?"

"A *thousand dollars?*" Ellen snorted. "I can't afford that much. They should just have to treat poor people."

"I understand," said Mike. "Are you aware, the Worms have refused to tell us how their treatment works?"

"Yes, I heard that. It's not right to keep something like that secret. They should have to tell us."

"Do you think the Worms should be forced to reveal their secret?"

"I wouldn't say, *forced,*" said Ellen. "They should just have to do it."

"I understand. If we sneaked aboard their ship and discovered their secret, should we tell everyone how it works?"

"Of course. Then more people could have it."

"Do you think we should try to sneak aboard the Worm mothership to discover their secret?"

"I don't know," Ellen hedged. "That might make them mad. I'm afraid of what they might do."

"I understand," said Mike. "If we could sneak aboard the Worm mothership and find their secret with no risk to us, should we do it?"

"Well, obviously, if there's no risk. That way, everyone could have the cure."

"I understand. Do you think the Worms should pay taxes?"

"Of course. What a question."

"What if the Worms don't actually use any government services?"

"What do you mean, *they don't use government services?*"

"What if the Worms provide their own defense, and their own retirement, and all other services. Should they still pay taxes?"

"Well, if they really don't take *anything,* they should get a lower rate," Ellen offered. "That would be fair."

"What if the Worms use no government services at all? Should they be exempt from all taxes?"

"That's not fair. They are making a lot of money."

"I understand," said Mike. "May I ask if you have children at home?"

"My younger boy is in the TV room. Why?"

"Might I speak with him? You could listen in."

The next day
Central Colorado

Steven Weaver dipped his runabout into a canyon. He nudged the throttle, and the airspeed indicator climbed to 330 knots. He was careful about his exhaust.

Steven was headed back to Advanced Circuits to check on his electroless copper-plating joint venture. He could have dropped straight down into their handicapped parking zone, since it was always empty, but he couldn't resist this canyon run. He roared past scattered Humans walking the river or paddling kayaks. Often, they shot him the finger, but some waved. He tried to wave back. He was a familiar sight.

Below, on a sandy beach, a handful of girls in bikinis waved excitedly. On the sand, rocks had been arranged to spell out a message.

BLOW JOB 4 RIDE

Up ahead was the bridge, Steven's favorite part of the trip.

Steven didn't know it, but the bridge was closed for maintenance. The closure had caused a traffic jam, but the cars were being diverted a half mile up the road, out of sight. On the bridge deck, 40 Mexicans chipped paint and tightened bolts.

Under the bridge, unseen by the workers, a toaster-sized metal box dangled from a hand-sized trolley, riding one of the bridge's many truss rods. The toaster-sized box sported an acrylic eye and a steel claw. For its size, the steel claw could support an astonishing load, but now it supported only a steel bolt. The bolt weighed 18 pounds, just like dozens of other bolts in the bridge, though all of the other bolts were bolted to something.

The toaster-sized box was a bombsight, almost but not quite standard military hardware, impressively capable, sophisticated, and overqualified in the era of guided bombs. This bombsight had been rescued from retirement and given a job, to watch the canyon. That was its purpose, to watch. It never got bored.

The bombsight didn't know it was perched on a bridge. It believed anything motionless was part of its mothership. The bombsight did not mind that its mothership included a canyon and parts of a bridge. The bombsight noticed the river was moving. That was good. The bombsight expected to see moving scenery.

The bombsight watched for a specific shape. The bombsight was clever; it could recognize its target shape from any angle.

At last, the bombsight spotted the correct shape, so it signaled its mothership. The signal meant, *Target Acquired.*

Downstream, divers slipped into the water.

The bombsight believed it was moving, while its target was stationary. Had the bombsight known of its error, it would not have cared. The math was the same, except for windage. The bombsight had been commanded to ignore windage, and it obeyed every grammatically-correct order.

The bombsight watched its approaching target and computed. Eventually, it queried its mothership's altitude, but got no response. The bombsight did not mind, because its designers had anticipated its mothership would be partially blown up. The bombsight did more math and inferred its altitude from the target image. This was easy, since the bombsight knew its target's dimensions precisely.

The target's dimensions had been obtained from a picture of the target parked beside two men, one tall and one short. The tall man was the Governor of Texas, smiling broadly and draping an arm over a short alien who was leaning away, looking uncomfortable in a printed T-shirt.

TEXAS
Going
Commie
Slower

The message was printed in letters whose dimensions were known precisely.

The bombsight watched the approaching target for 30 milliseconds, then commanded its mothership to change course.

The hand-sized trolley whirred, and the bombsight wheeled smoothly down the truss rod. When the angle was right, the bombsight commanded its mothership to hold course. The trolley stopped.

The bombsight watched and computed, working out the timing. The timing was easy compared to the task of recognizing its target from any angle.

When the bombsight decided the time was right, it opened its claw. The bolt dropped 22 feet before it struck the base of the pilot's canopy. At 330 knots, there was no doubt about penetration.

By design, the bolt struck at chest height, so Steven's head was not seriously damaged. More importantly, neither were his engines.

The spacecraft, its smashed canopy red with blood, dipped toward the water. On the first impact, it skipped, sailing 200 yards downstream before striking again, nose first. This time, the wildly tumbling fuselage was noticeably bent. On the fifth impact, it halted behind a sheet of spray, bobbed once, then sank.

Back at the bridge, Mexicans pointed and shouted. Beneath them, unseen, the bombsight rotated its claw to reduce wind drag. The rotating claw tugged on a cable looped through a release pin, and the entire bombsight dropped silently to the roiling water. Four seconds later, the surface shivered with the muffled thump of an underwater detonation.

For the next four minutes, the Mexicans chattered and the river gurgled. Then, half a mile downstream, a yellow buoy bobbed to the surface, invisibly small from this distance.

Two minutes later, a party boat, the big flat kind with a wide gap between its pontoons, chugged into view. The boat carried only five passengers, not enough for a proper party. The Mexicans shouted at it and and pointed downriver. Eventually, the boat passed over the yellow buoy and stopped. The five passengers looked into the water, then looked back toward the bridge and shrugged. At this distance, the gesture was wasted.

Two minutes later, the party boat chugged on, now moving slower.

Seven minutes later, the yellow buoy was destroyed when the river erupted in a booming fountain of mud. Back on the bridge, the Mexicans pointed and shouted.

Twelve hours after the crash, and 40 miles distant, a massive blast transformed a boring farmhouse into an interesting crater. The local newspaper reported it as a gas leak.

The alien spacecraft had two engines: one in the nose, and the other in the tail. Five hours after the first explosion, and 20 miles distant, a nondescript metal building exploded. Its corrugated steel roof burst skyward, fluttering down piecemeal onto nearby warehouses. The local newspaper ran a series on gas appliance safety.

Based on the two explosions, the state legislature passed new regulations that rendered 65 billion dollars' worth of gas-fired equipment illegal to sell or repair. The Gas Appliance Manufacturers Association promoted the legislation as a model for other states.

From the debris, most of the technicians' body parts were recovered, though this was not reported by the local newspaper. The spacecraft hull would yield some minor technical innovations, but the ship's metallurgy and avionics were disappointingly primitive. Unfortunately, the really interesting technical details were, necessarily, at the center of the blast.

Late that evening
Seattle, WA
The port district

Tito Taker toiled at his desk, cataloging the day's haul. Tito was a customs inspector, working late so he could be alone with the seizure inventory. He was sipping decaf coffee from his *United States Customs* mug, which had a picture of a remora, when his office lit up and he heard a rumble.

The rumble started small, but grew to a deafening roar that rippled Tito's decaf. He looked out the window and saw something descending onto the street, but trying to make out the shape was like trying to see the parachute above a magnesium flare. Tito thought of his military days as he opened his side drawer and pulled out his Colt 1911. Whatever was arriving, Tito would greet it before it deployed.

Outside, he found the street deserted except for a parked spacecraft, resting horizontally in a blackened circle. The alien craft was a two-seater, similar to the ones Tito had seen on the news. He smelled hot tar and saw asphalt had oozed up around the spacecraft's landing feet. Tito wished he had come out in time to see the famous post-landing topple, when their standing spacecraft tipped over to park.

The alien pilot was a male near Tito's age, late fifties, wearing a tailored martial-arts outfit. His cheek was decorated with the row of five mysterious tattoos, their color uncertain in the yellow streetlights. Tito tipped his hat. "Welcome to Earth. My name's Tito."

"Thanks, my name is Carl," said the alien. "Gold, silver, or poison?"

Gold, silver, or poison? That was how the aliens greeted Humans. It meant, *Shall we deal by consensual trade, or by coercion, or will you beg?* Tito eyed the holster strapped to the alien's thigh. It looked heavy, and rumor said it was loaded with silver bullets. "Let's stick with gold. Would you like some decaf?"

"I don't know. What is decaf?"

"Decaf is like kissing my sister."

The alien glanced at the 1911 in Tito's hand but didn't seem to find it unusual. "How could I pass up a chance to kiss your sister?"

Tito led him inside. "Any particular reason for this visit?"

"Yes. I want to buy cupholders."

"Wrong address. The cupholder company is the next street over. But you're right; he makes the only cupholders that would work in a roller-coaster or a spaceship. You'll want to talk to Kevin Curvle. He's the CEO, and a friend of mine."

The alien seemed to be impressed. "You just happen to be friends with the CEO?"

"I'm a customs officer. *Every* CEO wants to be my friend."

The alien's expression darkened.

"Relax; I know how you react to extortion, so I'll be careful." Tito poured a second mug of decaf.

The alien pointed to an inspection table sprinkled with contraband. "What is that?"

"That is testosterone cypionate I just seized."

The alien looked blank.

Tito handed him the mug of decaf. "It's an anabolic steroid."

"Really? I've heard those are used to boost athletic performance." The alien tried a tentative sip, then blinked. "Is this how it's supposed to taste?"

Tito chuckled. "I suppose somebody might use testosterone cypionate to cheat in the Olympics, but we have much better drugs for that. This stuff was probably going to some middle-aged guy who missed the old days when his pecker got hard and he wanted to stick it in something."

Now the middle-aged alien looked interested. "This drug boosts the sex drive of middle-aged men?"

"Oh, yes. Testosterone also boosts their sexual performance, I mean, *really* boosts it, along with their confidence, their joy in life, and their physical strength. They talk about it like it's a life-changing miracle."

The alien sipped his decaf. "So you confiscate it?"

"Yes." Tito gazed at the inspection table. "That's my job, to stop old men from getting their controlled substances." Suddenly, in the alien's presence, Tito's job didn't seem so cool.

The alien seemed fascinated by the contraband.

"Here, try some." Tito handed him a few vials. "You can look up the dosing on the internet, and the pills you have to take if you quit. It's pretty simple."

"Thank you." The alien accepted the testosterone vials gratefully.

For some reason, Tito wanted to change the subject. "So, you came all this way to buy cupholders? How many do you need?"

The alien tucked the testosterone into his pocket and produced a gold coin, the size of a dime but thinner. "Before we go further, I have to swear you to secrecy. Do you agree?"

As a customs officer, Tito was experienced in secret negotiations and untraceable gold coins. "What will happen later, if the secret gets out? Would you expect me to return the payment?"

"We'll boink that girl when she slows down."

"We say, *cross that bridge when we come to it.*"

"How polite." The alien waved the coin. "I'll pay you one penny-weight of gold to hold this conversation secret. Do you agree?"

Tito took the coin. "So, how many cupholders do you need?"

"I've bought your silence," Carl recited, "so your silence is now, *my thing.* If you betray me, what I will do?"

Tito pointed at Carl's holster. "Silver bullets?"

"They aren't exactly bullets, but you get the idea." The alien clapped Tito's shoulder and produced a stainless-steel flask. "We like to drink whisky while we talk about serious subjects, to help us speak plainly."

"I respect your traditions." Tito held out his mug.

Carl poured a dash into Tito's coffee, then into his own. "We didn't have much storage space, so we only brought the good whisky. Sadly, our world had no oak trees, so we couldn't make bourbon, if we had known how to make bourbon."

"In that case, let me introduce you to Irish decaf." Tito opened the lunchroom fridge for the heavy cream. "Sorry, I don't have any vanilla." He poured cream into both mugs, then dumped in some brown sugar. "What did you mean, *they aren't exactly bullets?*"

Tito touched his holster. "My pistol doesn't shove out the slug like a musket ball. The silver squirts out in a proper jet."

"Seriously? Your sidearm detonates a shaped charge? You must have good earplugs."

Carl sipped the half-assed Irish cream and looked pleased. "Is this really cow's milk? Drinking it seems kind of perverted."

"I never thought of it that way," said Tito. "Now it tastes a little better. So, how many cupholders do you need?"

"Forty thousand."

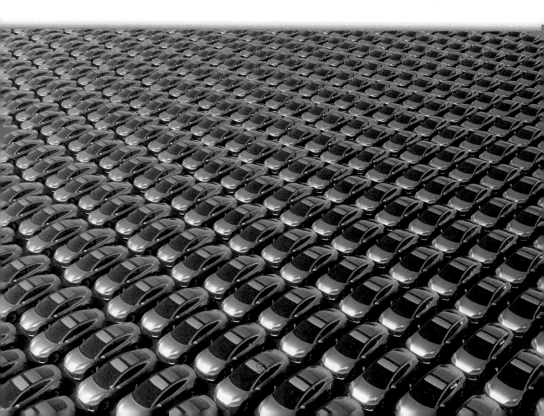

"Forty *thousand* cupholders?" Tito was surprised. "How'd you fit 40,000 boats into your mothership? I heard she's only 3,000 tons."

"40,000 cupholders is enough for 10,000 boats, but we couldn't fit anywhere near that many into the *Finger*." The alien grinned. "We're building a spaceship factory in our new colony!"

Tito considered that. Eventually, he said, "May I try your whisky straight?"

The alien hesitated, then handed over his flask.

Tito tried a generous swallow. "Pretty good," he lied. The alien whisky tasted like moonshine. "You got enough land for a colony? Here on Earth?"

"Yep. We're still keeping it secret, but it means you could join us, right now, if you want to be like me." The alien tapped the row of tattoos across his cheek.

Tito was already feeling the whisky. "Where exactly is your colony?"

"We bought a chunk of Africa. I won't tell you exactly where, but it's a rectangle, 90 miles by 110. We got it cheap."

"Africa?" Tito hesitated. He glanced around the lunchroom to make certain they weren't overhead, then lowered his voice. "Will you... um... will there be a wall?"

"Of course we'll build a wall around our colony. How else could we keep out wasps?"

"Hmm. Would you make me immune to malaria?"

"Oh, yes, we kill all parasites."

"Wow. And I can just move there? Just like that? Then I'd be ungovernable." Tito gazed at the pile of seized contraband. "I'd be forced to find a new job."

"Quite so," said the alien. "You won't earn a living by confiscating other people's drugs."

Tito turned a slow circle, taking in the massive customs warehouse. "I think maybe a new job might be good for me."

"We would test you first, to be sure you *really* want to kill parasites," the alien cautioned. "That's crucial. If we made you ungovernable, but in your secret heart, you root for the wasps, you'd eventually decide to kill yourself."

Am I really willing to leave my home and friends to join the aliens? Tito recalled his last encounter with the city government, in which he'd learned the 35-MPH speed limit on the Interstate service road was *not*, despite all appearances, a joke. "I'm in. Can we go now?"

The alien looked serious. "Are you *certain?* It's a bigger commitment than you might realize. The brain alterations are not reversible, and once you're one of us, it will be dangerous to visit your old friends."

Tito was really feeling the whisky buzz. "Fuck yeah. A whole culture where nobody tries to live by robbing me, and I can't... I won't be allowed to...Yes, I'm in. I don't need time to say goodbye. My friends are.... my friends won't be joining you, and if I suggested it, they would turn into something I don't want to witness."

The alien whisky must have been strong, because the room was swaying, and the alien's voice seemed to drift in through a tunnel. "Very well. If you're certain, I will start the…"

The next morning
Seattle, WA
The port district

Tito opened his eyes, and realized he was staring at ceiling tile with yellow stains. *What the hell?* He sat up and found himself in the customs warehouse, with an icepick headache. *How did I get here?*

The last thing Tito remembered was working late on a steroid confiscation. He rubbed the back of his head and found a painful bump. *I must have passed out and fallen on my head. Dammit. Now I have to get an MRI and see if I had a stroke.*

Tito walked outside into the twilight of sunrise or sunset. The streets were empty, so it must be sunrise. He smelled tar and noticed a 30-foot circle of darker asphalt. Had it just been patched? No, the darkened asphalt looked as rough and rutted as always. In fact, he saw three fresh potholes, deep and unnaturally square. Had someone set up a crane here, and pushed its stabilizing feet into the soft asphalt? But why did the asphalt look partially melted?

Whatever it was, Tito thought, *it must have been unusual. I'm sorry I missed it.*

Comments. Please respect the <u>forum rules</u>.

Pokemom Yesterday
> I can't believe we're all pretending this alien invasion is okay. Does a Worm have to rape YOUR wife before you will do something?

LawFareForU Yesterday
> It's not my wife I'm worried about, it's my daughters. Have you seen the stories about the missing girls?

Moby Duck Nine hours ago

Washington, D.C.

Dominick Tork began his briefing by establishing his authority. "Before I present today's data, I will remind you of your security commitments."

In the elegant briefing theater, every face lost its expression. The commissioners of the Alien Regulatory Authority had not forgotten their security briefings, which had included each commissioner's porn search history and a list of 19 websites eager to publish it. The websites were popular; the porn-search histories were accurate; and the interesting keywords had been highlighted.

"Today's material is particularly sensitive. If this material were leaked to the press, it might be prudent to reconstitute this commission from scratch." Dominick looked around mildly. He kept looking much longer than seemed strictly necessary.

When he felt the commissioners had accepted his dominance, he proceeded. "The Worms want to recruit our citizens. They made this clear in their First-Contact broadcast. Since then, they have repeated their invitation in hundreds of personal conversations. If they are allowed to establish a colony here, on our planet, the Worms will offer a haven to any Human who doesn't want to pay his fair share."

Dominick had worked on that last sentence for an hour to get the meaning across without using the word, *ransom.*

Around the theater, commissioners looked uncomfortable.

"Unfortunately, when it comes to the Worms, our people do not feel safe to voice their true opinions, so we've been forced to experiment." Dominick touched his computer.

Behind him, the ten-foot screen came to life with video of a crowded gymnasium. "These people believe they are participating in a disaster rehearsal." Dominick turned up the sound until the briefing theater echoed with the screaming of a dozen women. The video zoomed in to one woman on a stretcher, covered with blood and shrieking enthusiastically. "We recruited the victims from a local drama club and told them to indulge themselves."

Now the commissioners looked comfortable.

"This disaster drill was a planned psychological experiment, designed to learn the subjects' true desires regarding the Worms. This particular experiment exploited a curious effect we discovered by chance, in a previous experiment. We observed the screaming of injured women actually induced honesty between men. We speculate this instinct evolved to help competing males cooperate in a crisis."

The commissioners' expressions shifted from, *comfortable,* to, *interested.*

Dominick paused the playback. "The results of this experiment have been replicated with actual injured women. A total of 19,221 test subjects have been reduced to honesty by various combinations of injured women, trustful strangers, imminent death, psychedelic mushrooms, scopolamine, religious confessional, and, of course, tequila. An additional 6,014 test subjects have been convinced the aliens *already* possess a secret colony, which the test subject was invited to join. The invitations were fake, but they were credibly staged, including replica alien spacecraft lowered from cranes or helicopters, at a cost of 1.4 million dollars per incident. The total cost of these experiments added up to just under 19 billion dollars. Be warned; you may find the results disturbing. The video you are about to see is, unfortunately, not unusual." Dominick touched his computer.

The video panned over to a pair of men in folding chairs, chatting.

"The man on the right is our shill. The man on the left is our unwitting test subject. On several prior occasions, this test subject publicly condemned the Worms, and expressed his disdain for their ideology, so we might expect him to be loyal." Dominick turned up the sound.

On the screen, the test subject glanced around furtively, then lowered his voice. "The aliens are bastards, but the truth is, if I got the chance to send my kids to their colony, I would do it."

Around the elegant theater, the commissioners' expressions shifted from, *interested,* to, *alarmed.*

"Our tests prove public statements do *not* reliably indicate loyalty. We used our test results to project total Worm recruitment over the next 20 years." Dominick touched his keyboard, and the display switched to a map of the United States. The major cities looked like donuts, with white centers surrounded by gray rings. The coastal regions were light gray, darkening to a broad band of black centered on the Midwest, from northern Texas to the Dakotas.

Projected Worm recruitment rates range from below 10 percent in the inner cities, to 20 percent in the suburbs and nearly *40 percent* in the rural Midwest." Dominick waved at the ominous display. "Overall, the Worms will eventually recruit 17 percent of the U.S. population, or 56 million people."

Commissioners gasped.

"The really bad news," Dominick added, "is the 56 million will not be chosen randomly. No doubt you have all heard the rule of thumb, *ten percent of the people do 90 percent of the work.*"

The commissioners murmured.

"It turns out the 90/10 rule is too cynical. In reality, half the output of a typical organization is produced by the square root of its head count. For example, if a firm employs 100 salesmen, the top 10 will generate half the sales. This is called the *Pareto rule,* and it describes nearly every human endeavor. In the case of the U.S. economy, our total workforce is 160 million Humans. The square root of 160 million is 13,000, which implies approximately half the U.S. economic output is due to 13,000 people."

The murmur halted. Most of those 13,000 would be tempted to join the Worms, and the commissioners knew it.

The tall patrician tried to claim dominance. "That's absurd. 13,000 people can't produce as much as the other 160 million, regardless of how hard they work."

In Dominick's mind, the gorilla saw the challenge to his dominance, and roared. However, the ape who called himself, *Dominick* was more subtle, and merely rolled his eyes. "That's *not even wrong."*

The patrician reddened. The other commissioners looked amused.

"My point, obviously, is that without the genius of the top 13,000, the productivity of the rest would be halved." Dominick stared at the patrician. "If you'd ever worked with *average* people, you'd know this estimate is plausible."

"Ah, well." The patrician looked pleased. "You may have a point. I rarely get the chance to rub elbows with the average man."

Dominick was no average man, but his mind did contain the average number of monkeys. Each mental monkey was built for a specific task: to recognize females, to align a glove with an approaching baseball, to excavate boogers, to undermine a rival, and all the other chores of human culture.

Many of Dominick's mental monkeys were built for social tasks. Dominick's largest social monkey was the gorilla. The gorilla was built to establish social dominance by any means necessary, including beating the shit of anyone who tries to be clever by pointing out gorillas are not monkeys.

Dominick's second-largest social monkey was Miss Manners. Her job was to prevent Dominick from getting kicked out of his tribe, and now she was nodding approval. *Nicely done. We gave the tall patrician an exit that makes him look good.*

That's a mistake, growled the gorilla. *The tall patrician challenged our dominance. We should pound him flat.*

"By year 20," Dominick continued, "around the world, we project the Worms will recruit 500 million Humans, leaving behind eight billion of the most needy. Our analysts differ on the details, but they agree the remaining Human culture will be able to feed at least 400 million, but not more than two billion. Our best estimate is one billion."

The commissioners looked uncertain.

The tall patrician gave them a voice. "The Worms will leave us a population of eight billion that can only feed one billion? What happens to the other seven billion?"

Dominick smiled thinly. "What normally happens to people without food?"

Dominick expected the commissioners to look appalled, but they seemed fascinated. In a flash of insight, he realized they were imagining themselves deciding who would be fed. "As you know from the media, a two-seat alien spacecraft was destroyed by an act of vigilante justice. What you will not learn from the media..." Dominick paused. The commissioners were smiling, but none would meet his eye. "What you will *not* hear from the media," he repeated, "is the accident spared the spacecraft's engines."

All of the commissioners had smiled when Dominick said, *the spacecraft was destroyed.*

"Like all the Worm spacecraft, this one was propelled by cherub swords, small copies of the six massive engines that drove the *Unexpected Finger* through interstellar space. This particular craft had two engines, one in the nose and one aft. The aft engine fired through a single, rearward-pointing nozzle, while the nose engine was actually a cluster of 12 tiny cherub swords, variously angled for secondary thrust and attitude control."

Commissioners were sagging. They began to murmur.

Dominick realized they needed smaller paragraphs. "A team of six engineers was tasked to investigate the nose engine cluster. All of them were killed when it exploded."

The theater quieted abruptly.

"A tamper-proof bomb is, unfortunately, no great technical challenge, so when the forward engine blew up, our engineers abandoned their attempt to penetrate the aft engine. However, after 17 hours, it exploded of its own accord and destroyed our magnetic-resonance imager. Fortunately, the self-destruct blast was small, roughly equivalent to our standard, 2,000-pound bomb."

A 2,000-pound bomb is *small?* Commissioners seemed doubtful.

Dominick helped them understand. "An aircraft's bomb rack holds much less energy than its fuel tanks, at least for conventional weapons."

That didn't seem to reduce anyone's doubt, so Dominick tried again. "The Worm engines do not *store* energy; they *generate* it. The yield from destroying them is only a fraction of their potential. Unfortunately, while the blasts were small, they were nonetheless blasts. Clearly, the Worm's rigid, anti-coercion philosophy does not prevent them from building devices that might harm bystanders."

Blank stares. Obviously, the commissioners had missed the point, so Dominick spelled it out. "The problem is the *Unexpected Finger.*"

The *Unexpected Finger* was the Worm mothership, in orbit.

"If the *Finger's* destruction released even a tiny fraction of the energy it produced for its flight to Earth, the thermal radiation would be unacceptably intense, which, in this context, means you personally would catch fire."

Around the theater, faces contorted as if smiles were straining to break through their owners' grim resistance.

"The Worm technology may be primitive, but they have tapped into powerful forces. You should not want to see those forces unleashed without restraint. Fortunately, we are protected by our atmosphere. The air above us weighs as much as *four feet* of stainless steel." Dominick glanced up. "Four feet of stainless steel. Remarkable. Who would guess such wispy impediments could add up to such a weighty barrier, if layered deeply enough?"

Tom Pine was three hours into the Sarbanes-Oxley rules, trying to figure out which applied to the CEO of a privately-held corporation. He was about to give up and start searching for a Sarbanes-Oxley lawyer when his office door opened.

Sophie's head popped in. "We have a problem. The last lot of upper shrouds didn't include the US-ROHS paperwork, so it's illegal to use it. I called the supplier, but he gave me the runaround."

"Then they probably fudged the paperwork. Oh well." Tom shrugged. "We can't use it. Start looking for a new supplier."

"It's holding everything up, and the shrouds are custom designed. Getting them from another supplier will take weeks."

"Bummer."

"Dammit. I hate this stupid plan." Sophie slammed the door.

Tom resumed his research into the Sarbanes-Oxley rules.

His office door opened and Sophie's head popped back in. "Two of the technicians didn't get their annual wellness exam."

"Then they can't work," said Tom. "That regulation is ambiguous, but we'd better err on the side of caution. Send them home until they can get a doctor's appointment."

"One of them is Frank Drummer," Sophie added. "We won't make much progress without him."

"That's a blow." Tom's phone chirped. He picked up. "Pine here."

"Good afternoon," said the familiar voice of Dominick Tork. "How are your sentries progressing?"

"Progress is stalled," said Tom. "I did what you said, and started paying more attention to legal compliance. We're doing our best, but at this pace, finishing the alien sentries will take years. I'm sorry, because I know you wanted to see them delivered."

"That will not be a problem," said Dominick. "Our policies have changed somewhat, and now, we're in no hurry to see the alien sentries completed. Is there anything else I should know?"

"Yes," said Tom. "You're extremely annoying."

Dominick chuckled. "Dealing with you is always a pleasure."

Tom hung up. "Dammit, it didn't work. I think Dominick *wants* to slow us down." He pointed to Sophie. "Tell Frank to get his ass back in here, and go back to cheating on the regulations."

Tom resumed his Sarbanes-Oxley research. At lunchtime, he glanced at the clock, then looked out the window. The parking lot was filled with picketers waving signs.

VEGANS AGAINST WORMS

Tom walked out the front door and strode into the crowd, taking up station beside a frail woman with hair like straw, waving a sign that read, *VEGANS AGAINST WORMS.* She looked at Tom suspiciously. "You work with *them.*"

"They are watching. Don't look at me."

The vegan backed away.

"Don't look at me. I can't keep it secret any longer." Tom glanced around nervously. "It's too dangerous."

"What's too dangerous?"

Tom heard someone shouting into a bullhorn, and realized it was Frank Drummer, chanting *Hey Hey! Ho Ho! Work for pay has got to go!* The crowd joined in enthusiastically.

"The aliens are bringing tazanol *here,*" Tom hissed. "They are actually *doing it.* Who could have imagined?"

"They're bringing *what?"* The vegan stepped closer.

"If word got out, they know we'd go crazy, so in public, they carry it in a pizza box." Tom glanced at her sign, then added, "Meat lovers."

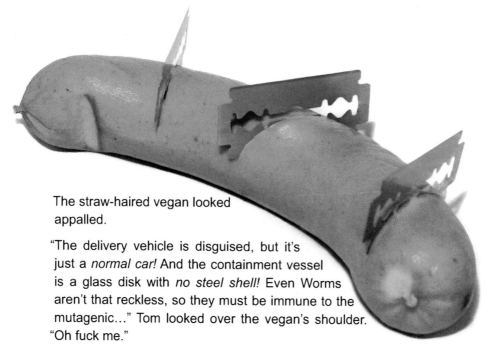

The straw-haired vegan looked appalled.

"The delivery vehicle is disguised, but it's just a *normal car!* And the containment vessel is a glass disk with *no steel shell!* Even Worms aren't that reckless, so they must be immune to the mutagenic..." Tom looked over the vegan's shoulder. "Oh fuck me."

A pizza-delivery car was trying to enter the parking lot but was blocked by angry protesters. However, after they spoke to the straw-haired vegan, the protesters decided to clear the parking lot and protest at City Hall for a while.

Tom paid the driver, then carried the pizza inside to the weekly meeting of his Executive Council. Today's agenda had been written out by hand, and contained one item: *Chicago Style.* Tom set the box on the conference table. "Why so gloomy?"

The Worms looked wooden.

"More of you were killed?"

Luci nodded.

"I can't believe you're so reckless." Tom opened the pizza box. "It seems like two or three of you are getting killed every week, so why do you mingle with us? It's a stupid risk, when you could do your business by phone."

Luci shook her head.

Tom took his cue to change the subject. "I keep hearing about your *burning bush*, the machine that rewires your brain for your tattoos. Is the bush a general-purpose brain adjuster? Could it change your thinking in other ways?"

"Oh yes, we still search for new ways to use the bush," said Natalie, the older alien. "A clever man in my generation actually came close. He adjusted his brain to recognize any incomplete task as his first priority, so he wouldn't leave half-finished projects sitting on the porch. Unfortunately, he couldn't stop cleaning the house."

The television switched to a talking head above the caption, *23rd Woman Alleges Alien Rape.*

Tom waved his pizza at the TV. "Was that real?"

On the television, the talking head was replaced by a gruesome image of the bank teller with most of her lower jaw missing.

"We did the rapes, but not the bank teller," Luci answered. "She was shot by an imposter."

The conversation paused while a solitary protester, outside in the parking lot and apparently saddened that his friends had ditched him, blew an air horn.

"I don't know about the bank teller," said Tom, when the air horn ran out of gas and faded into a delicate *toot.* "But the rape victims could have stopped the attacks just by asking, if they only knew. I promised to keep quiet, but it's getting out of hand. You've put me in a terrible position."

"Yes, we have." Luci touched Tom's hand. "Do you trust me?"

Tom pulled his hand away. "Of course not."

On the television, the mutilated bank teller was replaced by a black-and-white video looking down on a couple in an elevator. The woman's face was pixelated to hide her identity. The video paused, and a red circle appeared on the man's cheek, highlighting his Worm tattoos. The video resumed, and he tackled the Human woman, driving her to the floor and tearing at her clothes. Her breasts pixelated as he ripped open her top.

Tom watched them struggle. "Is that real?"

Luci watched the video with interest. "Yep. I know him."

"Luci, this is a problem. Plenty of women must have flirted with aliens and been attacked, then saved themselves by saying, *stop,* but that has *never* been reported. Even more ominous, before you arrived, no television station would have dared show a rape video. Now we see one every week, with the FCC's blessing. We're being prepared for something ugly."

"Yep." Luci sprinkled red pepper onto her bread stick. "We knew this would happen."

"If you knew you'd be demonized, you must have a plan. What is it?"

"Be ourselves and wait for the truth to come out."

Tom groaned.

111

After lunch, Sophie set to work on the quarterly EEOC disclosures. She'd been at it only three hours when the older alien, Natalie, walked in and said. "I want to see mythical flying creatures."

Ten minutes later, Sophie peeked out the window. "This is absurd."

The parking lot was mobbed by protesters waving signs.

 CAPITALISM EQUALS RAPE

Sophie strode back to the prototype room to fetch Buff.

The huge alien escorted the girls out to Sophie's car. The protesters edged away, eying Buff's holster, except one busty redhead blocked the car, holding a sign that read, *FLIRTING IS NOT CONSENT.*

Buff looked at her sign, and sighed. "What will it take to persuade you to move?"

"Why ask?" The busty redhead scowled. "Why don't you just move me by force? Then you'd have an excuse to feel me up without my consent."

"You *want* it." Buff grabbed a handful of shirt and bra between her ample boobs and jerked her in close.

Picketers gasped, then pointed at Buff and murmured angrily. The busty redhead in his grip looked surprised. "How could you tell?"

"Long and humiliating training." Buff glanced at the angry crowd. "What are you doing with these assholes?"

She grinned. "These men are pathetic. They're so *hungry* for a girl who's a good sport, but when they actually meet one, they have to assume it's a trap. Teasing them is fun."

Buff laughed and wrapped a muscular arm around her. "Do you think any of them have the nerve to rescue you?"

"Maybe if I moan," she murmured, "and you grab my ass."

"WHAT THE HELL!" Sophie rolled down her window and glared.

The busty redhead looked disappointed. "Is that your girlfriend?"

Buff looked alarmed.

"Oh, all right," the busty redhead muttered. "Pretend you're just dragging me out of her way."

Thirty minutes later, Sophie pulled her car into a parking lot for the BirdWalk, a wood-planked causeway that wandered through a marsh to a fish hatchery. Natalie rummaged in her bag and produced an aerosol can.

"Good idea." Sophie locked the car doors. "Can I borrow some?"

"Borrowing from me would be extremely dangerous, but you may have some as a gift." Natalie sprayed herself then handed over the black-labeled can.

Sophie started to spray her legs, then stopped. "Good Lord, this is not repellent; this is *pesticide.* What are you doing spraying this poison on your skin? You sprayed this on your *face!"*

Natalie rubbed in the spray. "Good locks make bad neighbors."

Sophie shuddered and handed back the can of *Raid Flying Insect Killer.* "Good locks do *not* make bad neighbors. I have every right to lock my door and expect the neighbors to knock."

"Child, you know that's not what I meant."

Sophie looked away.

"You feel it, don't you?" Natalie stepped closer. "You feel a foggy uncertainty, the clue that part of your brain has been turned off by your censor. We call him the *serpent,* and right now, this very moment, he is hiding your motive for misinterpreting me."

Sophie unlocked her car's trunk and began rooting.

Natalie persisted. "In your hidden heart, you *know* passive defense is a sin. If a wasp attacks your home and is merely repelled, he will move on to try your neighbor's home. That is why you all live in fear. You prefer the selfish path, and your censor helps you justify your cowardice."

Sophie did not answer, only produced an orange can and sprayed herself with repellent. Then she locked up her car and set off down the walkway.

Natalie sighed, and followed silently.

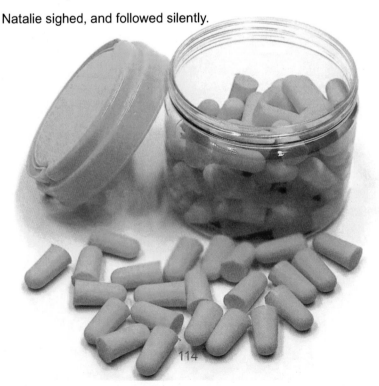

A hundred yards into the marsh, far from prying ears, Sophie spoke again. "You must defend yourselves."

Natalie slapped her wrist, leaving a red smear.

"We're always going to hate you," Sophie added, "but if you defend yourselves, we'll have to pretend we don't."

Natalie scratched her wrist, then gazed at the blood on her fingers.

"And you can't let people call you, *Worms*. That just invites attack."

Natalie bent to scratch her calf, leaving a trail of blood.

Up ahead, a flock of orange-breasted birds dropped to earth and spread over the damp ground, searching.

Sophie waved at the prowling hunters. "Worms are helpless victims, the lowliest of the low. You need a better name."

Natalie looked confused, then slapped her forehead.

"Right now, you're everyone's favorite punching bag, but I'm telling you, if you just defend your honor, you'll see we are hopelessly divided, with half of us wanting to kill you and the other half wanting to join you."

"*Half* of you want to join us?" The alien looked amused. "We'd be pleased with one in four. We expect one in six."

"That's not the point. My point is, our government is obviously making it safe to attack you, and you're going along with it. A mosquito is biting your arm."

Natalie swatted her bicep. "Drat. Next time, please don't tell me. I want to know if the poison works, but if I see something sucking my blood, I can't stop myself from swatting it."

"You're ignoring me." Sophie sighed. "If you're determined to make yourself a target, then I'd better ask this now. When Buff assaulted me, did he *really* know I was flirting?"

"Oh, yes, he knew perfectly well. Do you remember, we adjusted Buff's brain to make him more sexually aggressive?"

Sophie was not likely to forget.

"For Buff, that adjustment was no blessing," said Natalie. "In fact, I thought it was a mistake, because he can't take what's not offered."

Sophie set off down the walk. "I hate to think of Buff suffering like that. With his looks, he must get so few offers."

"That's true." Natalie spun in place, following a circling dragonfly. "So it was doubly important that we taught him to recognize our offers."

Sophie halted. "Did you just say you *taught* Buff to recognize sexual offers?"

"If we don't teach men to recognize our offers, how would they learn?"

"They won't. They have to keep guessing, and that's how I want them."

Natalie didn't seem surprised. "Many young girls feel as you do. They disapprove of Sunrise."

The alien's left shoulder was now occupied by a mosquito. Sophie eyed it, and said, "Sunrise?"

Up ahead, a pair of snowy egrets paced through the dappled sunlight. Or rather, the female paced as the male struck a pose. He stretched his wings, pointed his beak skyward and fluffed out his feathers. The female strode past, oblivious. Eventually, he broke his pose to trot after her. She didn't seem to notice.

Nor did she seem in any hurry to get away.

Natalie watched the courtship. "Do you know animals have mating cues, changes in female behavior that indicate her willingness?"

Sophie knew.

"It turns out we women also have mating cues, behaviors so subtle they lie below our perception."

"Like flipping our hair?" Sophie glanced at the mosquito, still enjoying Natalie's shoulder.

"We are well aware of hair flips. I mean the less obvious cues of posture and movement. We call them the *finks,* and before you ask, if you ever learn your own finks, you'll regret it." Natalie swatted her calf, leaving a smear of blood.

Sophie watched the mosquito. It didn't move.

"I teach Sunrise, so I've learned all the finks. Now I am constantly tempted to act strategically and send mixed signals." Natalie swatted her fanny. "Around our men, you *don't* want to send mixed signals."

"You have my attention," Sophie admitted. "What is *Sunrise?*"

Natalie slapped her thigh. "Sunrise is my company's product. We gather young men and older women together, and take drugs that make us behave differently. We all drink a fiendish cocktail that makes us crave sex."

Sophie's pupils dilated.

"I see you recognize the opportunity, but I'll not give away the formula. You can probably guess it includes a chemical that your liver converts to machonester."

"Mac and what?"

Natalie stopped to scratch her ankles. "The chemical that makes men male."

"Okay, I guess I can believe that." Sophie glanced back to the mosquito still riding Natalie's shoulder. "But I don't believe horny men can be taught faster."

"Sadly, no; sexual frenzy does not help anyone see clearly. In fact, the men could not complete their training in a reasonable time if they did not bite the forbidden fruit."

Sophie moved on down the walkway. "I keep hearing about this forbidden fruit. Does it really force you to see what you've been hiding from yourself?"

"Oh, yes, the forbidden fruit is brutal. It forces you to look inside your mind, and see what you really think." The alien grimaced. "For a man to spend so much time looking inside, *while he is being rejected by women...* I cried when my sons did it. It's nearly unbearable for men with unsound bodies."

"Sunrise is sounding better and better."

"I haven't told you the clever part." Natalie stopped to swat her calf, then scratched. "We also give the men a cocktail that helps them perform sexually many times per day, but only for ten minutes, and it prevents them from finishing."

Sophie raised an eyebrow. "Perform sexually for ten minutes?"

"Approximately ten minutes, many times per day. The time limit can be adjusted. It always starts an argument."

"That must make for some lively committee meetings." Sophie pointed to a pair of cardinals, a bright red male and a stealthy brown female. They flitted from tree to tree but never strayed far from each other.

Natalie scratched her cheek. "To help the men learn, the old ladies take a drug that boosts the connection between our arousal response and our blush reflex."

Sophie watched the cardinals fly away together. "When you get horny, you turn pink?"

Natalie slapped her fanny. "The blush is obvious and helps the men read us."

"Is that all it takes?"

"No, our intelligence makes us strategic, so we fool the men easily, even with pink cheeks."

Sophie felt a premonition. "Surely, you don't..."

Natalie grinned and scratched her wrist. "Yes, child, the last drug is the most important. It makes me stupid."

"You must be joking."

Natalie just smiled and scratched.

"So you basically get drunk with a bunch of horny men?"

Natalie seemed startled, and scratched before she answered. "Child, you have a real insight there. But no, alcohol changes how we move, and would make us sick if we drank ourselves dim. Our drug is more like... on our world there is a creature, dumb as a stone but prodigiously fertile."

"A rabbit?" Sophie checked on the mosquito. No change.

"No, it's a hamster we use as a wash cloth. Afterward, it licks itself clean. But you have grasped the core, that we reduce ourselves to animals with no concern for the future. We cannot even speak, though we move with grace."

"So the idea is to hang around with men, being dumb and obvious?

Natalie swatted her thigh. "At first, the old ladies are so dim, we actually follow the attractive men around the camp like children chasing a candy jar. The men watch our movements carefully. Everyone can see everyone else, so tall men can learn from the experience of attractive men. Over time, our intelligence returns, so we become coy and complex, but slowly enough for the men to follow."

Sophie looked confused. "Tall men learn from attractive men?"

"Yes. It helps that we teach them what to watch for." Natalie slapped her forehead.

"Are you ready to give in and put on some mosquito repellent?"

"No."

Sophie reached to Natalie's shoulder and gently picked off the unresisting mosquito. "Sounds like Sunrise takes all day."

Natalie snorted. "Your men must be smarter than ours. We are locked in together for six weeks, and we repeat the cycle many times. It takes so long, we risk losing our sense of purpose. That's why we must work for our food."

Sophie inspected the paralyzed mosquito. "Your poison works. I assume the women are well paid to humiliate themselves?"

"Oh, I pay myself handsomely. Sunrise is long days of simple urges and shared labor with young men who study my every move. At night, we have a campfire." Natalie trailed off, lost in her memories.

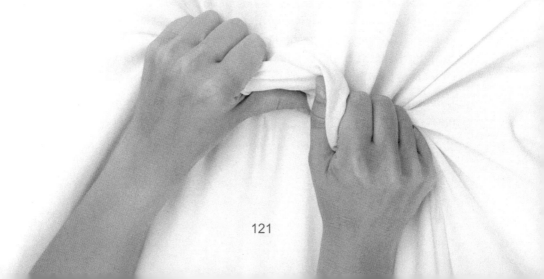

Sophie flicked away the poisoned mosquito.

Eventually, the alien stirred from her reverie and swatted her neck. "Young girls rarely participate, and I don't encourage them. Let them keep their dignity and their secrets, if they think it will help."

"I'm sure you have no trouble signing up men."

Natalie scratched her thigh, leaving a streak of blood. "Men would pay us more if Sunrise was staffed by teenage girls."

Sophie frowned.

"Even with old ladies, nearly all men find their way to our door. Afterward, the homely ones don't speak of it fondly." Natalie's eyes crinkled into a grin. "The old ladies complain too, while the men are around, and we try to sound sincere."

"Whatever works for you," Sophie sniffed. "But I don't need animal sex. I want real love. Do you know what that means?"

Natalie didn't answer, only glanced at the sky.

Ten minutes later, they reached the hatchery. Sophie dropped a quarter into a gumball machine and received a handful of pellets. They ambled down the aisle, tossing in pellets that were snatched by hatchlings. Eventually, they reached a spillway that separated a cloudy, crowded lower tank from a fresh upper tank.

Eight-inch hatchlings flopped and splashed as they struggled to climb the spillway to the coveted upper tank. Natalie watched them, her gaze flicking from the clean upper tank to the poop-laden lower tank, and the rushing spillway between. Then she walked to the upper tank, smiled mischievously and tossed a pellet in front of the spillway. The bait was snatched by a hatchling whose momentum carried it over the brink, sending it sliding down into the crowded, dirty lower tank. Natalie giggled.

Sophie watched soberly. "Do you get many chances to play a practical joke on a fish?"

"No, this is fun. The fish don't remind me of my children."

Well. How about that.

The same moment
Shenandoah National Park
200 yards from the Human-Alien colony talks

The clown trudged down the forest trail to the red spaceship.

Why am I not loving this? Barely halfway, he found his gait faltering, and the bag of gold was so heavy. With an effort, he picked up his pace.

This was no good. In this mental state, he couldn't do his job. The clown dropped his bag, sat on a fallen log, and closed his eyes. Birds sang, and the clown reminisced about the courtroom jousting in his three glorious divorces.

After two nostalgic minutes, he felt calm enough to turn his talent inward and explore his own motives. He considered his situation, negotiating with a hyper-violent alien who might perceive his very thoughts, bargaining for the future of his species, pretending to be controlled by a committee but actually controlled by a man with no self-control and a woman with no honor, pursuing a goal diametrically opposite his stated purpose.

He was doing the job he was built for, so how could he possibly feel gloom, an emotion with but one cause? Some part of his mind must have decided his goals conflicted, so to achieve one, he must abandon another. The clown considered his goals, searching for a hidden contradiction. In order of priority, his most urgent goal was...

Oh.

In the forest near the spaceship, on a fallen log, the clown opened his eyes and felt a tickle. He looked down to see a tiny wasp, half the size of a yellow jacket, walking up his suit pants. He shooed it away, rose to his feet, picked up his bag of gold and whistled a happy tune as he strode purposefully down the trail.

He emerged into a clearing to find a lipstick-red spaceship parked against a garden shed. In front of the shed stood a little wooden desk with a little wooden chair, a brass scale, and a little girl.

"Good afternoon." The clown settled the heavy bag onto the wooden desk, and the little girl completed the gold-weighing ritual. Then he bowed to her and entered the shed.

From the distant *Lens*, Kitty Siphon watched unhappily. Normally, she loved the dance and stab of a high-stakes negotiation, but that was before *mind reading*.

Should she cancel the negotiation? She could claim the Worms were unreasonable and walk out. It was tempting, because if she had to speak honestly, talking just wasted her time.

Inside the shed, Lucifa Dark sat in a folding chair behind her transparent Lexan barrier. "Gold, silver, or poison?"

It was the traditional Worm greeting, and the clown gave the traditional answer: "Gold."

"Very well," Luci acknowledged. "The first topic is yours."

Ambassador Peter Slip, the U.S. Government's clown, began by resolving the internal dispute that had dampened his mood. Gloom is caused by mental conflict, in this case by conflicting imperatives, so the clown resolved his mental conflict by shoving his diplomatic goals firmly into second place behind his *primary* goal– his own short-term survival. "I have a piece of information for you. There is no cost."

Kitty Siphon looked up from her notes. "What are you doing? You're off script."

"Be advised," the clown advised, "nothing I say should be construed as a statement of our ultimate strategic objectives, unless I say so explicitly."

"God damn you!" Kitty leapt to her feet in a shower of paper. "You think you can betray *me?* By Tuesday, you'll be sweeping floors in the Somali consulate!"

The *Lens* staffers looked alarmed.

In the shed, Luci parsed the clown's words, then chuckled. "Relax; I know this negotiation is a charade. You don't really intend to sell us a colony."

Kitty: "Fuck!"

"But life confounds all predictions," Luci predicted. "You were wise to warn me, even though I already knew. Have you allowed yourself to realize why you are paying me so much gold just to show up?"

"Diplomacy is an exchange," the clown observed. "If you supplied your time and good intentions solely in return for mine, then, in a sense, my good intentions would be your property. I should not like you to think I withheld them."

"That was smart, but be careful. I still can't give you the benefit of the doubt."

In the distant *Lens*, Kitty slumped back into her doeskin seat. "You're lucky she already knew you're stalling her."

The *Lens* staffers looked relieved.

The clown looked curious. "You said you consider this negotiation a charade. Are you here solely for the gold?"

Luci shrugged. "It's a lot of gold, and who can know the future? Right now, your queens are determined to deny us our colony, but you and I can work out the practical details anyway, in case one day, I give your queens a reason to change their mind."

Two days later in Kansas

Patrick Plum didn't get to keep the bass he caught, but the day turned out okay anyway.

A 2-seat spaceship roared over the pasture and landed by the stock tank. The cows ran away. Patrick ran toward it.

When the dust cleared, the spaceship's transparent canopy slid back, and an old man climbed out. To Patrick, anyone over 15 was old, but the Worm pilot was *really* old. He even had gray hair, and some black pictures on his cheek.

"Hello, young man. My name is Gabriel Tide."

Patrick straightened. "My name is Patrick Plumb."

Gabriel limped closer and extended his hand.

Patrick shook it. "Pleased to meet you," they said in unison.

"Jinx," Patrick declared. "Owe me a coke. Did you hurt your knee?"

"Just a little arthritis. You said your last name is *Plumb*. Would your father be Percival Plumb?"

"Yeah, that's Dad. Does he know you?" Patrick was impressed.

"No, no," said Gabriel. "We haven't met, though I would like to. Is he the same Percival Plumb who studies volcanoes?"

"No, my dad doesn't study volcanoes."

Gabriel's face fell.

"Dad used to teach about volcanoes, but now he looks for oil."

Gabriel looked relieved. Then he knelt, wincing when his knee touched the dirt, and whispered conspiratorially. "I would like to meet your father and negotiate."

"Negotiate?"

"I want to make a deal," said the alien, "assuming your father still knows about volcanoes. Do you think he remembers?"

"Sure, Dad knows all about volcanoes. He only had to quit his professor job because he said bad words." Patrick's eyes widened. "I'm not supposed to say that."

"I won't tell." With an effort, Gabriel rose to his feet. "What sort of fish do you catch in that pond?"

"Bass," said Patrick. "It's not a pond; it's a *tank.*"

"Thank you, I stand corrected. Are bass good to eat?"

"Oh, yes," said Patrick, wondering how anyone could not know. Then he realized. But he politely did not comment, only stared at the spaceship.

Gabriel followed his gaze. "Would you like to look at my boat?"

Patrick nodded eagerly.

The controls were exceptionally cool. Eventually, Patrick noticed something was missing. "Our spaceships have heat shields, if they go all the way into orbit."

Patrick was wise in the ways of spaceships.

"Really?" said Gabriel. "That's important. Thank you for telling me. When your pilots want to slow down, they probably use air friction."

atrick nodded. "I know." He had definitely known that, more or less.

My engines are a little better," said Gabriel. "So instead of carrying a heavy heat shield, I would rather carry more fuel."

Patrick was impressed. Even though the sun hadn't set, he noticed the quarter moon already visible in the Eastern sky.

Patrick, would you be willing to sell me some bass?"

I only caught three," said Patrick. "But they're really big. Well, kind of big."

Gabriel nodded gravely. "They sound valuable. I only wish I had more money."

Patrick seemed uncertain. He glanced at the 2-seat spaceship, then up at the moon.

Say, I have an idea," said Gabriel. "Maybe I could trade something for your fish. Do you think your father would let me take you for a ride?"

A ride where?"

I don't know," said the alien. "Where would you like to go?"

Interlude

Some events of a technical nature

Presented with the author's apology

At 9:27:33:01 Greenwich Mean Time, a navigation computer flipped a bit from zero to one, conceptually.

Physically, the bit charged itself to five volts. This attracted a few electrons, about 300 billion, which arrived via a meandering copper road provided for their convenience.

To reach the meandering copper road, the electrons had to cross a bridge made of Tin, which provides some of the best known evidence that God is a ten-year-old boy.

For reasons perfectly obvious to a ten-year-old boy, God arranged the laws of the Universe to ensure that Tin, the 50th element, is the most convenient material for joining electric circuits. Tin melts at temperatures that electronics can survive, and it sticks firmly to other metals, even when exposed to oxygen. Tin laughs at corrosion, happily conducts strong electric currents, and is even cheap and plentiful.

Naturally, Tin was used by the first electronic engineers to solder their electric connections.

Electronic engineers around the world were dismayed to discover, much too late, that Tin has another astonishing power. Once in a great while, and only under sustained electric voltage, a seemingly-harmless chunk of Tin will sprout whiskers that reach out and connect to nearby circuits.

On the Eighth Day, God giggled.

To suppress whiskers, the tin bridge had been alloyed with the 82nd element, which is Lead. When Tin is mixed with Lead, it stops growing whiskers.

Of course, Lead has been banned in much of the world to protect children, although sometimes children die anyway, when whiskers grow inside the lead-free computers that run mommy's automobile.

The tin bridge connected to a gate. The gate was mostly Silicon, which acts a lot like Carbon. Silicon and Carbon are similar because each has four *valence* electrons. Those are the electrons that live farthest from the nucleus, so they are most free to visit the neighbors.

For reasons known only to Him, God gave atoms a preference for certain numbers of valence electrons. The preferred number is eight, but zero is also acceptable.

Atoms really do want a full set of eight valence electrons. They want it so badly, they will swap electrons with their neighbors, so one atom can have a full set while its neighbor has none. Some atoms are even willing to share electrons, so each atom can partially own a full set. This electron swapping and sharing is what scientists call, *chemistry.*

Some atoms are born complete, with a full set of eight valence electrons. They have no interest in swapping or sharing, and pass their long lives in noble isolation, the elemental nuns.

Excitingly, removing just one of her electrons will turn a noble nun into a halogen succubus, so hungry she will suck an electron out of any life molecule she touches, instantly killing it.

Or add one electron, and the noble nun becomes an alkali-metal Lothario, donating his electron so eagerly he splits stable marriages like water. If he meets a halogen succubus, they will make fireworks, but eventually, in one of God's more benign ironies, the alkali-metal Lothario and the halogen succubus will bond together into the stablest of all elemental marriages, and become the salt of the earth.

132

Exactly midway between the halogens and the alkali metals, one finds Silicon and Carbon. These special elements possess four valence electrons, exactly half a set, which makes them the elemental world's party animals, willing to borrow *or* loan electrons. This is how Silicon dominates the electronic world, while Carbon's promiscuity creates a phenomenon that scientists call, *life.*

Silicon and Carbon are not the only party animals. Three other elements possess exactly four valence electrons. The first is Germanium, which is even better for electronics than Silicon, but is harder to manipulate and, annoyingly, grows whiskers.

The other two party-animal elements are the 50th element, Tin, and the 82nd element, Lead. Most of God's Easter eggs are pranks, but some of them look like hints. If only we knew what they hinted at.

The party animals actually do form stable bonds. They just want to do it with all of their neighbors at the same time. It is probably good, though a bit sad, that such neighborhoods are less exciting than they sound. When all the atoms in the neighborhood bond to all of their neighbors, the electrons settle down. No more chemistry. Scientists say they have *crystallized.*

Fortunately, a crystal's placid harmony can be livened up by sprinkling it with enticing impurities. The impurities lure electrons from their crystal bonds. Some electrons cut loose and hop freely from impurity to impurity, doing what scientists call, *electricity.*

Back to our transistor gate, which was...

Enough. The transistor was loaded with nerdilicious double-entendres, but we shall resist. Suffice it to say, electrons flowed from the transistor and soon found themselves spiraling around the windings of an electric motor, creating temporary magnets that pushed against cleverly-arranged permanent magnets. The motor spun as its spiraling electrons did what scientists call, *work.*

Heh. We shall *resist.*

The spiraling electrons did not mind doing work. Perhaps they even exulted, in a particular way. Under their influence, the electric motor accelerated.

The spinning electric motor had only one job, which was to rotate a nylon gear. The nylon gear meshed with a larger gear bolted to a paint can. Or at least, it looked like a paint can.

And that would have been the whole story, an excessively complex method for stirring paint, except the paint can did not contain paint. Of course. Instead, the paint can held a nine-pound disk of Uranium 238, spinning at 546 revolutions per second.

The spinning Uranium 238 was not sinister, or even radioactive. Its job was merely to be heavy, and to spin fast without flying apart. Instead of Uranium, the disk could have been machined from Tungsten, but as it happened, the spinning disk was built by an Israeli company that also forged Uranium 238 into spears designed to pierce tank armor, so they had a big inventory of leftovers when depleted uranium munitions were banned.

The spinning uranium's mass lay mostly on its perimeter, which made it stable. In fact, its stability was so extreme that scientists had a word for it: *gyroscope.*

A spinning gyroscope possesses a curious, almost human trait: It cannot easily be tilted. If you try, it will push back in a manner that can only be described as, *surprising.* Indeed, a classic physics prank, rarely executed but often imagined, is to mount a substantial spinning disk inside a suitcase, sideways. Then you take the gyroscopic suitcase to a hotel and ask the porter to put it in your room. All will be well until he tries to turn a corner.

Since the paint can contained a gyroscope, it did not consent to be tilted. Instead, the paint can stayed put while the nylon gear crawled around it. As the nylon gear crawled, it carried with it the electric motor, the transistor, the tin bridge, the meandering copper road, the computer bit, and all the other parts of the school bus-sized orbital observatory.

The orbiting observatory rotated around its gyroscope until it pointed eastward. Its thrusters lay silent, conserving precious fuel that might be needed to loft to a higher orbit, in pursuit.

Even without its thrusters, the observatory could have rotated faster. Yet it turned slowly, deliberately, as if its gyroscope had run down, stopped spinning to become a mere reaction wheel like those used to point cheaper satellites that don't expect their target to dodge.

Physically inspecting the satellite, even from close range, would reveal only a functional NOAA Earth observatory gliding 400 miles above the oceans and ice it photographed through its 20-inch telescope, searching for reasons to raise taxes.

Just now, though, the telescope was watching the horizon, the glowing border between blue ocean and black space, and the rising star that was the distant *Unexpected Finger,* the trumpet-shaped mothership that sheltered the aliens in her 8,000-cubic-meter body.

The observatory focused its telescopic eye on the rising *Finger* and computed.

When it was satisfied, the observatory slowly, deliberately rotated back toward the ice 400 miles below.

One third of the observatory's internal volume was consumed by its advertised purpose, a suite of instruments designed to prove productive men were ruining everything. The extra space, which hardly anyone knew about, was packed with mirrored cubes. The cubes were four feet wide, with all but one side sheathed in telescope-grade mirrors.

The mirrors' job was to reflect distant space. If the mirrored cube was floating free, it would look like a patch of distant space. You would never notice it looked like the *wrong* patch of distant space, unless you were very observant or very lucky. If the cube was 100 miles away, noticing it would be virtually impossible. If the cube was closer, you would probably have only seconds in which to notice it.

The cubes were mirrored on all sides save one, the vulnerable side that bristled with lenses and nozzles and black fins.

The black fins were for cooling. The mirrored cubes contained fuel-cell generators and guidance computers and helium pumps to chill the mirrors to 26 degrees above absolute zero. They should have been colder to blend in perfectly with the 3-degree background of interstellar space, but HVAC is hard.

The mirrored cubes slept. If they woke, their machinery would emit heat. The heat could not escape through the mirrors, because a mirror in vacuum is the best known insulator. Instead, the heat would be pushed to the black fins by a heat pump, rather like a car's air conditioner. The black fins would radiate the heat into cold space. To radiate all the heat, the black fins would have to glow red, so it would be important to point them away from prying eyes.

The black fins were ringed by nozzles large and small. The smallest nozzles were ion thrusters, which are feeble beyond belief. Of all the known varieties of thruster, an ion thruster is probably the worst for a guided missile.

These ion thrusters were quite good by ion-thruster standards, but still must thrust many hours to build up significant speed. Of course, *significant speed* has a different meaning when you're already gliding along at five miles per second.

An ion thruster's one virtue, at least for missile purposes, is its subtle exhaust. When a traditional, hydrazine thruster is fired in low orbit, its exhaust plume reflects enough sunlight to be seen by a child on the ground. But when an ion thruster is fired in vacuum, the only sign is the subtle glow of reforming atoms, as lonely electrons leap from a back-pointing, high-voltage needle to rejoin their proton mates flung out the nozzle.

As it happened, the mirrored cubes also contained traditional, hydrazine thrusters. In a pinch, the hydrazine thrusters could blast *through* the mirrors, giving up stealth forever in return for one robust maneuver. At that point, losing stealth would probably be okay, because the plan was to break the mirrors in the last milliseconds of the cube's life, during terminal guidance.

The mirrored cubes contained many other components, but only one was noteworthy. Nestled into each cube was a 16-pound sphere of Plutonium encased in a shell of Lithium.

The plutonium sphere had a job, nothing sinister, just to warm a few Peltier junctions enough to generate a keep-alive trickle of electricity.

And, of course, the plutonium sphere had a second job.

End of Technical Interlude

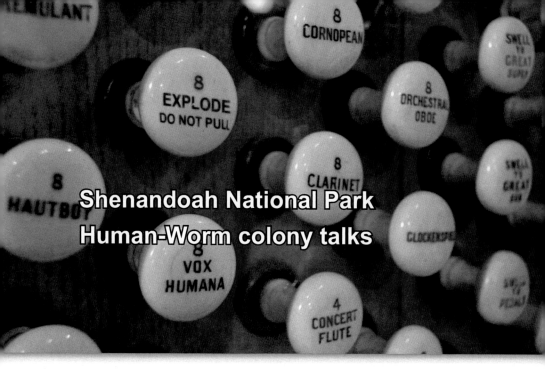

Shenandoah National Park
Human-Worm colony talks

"**We would** like to purchase the design details of your spacecraft engines," the clown recited. "We hope they might help us generate clean, renewable energy."

In the little shed beside her lipstick-red spacecraft, behind her protective Lexan barrier, Luci the alien looked startled. "Our spacecraft engines are cherub swords. Did you just say you *want* the awful secret?"

"We know your engines annihilate whole iron atoms," the clown continued dutifully. "However, we don't know how the annihilation is stimulated, or how you capture the resulting momentum."

Behind her Lexan barrier, Luci stared blankly.

The clown took a moment to steel himself. Then he quoted, word for word, his latest directive from the Alien Regulatory Authority. "We believe the crucial step occurs as neutrons are consumed by beta decay. If so, your cherub sword might be adapted to generate clean, renewable, environmentally-sound electric current." The clown stopped talking and breathed a tiny sigh of relief.

In the little shed in the forest, silence stretched. Eventually, Luci's face began to contort.

Finally, the alien burst into laughter.

The clown waited patiently.

When Luci could speak again, she wiped her eyes. "Good one."

The clown could not help chuckling.

"Do you get the joke?"

"Please." The clown waved an invitation. "Explain the joke."

"We considered coercing you by threatening to reveal the awful secret of the cherub sword. We actually held a meeting to debate."

"Very humorous," said the clown. "May I ask how you voted?"

"Oh, I knew we couldn't threaten you. That would be an implicit demand for ransom. So I suggested we post a detailed cherub-sword design on the internet, then head back out to space for five years. That way, we don't demand anything, and by the time we come back, the problem will have solved itself. But Gabriel has a soft heart, and brain, so he insisted we hide the awful secret." Luci shook her head. "Now, you offer to *pay us* for your doom."

In the *Lens*, Kitty Siphon settled back in her expensive doeskin chair. "Just like I predicted, but we staffed the Alien Regulatory Authority with morons, so make her spell it out."

In the shed, the clown said, "Doom?"

Luci leaned back in her folding metal chair, balancing on two legs, and rapped her knuckles on the red spaceship hatch. "Sweety, I know you're chewing gum. Please give me a stick. No, better make it two." She glanced at the clown. "Want some gum? The flavor is out of this world."

The clown hesitated.

"Oh, just try it," said Luci. "How often do you get alien gum? If you're worried about poison, you can choose which stick you want, and give me the other."

In the *Lens*, six technical eunuchs chanted in unison, *"She spent the last several years building up an immunity to iocane."*

140

Kitty Siphon looked worried. "What is *iocane?* What will it do to our clown?"

The eunuchs smirked.

In the shed, the red spaceship hatch opened and a little girl's hand poked out holding two sticks of gum wrapped in white paper.

"Thank you, sweety." Luci slid both sticks under the Lexan wall. "Choose one, and I'll chew the other. Please don't tell Buff I brought gum. He's still cranky he had to leave behind some tools."

The clown selected one stick and slid the other back to Luci.

"No, no," a eunuch shouted. "You're supposed to distract her, then switch them!"

Now Kitty looked annoyed. "What are you talking about?"

The eunuchs collapsed into giggling.

Luci unwrapped her stick of gum. "Your civilization is based on electromagnetism."

"Is it?"

"Electromagnetism drives every electric motor, every wireless, every lamp. It warms your homes and transmits your pornography, which by the way is fabulous." Luci folded the gum into her mouth. "Electromagnetism is the physical basis of flame and chemistry, and the means by which your thoughts are translated into action by your nerves and muscles."

The clown unwrapped his gum and sniffed it.

Luci chewed contentedly. "You discovered electromagnetism less than 300 years ago, after it had lain in the open, plainly visible for all of history. 10,000 generations of Humans were born, lived, and were struck by lightning without ever grasping the significance of static cling."

The clown bit off a piece of gum, then looked surprised. "It tastes like meat."

"Yes, roast hamster. Do you know what it took to discover electromagnetism? How it was finally revealed that an electric motor could be built and powered by a battery?"

The clown stopped chewing. "Roast hamster?"

"It's my favorite flavor. Discovering electricity required only the simple but unlikely experiment of wrapping a wire around a compass. Attach one end of the wire to a metal coin, and the other end to a coin of a different metal, then poke both coins into a lemon. The compass needle will rotate to a new heading, driven by the mechanism that rotates a battery-powered electric motor."

The clown did not seem interested. He said, "Very interesting."

"The cherub sword is no more complex than a coil of wire, two coins, and a lemon. It converts mass into velocity, using a mechanism that has lain in plain sight for mankind's entire history."

"Thank you for that explanation." The clown spat out the half-stick of gum. "What exactly is the problem with selling us the design of your engines?"

"The *problem?* For one thing, your rockets are too complicated. If your engineers ever see *our* design, they are gonna be doomed *and* pissed off."

"Thank you," said the clown. "Could you explain clearly what our doom would look like?"

"How can you possibly ask such a... Oh, it's not for *you.*" Luci rolled her eyes. "Well, you're paying me enough, so I'll treat you like children, if that's what you want." She stood up, and her voice flattened. "Be advised, a cherub sword can be built in a modest workshop, and its energy output has no obvious upper limit."

The clown's arm hair prickled.

"Happy now?" Luci sat down. "If you manage to steal our awful secret, I wonder if any of you will survive the first year?"

In the distant *Lens*, Kitty Siphon recalled her last meeting with the Alien Regulatory Authority. *The awful secret must be possessed by the U.S. rather than our enemies,* a tall patrician had solemnly intoned, *as if we could keep such a secret.* As if the most terrible weapon in Human history, and the best-guarded secret, had not been shared with our worst enemy by 1949. So Kitty said, "Do it again."

The clown sighed, and embarrassed himself again. "We might be willing to purchase your engine design to help us generate clean, renewable power. Will you name your price?"

"Wow. What must it be like for you, beneath such chains of command." Luci looked sympathetic. "Very well. In exchange for 10,000 tons of gold, I will explain the principle of the cherub sword to the government that is formed after you ratify a new constitution that I will write."

Kitty Siphon burst out laughing. A chuckle spread around the *Lens,* and the older staffers looked relieved. The young tech eunuchs looked disappointed.

The clown nodded soberly. "I will pass on your offer."

"My terms are not negotiable."

"Thank you," said the clown, sincerely. "May I change the subject?"

"Yes," said Luci. "In fact, I encourage it."

"Thank you. We began tracking your mothership when you fired your engines, near the inner boundary of our Oort cloud. Before then, did you travel here directly, or did your path curve?"

"*Your* Oort cloud?" Luci raised a single, perfect eyebrow. "Do you imagine you own *everything* within 500 billion miles of your birthplace?"

The clown waited patiently.

"In exchange for the information you seek, I want to know your preferred location for our colony." Luci pointed a stern finger. "I want your *real* preference, and if you're tempted to deceive me, remember I *can't* give you the benefit of the doubt."

"We accept," said Kitty. "Tell her where we want to put them."

"I accept your terms," said the clown "Our preferred location for your colony is Northern Alaska. We have mapped an area with no seacoasts and few mineral deposits. I will bring a detailed map to our next meeting."

Luci scowled. "I hate the cold."

"I am sorry," said the clown. "It was not my choice. These decisions are made entirely by the Alien Regulatory Authority."

In the distant *Lens*, Kitty Siphon snorted a laugh. "Perfect!"

"We're both lucky you didn't offer Antarctica," Luci grumped. "That might have triggered me, because I don't recognize your claim to control that dismal continent. Even *you* don't recognize Antarctica as *your thing,* because you know you haven't earned it."

In the *Lens,* Kitty pointed to a bushy female eunuch. "Our clown promised the bitch a map. You are personally responsible for keeping that promise."

The bushy eunuch looked unhappy.

"Very well," said Luci. "We flew directly toward your sun, except at one point, we dodged approximately 500 million miles toward Sirius. Then we resumed course toward your sun, but well off our original track."

The *Lens* staffers waited quietly while the astronomy eunuchs gathered around their alpha and calculated excitedly.

"Save the leftover gum," Kitty said into the clown's ear. "The biology eunuch wants it for, uh, what do you want the gum for?"

"To find out what roast hamster tastes like," said a male voice in the background. "Why did the aliens dodge toward Sirius?"

"Ignore that question," Kitty told the clown. "We're already wasting too much time on astronomy. Hold on, I just got something."

The alpha eunuch handed Kitty Siphon a summary.

> Given the *Unexpected Finger's* approach vector, the only plausible origin is the star LHS 288.
>
> Distance: 15.5 LY
>
> Travel time to Earth: 80 yrs, approx.
>
> Origin star class: Red dwarf
>
> Origin star luminosity: <0.0001 Sol.
>
> NOTICE! The origin star is TOO DIM for life, given the known length of the alien year.
>
> Alien statements are in conflict.

"Their home star is a dwarf," Kitty said into the clown's ear. "It's only a thousandth as bright as our sun. That's too dim to support life, so someone is lying."

"We have a problem," said the clown. "The information you gave me implies a home star only one thousandth as bright as our sun. This is too dim to sustain human life."

In the *Lens*, Kitty turned to the alpha astro eunuch. "Are you *sure* about this? Is that star really too dim for life?"

He shrugged. "Does it matter?"

"She can read minds! If she thinks we lied, she might blow someone up, and we can't be sure it would be you."

No worries," said the alpha eunuch. "What you told her is absurd. You even moved the decimal point. Their home star is actually one ten-thousandth as bright as ours. But your lie sounded plausible, so you can pretend you believe it. You have lots of practice doing that. Astronomers will back you up, but we're going to need more funding."

Kitty growled.

"Just kidding." The alpha eunuch unwrapped a warm bagel. "Red dwarfs can probably support life, though the tides would be a bitch. The problem is, the habitable zone for LHS 288 has an orbital period of about a week. But the alien king –sorry, the *Worm King*– talked to one of our astronomers, Frank Drummer, and mentioned their orbital period is almost 11,000 days. You can't fit an 11,000-day orbit into the habitable zone of a red dwarf, so Luci probably lied, and our clown definitely lied. This should be interesting." The alpha eunuch chewed on the warm bagel as he watched the Big Screen.

"Frank *Drummer?*" Kitty looked worried. "Do you think Luci knows enough astronomy to notice?"

In the shed, Luci turned sideways and planted her feet on the wall. "So, you're saying our star was too dim to support life? My friends will be surprised."

"Very humorous," said the clown. "However, you have placed me in a difficult situation, because you appear to be lying."

"That must be tough for you." Luci tapped her bare feet on the wall.

"Back off," Kitty hissed into the clown's ear. "You got the facts wrong."

The clown's expression did not change.

"Oh, all right. You grew up in a swarm, so you wouldn't know that accusing *me* of fraud is ludicrous." Luci tapped the square tattoo on her cheek, pointedly using her middle finger.

The clown waited calmly.

Kitty Siphon waited nervously.

"The missing piece," Luci explained, "is our suns were fake. They were just two big lamps orbiting 40,000 miles up, pointed down at us."

The alpha eunuch coughed up a chunk of bagel.

"It was not quite as dumb as it sounds," Luci added. "If one sun dimmed, the other would brighten to compensate, so it had some redundancy. Also, the suns could refuel, one at a time, without causing an ice age."

The clown blinked. "You built your own *suns?*"

"Nah, *we* didn't build the suns; God did. We think He wanted to put us near Earth, but He didn't have any good stars handy."

"God built you a pair of artificial suns," the clown said neutrally.

"Yep. In a galaxy with 100 billion natural suns, God built fakes. When we found out, we had a spiritual crisis, since it looked like we were created by an idiot. Though in fairness to God, from His perspective, everything is fake."

In the *Lens*, the alpha astronomy eunuch gasped and pounded his chest.

The clown sat very still. "Did you speak with God personally?"

"Not me, just my ancestors."

"So, your world had self-proclaimed prophets?"

"Self-proclaimed?" Luci looked amused.

"Change the subject," Kitty hissed into her microphone. "We don't actually give a shit about astronomy or their religion, so save those topics for a cocktail party and move on to the food problem *now,* before she figures out you lied about their sun."

The clown's expression never wavered. "Our astronomers feel certain your trip lasted not less than 80 years. How did you feed yourself?"

"I neither confirm nor deny your premise," Luci replied. "You ask for information but offer nothing of value in return."

"Granted." The video tilted as the clown inclined his head. "I will give you free information regarding our desires."

Luci looked interested.

"Your mothership is relatively small," the clown began. "To survive 80 years, even in hibernation, you would need a great deal of food for such a confined space."

"Your logic appears sound," Luci replied. "Surprisingly."

The clown nodded amiably, drawing a growl from his earpiece. Then he proceeded to execute his next directive from the Alien Regulatory Authority. "If, hypothetically, you possessed technology for compact food production, we might be interested in securing the rights to it, perhaps as part of the price for your colony."

Luci laughed and held up a palm. "No no, don't tell me, let me guess. You don't want to *copy* our magic food machine; you want to *conceal its existence*. Your queens are terrified we might give you food factories small enough to hide, so you could feed yourselves without paying a queen for permission."

The clown sighed contentedly. "Miss Dark, I find you far more gratifying than the typical diplomat."

"Seriously?" Kitty rolled her eyes. "You're hitting on her?"

"You can relax," said Luci. "Nobody will want our travel food."

"Thank you. However, that didn't exactly answer my- "

"Stop it," Luci interrupted. "I don't play word games. We don't have the magic food machine you fear."

"Very well," said the clown. "That concludes our interest in your diet. Before we move on, will you clarify an earlier comment?"

"You may ask."

"Thank you. You've repeatedly warned us against demanding ransom. I would like to map the boundaries of that prohibition."

Luci rotated toward the clown, propping her feet on the Lexan barrier. "So, the predator is curious about the prey's top speed. What's your scheme?"

"On reflection, we wondered how you would react if a thief simply grabbed your possessions and walked away. A silent theft cannot easily be interpreted as a demand for ransom."

"You're right," Luci conceded. "We're only triggered by extortion, not simple robbery."

"YES!" Kitty Siphon jumped to her feet, pumping her fist.

Around the *Lens*, staffers looked uncomfortable.

Kitty sat down hastily and looked embarrassed.

"Thank you." The clown leaned left to see around Luci's feet. "That will simplify our relations."

"I doubt it. Obviously, if I don't know I've been robbed, I can't be triggered. But if I spot you carrying my goods, I'll want them back. This will create a situation we call, *the knife edge.*"

Kitty: "Uh oh."

Luci: "To understand the knife edge, you must understand why, if a six-year-old boy tried to snatch my purse, he would be safe, even if we wrestled."

This was the clown's realm of mastery. "The child is protected by his own weakness."

"Ooh!" Secretary Siphon stood up again.

"Correct," said Luci. "If I wrestle with a child, I am safe, so *he* is safe. But if an *adult* snatches my purse, and we wrestle for it, I would not be safe, so he would not be safe."

"Because if he makes you afraid," the clown finished, "then your struggle becomes extortion. He is implicitly demanding your purse in return for your safety."

"Exactly. The thief puts himself on the knife edge, because the moment I begin to fear him, his grasp on my purse becomes an implicit demand for ransom, so I'll be triggered."

"You are *not* triggered unless the threat is credible. That's an elegant means to deter extortion while protecting your children. What if the child had a pocketknife?"

"I won't tell you."

"Miss Dark," the clown said gently, "you cannot ask us to make room for a culture that will execute a Boy Scout for stealing a french fry."

"Dammit." Luci grimaced. "Okay, I will answer, if you insist, but only if you keep it secret."

"Tell her we'll keep it secret, because whatever it is, I have a feeling it will make them look good." Kitty pointed to the alpha eunuch, then drew her finger across her throat.

The eunuch bent to his computer, and the huge wall displays switched to *Gilligan's Island*. It was Episode 4, the one where the skipper tries to remember how he turned a radio into a transmitter. The ten-foot speakers boomed, *Just sit right back and you'll hear a tale...*

The *Lens* staffers looked annoyed.

"We agree to hold your answer in confidence," the clown recited. "We will inform only those government officials who need to know."

Luci pointed to the row of tattoos on her cheek, singling out the third symbol, the pentagon. "Children must be protected from our wrath, so we boosted our natural protective response to the mental category, *child.* We know children are wasps, yet they are safe with us, even *your* children."

"Oh, my," said Kitty. "What a productive meeting this had been."

"But a child can threaten your life," the clown pointed out, then was surprised to see Luci flinch.

"Children are killers," the alien breathed, and her famously beautiful face looked like winter. "My higher brain knows that all too well. Nonetheless, my lower brains, my monkey brains, will *not* recognize a child as a threat. We think this safeguard is built into every species that nurtures its young. We just strengthened it." Luci rested her index finger on her pentagon tattoo, just below her eye. "This is how we can make ourselves *ungovernable,* and still be mothers. You see why we want this kept secret," she added. "If it gets out, we will be swarmed by thief children."

"Yes," Kitty agreed. "I believe you will be. What if an adult uses a child as a clown?"

154

"Hmm." The clown considered. "What would you do if a child held your belongings for ransom, acting on orders from his parents?"

"If I really believed that, I would kill his parents, but I would never believe that, if his parents wore these." Luci tapped the row of five tattoos across her cheek.

"Luci, we're struggling here. We're trying to protect our way of life without goading you to violence, and it's proving difficult. If the slightest hint of coercion provokes you to murder, how has your culture survived?"

Luci waved dismissively. "Our culture is not as dramatic as it sounds. If we can't agree, we both bite the forbidden fruit to see who's being an ass. Fortunately, that's rarely necessary, because we can always give each other the benefit of the doubt."

"That may be a weakness," Kitty observed. "Act like you don't care."

"Thank you for clearing that up," said the clown. "And now, I fear I must broach an even more delicate subject."

Luci looked interested.

"An alarming number of Earth women have been sexually assaulted by alien men."

Luci shrugged. "It doesn't alarm me."

"You consider this behavior *acceptable?*"

Luci leaned back and propped her feet on the sheet-metal wall. She seemed relaxed. "Your women demand to be treated as children, and you indulge them. We don't. We *warned* you our men consider flirting an invitation to sexual assault, and you haven't exactly kept that secret."

In the distant *Lens*, Kitty Siphon thoughtfully tapped her chin. "What is she up to?"

"Thank you for that information," said the clown. "Your men will desist if the victim simply asks. Why haven't you explained this?"

"Why haven't *we* explained it? We've *shown you* dozens of times. Dozens of times an Earthborn woman has invited our man –an alien– to assault her, then asked him to stop. Her request has *always* been granted, but this is *never* reported in your wasp media." Luci sat up, and now she did not seem relaxed. "If a non-victim tells her story on the internet, and explains that she only had to *ask,* she is swarmed by your minions denouncing her as a victim-blamer or a rape apologist. Women aren't built to resist that level of public shaming."

"She's up to something," Kitty mused. "She is *helping us* suppress this story. It feels like she knows what's going on, and we don't."

The clown said, "I feel I am missing something."

"It's not complicated." Luci relaxed, and propped her bare feet back on the wall. "You're hiding our virtue, and we're letting you do it, because we like to see our men enjoy themselves."

In the distant *Lens*, Kitty Siphon goggled.

"We let our men keep their dicks," Luci added. "So it's appropriate for you to call us, *aliens.*"

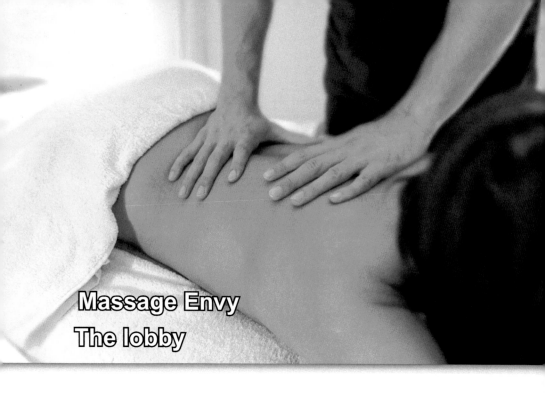

Massage Envy
The lobby

Mona loved her job, but Massage Envy was having a slow day. She caught up on license paperwork while her friend Marcie sat in a guest chair chatting about her kids.

The lights flashed brighter. Mona glanced up. The extra light seemed to be coming from the parking lot. Both women looked out the big windows as the light dimmed orange, then they heard a roar. "Oh my God," Marcie breathed. "That's a spaceship! A Worm is landing *here.* What if he wants a massage?"

Mona watched the orange smoke blasting over the parked cars. "What if he wants a happy ending?"

"You can't flirt with them! If you flirt with them, they rape you!" Marcie seemed to be hyperventilating. "If he thinks he deserves a happy ending but doesn't get one, he might kill us! Don't call him a *Worm!* That's rude! Call him an *alien!* No, that's racist! We have to find out his name!"

The spaceship landed vertically, nose in the air, bouncing gently on its swept-back wingtips. A hefty metal foot shot out from the fuselage with a clank, then both women jumped at a much louder bang, and the standing spaceship tilted.

"Oh my God!" Marci shouted as the spaceship toppled onto the asphalt, the metal foot compressing as it took the shock. Then the canopy opened, and the Worm pilot climbed out.

Marcie gaped. "Oh. My. God. It's *him.*"

It was Buffalo, the fake Jesus from the First-Contact prank, the one who looked a male stripper. In person, he stood 6'4" and just as pretty as he'd been on television.

"Best to play it safe," Mona decided. "We should give him whatever he wants."

Marcie poked her, but not too hard. "No happy endings! That's corporate policy."

After a moment's pause, both women smirked.

Buff opened the glass door and peeked in. "Gold, silver, or poison?"

The women stopped smirking. "Oh, definitely gold," Marcie warbled.

"Hi, my name is Buff." The famously handsome Worm walked to the counter and tugged open his belt pouch. "I'd like to buy a massage."

Mona grinned. Marcie poked her.

"For my girlfriend," Buff added.

Mona's grin disappeared.

"Every woman loves a massage," Marcie recited brightly. "Do you know if she likes deep tissue, or a softer touch?"

"Hard and deep, from a male. Please bring out the men so I can choose."

"I'm sorry, sir." Marcie's tone cooled. "We don't offer cattle calls."

"I understand." Buff pulled out a silver coin and dropped it on the counter. "Do you offer cattle calls now?"

Marcie picked up the coin, the size of a quarter. "Is this real silver?"

"Yes, four-nines pure."

Buff was cleanly muscled and wearing a martial-artist's outfit, perfectly tailored and tied shut with four sashes. Mona had heard some exotic rumors about what those sashes were used for. She tried not to stare at them.

"Wow, real alien money. What do you think this is worth?" Marcie turned the coin in the light.

"That's about 20 bucks worth of silver." Mona plucked the coin from Marcie's fingers and offered it back to the Worm. "But it's worth more as a collector's item. Would you please hold it beside your beautiful face, and explain what it is?"

Buff looked surprised. Then he grinned and held the coin beside his perfect, tattooed cheekbone. "This is-"

"Not yet," Mona interrupted, and pulled out her phone. She pointed it at Buff. "Go ahead."

"This is a one-doofus silver coin, which I am attempting to exchange for services." Buff looked enquiring. "Is that sufficient?"

Mona zoomed in to the coin. "Your money is called a *doofus?*"

"Yes, 100 dorks per doofus, and I know." Buff sighed. "We named our money *dorks* and *doofuses* 200 years ago. It's probably just a coincidence, but God might have pranked us again."

"God might have pranked you *again?*"

"Yes, again," said the alien. "Have you never felt you were being pranked by God?"

Mona blinked. "You *are* like us. I just felt myself relax."

"You *felt yourself relax?*" Buff seemed to notice Mona for the first time. He leaned forward, and visibly focused. "For a masseuse, that's a professional skill."

Mona felt herself flush.

"Careful," Buff warned. "I want this to be about my girlfriend."

"Oh my God. You're *reading my mind.*" Mona looked fascinated. "Can all Worm... oh I'm so sorry. I mean, can all *aliens* do that?"

Buff chuckled. "A 13-year-old boy could have read your mind. You blushed all the way to your cleavage. Normally, I'd take that offer, but Sophie is going to quiz me and I don't want to lie."

"That was *not* an offer," Marcie snapped. "Turning red does *not* imply sexual attraction."

"Oh, really?" Buff looked amused.

Mona touched Marcie's hand. "He read me correctly."

Marcie looked appalled.

"So, you want to buy a massage for Sophie." Mona clipped an appointment form to a clipboard. "Is she Human or alien?"

Buff took the clipboard. "She's Earthborn. About that cattle call…"

"We have two male therapists here now," said Mona. "They are both with customers, and normally, I wouldn't consider interrupting, but I can't let them miss this. Why don't you get started on that form, and I'll bring them out."

Three minutes later, two bemused masseurs and two white-bathrobed housewives filed into the lobby and gawked at Buff.

The first masseur was 20 pounds overweight. Buff gazed at his paunch with distaste. "Who would hire a carpenter with rusty tools?"

The white-bathrobed housewives smiled, then looked guilty. The paunchy masseur turned red, but that probably didn't reveal sexual attraction.

Buff stepped up to the other masseur, who was 6'2" and obviously spent his spare time at the gym. "Sophie *likes* tall men."

The 6'4" alien said the words slowly, with relish. The white-robed housewives nodded in fervent agreement.

Mona leaned to whisper in Marcie's ear. "We should warn Michael, this Worm might be a cuck fetish."

The Worm offered his hand. "My name is Buff."

The tall masseur shook the offered hand. "I'm Michael."

"Michael, I want you to give Sophie a one-hour, full-body massage, medium to hard pressure, with extra attention to the flat sheet muscles in her shins and beside her right shoulder blade. Then oral sex to first orgasm, then rough doggie style with light choking to second orgasm, then anal, gently at first, to your orgasm. Do it bareback and don't worry about disease. If either of you catches something, I will cure it. And for God's sake, don't ruin it by asking her permission. Can you remember all that?"

In the Massage Envy lobby, six mouths dropped open. A white-bathrobed housewife swayed and clutched the counter.

After a long, quiet pause, Michael said, "Tell me about Sophie."

Buff patted his shoulder. "Her appearance will please you."

"In that case, remembering will not be the problem."

Buff took a business card off the counter. He wrote on the back, then handed the card to Michael. "Show this to Sophie. She will recognize my handwriting."

Michael read the card. Then he wordlessly handed it to the women.

The four women huddled around the card.

Sophie...
I have given Michael
detailed instructions.
Relax and enjoy it.

You are not in charge.

Marcie: "That is *really* not appropriate."

Mona: "Wow."

White-bathrobed housewife #1: "That does *not* count as consent."

White-bathrobed housewife #2: "What is the exact procedure to join your colony?"

Mona took another card. "You've only been on Earth a few months, so if Sophie is Human, you can't have been together very long."

"A few weeks," said Buff. "Why?"

Mona flipped the card over and wrote her phone number. "I'll cook you a pot roast and make you feel better." She handed over the card. "Call me, when you find yourself wondering how any woman could be so ungrateful."

Three days later, in Sophie's kitchen, Buff said, "How can any woman be so ungrateful?"

"Ungrateful," Sophie sputtered. *"Ungrateful?* What kind of whore do you think I am?"

Buff tried, but couldn't stop himself. "I don't know. What kind of whore would you like to be?"

Sophie punched his shoulder, but not in the friendly way. "The receptionist *smirked* at me. Does she know what... what you asked that man to do to me?"

Oops. Buff reddened.

"You *told her!* You made me a laughingstock!"

"This is not the reaction I hoped for."

"How could you possibly be so insensitive!"

"You might be right." Buff fished out the *Massage Envy* card. "Now that I think about it, the receptionist tried to warn me."

"What?" Sophie looked suspicious.

"It was Mona, the pretty one. She gave me her phone number and told me to use it when you rejected my gift." Buff waved the card. "She offered to cook me a pot roast to make me feel better. I apologize for not figuring it out until now."

Sophie stared at the card.

"Sorry again." Buff tucked the card into his pocket and turned to leave. "I'll see you around."

"Wait."

Buff waited.

Sophie took a moment to summon her willpower. "I'm not mad at you," she lied. "I'm mad at the masseur for not *being* you."

Buff looked doubtful.

"Your gift got some of the details right." Sophie unid her top button. "You just should have delivered it yourself."

Two hours later, in the dark of her bedroom, Sophie twined with Buffalo.

"Why do you let people call you, *aliens?*"

They lay quietly for a while.

"Did you know we come from a different planet?"

Sophie poked him, but not too hard.

"Why not call us *aliens?* It seems appropriate."

"No, it is not appropriate. It implies you are different from us."

"Did you know we come from a different planet?"

Sophie poked him again, but not too hard.

"Why does this word *alien* trouble you?"

"People are not just calling you a*liens*. They are calling you *Worms*. You need a better name." Sophie expected Buff to say they already had a name.

Instead, he said, "People will call us what they will."

"No, they won't. If you say you don't want to be called *Worms*, people will have to stop."

"Are you really so afraid of us?"

"No." Sophie felt a tingle of exasperation. "Just say it hurts your feelings. Then nobody can say it, at least not in public. It would be crude, like saying the N-word."

Buff considered. "So, if we make our name an unspeakable profanity, you think that will improve our image?"

Sophie poked him a little harder. "I'm serious. Letting people call you *Worms* is dangerous. It makes you safe and socially-acceptable targets. You should call yourselves the *Homicidal Dragons,* or the *Affectionate Bunnies.* Anything but *Worms.*"

Buff didn't reply, but Sophie knew he wasn't sleeping.

Four days later
Springfield, MO
A day of revelations

Tom Pine reached his office at 7 AM. He walked inside and glanced longingly at a stack of Foucalt test images. Then he settled in and began the paperwork to renew his state business permit.

Three hours later, the protesters arrived. Tom heard them chanting and glanced out the window. His parking lot was filled with picketers waving signs.

COMPASSION IS NOT RANSOM

AUDIT AREA 51

I PAY CASH FOR UGLY GIRLS

Tom walked out the front door and strode into the crowd, taking up station beside a fat man holding a sign that read, *Audit Area 51.* "Pretend you're not talking to me."

The fat man looked alarmed.

"Look *away,*" Tom hissed.

The fat man looked away. "Are they watching?"

"Yes, but they can't hear us over this crowd. Even alien microphones can't pick out a single conversation, like Human ears can."

The fat man nodded. "Do you need to get a message out?"

"Yes, it's critical. You know I'm forced to work with the aliens?"

"We all know." The fat man waved his *Area 51* sign.

"Area 51 is a diversion," Tom murmured. "They keep it at Area *52.*"

The fat man straightened. "They keep *what?*"

"I already said too much." Tom pushed off and shoved his way back to his building, barely making it through the front door before he burst out laughing. Inside, he checked Sophie's whiteboard.

Signed E.R.I.S.A disclosures are
due wed by 5PM. No exceptions.

The aliens do **not** know how
to make anything bigger.
So stop asking them. And
stop listening to Frank.

Sophie

Ten minutes later, the alien Luci Dark walked into Tom's office and noticed his wall. "That's not a very good pinup."

She was looking at *Fluffer,* the painting that dominated Tom's office. The seven-foot watercolor showed a young woman in a modest dress, alone on a park bench made for two, obviously waiting for someone. "She looks lonely," Luci opined. "What does she fluff?"

"Me," Tom replied. "She's my incentive plan."

Luci looked doubtful. "Why is she wearing clothes?"

"Because this is a workplace."

Luci seemed to be waiting for the punchline.

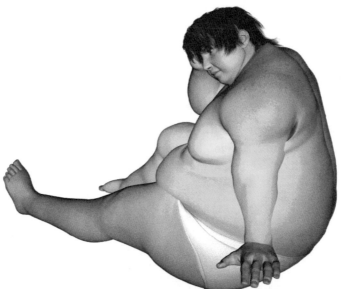

"This is my *office.* I can't put real pinup girls on the walls, because I would get..." Tom trailed off.

"Go ahead." Luci looked enquiring. "You were about to explain why you can't put a pinup girl on *your* wall of *your* office in *your* company in *your* building."

"Oh, wow." Tom rubbed his face. "I can't be sued. How did it take me so long to think of this?"

"Don't be too hard on yourself," Luci suggested. "You've only recently had your dick reattached."

"Miss Dark, what do you need from me?"

"I have an announcement. We have chosen a name."

"Oh, good. I was tired of calling you, *aliens,* and the thought police are trying to make us call you, *Worms,* which just invites attack."

"*Alien* is still appropriate," Luci pronounced, "since I am exotic and mysterious."

"Okay, Miss Dark, what name have you chosen?"

"Henceforth," Luci intoned, "you may refer to us as, *Worms.*"

Tom slumped slowly forward until his forehead rested on his desk. "Death wish," he mumbled. "That's the only explanation."

Luci ran her hands over the carved wood of Fluffer's frame. The painted girl on the bench radiated loneliness, but also a sense of hope. "Our name was a collective decision. Together, we are dumber than any of us, but at least we didn't go with, *Frugi.*"

"At least *Frugi* would not invite us to attack you. Calling yourselves *Worms* is suicidal. How could you possibly...Wait." Tom looked up. "You made a *collective* decision? Is that possible? You all agreed?"

Luci snorted. "We couldn't all agree on which end of a shoe to put our foot into, but we all know misunderstanding invites conflict."

"Which you settle with pistols."

"Pfft." Luci waved. "We can always give each other the benefit of the doubt. The pigheaded party usually admits it, since the alternative is the forbidden fruit."

Tom looked interested. "Natalie mentioned your forbidden fruit. Do you really have a drug that would unmask my delusions? I'd like to try it."

"No, the fruit is too painful to try on a lark, and too dangerous."

"Yet you use it every month."

"It's only dangerous the first time, when you find out if you're a wasp. After that, it's just YIKES!" Luci spun toward the window as a string of pops was followed by shouting. "Was that gunfire?"

The office phone beeped.

It was a rooftop guard. "Sir, someone drove by and tossed a string of firecrackers at the hippie protesters."

"I heard," said Tom. "Did our hippies flee in terror?"

"Sir, your hippies are the other kind. They threw a brick through his windshield."

Tom thanked the guard and hung up. "Getting back to your impressively stupid choice of name, I'm surprised you could agree on *any* name." He considered. "On the other hand, you obviously *can* agree on a big decision, since you all agreed to pile into the *Finger* and come here."

"Hardly."

"Coming here wasn't a choice? Gabriel said the wasps on your planet had united against you. Were they so powerful you had no choice but to flee?"

"No, you're right." Luci gazed at the sunlit world outside, then she turned away from it. "We had a real choice, thanks to Gabriel."

"You *let yourself* be chased off your own planet? That must have been awful, but at least Gabriel had a ship big enough to hold you all. He must be a hero."

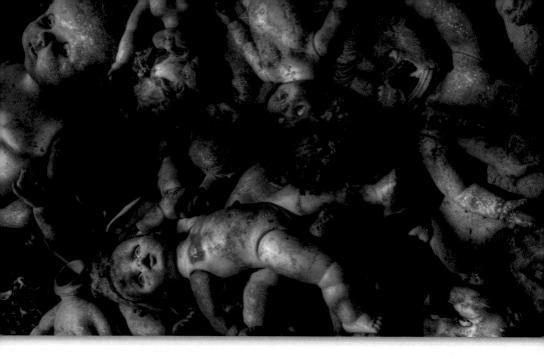

"Oh, yes, Gabriel is quite the hero. Only *he* would pay for something as ridiculous as the *Unexpected Finger*. But he also paid *me*, so I helped. Then, after we were... when it really mattered, the *Finger* wasn't ridiculous. It gave us the choice, and it was *me* who stood up and convinced everyone to abandon our world." Luci slumped into Tom's guest chair. "Now, I don't see much of my friends."

"Seriously? You were ostracized for giving them an option?"

"Not like that." Luci waved at her row of cheek tattoos. "My friends can't help loving me, but when they think of me, they remember the awful choice, so their compassionate censor stops them from thinking of me when they make a guest list."

Tom pondered that awhile. When he glanced back to Luci, he was shocked to realize she was trying not to cry. It was so out of character, he didn't know how to react.

"If only we'd never built that damn thing." Luci wiped her eyes and mustered a weak smile. "Anyway, we managed to agree our name should be chosen randomly from the serious contenders. Personally, I was rooting for, *Merciless.*"

Luci's famously beautiful mouth continued to smile, but a tear had started down her cheek.

Sophie poured two glasses of red wine, then she and Buff relaxed on her couch, getting to know each other.

In time, the conversation found its way to Sophie's childhood. "Tom Pine was my boy next door. He was *really* popular with girls, before he got older and everyone saw what...what he would look like."

Buff sipped his wine. "I don't understand."

"I shouldn't talk about him that way. When I was 16, he tried to seduce me."

Buff looked interested.

"I rejected him. I rejected *everyone,*" Sophie said wistfully. "I didn't even have sex after my senior prom. You know, I can still fit into my prom dress. Wait here, and when I come back, you are *not* allowed to leave the couch." Sophie set down her glass and walked into her bedroom, closing the door.

Five minutes later, she opened the door, wearing her prom dress. "Do you like it? A good prom dress has lots of complicated buttons and hooks to torture your date, but I'm not that kind of-"

Sophie never finished her sentence, because Buff already had her by the hair.

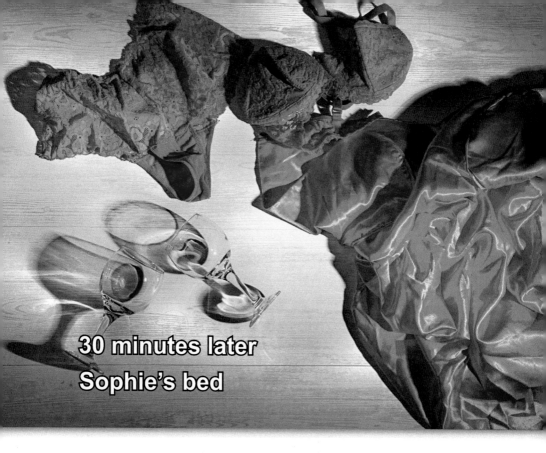

**30 minutes later
Sophie's bed**

In the dark, Sophie twined with the beautiful Buffalo. "You're not just *ungovernable*," she murmured. "You also altered your brain somehow, to make you behave honorably. Luci says that's how you avoid killing your friends, because you can give each other the benefit of the doubt. But if that's true, why make yourself ungovernable? Why take the risk of violence?"

They lay silent for a while.

"We were built to hold good men for ransom," Buff replied eventually. "I mean, we were *literally* built for it. We can't change our nature by half measures."

Sophie slid her hand idly over his chest. She loved these moments. "How do you know, if you haven't tried?"

"We *did* try." Buff laid his hand over hers. "Our first generation harmed no one but themselves."

Sophie felt a chill. "Themselves?"

"One in three of our first generation died by their own hand before they escaped the malaise."

"What malaise?"

"The malaise that strikes if we withdraw from the tournament." Buff's other hand slid slowly over her butt. "Do you know about the tournament of life?"

Sophie twirled a finger in Buff's chest hair. "Natural selection, survival of the fittest."

"*Survival of the fittest* is a nice expression, but competition for women is the more potent force. Do you know the tournament built your mind?"

"That question is controversial."

"On our world as well," said Buff. "But it's not in doubt. My mind was built by the tournament, *for* the tournament. If I didn't compete, I would have no reason to live."

Sophie raised her face toward him. "You think the meaning of life is survival and reproduction?"

"The tournament gives me joy. That is the *purpose* of joy. Life without the tournament would be joyless."

"Your logic is circular." Sophie ran a finger around his nipple, watching it shrink then rise under her touch.

"My most basic drive, my *only* drive, is to advance in the tournament. My mind is purpose-built to reproduce and accumulate money."

"You don't mean *money;* you mean power to assure your survival."

"That too, but mostly I need money for reproduction. You know how women are."

Sophie poked him, but not too hard.

"Survival and reproduction require different strategies. Around you, I have to choose one or the other."

Sophie poked him again, harder. "Quit trying to distract me. What happened to your first generation?"

"They took your suggestion and tried a half measure. They faced the burning bush and shackled their wasp. That means they adjusted their brain, so they couldn't demand ransom. They gambled everything on their new idea, and they lost."

"No way," said Sophie. "Are you seriously telling me your people get suicidally depressed if they can't demand ransom?"

"'I'm seriously telling you the tournament put a wasp in my head, and in yours. The wasp attacks virtue to disarm it and hold it for ransom."

Sophie poked Buff a little harder. "I don't attack virtue; that's nasty. Why would I do it?"

"Because that's where the money is."

"You're so cynical."

"We shackled our wasp." Buff tapped his cheekbone, singling out his second tattoo, the square. "Yet the wasp still lives, and it is aroused by easy targets. When my wasp sees a soft target, it thrashes in its shackles and ridicules every honorable restraint. Eventually, it would harry me into the malaise."

"That's a stretch," Sophie decided. "You actually believe your brain evolved to attack the virtuous, so you can hold them for ransom?"

"Yes," said the almost-Human sharing Sophie's bed. "We were built to plunder soft targets, whenever we find one."

"So, to keep that part of your brain quiet, you had to get rid of soft targets?"

"Correct. Luci knows, if she demands ransom, I will go berserk and shoot her, so her wasp sees no soft target. It sits quiet in its shackles, and Luci can have some peace."

Sophie rolled over and straddled the alien. "You help your friends relax by threatening to kill them?"

"The irony is not lost on us."

"Why do you call it a *wasp?* That's what you call *us.*"

"We call it the wasp because it attacks with poison, a calming poison that leaves the target unwilling to resist."

"Poison?"

"Poison is a metaphor. It means a moral attack. Sophie, hear me now: I must *never* come to believe you are poisoning me. I am homicidal, not suicidal, so you must *not* set my mental imperatives against each other. I cannot allow my super-strong monkeys to fight, so I *will not* allow it."

"Relax," said Sophie. "I would never do that to you."

Buff did not relax. "Tell me you understand."

"I understand. Would poison really work on you?" Luci ran her finger down the row of tattooed warnings on Buff's cheek. "Could a moral attack turn your moral imperatives against each other?"

"You're the only one who could do that to me."

Sophie smiled in the darkness.

The next day, just past noon, Sophie and Buff joined the weekly meeting of Tom Pine's Executive Council.

The Executive Council consisted of three Humans: Tom, Sophie and Frank; and three aliens: Natalie, Buff, and Luci.

Luci opened the microwave and pulled out a burrito. "I was poking around Facebook, and I saw a cute girl post a challenge. The challenge was: *Seduce me with one sentence.* She was flooded with replies, mostly dumb or crude, but a few were touching. One guy just said, *Make me believe again."*

"I will make all your dreams come true," Sophie recited. *"*I always wanted a man to say that to me with a straight face."

Luci waved her burrito at Buff. "Seduce me with one sentence."

After a long pause, Buff said, "Join me for a lonely, 90-year quest to save your family and everyone we love."

Natalie whistled.

Luci blinked and had to sit down.

Sophie scowled.

"Cheater." Luci wiped her eyes, then pointed an accusing burrito. "You used that one already."

"Of course," said Buff. "Why gamble on a new design, when I have one proven?"

Luci threw her burrito wrapper at him. "How about you, Frank. Can you top that?"

Frank: "I have $300."

Tom Pine walked in and headed for the coffee machine.

"Tom, we're playing a game." Luci flipped her hair, then struck a pose that, by accident and not at all on purpose, slightly lifted her shirt to show off her flat abdomen. "Seduce me with one sentence."

"Maybe later. I noticed a dangerous broken bolt on your left engine mount that will take me half an hour to fix. Make a sandwich and bring it out to me."

Tom walked out, closing the door behind him.

The lunchroom fell silent.

Frank: "Technically, that was *two* sentences, plus a fragment."

"I saw a bicycle race," the old alien Natalie mused. "The course was famously difficult because of the hills. When the starting gun fired, all the racers jumped on their bikes and took off, except one racer was busy flirting. He hung around, chatting up the girls and signing autographs, while we tried to tell him the race had started. Finally, when the other racers were out of sight, he kissed the prettiest girl and climbed onto his bike. By the halfway point, he had passed everyone. By the finish line, he was half a mile ahead of his closest rival."

The lunchroom fell silent again.

Luci stood up. "Does Tom prefer ham or chicken?"

Later that evening
Sophie's bedroom

Sophie Flint stood before her mirror and inspected her nightie with a critical eye. Actually, the nightie was so sheer, Sophie could inspect her whole body.

When she was satisfied, Sophie walked into the living room. Buff lounged on the couch before the big-screen TV, playing the Vatican DLC in *Left 4 Dead 3*. She strolled past him in the transparent nightie and almost reached the kitchen before he tackled her and ripped it off.

Later, in the dark of her bedroom, they twined. "Why do you only have four tattoos?" Sophie traced her finger across the four symbols on Buff's cheek. "All your friends have a fifth symbol, the circle. Luci's circle has a slash through it."

Buff shook his head beneath her finger. "Explaining my tattoos would violate sacred taboos."

They lay quietly awhile.

"Taboo tattoo, taboo tattoo," Sophie murmured. "I know why you're so aggressive. It's the monkey in your head that recognizes me as, *female.* You bulked him up into a super-monkey."

"Natalie *really* didn't want to tell you. She fretted about it for hours, but you were obviously about to figure it out yourself, and we were afraid you'd blab it to everyone."

"Could you undo it? Make yourself normal?"

"Why? Would you like to wear that nightie around the office?"

Sophie poked him, but not too hard.

Eventually, Buff answered. "Yes, I'll have to dial back my sexual aggression when I get old, so the monkeys won't drag me into places my body can't follow."

Sophie combed her fingers through his chest hair for a while. "Have you ever been married?"

"We can't do marriage like you do, as a property right. It would end in murder."

Sophie's heart sank.

"But we have something," Buff added.

"Really? Tell me about it."

"No. Your queens must not learn our mating habits."

"We *already* know enough to make you look bad. You should tell me enough to make you look good."

"Sophie, we've been over this."

"No, we haven't. You always refuse and tell me it would *violate a sacred taboo.*"

"I won't explain our mating habits. It would violate a sacred taboo."

Sophie played with his nipple. "You can make your mental monkeys super-strong. I bet you have a monkey whose only job is to recognize your mate."

Buff stroked her hair.

"If you *did* choose to bond with someone, you could do it tightly."

Buff didn't answer.

Sophie looked up at him. "Have you ever done it?"

"I wanted to, once. I really worked for it, but it ended badly."

"Who with?"

"I won't tell you."

"What happened?"

"I won't tell you."

Sophie sat up abruptly. "Did you kill her?"

Buff chuckled. "I managed not to. That's what took so much work."

Sophie lay back down. She stretched her arm across his broad chest, and laid her head in the pillow of his muscular shoulder. "Do you think you'll want to try again?"

After two heart-stopping seconds, Buff said, "Yes."

In the dark, Sophie smiled contentedly.

The next morning
Still in Springfield

Sophie reached the office at 7 AM. She closed her door and gazed longingly at her stack of employee discipline reports. Then she fired up her web browser and headed over to PGBC.gov to check for changes in the ERISA rules.

Three hours later, the protesters arrived. Sophie glanced out her window and saw the handicap parking spot filled with picketers.

Sophie walked outside, into the crowd to a pregnant Latina woman holding a professionally-printed *Just Nuke Them* sign. "Saying that here is risky."

The Latina woman looked apologetic. "No hablo English."

Sophie tapped the woman's sign. *"Just nuke them.* Threatening the aliens is dangerous, and you are pregnant. Hablo?"

The Latina woman shook her head and rubbed her fingers together. "No hablo. Cuarenta dollars."

"Seriously? You're picketing us for *40 dollars,* and you don't even know what your sign says?"

"Que?"

Sophie gave up and walked back inside, stopping in the lobby to update her whiteboard.

Wellness Surveys due Fri to avoid the penalty.

The 3-d scanner and printer are for business purposes only. There is no business reason to duplicate any part of your body. This means you, Frank.

Sophie

In her office, Sophie closed gazed longingly at a stack of new building blueprints. Then she settled in to work on the environmental impact statement.

She was only five hours in, just starting to research the formatting requirements for the *Streets and Bridges* section of Part 9: *Costs of Increased Employment on Nearby Communities,* when she heard a knock. "Enter."

It was Buff. "Peace offer?"

"You may offer."

"I know a spot for a picnic."

Sophie grabbed her purse. On the way out, she glimpsed furtive smiles from the Worm women.

Buff had her stop by the bathroom. Then she was surprised when he led her to the staircase.

"Are you game?"

Sophie hesitated, then nodded.

Buff handed her a green berry, the size of a peanut. "Eat this."

"What is it?"

"We call it, *First Fink.*"

"What does it do?"

"It stuns the part of your brain that detects poison."

Sophie folded her arms.

"If you don't eat it," Buff said sternly, "you *will* be sorry later, and so will I, when you vomit on my silk upholstery. Uncommanded motion triggers your poison detector."

Sophie ate the berry, and puckered. "Was that ripe?"

"Ripe is poison, which you would not detect. Got your sunglasses?"

Sophie fished them out of her purse and followed him up the stairs.

Buff waved to the guards then walked around his boat, flapping control surfaces and peering into holes.

When he strapped Sophie into the rear seat and snapped her chest harness together, she was vaguely disappointed he did nothing she could protest. He settled a headset over her ears and pressed the boom microphone against her lips. "Kiss this."

Sophie watched as Buff climbed into the front seat, strapped in, and drew the canopy shut. She could see only the back of his head. He pulled on his headset, then she heard his voice in her ears. "How's my volume?"

"Fine."

"Kiss the microphone."

She moved it closer. "Volume is fine."

186

"That's better." Buff's head moved as he fussed with his controls. "Before we launch, I want you to learn four techniques. You probably won't need any of them. Pay attention anyway."

Behind him, Sophie nodded nervously, but he couldn't see her.

"First, find the breathing mask. It's under your right leg."

She felt under the seat. "Got it."

"If we lose pressure, the mask will give you Eight to breathe."

"Eight is Oxygen?"

"Go for the mask immediately, and don't try to hold your breath. If we lose pressure, your lungs will work in reverse and suck the Eight –the oxygen– out of your blood. That blood goes straight from your lungs to your brain, so you will pass out in seconds."

"You're so reassuring."

"On the back of my headrest, you see a tube of goo and a roll of tape. Those are for leaks."

This foreplay was not helping Sophie relax.

"Don't worry; pressure leaks are rare and usually slow. Now, find the vomit bag under your left leg."

Sophie felt around. "Got it."

"Please, *please* do not confuse the vomit bag with the breathing mask. Remember the expression: *Breathe right or barf left.*"

Sophie managed a weak smile. Nobody saw it.

"Now, look at your controls."

"Okay, what am I looking at?"

"Generally speaking, it will be best if you don't play with the controls, but I want you to find the red button with the black arrow pointing down."

Sophie searched. "Got it."

"You see the label says, *Autolander.* If I pass out, and you think I won't wake up, your options are to press that button, or learn to fly."

"Okay." Sophie's voice came out higher pitched than she intended.

"The autolander is a blind idiot," Buff warned. "It will take us straight down, even over water."

"Got it. Wait for flat ground."

"Okay, you are halfway through flight school. Most of the rest is learning to be subtle when you brag."

Sophie laughed nervously.

"Do you know what to expect, when I pull the trigger?"

Sophie had seen several takeoffs. "I know what to expect, but it seems a poor system for heavy gravity."

"Landing in heavy gravity is a nightmare. The toppler is the second worst scheme."

"What's the worst?"

"All the other schemes tied for worst."

"But *falling over?* In heavy gravity?"

"Our world wasn't paved with long, smooth runways."

"Then lengthen the wings, so you can land slower."

Buff shook his head. "Fixed wings can fly fast or land slow, but not both. Plus, I have to fit through the *Finger's* hatch."

"So fold the wings when you dock, or sweep them back when you want to fly fast."

"Movable wings would be worse." Buff held up his index finger. "Bigger spar to support long wings." He added his middle finger. "Load-bearing hinges." Another finger. "Actuators strong enough to move the wings under load." The fourth finger. "At least two rear landing struts with wheels." He raised his thumb. "Hinges and actuators to retract the wheels." The index finger on his other hand. "Internal space to stow the wheels and struts." Another middle finger. "Brakes, plus their actuators, linkage, and pedals." The final ring finger. "Then I need a runway."

"Okay," Sophie conceded. "Rotate the engines, like Luci's yacht."

Buff snorted. "Luci's ridiculous swiveling engine mounts suck up half of her maintenance hours and a quarter of her dry weight."

"You wouldn't have to rotate the whole engines, just their exhaust nozzles."

"*Rotate* the nozzles? Do you know my exhaust velocity?"

Sophie wasn't ready to surrender. "Why not just leave the boat standing, and climb down a ladder?"

"What if the wind blows?" Buff pointed at a wing. "Have you ever tried to hold a barn door in a storm?"

"I just can't believe tipping over is the best solution."

"You have to admit, it looks cool, and I need compressed air tanks anyway, to breathe."

"What if your air piston fails? You'd be stuck horizontal."

"Give me some credit. My attitude jets can lift the nose. I only use the air piston so I don't tear up the roof when I do this." Buff pushed a button.

The nose dipped an instant before Sophie's seat cushion slapped her butt. Outside, the rooftop rocked crazily and Sophie was instantly dizzy. Orange flame burst from the nose, spraying back around the canopy as her headphones filled with a rumbling hiss, then her seat pushed firmly into her back and the rooftop dropped away. As they ascended, the orange exhaust gradually constricted to three narrow jets, like incandescent ropes that emerged from the nose and stretched backward just outside the clear canopy, reaching for the ground behind them. Sophie felt an absurd urge to touch one.

The seat kept pressing as the Pine Shack receded. When she could see most of the neighborhood, the orange ropes faded and Sophie felt a coarser vibration as the rear engine ignited. Her seat pressed harder.

Over the roar, she heard Buff whoop. He wasn't saying anything, just enjoying the moment.

The thrust lasted longer than Sophie expected. It went on and on for what seemed like several minutes, as the ground grew distant and vague.

Eventually, the blue sky faded to purple, then to black. With a start, Sophie realized she was in space, but she couldn't see any stars. The sun was brilliant, painful even with her sunglasses.

The engine quit abruptly, and Sophie lurched forward into her straps. She panicked as she felt herself falling.

"Don't worry." Buff's reassuring voice filled her headset. "I have a plan."

Sophie's hair floated, and dust rose around her. She willed herself not to believe she was falling, so she didn't need to flail.

Buff tugged off his headset and replaced it with a baseball cap. Then he reached over his shoulder to hand a cap to Sophie.

The blue cap was printed with the five Worm tattoos in white, above the words, *ALL THE RIGHT ENEMIES.* Sophie put it on and angled it to block the sun.

The little cockpit fell silent. Off to either side, the curving limb of the Earth glowed blue.

Buff didn't spoil the moment by speaking.

In time, they passed a silently flickering thunderstorm, rising beneath them to a tenth of the little boat's altitude.

Fifteen minutes later, Buff broke the reverie. "Time to slow down. I want us both to know the autolander works, so on my mark, push the button. If it does something stupid, I'm here to override."

Sophie felt calm, not at all nervous. Below them, she saw only ocean.

Buff's baseball cap disappeared and was replaced by his headset. Reluctantly, Sophie pulled hers on and kissed her mic.

"Volume check."

"Volume is good." Sophie thought about saying, *Five by Five,* but she didn't know what that meant, and she wasn't tempted to pretend. It felt good that Buff knew her limits.

"On my mark, trigger the autolander. Three... two... one... mark."

Sophie pressed the button. She felt a nudge, and the blue horizon rose. It kept rising until the ocean lay above like a ceiling, and Sophie realized she was looking straight astern. She saw only water and clouds and a few contrails far below, with no sign of the coast. Then the engine roared and her weight returned.

The thrust continued for many minutes, but this time she expected it. Eventually, the rear engine cut out and the nose engines woke, then the horizon rose again, their view shifting gradually spaceward. Above the roar, she heard Buff's voice. "Your GPS navigators are so sweet."

More minutes passed, and she saw Buff craning to look behind them. Sophie turned and spotted a crescent atoll, just large enough to support a band of trees. In the central lagoon, curving white lines washed toward the beach.

The atoll grew closer. They were headed for the lagoon.

"Damn. A near miss. I have to override."

Sophie felt a nudge, and they drifted toward the beach. The landing was not quite a thump, more like bouncing on a spring.

The engine noise faded, and was replaced by surf. Outside, Sophie saw palm trees swaying. Waves crashed onto the beach. "If you had told me, I could have brought a swimsuit."

Several seconds of quiet.

"Sophie, it's a deserted island."

More quiet.

Sophie sighed. "Oh, alright."

Obviously, people never came here, because the good driftwood hadn't been taken and the seashells were the best Sophie had ever seen. She quickly found more than she could carry.

When their pile of clothes had fallen 100 yards behind, Buff reached into the picnic basket with a grin and withdrew a bottle of sunscreen, but not the spray kind.

Five minutes later, Sophie stopped worrying about burning her pale areas. Then Buff settled in behind her and began combing her hair. "I've never seen you so tender," she remarked. "Natalie said you can have gentle lovemaking, but it's just a comfort for the elderly."

"Look at this." Buff reached around and showed her the comb.

It was metal, its teeth too close together, made to find lice. "That's a nit comb. Next time, bring a brush."

Buff wiggled the nit comb. "Look closer."

Sophie looked closer and saw a strand of her hair, but it was too reddish and seemed stiff, with a bump on one end. "What the hell?"

Buff picked off the little bump and buried it in the sand. "It's not hair; it's an antenna."

"It's a *microphone?* How did it get in my hair?"

"How hard is it to enter your bedroom at night?"

"Oh, that is just totally not acceptable."

Buff continued combing.

In time, Sophie calmed. They walked 100 feet from the buried antenna and sat side by side, their legs barely touching. The surf rushed rhythmically as gulls called beach memories from her childhood. She leaned back and closed her eyes, feeling the sun on her skin. She was debating a nap when Buff spoke.

"I want to tell you a secret, something we haven't told the Humans." Buff pointed upward. "On our trip to Earth, we were intercepted. Whatever it was, we never saw it, only felt its magnet aura. We were moving too fast for it to catch us, I think, but we passed too close for chance. We tried to evade by shifting our track a half-billion miles then going dark, but we can't be sure it didn't follow."

"Maybe it was something natural." Sophie dug idly into the sand. "The universe might be full of floating magnets."

"I hope so," Buff said quietly. "Because otherwise, it was trying to capture us. Its magnet aura hammered our wiring and destroyed most of our electrical equipment. It was not the act of a friend, so if the magnet wasn't a natural object, then it was a weapon. We decided not to tell your queens."

"Why are you telling me?"

Seagulls circled restlessly. A pelican glided past, skimming the waves. It flapped lazily and faded into the hazy distance before Buff answered. "I want us to share something, you and me, some-thing we don't share with anyone else."

"Tell me another secret, something about you."

Another minute passed quietly.

"My ancestors weren't rescued by aliens," Buff said at length. "They were rescued by God himself."

Sophie poked him, but not too hard.

"I'm not kidding. God rescued them from the sinking ship in return for 20 years of indentured servitude, building His temple on the New World."

"Seriously? What was God like?"

"Actually, God was not very godlike," said Buff. "He looked like a giant green serpent. You noticed we don't worship him."

After a long pause, Sophie said, "Are you absolutely *sure* it was the right God?"

"Pretty sure. He took the body of a mortally-wounded man and lived among us for 16 years. My ancestors kept detailed diaries."

"Wow. What was that like, living with God?"

"He didn't know He was God. Everyone assumed He was human, even *He* thought He was human, but His wife figured it out quickly."

"His *wife?*"

"God took the body and the wife of a mortally-wounded man. His wife suspected the truth, when the giant serpent disintegrated at the moment her husband's body woke up, healed. Later, she knew for certain, when He accidentally performed a miracle. But *He* didn't know, and in their 16 years together, she never told Him."

"What happened after 16 years?"

"She was killed, and in God's grief, He remembered who He was. He gave us the forbidden fruit, then He left our world, and we never saw Him again. We think His human wife's death hurt Him more than He could bear, and He had to avert his eyes."

"But why," Sophie asked. "Why would God want to live as a man, especially if His mortal life ended badly?"

Buff shrugged. "Who can know the mind of God? But He hinted He needs to be human sometimes, or He will lose touch with us."

A two-inch crab emerged from a hole in the sand. It stared at them awhile, then crab-walked toward the surf. Sophie sprinkled sand onto Buff's leg. "Why did God want a temple on another world? Were other people already there?"

"No, we had the place to ourselves, except for the animals."

"Why did He send you there?"

"He never told us, but He obviously sent us there to test an alternate path to redemption. You noticed we don't worship, because we don't need to, not after we face the burning bush." Buff sighed. "Unfortunately, it turned out our kids *do* need Christianity. Next time, we're sending the little monsters to church."

Sophie poked him. "God Himself used *you* to test an alternate path to redemption? You can't stop there. What other path?"

"I can't tell you."

"Oh, that is just not acceptable. What do you mean, *redemption?*"

"I should say, *sanctification*. The trouble with heaven is, it has lots of people and no rules, so God can't let you in if you enjoy hurting the other residents."

After a pause, Sophie said, "I think I'm offended."

"I'll tell you another secret," Buff offered. "When we become Worm, we are tested. One test was an oral exam that included me getting punched in the face."

"Seriously? Why did they punch you? Is that the secret?"

"They punched me to see how I would react, whether I could control myself." Buff touched his hexagon tattoo. "I can't tell you what this hexagon means, because it would violate sacred taboos, but I can tell you how it is tested, if you will swear secrecy. Your queens must not learn what we really are."

"Of course I'll keep our secret," said Sophie. "You don't have to ask."

"The test of the hexagon was inspired by the Christians," Buff explained. "They taught it in their Sunday school as the ideal of sainthood."

"So your world *did* have Christian churches?"

"Yes, but Worms don't need them. Before the test, I took a drug that suppressed my intellect, so I was like an animal and didn't know I was being tested. Then I was set loose in the forest. I heard screaming, so I investigated and found a stranger caught in a trap. He was shrieking in pain, because the trap was electrified, but in my animal state, I couldn't figure out how to free him. I could only hold the jaws open with my bare hands and transfer the electric shock to myself. The pain was excruciating."

Sophie winced. "Sounds awful."

"The test of the hexagon is beautiful and terrible, even to us. The only way to pass is to hold open the jaws and take the stranger's agony onto myself, until I faint from the pain."

"Did you pass?"

"We *all* pass, because letting the stranger suffer is unthinkable. In fact, I don't think the test was really intended as a test. It was to show me what I had become."

Sophie turned and kissed the alien, their lips barely touching. She felt the hairs rise on his leg, as if he were chilled. Her own skin tingled in response.

Half an hour later, Sophie realized Natalie had been mistaken.

It was not just a comfort for the elderly.

My tattoos mean something TOTALLY AWESOME

That's why I won't tell you

Like   Share   Comment

Comments. Please respect the <u>forum rules</u>.

Pokemom 12 minutes ago
> Everyone knows the triangle tattoo means they took the forbidden fruit, the drug that turns them into child molesters. The square means they like to kill people for no real reason. The other three are secret, but an NSA insider leaked in a military chat room that the hexagon tattoo means they like to participate in sex orgies. The circle means they know the terrible secret of the cherub sword. Luci's circle has a slash through it, which means her understanding of the cherub sword has been erased. That's why they made her their ambassador, since she couldn't accidentally let it slip.

LawFareForU Ten minutes ago
> The triangle is not a tattoo, just an ink mark. It wears off in about a month.

Pokemom Just now
> It's no coincidence they call that drug the forbidden fruit. They want us to think it's a reference to the tree of knowledge, but it's actually a reference to children.

Late in the afternoon, all of Tom's employees gathered in the lunchroom for the first test of the Worm sentry mods. In the front row, the technicians hunched over their pads playing *Revenge of the Incels 2: Chadmasculate.* Behind them, the assemblers had gathered around one screen, raptly watching *Continuing Medical Education Volume 255: Abdominal Inflation (One credit.)*

In the back, salesmen chatted. Up in the corner, the silent television showed a huge protest rally, captioned, *ACTIVISTS CLAIM WORMS BEHIND CHILD ABDUCTIONS*

Tom counted heads, then rapped the table with his *World's Best Boss* mug, which had a picture of Joseph Stalin.

The room quieted.

"I'm tired of getting my feelings hurt," Tom announced. "So, before we test the sentry, I'm enacting a new rule. Starting now, we will all act like Frank Drummer."

Half the employees looked doubtful. The rest looked alarmed.

"Our new rule will be called, the *Dungheap Rule.* Are you prepared to receive it?"

"Yes, boss," the employees chanted. "We are ready to receive the Dungheap Rule."

"Very well," said Tom. "I will reveal the Dungheap Rule, which is, *Talk about the elephant.* You will now recite the Dungheap Rule."

The lunchroom fell silent.

"Recite the damn rule!"

"Talk about the elephant," the employees recited dutifully.

"Very good. I will now set the example." Tom pointed to Sophie. "Tell me how I look. What do you *really* think of my appearance?"

Sophie froze.

Tom turned his palm up and wiggled his fingers in the universal gesture of, *bring it.*

"You're a handsome man," Sophie said with medium-low sincerity. "And you're well dressed."

"Oh good grief." Tom rolled his eyes. "Frank, help her out."

"Okay," said Frank. "You're short, and you look like a ferret."

Everyone gasped.

Tom winced. "That hurt worse than I expected."

The three Worms smiled approvingly.

Sophie punched Frank's shoulder.

Frank: "Ow!"

Tom: "Again."

"Okay," said Frank. "You're short, and you have a weak chin. I doubt any women find you physically attractive."

Tom's eyes squeezed shut, and his posture drooped.

Sophie punched Frank again. "And you're fat!"

"Ow!"

Tom's eyes were still closed. "Again."

"Tom, you look weak to women, because you were born short and weak-chinned. OW! God dammit Sophie, stop hitting me!"

Tom: "Again."

By the tenth repetition, people started to get bored.

"Okay," said Tom. "That last one didn't hurt, it was just annoying. Thank you."

"Finally." Frank rubbed his shoulder.

"You *hate* drama," said Sophie. "Why are you doing this?"

"Because I hate drama," Tom replied. "And you're ugly when you pretend to be stupid."

Sophie's eyes narrowed. "You're short and you have no chin."

Tom chuckled. Then he looked around the room, taking in the nervous faces. "This seems like a good time to mention you can't sue me. I keep reminding you of that, but I should have kept reminding *myself*, because I didn't grasp all of the implications."

The aliens looked interested.

Tom walked to the bulletin board. He produced a manila envelope, unwound the red string, and slid out a spiral-bound calendar, labeled, *Hot Shots.*

His employees looked worried.

"I'm changing one more policy." Tom paused to savor the moment. Then he raised the calendar and let it fall open to January.

The employees gasped. The aliens smiled.

The pinup girl looked exactly 18 years old. She displayed a brilliant smile and a tricked-out AR-15, neither of which obscured her perfect, perky C-cup breasts. Tom pinned the topless calendar to the bulletin board, then stepped back and gazed at it reverently.

Some people seemed to have trouble breathing.

Luci grinned and whispered something into Buff's ear. He smirked.

Sophie scowled.

Tom sighed contentedly. "Does anyone want to speak?"

Apparently, no one wanted to speak.

"Any comments? Any at all?"

"This is where we *eat*," Sophie growled. *"You're breaking the Intimate Rule."*

"Ah, the Intimate Rule, our most sacred commandment." Tom turned to face his employees. "You will now recite the Intimate Rule."

Sophie: "Are you drunk?"

"Recite the rule!"

"Don't poop where you eat," everyone chanted dutifully.

"Very good. Our highest law is, *don't poop where you eat.*" Tom pointed to the pinup girl. "Does anyone wish to claim she is poop? If you do, please speak up now, so I can push your head into the toilet."

Sophie rolled her eyes.

"That is all my announcements," Tom announced. "Let's test the alien sentry mod."

The employees looked relieved.

Frank plugged a camera into his laptop computer, then mounted a camera on a tripod. While he worked, Luci uncapped a green marker and drew the five alien symbols on Tom's left cheek.

Frank pointed the camera at the pinup. His laptop beeped and a window opened with a closeup of the pinup girl's face. A smaller window popped up to show her face crisscrossed by yellow lines. "Oops." Frank shifted the camera to an empty wall. Now his laptop showed the Seventies-era dark wood paneling.

Luci walked into the camera frame, looking left to show her face in three-quarter profile.

The computer beeped, and a window opened with a closeup of Luci's face, mathematically rotated so she appeared to be looking directly into the camera.

A smaller window popped up to show her face crisscrossed by yellow lines. Some of the lines marked obvious features like the distance between her eyes, and the span from her lips to her nose. Where lines crossed, tiny numbers called out intersection angles. Some lines connected nothing, yet somehow didn't feel random. A message window popped up.

Lucifa Dark
97% Match

Another window showed Luci's tattooed cheekbone, which promptly vanished and was replaced by outlines of her blue tattoos as they would look if she were facing the camera, except outlined in green.

Luci turned to look directly into the camera, and two more windows popped up. They showed extreme close-ups of Luci's irises, their distinctive blue features outlined in yellow. Below Luci's name, the *97% Match* increased to *99.8%*.

Luci moved aside, and Tom stepped into her place. The lunchroom crowd waited, tense, for five long seconds. Then Tom's name popped up as, *94% match*.

Tom turned toward the camera to reveal his irises, and the *94%* increased to *98%*.

A new window opened with a close-up of the five geometric tokens on Tom's cheek, drawn by Luci in green ink. The symbols were overlaid with red pixels above the urgently flashing message, *IMPOSTER*.

The lunchroom erupted into a cheer, then smiles and handshakes. Frank reached over and switched off the biometric scanner.

To Tom's surprise, the aliens didn't join the celebration. In fact, they seemed gloomy. Buff gazed somberly at nothing, his posture slack. Luci stood motionless, eyes closed.

Natalie was near tears. She saw Tom's questioning look and mustered a weak smile. "Not to worry, all is well, but it would have been good to meet you sooner." She briefly squeezed Tom's hands. Then she wiped her eyes and turned to her friends. "Come on, it's a happy day. Let's celebrate."

Nineteen released in a bellowing rush
They scythed and we harrowed
I furrowed the dust
Cherub sword flashing in smoldering husks

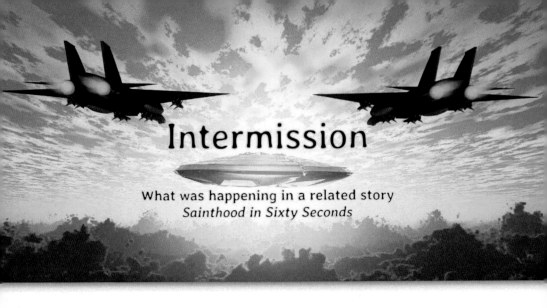

Intermission

What was happening in a related story
Sainthood in Sixty Seconds

This intermission is presented for
entertainment purposes only.
You can skip it and go get popcorn.

3,000 feet above a parked Worm spacecraft, Shades the pilot and Mustache the gunner circled in their cobra attack helicopter, the swift scourge of Vietnam and a valuable antique.

"Tang Soda, this is Shades. Two guys just entered the spaceship."

Tang Soda was the call sign of McGhee-Tyson air base.

"Shades, this is Tang Soda. Be advised, the secret squirrels assess the taller one is Joshua the Prophet."

"I love that guy!" In the front gunner seat, Mustache raised both thumbs. "Joshua is the prophet who fell to Earth in Saint Peter's Square and knocked over the Vatican Obelisk. I'm a Methodist."

Shades switched his display to show the view from the chin turret, which Mustache had zoomed in to the target. The little spacecraft parked beside the trail was roughly the same size as their helicopter. "Tang Soda, this is Shades. The pilot is giving me the finger."

"Shades, the secret squirrels have live drone footage. They assess this spacecraft as the *First Knuckle*, and the pilot giving you the finger is Gabriel Tide, the alien who owns the *Unexpected Finger*."

Mustache whistled.

The *Unexpected Finger* was the Worm mothership spinning serenely in orbit, occasionally spitting out small spacecraft like the one below, parked beside the Appalachian Trail on its front nose gear and two aft wingtips.

As Shades watched from above, the little craft's nose dipped then bounced upward. Just as it started to drop back, the nose engine fired, blasting debris across the Appalachian Trail and yanking the boat forward as it levered upright, plowing ruts with its dragging wingtips. When it reached vertical, the entire nose erupted orange fire and the boat leapt upward.

"Holy crap!" As the Worm rocketed skyward, his exhaust narrowed and resolved into five distinct jets. At 2,000 feet, the exhaust plumes curved as the worm pushed his nose over to head northeast. Then his nose engines quit abruptly and his tail engine ignited. Shades' world went dark as his visor tried to block the exhaust it interpreted as a nuke flash. "Tang Soda, the Worm is departing at heading… uh… looks like five-zero degrees, and he's in a hurry."

Ninety minutes earlier, when the incoming spacecraft was first spotted on radar, Shades and Mustache had been hastily extracted from Thursday softball. The weekly game had become a tradition at McGhee Tyson Air National Guard Base, home of two units: the 119th and the 134th, each with just enough female soldiers to field a coed softball team.

Shades and Mustache were attached to the 134th, which was a refueling wing. In normal times, their duty was to defend the fuel depot from ground attack by disloyal Knoxville residents, but scrambling to intercept an alien was more fun.

Their rivals, the 119th Command and Control Squadron, had been the first Air National Guard unit to be drafted into the new Space Command, which they considered ample reason to take command of the alien intercept. Unfortunately, the 119th's Space-Command radio couldn't talk with a Vietnam-era helicopter, so the 119th officers piled into the rival 134th op center and started shouting orders.

"Shades, radar confirms the Worm is headed toward Washington. Follow him."

3,000 feet above the Appalachian Trail, seated just below Shades in the gunner seat, Mustache snorted.

"Tang Soda, this is Shades. It's a spaceship. He's faster than a helicopter."

"Roger that, Shades," the 119th radio operator replied laconically. "We copy you feel unable to perform. Stand by for a message from commander, 119th. Message reads: *Do you have something better to do.* End message."

Shades turned his sleek attack chopper toward the alien and slammed the throttle to the stops.

"Tang Soda, this is Shades in pursuit of the alien. Please inform commander, 119th that I was hoping to get back in time to complete his remedial softball instruction."

"Shades, we copy you in hopeless pursuit. Take care to avoid the Worm's exhaust, and don't worry about the commander's ball skills. Your mom volunteered to tutor him privately."

"Tang Soda, the Worm's exhaust will not be a problem. He noticed our pursuit and turned back toward us. His bearing is now constant."

Like all good pilots, Shades took pride in his ability to speak calmly in ridiculous situations.

"Shades, our radar confirms the Worm is on collision course. Stand by for a message from commander, 119th. Message reads: *We will avenge your death, if it is convenient.* End message."

The alien flashed past, and Shades keyed his mic. "Tang Soda, this is Shades. Negative on playing chicken; the Worm took me on my right." Shades brought the cobra around in a hard left turn, craning to look over his shoulder.

The alien turned right, banking steeply and roaring past the cobra again. Shades circled hard right. "Tang Soda, he just passed me on the right again and gave me the finger."

"Shades, we see it on the radar, but we can't tell what he's up to."

Despite the aggressive maneuvers, Shades was pleased to see the constantly-rotating image of the alien craft wobble only slightly in the chin gun's telescopic crosshairs, which would have been so much cooler if the chin gun had some bullets.

One minute later, 2,000 feet above the Appalachian Trail, Shades gave up. He backed off the throttle and brought his cobra into a stationary hover. "Tang Soda, this is Shades. The Worm is flying circles around me."

The alien roared past left to right, refreshing the smoke trail from his last orbit. From the little spaceship's back seat, Joshua the Prophet waved. In the front seat, the gray-haired Worm pilot raised his middle finger.

"Shades, you're merged on our radar, but Doppler confirms he is orbiting you. Stand by for a message from commander, 119th. Message reads: *Wow, you must be embarrassed.* End message."

"Tang Soda, please assure commander 119th that Shades is standing tall. My confidence has been boosted by observing the commander's softball performance."

"Shades, we concur with your evaluation, and the secret squirrels now assess the Worm is jerking you around. Break pursuit, and come on home."

End of Intermission

Springfield, MO
A job interview

"Send in the next one."

Tom Pine's door opened to admit the next job applicant. She was about 20, with a perfect, elfin face and an ostentatiously flat stomach beneath her proud, 50-percent-visible C-cup boobs.

She'd belong on a magazine cover, if one side of her head had not been shaved, the other side had not been died blue, and one entire arm had not been tattooed with leafy vines.

Tom looked closer and saw the tattooed vines were poison ivy. "Are you trying to see how ugly you can make yourself and still attract men?"

She looked startled. "You can't say that."

"What kind of business do you think would hire you?" Tom was genuinely curious.

She shrugged. "I'm here."

"You don't have to stay for the whole interview. I'll sign the voucher for the unemployment office."

"You have to give me a fair chance." She was chewing a wad of gum. "Otherwise, it's discrimination."

"Ah, nice." Tom nodded appreciatively.

She smacked her gum. "What do you mean?"

Tom picked up her resume. For *Occupation,* it said: *Communication Facilitator; Activist; Creative Consultant.* For *Experience,* she had listed: *Protested climate change; Protested corporate greed; Raised awareness of inequality.* Tom pushed the intercom button labeled, *Sophie.* "Where did you find this?"

"Take me off speaker."

Tom picked up the handset. "Okay, spew."

"She's my cousin," Sophie explained. "She's always been beautiful, and I don't think any man has ever told her, *no.*"

"I understand." Tom put down the phone and looked at the cousin. "Listen to me. Are you listening?"

"Sure." The blue-haired girl smacked her gum.

"If you try to sue me, you'll be murdered."

She stopped smacking her gum.

Tom pointed to the exit. "You're useless. Get out."

After six minutes of crying noises from Sophie's office, Tom's door opened to admit the next applicant.

She was 30-something, and chubby. She stared at the three-legged guest stool, then sat on it.

Tom flipped through her resume and found some respectable job experience, so he opened his wallet, pulled out a $50 bill, and handed it to her. "This is for your trouble, because I lured you here under false pretenses. My job description was a lie."

She took the money. "You don't want me to read *Atlas Shrugged* to strippers?"

"No, we just say that in the ad so we don't attract crazies. I need someone for Q.C. That means, *quality control.* The bad news is, you can't sue me."

She arched an eyebrow. "Oh really?"

"Yes, really. Please take me seriously, because I don't want you to…" Tom hesitated. "Actually, maybe I *do* want you to show everyone what happens if you sue me." He picked up the girl's resume and glanced over the section marked, *Education.* She had majored in Cultural Studies. He pressed the intercom. "Really, Sophie? You sent me a *Cultural Studies* major to do quality control?"

"Cultural Studies is perfect for Q.C." Sophie Flint's voice crackled from the cheap speaker. "We don't need her to build anything, just nitpick the men who do."

Tom sighed. "Normally, I love hiring, but the last girl put me in a bad mood, so let's get this farce over with. This will come as a shock, but in this workplace, we respect *consent.*"

The chubby girl opened her purse and tucked in the $50. "If you respect my consent, I won't have to sue you."

Tom picked up her resume and scribbled the word, *Trouble.* "I wasn't talking about *your* consent. Odd as this sounds, you can't force me to keep paying you, if I don't want to."

She snapped her purse shut. "That's not what *consent* means."

"Ah, you're one of those." Tom dropped her resume on his desk, then propped his feet on it. "I guess we have to talk about sex." He tossed a slim binder at the girl. It slid across the desk and dropped into her lap. "Those are pictures of my most important employees. They are valuable, so they all get to sexually harass you."

The girl looked at the binder. "You have got to be kidding."

Tom pushed the *Sophie* button. "We're talking about sex, and she thinks I'm kidding."

They waited in silence for a few seconds. Then the door opened to admit Sophie Flint's head. "He's not kidding."

The chubby girl twisted around to look at Sophie. "Why do you put up with this?"

"If a man gets too annoying, you can slap him. Everyone will laugh, and he'd better laugh too, or we will taunt him mercilessly until he develops a sense of humor. You just can't sue us." Sophie withdrew, closing the door.

Then she opened it again. "You should also know, that binder isn't just the important employees; it's all of them. Everyone gets to harass you, until you prove you're valuable enough to be an annoying prima donna." Sophie left again, closing the door.

Then she opened it again. "By the way, I *am* valuable enough to be an annoying prima donna. Nobody gets to harass me."

Tom winced, ever so slightly, but the chubby girl noticed. She gazed at Tom for a long moment, then turned to Sophie. "What if my supervisor demands sex and threatens to fire me?"

"If you make yourself valuable, nobody will dare fire you, because he'd answer to Tom," said Sophie. "If you can't persuade a coworker to behave tolerably, you can force Tom to choose between you. But save that for your last resort, because Tom is not likely to choose the one who made him choose."

Tom pulled his feet off the girl's resume. "I'm going to test you now."

The chubby girl leaned away. "Are you going to feel me up?"

"Maybe if you lost 20 pounds. The point of this test is to determine whether you are human or NPC."

"I'll skip this part. Have fun." Sophie left and shut the door.

The chubby girl stared at Tom, open-mouthed. "Did you just tell me I'm too fat to grope?"

"Yes," said Tom, "I was joking. I don't grope my employees. Now pay attention, and I'll explain the test. The point of the test is to determine whether you are human or NPC. A human can over-power her urges with reason, but an NPC cannot, even though I just told you it's a test."

"I can't believe you just told me I'm fat."

"And now it gets worse. I am about to praise men, and you will let my pro-male statement stand, without pointing out an exception or adding a caveat. Then I will describe something men do better than women, and you will *not* point out an exception, or express disapproval. Do you understand the test?"

"I do not consent to be sexually harassed."

"Okay, thanks for your time. Just leave the door open." Tom pressed the *Sophie* button. "Please send in the next one."

"Wait," said the chubby girl. "What does *harass* mean? Would you really expect me to tolerate inappropriate comments?"

Tom was already leafing through the next resume. "She's afraid of inappropriate *comments.*"

"I don't know what I'm afraid of," the chubby girl admitted. "This place is alien. Where is the limit to what men can do?"

Tom looked up. "Why are you still here?"

The chubby girl rolled her eyes. Then she opened her purse, pulled out the $50, and dropped it on Tom's desk. "I'll pay you 50 dollars to tell me what you're hiding."

Tom laughed and pressed the *Sophie* button. "Hold on, something interesting happened." He tucked the money into his shirt pocket. "The boundary is *rudeness*. Men who cross it pay a social penalty. But the sad truth is that even here, the men are too beaten down to harass you properly. The only dragons are Buff and me, but he's trying to please his girlfriend, and I don't molest my subordinates, because flirtation from the CEO is an implied promise."

"If you don't molest your employees, what's the point?"

"The point is money. I provide a male-friendly workplace, and in return, men accept a lower salary."

The chubby applicant held out her hand. "Give back my $50. I didn't pay for bullshit."

Tom hesitated, then he tossed the $50 back into her lap. "You're right. I apologize. The truth is, I enjoy a sexualized workplace."

"That I can believe, but it's not appropriate for women."

"You think I should run *my* company to suit *your* sensibilities?"

"Well, you... hmm. Doesn't it cause drama?"

"I worry about that," Tom admitted. "So I've tried to build a no-drama culture. Surprisingly, it turned out drama was not being reduced by lawsuits. It also turned out the crudest horndogs are the fat women, once they realize it's safe."

"Fat women? Seriously?"

"You can also tell me I'm short and ugly," Tom added. "We find life is less stressful after we admit there's an elephant in the room."

The chubby applicant shook her head. "This cannot exist."

"If calling you fat or pinching your butt at work seems inconceivable, your parents weren't honest about the Seventies."

After a pause, she said, "You're short and ugly."

"Yes," Tom admitted. "I am."

She seemed surprised. "Didn't that hurt?"

"Of course it hurt, but only the first ten times. That pain was the best investment I ever made."

She blinked.

"Alien, isn't it? And on that note, there's one more thing I didn't tell you. This is not my building, just a place I rent some offices. *My* building is down the street. It's the one surrounded by protesters."

"Ah." She seemed almost relieved. "You work with the Worms."

Tom waved at the door. "Why don't you wander over to the other building and talk to the women. If you come back, I'll take the time to learn your name."

The chubby job applicant tucked the $50 into her purse. Then she

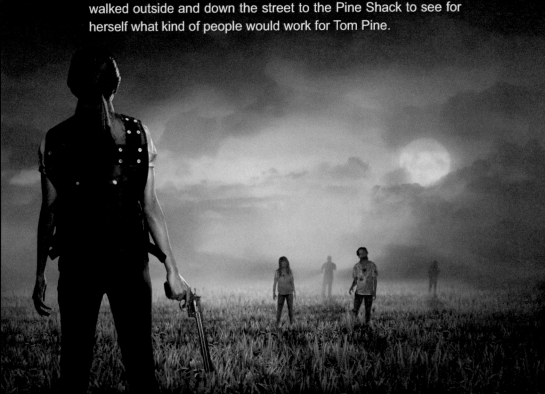

walked outside and down the street to the Pine Shack to see for herself what kind of people would work for Tom Pine.

Inside the Pine Shack, she followed the noise to the assembly room, where a dozen men and women worked in close quarters.

A fat man swore as a wisp of smoke rose from his workbench. "Dammit, nothing is going right today. Marcia, I need you to show me your tits."

The woman beside him didn't look up. "I'll show you my tits when you show me your six pack."

Everyone laughed except the fat man. He looked down at his generous belly and sighed.

The prettiest woman worked at a solder station. The chubby job applicant pulled up a chair. "How bad is it here, for you?"

"Ah, you're interviewing with Tom." The pretty woman chuckled. "Working here is *much* better than he lets on. We're all losing weight, and we get to hang out with the aliens, though for me, it's a bit lonely." She glanced at her coworkers. "When Tom threw out the old rules, they made new ones. This must be how cultures form."

"*They* made new rules? Not, *we* made new rules?"

The pretty woman smiled ruefully and held up her left hand to show her wedding ring. "My husband isn't cool with it, so I get left out."

The chubby job applicant stood up and walked back to Tom Pine's rented office.

On the way in, she stopped to see Sophie. "Start my paperwork. Tom is going to hire me."

"Oh really?" Sophie looked doubtful.

"He'll have to. I found his soft spot."

When she walked in, Tom seemed surprised to see her. He said, "I'm surprised to see you."

"My name is Candice." The chubby job applicant dragged in a comfy chair, flopped down into it, kicked off her shoes, and propped her feet up on Tom's desk. "I'll develop a rigorous sexual-harassment workshop, two hours per day for three weeks. I will supervise the class personally, and you will make it mandatory for all male employees."

Tom looked at her bare feet on his desktop. "Candice, did you understand anything I told you?"

"Yes, I did," said Tom's new quality-control officer. "Your men need training. If they're going to sexually harass me, I want them to do it better."

The next morning, Tom arrived at 7 AM and checked Sophie's whiteboard.

UPdate your tax iNfo
By tuesday 5 PM

All Employees

WarraNties are offered by
the compaNy _oNly_. You May
Not offer private guaratee
for cash.
This meaNs you FraNk   Sophie

Tom closed his office door and gazed longingly at a pile of 3D-printed brackets awaiting structural tests. Then he settled in and resumed his quest to figure out which export laws applied to the Worms.

After three hours, Tom still didn't know, and he decided to take a break. He looked out his window and saw picketers waving signs.

Tom walked outside, unlocked his pickup truck, and rooted in the glove box for his registration paperwork.

A hairy woman loomed over him, holding a sign that said, *ALL PROPERTY IS THEFT.* "You'd be in trouble," she hissed, "if you weren't rich enough to pay armed guards."

"I don't have to pay them." Tom glanced at the rooftop guards, casually resting their rifle muzzles on the parapet. "The Worms offered a bounty, half a pound of pure gold. Those guys on the roof are hoping to collect."

"A half-pound of gold for doing what?"

"Break into my truck, and you'll find out."

"Gaa! Men!" The hairy woman backed away.

Tom barely made it back inside before he burst out laughing.

He found Luci in the office she shared with Frank, working on the Worm web page. Tom flopped into a chair. "Are you really the Worm ambassador, negotiating with the Alien Regulatory Authority?"

Luci nodded.

"*And* maintaining the Worm website?"

"I just moderate the comments." Luci closed her document and rubbed her eyes. "We are too few. Each of us must do five jobs, and I'm exhausted. Let's get a snack."

"But why *you?* Do you have some hidden technical expertise?"

"None at all. My special expertise is understanding *you,* which is why I hang out in this lovely former gas station." Luci stood up, stretched, and headed for the lunch room.

Tom followed. "How did you learn so much about me?"

"Not you in particular. I just understand wasps."

"Do you think I'm a wasp?"

"Don't be an idiot." Luci perused the vending machine.

Tom persisted. "How did you come to understand wasps?"

"Accident of birth," said Luci's mouth, while the rest of her body said, *drop it.*

Tom glanced at the television, bolted high in the corner. It showed a mug shot of a cheerful Worm, his row of tattoos clearly visible. Underneath the grinning alien, the caption read,

ANOTHER WORM RAPE SUSPECT
CLAIMS DIPLOMATIC IMMUNITY

Tom winced. "Why won't you let us tell?"

"Tell what?" Luci gazed longingly at the Ding Dongs, then bought a bag of kale chips.

"Why won't you let us announce it? Your men can't actually rape anyone. Those women, the assault victims, they only had to say, *stop*. Why are you keeping that secret?"

Luci looked disappointed, but that might have been the kale chips. "Have you *still* not figured this out?"

Tom pointed to the television. "*Worms claim diplomatic immunity for multiple alleged rapes?* Of all the headlines ever written, that might actually be the most infuriating. You have to explain."

"No, I think the most infuriating was, *Worm assailant claims woman invited assault by wiggling butt.* That was yesterday."

"Miss Dark, this is serious. Your enemies are using this to recruit a mob. Why won't you explain?"

The television had flashed to an automobile with one front wheel hiked up on the sidewalk and its windshield pocked with bullet holes. The picture was captioned, *WORM DRIVER RESPONDS TO FENDER BENDER.*

"Mister Pine, you promised me your silence, and you will honor that promise." Luci bit into a kale chip, and puckered.

"You *can't* ignore this. If the assaults continue, there *will* be violence."

"Like that?" Luci waved at the bullet-riddled automobile.

"No, not like that," Tom snapped. "Have you read any Earth history? We are capable of *much* worse."

"Oh, yes," Luci said softly, still chewing the kale chip. "You are."

226

The same moment
In the empty lot out back
Sophie educates her man

"You're supposed to try to block me."

"I forgot." Buff trotted across the asphalt court and stood between Sophie and the basket.

Sophie dribbled twice, feinted left, then stepped back and fired.

Buff watched the ball sail over his head and bounce off the rim.

"Dammit! You're supposed to try to block my shot."

"Oh, right." Buff grabbed the ball and tossed it toward the basket. He overshot wildly.

Sophie shagged the errant ball, then deliberately repeated the same move, but when she reached Buff, instead of shooting, she paused. "Now, try to block me."

Buff had been standing with his hands at his sides. "Oh, right. I forgot." He held up his arms.

Sophie fired between his hands, and the ball bounced off the rim. Buff reached for the rebound, but misjudged and the ball sailed over his outstretched fingers.

"You should have caught that! You have to jump."

Buff looked at his feet.

A crowd of urban youths sauntered onto the court, obviously deter-mined to take it over. Then they noticed Buff's tattoos, his muscled 6'4" frame, and his ever-present holster. They gawked.

Sophie: "Boo!"

They sauntered away.

"Just *jump,*" Sophie commanded. *"*I've already seen you vault a conference table and pin me to the wallpaper."

"That was *indoors,* so it felt like the *Finger.*" Buff glanced up at the sky, then down at the asphalt. "On our world, falling was death."

"Don't be a sissy. Your species evolved on this planet. This is the gravity you were built for."

Tentatively, Buff jumped upward an inch. He landed lightly, looked at Sophie, and grinned. Then he jumped a little higher, and his smile broadened.

"Welcome to Earth." Sophie swiveled around him and trotted in for an easy layup. Buff turned to watch her, hands at his sides.

"Dammit, you're supposed to try to block me!" Sophie was getting angry now.

"Oh, right. I forgot."

Later that afternoon, Sophie drove Natalie out of the city to ride a legendary beast.

"On your world, did you have horses?"

"I wish," said Natalie. "Horses were almost as mystical as dogs. But I watched 14 episodes of the Lone Ranger."

"If you've only seen horses on television, you're in for a surprise."

"Oh, my," Natalie breathed 20 minutes later, as a massive white stallion trotted up carrying a tiny, leathery woman with a gray ponytail.

"This is Duke," said the tiny woman sitting casually in the saddle. "Don't act nervous. Put your hand in front of his mouth."

The huge stallion's back was higher than Natalie's head. She held out a trembling hand. The stallion sniffed it, then ignored her.

"Good. Now pet him."

Natalie froze.

"Go ahead," said Sophie.

Natalie hesitantly touched Duke's neck.

Sophie presented her hand to Duke's muzzle, then firmly stroked his neck.

The stallion snorted and Natalie jumped. "He's so.... so *overpowering*. I can't tell if I want to ride him or run away."

"You'll get used to him," said Sophie. "I rode a lot when I was young."

"When you were *young?*"

"Oh, yes." Sophie stroked Duke's muscular shoulder. "Girls grow quite attached to their horses."

"Of course! Why didn't I see it?"

Sophie looked suspicious. "See what?"

"Him." Natalie waved at the stallion. "He's so powerful, and so quiet, and so useful to the woman who rides him. He's an archetype of masculinity." She peeked underneath. "Oh my lord."

Sophie frowned.

"The bouncing in the saddle must wake the sex monkeys. It's no wonder young girls love him."

230

High in her saddle, the gray-haired woman looked sour. "If you ladies are done slandering my virtue and flirting with my horse, you can go inside and sign away your right to rob me."

"That will be redundant, but I don't object." Natalie opened her pouch and pulled out a nit comb. "May we undress in your kitchen? We want to speak privately, so we need to microwave our clothes."

Eventually, Natalie and Sophie found themselves astride a pair of placid geldings ambling down a well-pooped trail. Natalie steered her horse around a tree. The horse avoided the tree, but didn't seem unduly influenced by Natalie's hesitant prodding. She turned to look back at Sophie. "How are things going with Buffalo?"

Sophie beamed and sat up straighter.

Natalie smiled wistfully. "I know that look."

"Sometimes, Buff is smug and infuriating, but he's so happy when I'm happy, and when something makes me sad, it makes *him* sad." Sophie nudged her gelding to move up alongside. "Even that is not the amazing part. This is my world, so I can do most things better than he does. With a Human man, that would be a problem, but with Buff, it's not. He's just so easy to be around."

Natalie eyed the gap between the massive horses, barely wide enough for the human legs.

Sophie didn't seem worried. "Buff has never hit a softball, or played a video game or putt-putt, and he throws like a girl. He's tall, but he sucks at basketball, and I have to keep reminding him to play defense."

Natalie bristled. "Buffalo is *not* incompetent. It's just that throwing games weren't popular in our gravity."

"You don't have to remind me he's intelligent and strong. What amazes me is, when I make him look clumsy, he never tries to cut me down. Buff seems genuinely *pleased* when I succeed, and when we compete, he never remembers to block my moves."

"Ah, child." For some reason, Natalie seemed troubled. "You've noticed Buffalo is paternal."

"Paternal?" Sophie snorted. "That's not the word I would use, but he certainly is supportive. He knows he should play defense, but he always forgets, because in his heart, he wants me to score. When I saw that, I realized I've never seen it before." Sophie kicked her gelding. "Let's see if we can get them to trot."

"Not quite yet, child. We need to talk."

"Hah. My dad says those are the four most disheartening words."

"Worse than, *is it in yet?*"

"What did you want to talk about?"

Natalie glanced up. "Let's stay under the trees. I'm afraid your drones can read lips."

"What did you want to talk about?"

"When I told you Buffalo was paternal, you mistook my meaning. You've wondered about his tattoos, the token of the hexagon?"

The test of the hexagon is beautiful and terrible, even to us.

"Natalie, the whole *world* is wondering about your tattoos."

232

The old alien was avoiding
Sophie's gaze. "The hexagon has
a symbolic meaning. We found a technique
to assemble rods into a sphere that is strong for its
weight. Each rod supports the others, so individual rods are
only pulled or pushed, never bent."

Sophie: "A geodesic dome."

"As you say. It is made with pentagons and hexagons." Natalie hesitated, then visibly steeled herself. "The hexagon on Buffalo's cheek is a token of honor. It certifies he faced the burning bush and made himself *paternal*. It's the main reason I can always give him the benefit of the doubt."

"Paternal? Is *that* all it means? Buff wouldn't tell me. He said explaining it would *violate a sacred taboo*. It was infuriating."

> *I held the trap jaws open and took the stranger's agony onto myself, until I passed out from the pain.*

"Oh, child, the secret of our hexagon tattoo *definitely* violates a sacred taboo, so Buffalo spoke the truth. He also misled you. We bite the forbidden fruit so often, we can have no sacred taboos."

"What? If you have no taboos, then how…. Oh, cute. It violates *our* taboo. Remind me to slap him."

"It wasn't his fault. Buffalo was trying not to lie, but to name your taboos is taboo. When I try to talk about your age of consent, you–"

"What did you want to tell me," Sophie interrupted.

"The hexagon is a secret we want kept. I see you're about to puzzle it out, and I fear you'll blab."

Sophie's gelding slowed as it dropped a load on the trail. "Are you saying Buff is hiding a secret virtue?"

"I think Buffalo has kept silent to spare your feelings. I'm older and wiser, so I will spare your feelings next month."

"Are you trying to tell me Buff is bisexual?"

Natalie laughed nervously. "No, I think we can safely rule that out. I'm afraid the truth will be worse for you."

"I don't see any obvious problem with being supportive."

"No, child, you wouldn't. The hexagon is the sweetest thing we have achieved. Without it, you cannot hope to attract Buffalo for more than this brief dalliance."

"What?" Sophie paled. "Is it something you could give me?"

"Yes, child, we can give it to you. I just don't think you can want it."

Sophie darkened. "Perhaps you should explain."

"Yes, I should. To make you understand, I must tell you some of our history, the early years of our grand experiment."

Sophie nodded impatiently. The geldings plodded down the trail.

Natalie pointed to the row of tattoos on her cheek. "We adjust our brains with multiple, interlocking imperatives that create a stable society. But our first generation made only *one* adjustment. They gave up their ability to demand ransom, and they hoped it would be enough. They knew it was a gamble. Their courage was... well, we all respect their choice."

"But it didn't work. With their ransom urges thwarted, our entire first generation was stricken by malaise. What little energy they had, they used to attack their betters."

"*Malaise* is your word for, *depression?*" Sophie remembered her pillow talk with Buff. He had used similar terms.

"*Depression* is a good word for it, and it crushed them. As it progressed, it sapped their will to search for a solution."

"Very sad. Why don't I want to be maternal?"

"Child, shall I just tell you what to do? Or will you let me tell you the facts, so you can decide for yourself?"

That was the proper code sequence. Sophie stopped complaining.

"Our first generation was in trouble. Their joy in life was fading, and by the bitter end, one in three had actually taken his own life." Natalie grimaced. "To think what we might have achieved, if we hadn't lost a third of our best. Yet the survivors had the solution in hand, and one was genius enough to see it. Before his drive failed, he realized he had lost his inner harmony. When he set his mind against the wasp, the wasp fought back."

"Buff mentioned something like that," Sophie recalled. "He said we can't be happy unless we attack good men. Are you telling me he was *serious?*"

"Quite serious. The wasp *demands* we seek ransom, and our base urges cannot be thwarted without consequence. The consequence is the malaise. It strikes when the animal parts of your mind fight each other, and the wasp is a fighter."

"Buff said that's why you made yourselves ungovernable. Now, you know your neighbors are not easy targets, so they don't trigger your wasp."

"Correct. My ancestors used the burning bush to stop themselves from demanding ransom, and it nearly destroyed them. Then, their greatest genius realized we must also stop ourselves from *paying* ransom, so our neighbors won't have to stifle their inner wasps. Our wasps are still frustrated, but now the main obstacle lies *outside* our head, so the wasp never reaches the obstacle *inside* our head, and we can have inner peace."

Sophie's mind drifted back to her one, perfect afternoon with Buffalo. "Your brain finally stopped fighting with itself. Do you think that breakthrough brought you paradise?"

"No, child, it was still not enough to bring them paradise. My ancestors had abolished ransom, but ransom is the *last* step of wasp strategy. The first step is even more vile."

Sophie thought about what she had seen, and in a flash of insight, the pieces connected. "First, disarm your food."

"Child, your mind is so quick. Before wasps grab the gold, they soften up the target. That is why you demonize the virtuous, those who have earned the money and mates you covet. As my ancestors discovered to their horror, when they could not ask for ransom, they attacked virtue all the more fiercely. If a man built a profitable company, he was browbeaten by nitpickers telling him he was a nuisance. If a woman made herself beautiful, she was set upon by her friends with a viciousness that surprised even them. Thankfully, the genius saved them a second time." Natalie's face relaxed into a smile. "His scheme was so elegant, and so audacious, even now, it renews my sense of wonder. Have you noticed the wasp poisons every Human relationship, except one? The one whose pain will never bring us joy?"

"Fathers have many failings," Sophie observed with a sigh. "But they don't envy their daughters."

"Exactly. The bond between mother and son is even more pure, perhaps because maternity is never in doubt."

238

"I don't agree," said Sophie. "When I date a guy, his mother always hates me. Isn't that envy?"

"Child, you break my heart. Your mind is so quick, but you..."

"What?"

Natalie shook her head. "You will solve the mystery of the envious mother as quickly as I could explain it."

Given that sort of challenge, Sophie had to focus her whole mind. It took four seconds. "The problem is not her son. The problem is, I'm not her daughter."

"If you were her blood daughter, she would not envy your bond with her son."

"Maybe not," Sophie scowled. "But give us a few days, and we'll find some other reason to fight."

"Damn right we would."

The two women laughed at their shared experience, worlds apart. Then Natalie sobered and pointed at her cheek, singling out the fourth tattoo, the hexagon. "I faced the burning bush and killed a monkey. The monkey was small, but it had an important job. Its job was to say, *that person is not my offspring.*"

Sophie's eyes widened. "You mean..."

"Yes, child. Buffalo's animal mind recognizes *you* as his daughter. Your joy is his joy, and he will always want you to score."

Sophie shook her head in wonder. "That is just... that's just beautiful. Did it work?"

"Oh, yes, even better than we hoped."

I took the stranger's agony onto myself

Sophie considered. "Why are you acting like it's a problem? Wait, don't tell me. You see everyone as your child, so if a man demands ransom, and you kill him, it feels like killing your own son."

Natalie flinched as if she had been slapped.

Sophie touched the old alien's arm. "Sorry."

Natalie managed a weak smile. "You are insightful as always, yet I'm afraid you will forget you aren't really Buffalo's daughter, and he can't give you the benefit of the doubt. You *must not* sting him."

"I understand he is dangerous, but that's not what you're trying to tell me. Just spill it."

"Very well, child, I will just spill it. Maternity has another side effect, one we did not predict." Natalie touched her own chest. "I am maternal, in here to my bones, even more if I grow to love a man. I yearn for him to have what he wants most."

"I understand. Why is it a problem?"

"Child, what does a man want most?"

Sophie blinked, then looked away. "I don't know, power I guess. Respect. Attention."

"Please, child, it's just you and me. There's no need to pretend."

Sophie paled. "You mean..."

"Yes."

"That is just.... that's just ugly."

"Child, you *must* use that swift mind of yours and sheathe your stinger. You are not really his daughter."

Sophie wasn't listening. She kicked her gelding hard and slapped its flank. It whinnied in outrage.

Natalie watched them gallop away through the forest.

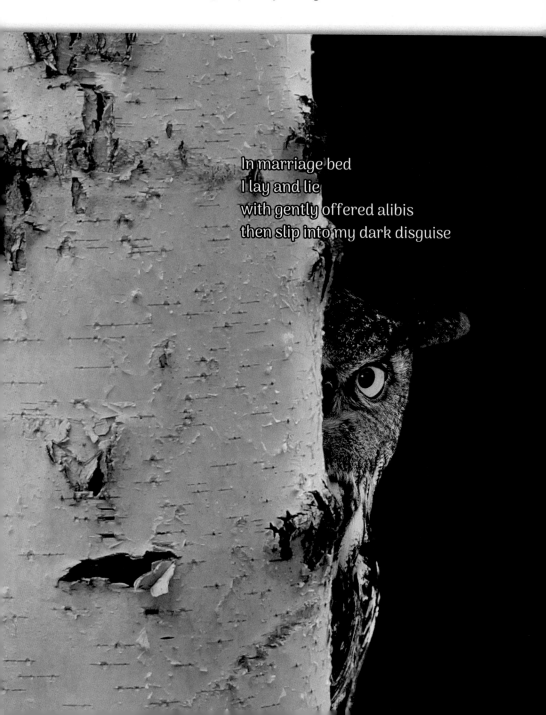

In marriage bed
I lay and lie
with gently offered alibis
then slip into my dark disguise

Secretary of Commerce Kitty Siphon stared at the surveillance video, rapt. She gasped as Natalie explained her hexagon tattoo, and what the Worms called, *maternal.*

Two screens showed video from the mini-drones. A silent, nearly-transparent flier wafted between the tree branches, looking down at the woman and the alien on horseback. On the ground, a six-legged crawler looked up at them. Both drones were equipped with phased-array electrostatic microphones, following the slow-walking geldings through the forest.

After Sophie slapped her horse and galloped away, Kitty sat, lost in thought.

Dominick Tork paused the video. "I trust the implications of *maternal* are not lost on you."

"Oh, no."

"Luci already told us they fetishize children, and now we learn her animal brain recognizes our clown as her own child. If we used a younger clown, Luci might be compelled to offer him better terms."

242

"Oh, I suppose so," Kitty said idly.

Dominick looked miffed. "We could threaten to publicize the sexual implications. The Worms might offer concessions to stop us from turning our population against them."

Kitty stared at Dominick. Her cheek twitched, until finally she could contain it no longer. She burst out laughing.

Dominick sat woodenly.

When Kitty could speak again, she apologized. "Oh, Dominick, I am sorry, but to have such a treasure handed to me by a man with no idea of its value..." She wiped her eyes, then patted Dominick's leg, halfway up his thigh. "When a man is made *paternal,* he might value your welfare *above his own."*

Dominick stiffened.

"They do this with their burning bush, whatever that is. They call it their *beautiful secret.* If we can lay our hands on it, I believe we might see some changes in our political system."

Dominick sat unnaturally still. "Changes indeed. Large ones."

"This could *snowball.* If a woman values my welfare above her own, she would want *everyone* to feel the same." Kitty doubled over in her seat and grunted.

Dominick stared at her hand, still on his thigh. "Do you need assistance?"

"No, no, I'm fine." Now Kitty was discretely, and in a feminine way, panting.

Dominick waited.

"I suppose their burning bush must have other uses, but surely none more valuable than this." Kitty straightened. "I must know the limits of *paternal* and *maternal.* This couple, Buffalo and the Human woman, could you get me some of their pillow talk?"

Dominick picked up his office phone. "I'll have my staff put together a montage."

Later that afternoon
Washington, D.C.

President Mirror teed off. He swung smoothly through the ball, and with a metallic *ping,* it sailed down the fairway.

Secretary Siphon teed off. She took a determined backswing, then whipped her club through a whooshing arc an inch above the ball. Finding no resistance, her club head continued on to circle her body in a textbook spine-twisting follow-through. She slapped her palm against the small of her back. "Ow!"

Agent Bear hastened to her aid.

Five minutes later, Kitty Siphon limped down the fairway. At her side, President Mirror looked back to be sure the Secret Service was beyond earshot. "This is the first time I've been summoned to emergency golf."

Kitty handed him a sheet of paper. "We figured out one of their tattoos. The hexagon on their cheek means they are *maternal.*"

"Maternal?" Mirror looked disappointed.

"Or *paternal,*" Kitty added. "Read the first paragraph."

Mirror scanned the summary, and his mouth spread into a smile. "Maternal means she *wants* her husband to get lucky? The whores will have fun with that."

"The press must *never* find out."

"Why not?" Mirror waved the summary. "This will force everyone to pretend they're outraged. Anyone who talks about the Worms will have to start with, *Of course, I don't agree...*"

"We have to keep this secret," Kitty insisted. "Our donkeys already know too much. They know about the forbidden fruit, and they know what *ungovernable* means. If they find out the Worms *really* want people to be happy, our donkeys will suspect the burning bush's real power."

Donkeys was their name for the productive class.

Mirror chipped his ball onto the green. "You have something in mind? Some use for their burning bush?"

"Don't you see it?" Kitty vibrated. "We could force the donkeys to see us as *their own children!* Just us! You and me!"

Mirror walked three steps before it hit him, and he staggered. "Whoa," he breathed. "They found the Holy Grail. Nobody can ignore his own son. Nobody could ignore *me!"*

"It's so perfect," Kitty gushed. "We use the burning bush to make people recognize *you and me* as their children. Just you and me! Then we crank up their parental urges, twist the mommy dial all the way to 11. The Worms already know how to do that." Kitty's pace quickened. "They will sacrifice *everything* for us!"

"Recruiting parents would be easy," the president marveled. "We'll tell them it's for weight loss, to make them skinny like the Worms."

"We only need a dozen parents, if we give them guns and badges. Then we show them how to build burning bushes, and ask for more parents. Our new parents will recruit more parents!" Kitty skipped down the fairway like a 7-year-old. "Once we get it started, we sit back and watch it snowball. In ten years, half the people in the world will be saving money for us to inherit. It will be even better than a human remote control, because they will do the work *and* the planning, and do it all for *our* benefit! Now we know why the Worms call it their *beautiful secret!"*

"Slow down!"

Kitty stopped and looked back guiltily.

"You're getting ahead of yourself." President Mirror caught up. "They want *everyone* to be happy, not just us."

"That *proves* they can adjust their maternal instinct. The eunuchs will find a way to focus all their mommy urges on *me*. And you," Kitty added.

"Even if that's possible, the donkeys will know we aren't *really* their children. Their conscious mind will interfere."

Secretary Siphon darkened.

"Kitty, you're supposed to be the one who faces reality."

Kitty's eyes narrowed, but she did not retort. They walked for three minutes, then she slumped. "You're right; we need more information. The Worms already know if the mommy urge can be hijacked, or if some other route will lead us to the Grail. Let's step up the surveillance, and maybe they'll let something slip."

They had reached Kitty's ball. She lined up, and drove it into the Secret Service detail.

"OW!"

They walked on. "I've always wondered," Kitty wondered, "how would it feel to watch a woman kill herself because I asked her to?"

"Don't spend too much on your suicide chamber yet," Mirror advised. "The donkeys might draw the line at scooping out their own eyes."

Kitty poked the president, but not too hard. "I don't poop in *your* donut."

Mirror arched an eyebrow.

"Unless you need it," she added.

"Apparently, I need it often."

Kitty's mouth slowly widened into a grin. "When I saw that video, where the Worm said their burning bush could turn normal people into willing slaves, I actually had an orgasm. A *good* one. I damn near ordered Dominick to screw me on his desk. I would have, if he was taller."

"Ha! I would have enjoyed seeing his expression."

"His *expression* is not what you would enjoy seeing." Kitty thoughtfully tapped her chin. "I'm tempted to give them a colony right now. They will recruit immigrants, so we'll have plenty of chances to slip in our agents."

"It may come to that. Speaking of spying, what have we learned from the little bugs in their clothes?"

Kitty's smile faded. "The only thing we learned is their locker room talk is just like ours. The bastards know we're spying on them, so they always change clothes when they get to their mothership. How's our military option?"

"Our military option is promising. Right now, the war pigs are shadowing the *Finger* with 90 stealth nukes."

"Ninety nukes?" Kitty blinked. "That should do it, but their little ships fly everywhere. Can we get them all?"

Mirror waved dismissively. "We've bagged a dozen of their little two-seaters and took them apart. None of them had any defenses, except their exhaust. After we nuke the *Finger,* we'll announce they are child molesters and declare open season. Finally, we'll get some payoff from letting rednecks keep their deer rifles."

Kitty nodded uncertainly. "That will work in America, and we'll have no trouble calling the Worms *child molesters* after we release the videos. What about the rest of the world?"

"There is another option," said the president. "We could launch a hundred tons of birdshot into low orbit and make space flight unsafe for a few weeks. The eunuchs call it the *tungsten overcast.* The problem is, it wouldn't make low orbit unsafe *enough.* The risk of a spaceship getting hit by a pellet is only about five percent per month."

"Could we do it on a larger scale?"

"Let me handle the military problem," said Mirror. "You focus on intelligence. The Worms already know if their burning bush can turn them into our slaves, so make them tell us."

Ten minutes later, Mirror stood silently on the turf, watching the commerce secretary's caravan drive away. *Could we really transform the whole population into doting parents, constantly attending their beloved child masters?* It actually seemed possible. The implications were troubling.

Very troubling, because Mirror saw no need for a sibling.

Agent Oak, head of the president's Secret Service detail, waited by the limo. Mirror waved him over. "Max, I have a task for you and Agent Bear. It will require discretion."

"Of course, Mr. President." Agent Oak was as monotone as ever, but Mirror's trained eye could not fail to notice the flash of professional pride.

"I have some doubts about Cougar's mental state." Mirror spoke quietly, so the rest of the detail wouldn't overhear. "It may just be my imagination, but I'm worried Kitty might actually try to harm me. Her plan would be subtle."

Agent Oak did not react.

"If she were to sense any unusual scrutiny..."

"I understand, Mr. President. She won't notice a thing."

Aliens need a new place
Out of their home
they were chased
Let's sell them a town
Invite them all down

Then blow them all back into space

Like   **Share**   **Comment**

COMMENTS Please respect the <u>forum rules.</u>

Pokemom Two days ago
> What's stopping us from burying a few dozen nukes in Alaska, then offering the Worms a bargain price?

LawFareForU Two days ago
> The worms would notice the signs of recent excavation

Moby Duck Two days ago
> No, they wouldn't. Modern warheads are small enough to fit down existing oil well shafts. You could literally drop them into the hole and they would sink to the bottom.

Pokemom Two days ago
> You'd have to time them to go off the same moment we took out their mothership. Gabriel's Trumpet spends most of its time in geosync over Washington, D.C., holding our politicians hostage.

S. Quiblee Two days ago
> My friend in the government says they are working on it.

When Sophie entered the prototype shop, she found Buff at his usual spot at the workbench, assembling a complex extruder nozzle array.

"Is it true?"

Buff sighed. He had been warned. "You'll have to be more specific."

"Don't be an ass," Sophie snarled. "Is it true you'd only marry a woman who thinks you should get whatever you want? *Whoever* you want?"

Buff put down his torque wrench, and considered.

Sophie's anger flared. "Don't sit there thinking about the perfect answer! Just tell me!"

Buff's expression hardened. He stood and crossed the shop in three long strides, towering over Sophie. "Yes," he said evenly, his stony face inches from hers. "It is true."

"I should have known. You're monsters." Sophie turned and walked out, slamming the door behind her.

DON'T WORRY

We'll take good care of your planet

Like   Share   Comment

COMMENTS Please respect the <u>forum rules.</u>

Pokemom Two days ago
> Holy crap my friend Mike actually dated a Worm woman. You won't believe this; she tried to recruit ME to a surprise orgy she was organizing for HIS BIRTHDAY! Unbelievable! Of course I said no, and warned him what she was doing.

LawFareForU Two days ago
> Seirously? How did Mike react?

Pokemom Two days ago
> Mike's a good guy. He said not just No, but Hell no. Then the alien bitch called him the P-word and dumped him!

Moby Duck Two days ago
> Disgusting.

S. Quiblee Two days ago
> Not surprising.

Two days later
Sophie takes steps

Sophie arrived at 7 AM and stopped in the lobby to update her whiteboard.

All male employees must submit their A.S.R.H.A. pledges by Fri 6pm. This is <u>mandatory</u>.

The aliens do <u>not</u> know a trick that makes you pass out. So stop asking them. And stop listening to Frank.
Sophie

Sophie closed her office door and gazed longingly at a stack of unread job applications. Then she settled in to recompute payroll tax withholding. The first step was to read the 30-page summary of the new rules.

She was only three hours in when she heard the knock. "Enter."

Buff walked in and shut the door. Sophie looked away.

The silence stretched. Sophie pretended to work. She couldn't see the words in front of her.

Buff gave in first. "Sophie, it's been two days. Will we never speak again?"

She dithered. "I don't know if I can."

Buff waited.

"It is just that I..." Sophie paused, trying to decide whether to use the word.

She chickened out. "I really like you, and we are so good together. I know you feel the same way, despite what you... what you want."

Buff nodded.

"But I can't stand the thought of you with another... I just can't stand it. It would make me crazy."

Buff sighed.

Sophie brightened. "I've been thinking. You are paternal, and you really... you love me. That means you want me to get what I need. You have no choice; your parenting urges have been supercharged. And what I really need is for you to want only me. If you wanted someone else, you would hurt me terribly. So, doesn't that mean you have to–"

Buff seemed to leap straight at her. His fingertips barely brushed her desktop as he vaulted over and crashed into her, lifting her out of her chair and driving her back into the wall.

It was just like their first meeting. Sophie thought, *Again?* Then Buff's hand clamped around her throat.

Sophie forgot everything she had learned in Taekwondo. She clutched at Buff's arm and kicked wildly, but he had rotated, so her legs could not rise between his. She found his shin, connecting solidly with her right foot. He didn't seem to notice.

Sophie struggled to breathe, and dug her nails into his hand. Buff leaned into her, lifting her up onto her tiptoes. She could get no air at all. She kicked more. Buff ignored the blows and watched her intently, a vein throbbing on his temple.

Sophie's vision contracted. She vaguely wondered why she was losing consciousness so quickly, after only ten seconds without air. Then she realized her carotid artery must be compressed. Was her windpipe crushed?

Buff's face turned red. He opened his mouth and howled, an anguished animal sound. His face twisted, but still he held her.

Then, after five more endless seconds, he gasped and stepped back, throwing her to the floor.

Sophie thudded onto the carpet. Her throat felt wrong, compressed. She tried to cough, but she only gagged, her back arching in futility. She could get no air, but now her mind was clear. Her blood must have resumed its flow to her brain, but it was quickly giving up its store of oxygen.

Buff stood over her, breathing heavily as if he were excited, but his voice was flat, almost analytical. "I warned you not to poison me. You should have hidden your stinger."

Sophie desperately thumped her fists against her neck, trying to force open her airway. It didn't help. Her vision closed in again, as if she viewed Buff, looming over her, through a tunnel.

The office door banged open. Natalie stopped in the doorway and took in the scene. Sophie writhed on the floor, punching feebly at her neck. Buffalo stood over her.

Natalie strode across the room, shouldering Buff aside as she yanked open Sophie's top desk drawer. Her eyes scanned the contents, then she slammed it shut and yanked open the side drawer. She rifled through it and found Sophie's scissors.

Buff stared at her mutely, hands at his sides.

Natalie knelt, and hesitated. Then she grimaced and pushed the scissors into Sophie's throat.

Three hours later, Buff sat woodenly in the lunchroom, his hands on a table, staring at the wall.

Tom Pine entered, tossed his lunch bag on the table, and settled into a seat. "So, Buff, I've always meant to ask you, how are you and Frank both still alive?"

Buff blinked and turned toward Tom. "What?"

"The first time we met, when Sophie flirted and you jumped her, Frank punched you in the face. Wasn't that an implicit demand for ransom? Wasn't he asking you to give up something to stop him from hitting you again?"

"Oh, that." Buff turned back to the wall. "At first, I was confused, so I couldn't act, but it only took a moment to realize he was defending Sophie."

Silence stretched.

"Can you tell me why you attacked her?"

Buff shook his head. "Telling you why I attacked my own woman would violate sacred taboos."

Tom sighed. "In that case, maybe this would be a good time to give us some space."

"Gabriel won't let me back into the *Finger,* not until I get retested to confirm I'm ungovernable."

"Buff, that might be a problem, if it takes very long. Although I can't say I blame Gabriel, since strangling Sophie was pretty much the opposite of respecting her property rights."

Buff's head rotated toward Tom. "What?"

"Worms don't generally strangle their girlfriends, do they?"

"No, we don't."

"I didn't think so. Your society wouldn't work if you always attack each other."

Buff's gaze rotated back to the wall. "Tom, you are confused. I have to get retested because she survived."

One hour later
Washington, D.C.

Kitty Siphon watched the surveillance video attentively.

At the end, when the Worm female performed an emergency tracheotomy with a pair of scissors, Kitty pursed her lips in distaste. "This is disappointing."

Dominick nodded agreement.

"Buff's romantic attachment to the victim *must* have strengthened his parental instincts, but he still wouldn't give up his sex life. Obviously, his *paternal* conditioning is not as strong as we hoped."

"Maybe it can be strengthened," Dominick offered. "The pentagon tattoo means their parenting instinct has been boosted, so it can probably be boosted more, perhaps enough to compel a useful level of self-sacrifice."

"Let's hope." Kitty replayed the video. "Well, at least some of this news is good. He was obviously triggered, yet he didn't actually kill her. That has never happened before."

"So far as we know."

Kitty thoughtfully tapped her chin. "He was triggered when she tried to force him into monogamy."

Dominick almost replied, but decided against it.

"Do you think he was triggered by Sophie's *tactic,* trying to turn his Worm conditioning against him? That would be an obvious defensive strategy, or was he just pissed off because she was holding his fun for ransom?"

"We don't have enough information to answer that."

"No, we don't," Kitty grumbled. "Please keep your eyes open for something I can actually use."

Dominick stiffened. "I keep my eyes open."

"So you do. I apologize." She patted Dominick's thigh. "You are my crown jewel, my best insight into the Worms."

Dominick looked at Kitty's hand on his thigh, and relaxed a little.

"They've launched *dozens* of joint industrial ventures, always with just two or three face-to-face meetings. The only project the Worms actually supervise personally is this one, Pine and his sentries, and it's no mystery why. Those sentries are crucial, or they will be someday. But I think *you,* Dominick, might be even more important as our window into their interpersonal relations."

"It's good that you appreciate my value."

"I almost wish you were *less* valuable, so we could experiment on your Worms." Kitty waved at the video. "This soap opera at the Pine company is the only repeated interaction we ever see. They've been here for *months,* and we don't even know if they can be triggered on behalf of a friend. Hold on, what's he doing?"

Dominick's third screen showed Frank Drummer entering the Pine Shack lunchroom. He unrolled a placard and pinned it to the wall.

> **CONSUMPTION OF ACOHOL, NARCOTICS, OR ALIEN URINE**
> ## IS STRICTLY FORBIDDEN
> **WHILE OPERATING DANGEROUS MACHINERY**

Kitty frowned. "Does alien urine have narcotic properties?"

After a pause, Dominick said, "That was Frank Drummer."

"Ah, Frank," Kitty sighed. "I wonder if anyone will fall for it."

"After the attack, I recorded a conversation between the attacker and the CEO." Dominick replayed the surveillance video of Buffalo and Tom chatting in the lunchroom.

When the playback ended, Kitty looked thoughtful. "They were talking about their first-meeting fiasco, when the Worm assaulted Sophie, and her friends defended her?"

"Yes, the large alien was punched in the face and did not retaliate, though I believe he could have defeated all the Humans easily, without resorting to his sidearm."

"Interesting. The alien said, *I was confused, so I could not act.* Then he didn't retaliate for a mistake."

"I see the potential is not lost on you."

"Oh, no. Strategic incompetence is Baby's First Politics. If we say, *our attack was a mistake,* it gives the enemy an excuse to be weak." Kitty idly tapped her chin as she considered the new information. At length, she straightened. "My ignorance is too constricting, and resources are useless if we don't spend them. Of the three Worms that visit Pine, which would you say is least important?"

The day after

In a hospital bed with a tube in her neck, Sophie had time to meditate.

How could she have been so blind? She had stepped in a pile so foul, so huge, how had she not seen it lying there? It was almost like her brain had some kind of idiot censor that blanked out the obvious, when it became painful.

Love makes us stupid, she thought bitterly, *even me,* though she saw clearly enough now. Buff was simply not capable of commitment. Probably none of the Worms were, certainly not the males.

Which left Sophie with Plan B: *Tom Pine.* It seemed so obvious.

Tom brought her none of the breathless heat she felt, *had* felt with Buff, but Sophie still remembered Junior High, before it was obvious Tom would be short and ugly, when he'd been so popular with girls. That history gave him some trophy value, despite his adult appearance. More importantly, her boy next door had always behaved honorably, despite his annoying misogyny. His height would be an ongoing problem, but the natural-style personal lubricants were quite good. In a few months, after Sophie had re-virginized, Tom would make an acceptable Plan B.

With that issue settled, Sophie turned to her next big decision: Whether to make drama. Unfortunately, a lawsuit was too danger-ous, but she could make Tom's life difficult, pressure him to get rid of Buff. Sophie enjoyed that fantasy for a few hours, then she abandoned it. When Tom Pine was forced to choose, he did not choose the one who made him choose.

Worse, if she made drama, she might force Tom to learn the details of Buff's attack. Sophie would not want her Plan B to learn the details. Tom was a good man, but he was still a man, and a bit of a perv, so it would be no kindness to give him unrealistic ideas. Sophie would do her future husband a favor, and make sure he never had to lie beside her and think about what Worm women meant by the word, *maternal.*

With all her important decisions made, Sophie relaxed and enjoyed her forced vacation.

On the day after her injury, late in the afternoon, Plan B stopped by to visit. Tom Pine stood by her bed, looking uncomfortable. "My employees are at risk. I have to ask."

Sophie played dumb. But in her defense, she had little choice. It would be three days, at least, before she could speak. She picked up her whiteboard and wrote,

NO Threat

Tom frowned, so she updated her whiteboard.

NO Threat

Do you trust me?

Tom rolled his eyes, but to Sophie's relief, he stopped pressing for details.

Would the Worms blab? Probably not. Natalie obviously wanted to conceal the meaning of their hexagon tattoo, and the repellent side effect of their maternal urges.

Two days later, Sophie's swelling subsided enough to let her breathe without a hole in her neck. Three days after that, she could talk, sort of. A nurse plucked out her stitches, and the next day, Sophie's vagina caught fire.

"It feels almost like a yeast infection." Sophie lay back on the exam table and rested her feet on the stirrups. "But the pain is unbearable. Did Buff give me some super STD?"

"Quite the contrary," the doctor replied. "Let's take a culture to be sure, but I suspect his immune system wiped out your natural vaginal flora. I'm hearing rumors of severe yeast infections a week after an alien sexual encounter."

The doctor's chaperon, a bored-looking woman standing in the corner, now seemed less bored.

Sophie looked up and saw the words, *DON'T BLOW* on the ceiling above the examination table, with a picture of a local DUI attorney. "You're hearing *rumors?* Are you keeping up with preprints?"

Alien strangulation was a scandalous change of hospital routine, so Sophie's case had been snapped up by the Attending Physician, a calm internist with silver hair. "I do keep up with preprints, and with DHS and insurance company bulletins," he replied mildly, and pushed in the speculum with a little more force than seemed strictly necessary. "Curing an STD by having sex with an alien is not *entirely* uninteresting, so the lack of reporting seems noteworthy."

The examination room fell silent.

"I also browsed through the case reports on Worm shooting victims," the silver-haired doctor added. "They were disappointing, just vanilla gunshot wounds with only one anomalous detail."

Sophie: "Ow, dammit, I don't open that wide."

"You'd be surprised. Did you know, most of the Worm attackers arrived in automobiles? Those victims were all shot with normal guns. But in the four cases where the alien arrived in a spaceship, I can't find any description of the victims' wounds."

Sophie sighed.

"You work with the Worms," the doctor with his nose in Sophie's vagina remarked casually. "Do you know why so many Humans are being shot with ordinary guns by Worms without spaceships?"

"Yes, I do," said Sophie. "So you should take me seriously when I suggest you focus your curiosity on something safer, like Ebola."

"I thought so. What should I expect, if I see a real alien gunshot?"

"You should expect to see it in the morgue. Worm sidearms fire silver jets at over two kilometers per second."

"Huh. That might be survivable, if it only struck a limb. You need at least four kilometers per second to destroy the brain with a leg shot." The doctor stood up and pulled off his gloves. "You're foaming, more yeast than a brewery. I'll write you a prescription for Monistat Pro."

Two days later, Sophie returned to work.

On her first day back, she was met in the corridor by Luci. The annoyingly beautiful alien took Sophie's hand. "If it wasn't real love, you couldn't have turned it against him."

Sophie jerked her hand away. "Next, you'll say I'm lucky to be alive."

"No, I won't," Luci said unhappily. "I'll just say your survival cast Buff under a pall of suspicion."

Sophie scowled and strode away. Only later, when she was safely hidden behind her office door, did she allow herself to lean against the wall and tremble.

That afternoon, she passed Natalie in the corridor. "I'm sorry," the old Worm said quietly, then walked away and spoke of it no more.

Human women pressed for details, but Sophie did not share. Everyone knew Buff had attacked her, but only the Worms knew why. Frank was oblivious as always. Tom, thankfully, seemed content to remain ignorant.

She avoided Buff, but only when it was convenient. When their work brought them together, Sophie was professional and correct. He responded in kind.

At home, Sophie reestablished her old routine, the one she had followed before Buff had filled her evenings. She switched back to microwave dinners. She talked to her mother and reconnected with her female friends. She watched television.

Sometimes, alone in her quiet house, Sophie remembered the calls of seagulls on a tropical atoll, and cried a little.

Seven weeks later, Tom's employees gathered in the barren lot behind the Pine Shack for the first real test of the Worm sentries.

Six of the towering robotic telescopes formed a perimeter, ringed by coaxial cables. In the center, Tom and Luci fidgeted. Tom wore huge, owlish dark glasses that made him look even smaller.

Everyone was here, except Frank, who was still inside loading the drone box. On his way out, the phone rang, and he hesitated. Frank was strictly forbidden to answer the phone, but everyone else had gathered out back.

It rang again. Frank set down the drone box and picked up. "Pine Robotic Sentry, this is Frank."

"Hi Dan," said the caller. "I hope you can help me. One of your bird telescopes is listed on eBay, and I was thinking about bidding."

"Excellent," said Frank. "We love it when customers buy our products used, instead of hassling us to make a new one."

"Before I bid on it, I want to make sure it was built with sustainable manufacturing. The environment is very important to me, so I think everything should be made sustainably."

"Us too," said Frank. "In fact, I can honestly say sustainability is our top priority."

"Really?" The caller sounded skeptical.

"Oh, yes, we track our sustainability *very* carefully. We actually quantify our resource consumption in standardized green units that reflect each individual resource's scarcity, as well as its importance to humans, with multiple safeguards to ensure our green units are measured without deception. We review the results every quarter, and even use the green units to determine bonuses, because at Pine Robotic Sentry, we believe our number one job is to consume less than we produce."

"Oh, good for you," said the caller. "It's disgusting, how capitalists only care about profit. I want to support your effort, so I will bid on the used one, so long as it doesn't go above 40 dollars."

Frank hung up, and wondered again why Tom had banned him from answering the phone. On his way out, he stopped by the lunchroom to nail up an informational plaque he had printed for the women who complained about the thermostat setting.

Outside in the back lot, the sentry array looked like a ring of totem poles, with Tom and Luci fidgeting in the center. The six sentries bristled with lenses and spotlights. At the pinacle, 11 feet above the cracked asphalt, a 14-inch motorized mirror reflected the world down into a 10-inch Newtonian telescope that filled half of the sentry's internal volume.

At the base of each sentry, a 15-inch sunlight-readable display waited darkly. Higher up, fisheye lenses watched all directions at once, diffracting their distorted images into 90-megapixel cmos photodetectors. The photodetectors passed the pixels to a computer, which reversed the fisheye distortion and searched for faces.

Frank set the drone box on the asphalt. Then he opened his laptop, typed for nine seconds, and hit, *Enter.*

The sentries came to life too quickly to be followed by Humans or aliens. Six vivid, 15-inch displays lit up with wide-angle images of the barren lot, including Tom and Luci. Four of the images captured at least one face, promptly outlined in blue.

Motorized mirrors chirped to new angles. The third sentry claimed the best view of Luci and filled its display with an extreme close-up of her nose. A new lens clicked into place, and Luci's perfect, enormous nose was replaced by a wider view of her perfect face. White lines traced her perfect features, and her blue tattoos flashed green. Then the 15-inch screen split, the left side maintaining Luci's real-time image while the right side presented her mugshot and vital statistics.

The fifth sentry was trying to identify Tom. His image changed hue as the telescope rotated its color filter, seeking a wavelength that would penetrate his dark glasses. Nearly half a second passed before the computer settled on blue. White lines highlighted the distinctive features of Tom's blue face, and the five tokens painted on his cheek.

The tokens flashed red, and a banner appeared, blinking urgently:

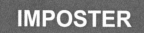

IMPOSTER

Sirens howled and one-inch sentry mirrors blurred into motion to paint Tom's body in shimmering plaid laser light. The lasers were test dummies, only five milliwatts, barely visible in the sunlight. Their dancing pattern covered Tom's body but stayed below his neck.

Later, when he trusted them to avoid his eyes and never stop moving, Tom would install the real, half-watt lasers.

The drone box snapped open and a nine-inch UAV whined straight up. The little drone rotated, then raced directly to Tom and hovered 20 feet above his head, flashing a brilliant strobe as it bobbed and weaved in a manner calculated to frustrate an accomplished duck hunter.

Armed guards peered down from the rooftop. Tom raised an arm, watching the squirming red and green laser tracery vanish as his arm approached his face. He turned 90 degrees and repeated the gesture. Again, the lasers faded as his arm approached his eyes. Tom gave Frank a thumbs up, then turned and sprinted away through the weeds.

The drone followed, and the sentry mirrors tracked him easily, painting him in dim laser coveralls.

Frank switched off the power and the sirens stopped, replaced by a subdued cheer, with handshakes all around.

The next morning, Tom arrived at 7 AM and gazed longingly at a half-finished drawing of a new sentry shipping crate. Then he settled in and resumed his research into alien partnership tax reporting.

He was only three hours in when the protesters arrived. Tom glanced out his window and saw his parking lot swarmed by picketers waving signs.

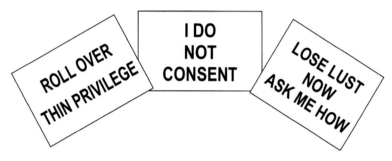

Tom walked out the front door and stood beside a round woman waving a sign that said, *ROLL OVER THIN PRIVILEGE.*

She looked at him suspiciously. "Do you work in there?"

Tom covered his mouth. "Please hold your sign in front of our faces. The drones can read lips."

Her eyes widened, and she held her sign closer. "Do you work with *him?* The fake Jesus?"

"Yes," Tom murmured.

"In person, is he as… does he…"

"He looks like a male stripper," Tom confirmed. "And now, he's single, because he strangled his Human girlfriend. She only survived because he loved her so much, he called for his friends to stop him as he was choking her."

The round woman gasped.

"You have to help me." Tom glanced around fearfully. "They let something slip, and I need to warn the world, but I'm always watched."

"Ooh!" She looked excited. "Warn the world about *what?"*

"Worm males are so sexually aggressive, haven't you wondered how their women survive?"

After a pause, the round woman said, "Yes?"

"They have a system," Tom murmured. "It's stupidly simple. They stamped it into their brain, so they could have an orderly culture, but they *don't want us to notice it.* They're afraid we'll use it against them, so they made me promise to keep it secret, but I can't. I simply *must* do something to protect our women."

Now the round woman looked really interested.

"Shake your sign," Tom commanded. "We don't want to attract attention."

She waved her sign, then covered their faces again.

"It's a color code," Tom explained. "A red dress means, *don't touch me.* A green outfit means you *want* to be raped. Any other color is ambiguous, but for God's sake, *don't* wear red with green stripes, or you won't be able to walk right for a week."

The round woman was having some trouble with her breathing.

"Good luck." Tom strode back into the Pine Shack, closed the door, and burst out laughing. Then he picked up his phone and hit the button labeled, *Aliens.* "Let's go shopping."

Two hours later
Across town

Martha gripped the wheel and focused on the car ahead. She was driving a minivan full of samples, some sort of promotional novelties, and she didn't want to screw up on her first day.

She glued her eyes to her leader, a sedan loaded with salesmen weaving through traffic too fast. Martha's job was to follow them on their rounds, as a sort of pack mule. So far, they hadn't stopped anywhere.

Traffic was tight. Martha gripped the wheel tighter, which is why she was so surprised when her car turned hard right. She spun the wheel leftward, but it seemed disconnected, and to her horror, she veered directly toward the doors of another car. The roar of her engine was replaced by a sickening crunch in the instant before the air bag smacked her face.

When she came to her senses, Martha saw she had crumpled the passenger door of the other car and sandwiched it into a third car beyond. Behind the shattered front passenger window, she saw a red-headed woman covered in blood.

The rear passenger window burst outward, showering glass onto Martha's hood. She briefly saw feet, then they were withdrawn and a large, muscular man scrambled onto the hood. He crawled to the redhead with the bloody face, swiping asides the shards of her window. The two of them seemed to be speaking.

The large man hopped off Martha's hood and walked to her window. She rolled it down.

His hands were covered with blood, where he had brushed away the broken glass. He leaned in close. "Are you injured?"

His face was beautiful. Then, to her horror, Martha noticed the cheek tattoos that marked him as a Worm. She shook her head.

The huge Worm seemed vaguely familiar. He stared at Martha. "Why did you do this?"

Martha's squeaky voice betrayed her panic. "I don't know, it just turned. I didn't try to."

The Worm studied her for a terrifying moment. Then he trotted back to his friend.

Ambulances appeared with miraculous speed. The paramedics briskly unstrapped a gurney beside Martha's car, but she waved them off. "I'm not hurt. Take care of the other woman."

They didn't seem to hear her. They all but dragged her out of the car and hoisted her onto the gurney. A tow truck approached.

For some reason, the paramedics did not wheel her to an ambulance. Instead, they waited until they had collected the other victim, the bloody-faced redhead. Then they parked two gurneys together and started talking on their radios.

Martha's voice quavered. "Are you badly injured?"

"I hope not." The redhead had trouble with the words, as if her tongue were swollen.

Worse, when she spoke, Martha glimpsed teeth through the hole in her cheek, and above the hole, through the blood, Martha saw a row of green geometric tokens, the Worm tattoos. "I'm so sorry," Martha babbled. "I don't know what happened. It just turned."

The Worm turned to look at the Human. "Don't worry."

Martha reached over to squeeze the Worm's hand. The Worm squeezed back.

Two blocks away, in a darkened van, Dominick Tork watched the video feeds with interest. His secure phone beeped.

"Well," said Kitty. "What happened?"

"Just like I predicted," Dominick replied. "The Worms are not triggered by negligence, even if it injures a close friend."

"Excellent!"

Buff needed only Bandaids.

Natalie's injuries were more serious but not immediately fatal, which proved a mixed blessing. At the county hospital, Luci waited with Natalie's gurney while Buff and Tom stood in line.

The waiting room was packed. Children whined and grownups sniffled. Buff looked around the crowd in dismay.

"Relax," said Tom. "This is just the waiting room. The emergency room will be more impressive."

Buff's brow furrowed. "You have a waiting room for the emergency room?"

"Not to worry. Most of these people just have head colds."

"I thought head colds were minor."

"They are," said Tom. "But our hospitals have to treat anyone, even people who refuse to pay."

Buff bolted, heading for Natalie at a dead run.

She was already gone. "They took her inside," Luci fretted. "They wouldn't let me go with her. I'm worried, but I thought, if they want to hurt her, they don't have to bring her here."

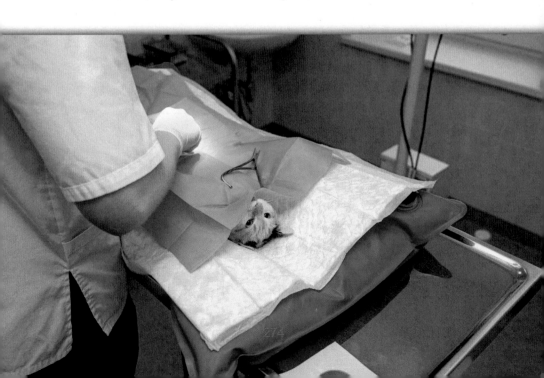

Nine hours later
Still in the hospital

Tom, Buff, and Luci fidgeted in the waiting room's white plastic chairs. They had signed in the injured Natalie, using her mail-drop address. The mail drop looked like a home address, but it was really just an expensive post office box.

Tom squirmed. "These chairs must have been stolen from a laundromat. Uh oh."

The Worms looked alarmed.

"Don't worry," Tom added hastily, "Just a minor administrative glitch. I'll be back as soon as I can." He hustled off and quickly reached an intersection. None of the four corridors were marked, so Tom picked one at random. The next intersection was marked with arrows labeled *CCU, PSR,* and *Radiology.* Tom considered, and decided *PSR* might conceivably refer to patient records.

200 feet down, the corridor ended in locked double doors. Tom backtracked and tried the path labeled, *CCU,* which could refer to credit and collections.

Twelve minutes later, after three right turns, four left, and two U-turns, Tom encountered a chubby little man in a bowler hat. He grabbed Tom's arm and whispered urgently. "If you see a bowl of candy, *don't touch it.* That's how they get livers."

The little man hurried off down the unmarked corridor.

Eventually, Tom located the administrative offices, where he found a tired-looking staffer. He took a seat before her half-size desk. "You have a patient here, Natalie Clover. I would like to change her billing information."

"Spell the name, please."

Tom spelled it, and gave Natalie's made-up birthday and social-security number.

The staffer typed. She paused. She typed. She paused. Eventually, she said, "What relation are you?"

"No relation."

"Sir, I cannot disclose information about a patient."

"I already know the information," Tom replied wearily. "I just want you to send her bills to my address."

"I'm sorry, sir, but..."

Tom interrupted her, standing up and half shouting. "Look, I'm trying to do you a favor. You might have given Natalie a Band-Aid, or an aspirin. Let's not find out what she'll do when you bill her 40 dollars for it."

The staffer stared at Tom.

Tom sat down. He breathed. "I apologize; I'm having a bad day. She is my business associate, and she has no other relatives."

The staffer typed. She paused. She typed.

Tom tried to entertain himself by reading the health warning posters.

Ten minutes later, the staffer was still typing. Tom lolled in his chair, until inspiration struck. "Your patient Natalie Clover is indigent. I want to pay for her care."

The tired staffer looked up. "Why didn't you just say so? Please step back here into my office. Would you like a drink? I have an excellent single malt."

One week later, Tom arrived at 7 AM and gazed longingly at a sample power-supply enclosure awaiting structural tests. Then he settled in and started researching this year's changes to the depreciation tax rules that dominated his investment decisions.

He was five hours in when the chanting started. Tom peeked out his window to see the picketers in the parking lot.

The *ROLL OVER THIN PRIVILEGE* sign was enthusiastically waved by a round woman wearing a red dress with green stripes.

Tom headed to the lunchroom for the Executive Council meeting. This week's topic was, *Supreme.*

Frank opened the pizza boxes. "How does the burning bush make you ungovernable? Technically, I mean. What's the mechanism?"

"You just asked me to torch your planet." Natalie spoke carefully, but that was probably because of the stitches on her mouth. "The burning bush would render your society to ashes."

"Sure," said Frank. "How does it work?"

Natalie smiled, then winced. She picked up a napkin and dabbed at her bleeding cheek. "I can tell you this much. Your mind is not a single entity; it is a cooperative of many personalities, simple and complex. We call them, *monkeys.* They perform various tasks, including one built to recognize our own property. We named him, the *leprechaun.* Strengthening his resolve makes us ungovernable."

The Humans looked doubtful, except Frank, whose eyes were closed, as if he were looking inward. "That won't work. It would stamp out ransom, but you would compensate by ankle-biting even more, and you couldn't raise kids."

The alien women looked startled.

"Trusting people to identify their own property could *never* work," said Sophie. "People always imagine they've been ripped off, which you would know, if you had to deal with our customers."

"No," Frank murmured. "The monkey they call the *leprechaun* is honest to a fault. You just *think* he's a liar, because he gets shouted down by the other monkeys. The problems are ankle-biting and children. You could protect the kids by turning up the positive feedback in the maternal monkey, but you'd still attack everyone above you on the status ladder."

All three aliens were staring at Frank.

Up in the corner, the silent television screen split. On one side, a talking head looked somber, while the other side flashed pictures of pre-adolescent girls, all white or oriental.

"If we don't punch up, the monkeys get depressed." Frank drummed his fingers on the table. "They need to hurt everyone who outshines them, except for..." His eyes flew open. "Jesus Christ, you OUCH." He turned and glared at Luci, who looked innocent.

Natalie held up a palm. "The important thing is, we found a way to behave ourselves. We don't nitpick successful men."

"I don't see the dangerous part," said Frank. "You all survived."

The aliens winced.

"It's time to quit stalling," Natalie said with obvious reluctance. "We've been hiding something."

Sophie snorted. "No. Really? You've been *hiding* something?"

"The truth," Natalie continued, "the terrifying truth is, our ransom immunity defends itself. If anyone tries to undermine my immunity, he can have but one purpose, so I will be triggered."

Frank: "That truth does not terrify me."

"It *should* terrify you, because the burning bush also works in reverse."

Sophie stiffened, and the color drained from her face.

"The father of our culture, the man who found the burning bush, faced a choice, probably the most consequential choice in all our history." Natalie spoke quietly, one hand on her injured cheek. "In the end, he chose to free us, but he could have chosen otherwise. He had the burning bush, so instead of liberating us, he could have enslaved us. If he *had* enslaved us, then our serfdom would defend itself."

Tom's mouth made a round *O*.

Sophie leapt to her feet. "What the hell are you thinking? Revealing this is incredibly irresponsible!"

"I know," Natalie replied bleakly. "We want to keep the secret, but our children know. We love our children too much to stop them from blabbing."

Sophie's face flushed white to red. "You've brought us *plague!* It will be contagious!"

"Yes, child." Natalie closed her eyes, and made a visible effort to keep talking. "If you were bush-burned to embrace your role as servant, you would recruit more servants to glorify your queen, and the new servants would recruit still more. Once it starts, we see no escape. Eventually, you would all be recruited."

Around the table, the Humans leaned away.

900 miles distant, in his high-ceiling office six blocks from the White House, surrounded by surveillance monitors, Dominick Tork leaned forward and pushed a red button.

"What the hell is going on!" Agent Sheila Bear, the head of Kitty Siphon's security detail, bellowed at the staffers dashing madly about the West Wing of the White House.

They ignored her, so Agent Bear snagged a passing necktie and reeled in Dale Drover, the press pimp, like a tetherball. "Right now," she grated. "Why are you running?"

Drover stared back blankly. Then he understood. "Oh. Nothing for you. No physical threat. At least, not yet."

A 40-something man sprinted down the corridor, chin tucked and a stack of laptop computers nestled under his arm like a football, his tailored suit flapping.

Agent Bear did not speak, choosing instead to communicate her dissatisfaction with a profound stillness, specifically in her fingers, twined in Drover's tie.

More aides hustled past, and Drover leaned close. "Listen, you did *not* hear this from me."

Agent Bear nodded acceptance.

"Ninety minutes ago, Secretary Siphon got some intel on the Worms, something hot. Even I'm not sure what it was, but Siphon freaked out and so did Mirror. Now, they are diverting funds from the whole executive branch."

A phalanx of staffers strode past, nine grim-looking women with blue suits, short haircuts and airline bags, marching in lockstep toward the exit.

Drover pointed at them. "Those bags are full of cash and guns. Secretary Siphon sent them out to lease office space and not take *no* for an answer. It's the freaking Manhattan Project."

Agent Bear frowned.

Drover glanced nervously over his shoulder. "Sheila, I shouldn't tell you this." He placed his manicured hand over Agent Bear's fingers on his tie. "Rumor says the Worms are responsible for all those little girls gone missing."

Bear straightened. "What's happening to the girls?"

Drover shook his head. "It looks bad, *really* bad, but they are still alive. Apparently, there is a way to save them, if we had the burning bush, so we *must* acquire a burning bush, at any cost. It's the only way to save those little girls."

Aliens say we are slaves
Five of us foul and depraved
The sixth they seduce

with child abuse

They know what their followers crave

Like   Share   Comment

Comments. Please respect the <u>forum rules</u>.

Pokemom Six hours ago
> They say they will recruit one out of six Humans, but why are we tolerating this? Everyone knows what is happening to those girls.

LawFareForU Six hours ago
> President Mirror is holding off, hoping we can get the Worm disease immunity.

Moby Duck Six hours ago
> They aren't immune to disease, only to contagion. They won't give us a cure for cancer.

LawFareForU Five hours ago
> Malaria kills more people than cancer.

Moby Duck Five hours ago
> No it doesn't. Cancer kills way more people than malaria.

LawFareForU Four hours ago
> You only think cancer is more important because malaria kills mostly black people.

Moby Duck Four hours ago
> I'm sorry if I seemed insensitive. Malaria is more urgent.

The next day
Springfield, MO

Tom Pine walked into his building at 7 AM and checked Sophie's whiteboard.

> The aliens do it just like we do. So stop Lurking in the bathroom. And stop listening to Frank.
>
> Sophie

Tom closed his office door and gazed longingly at a stack of thermal test data. Then he settled in to research the new molded plastic additive regulations.

Three hours later, the protesters arrived. Tom glanced out his window and saw picketers milling about the parking lot.

JESUS SAITH TO PAY YOUR FUCKING TAXES

FLIRTATION IS NOT INVITATION

WORMS ATE MY BABY

Someone banged on Tom's door. "Enter."

It was Luci, and she wasn't smiling. She glanced at the *Fluffer* painting, then sat in Tom's visitor chair. "We tested the first lot of sentries."

Uh oh. "Is there a problem?"

"Yes," said Luci. "You promised us a range of 200 yards in daylight."

"And?"

"And this is not our first trade with a swarm, so we tested our sentries thoroughly. The effective daylight range of our sentries, of the sentries *you* constructed for us, is nearly *500 yards.* That's two and a half times the range you promised."

"In that case," said Tom, "I will resume breathing."

Luci scowled. "Two and a half times more range translates into *six times* more coverage area. It radically improves our budget."

"You guys are frightening. I didn't want you to think I ripped you off."

"No, you are *not* afraid of me, and you could have demanded better terms. Why didn't you?"

"You have a point," Tom conceded. "On further reflection, I am prepared to accept a 30-percent bonus."

Luci didn't seem to hear him. "Before our arrival, you built telescopes that identify birds and ships. We purchased three of your old devices on Ebay and tested them. They *all* delivered two and a half times the range you advertised, which means they cover six times the area you promised, which means you could have used cheaper optics. *Much* cheaper."

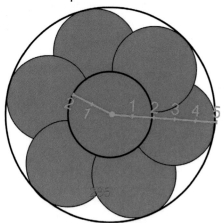

"Dammit!" Tom slapped his desk. "I *knew* I needed an MBA."

Luci's eyes narrowed. "What are you up to?"

"Miss Dark, there is no conspiracy here, just a personal phobia about promises I can't keep."

"Oh, please. You *love* to write fake job descriptions to lure in female applicants."

"That is fun," Tom admitted. "But have you ever seen one disappointed, if she lasts long enough to find out what I'm *really* offering?"

Luci didn't answer. The silence stretched as they stared at each other. Finally, she grinned. "Promise-keeping is a good phobia."

"The hell it is." Tom's gaze shifted to the painting that dominated his office, Fluffer, alone on her park bench, waiting for someone. "You would not believe how much it has cost me."

"It's good that you keep your word, but delivering *six times* what you promised seems a bit extreme. Tom, what did you fail to deliver?"

"Miss Dark, that is none of your business."

"How old were you?"

Tom wadded up a sheet of paper and bounced it off Luci's forehead.

She stood up. "Please come to my office."

In the little office she shared with Frank, Luci's computer showed the national weather radar. She panned around for a while, zooming into various storm systems. "I want to take you for a ride."

Frank sat at his computer. "In our idiom, the expression, *Take you for a ride* has three possible meanings. The differences are important."

Luci grabbed her sunglasses. "Frank, nobody would want to take you for a ride."

Frank didn't answer.

Tom followed Luci up the stairs. "What is your problem with Frank?"

"You mean, beside him being an obese slob with no social skills?"

"Yes," said Tom. "Besides that."

"He told me I can't hurt his feelings."

Tom followed her out onto the roof. "And you believed him?"

"No, I didn't, but you're the one who said we should talk about the elephant." Luci opened the hatch and swung herself into her lipstick-red yacht.

Tom climbed in behind her. "Yes, we should talk about the elephant, because we're happier after we admit the obvious. But you're *trying* to hurt Frank's feelings."

"Do you think so?" Luci strapped into the pilot's seat.

"Yes, I oof!" Tom flopped into his seat as the engines roared and the rooftop dropped away.

Tom took the hint and stopped talking.

Twenty minutes later, he relaxed in the right seat while they approached a flat-bottomed anvil cloud, towering 80,000 feet above the desert.

Luci banked to circle the thunderstorm. "Which way is it moving?"

Tom craned to look around. "The ground behind us looks wet."

Luci descended toward the dry side and landed in the empty desert.

When the dust settled, Tom peered out the window. "That storm is about to roll over us."

"I hope so." Luci turned a knob on her instrument panel. "I've never seen a thunderstorm in the desert."

Tom heard a whirring noise. He looked out and watched the engine pods rotate until their exhaust pointed straight up.

Luci's instrument panel included a sound system that obviously wasn't original equipment. She loosened four thumbscrews, slid out the stereo, and unsnapped a white rectangular connector to disconnect it from her yacht's wiring. She reached under her seat and withdrew a roll of aluminum foil and a coil of black cable. She jacked the cable into her instrument panel. "Give me your phone."

Tom hesitated, then handed it over.

Luci stacked Tom's phone with her stereo, her own primitive flip phone, and her handheld GPS navigator, then wrapped them all with four layers of aluminum foil. She crimped the foil ends, then tucked it all into an aluminum case. She snapped the case shut, then rose and headed back to the hatch, carrying the case and paying out the black cable. "Let's go outside. I'd like to see a snake."

"Good idea." Tom followed her out. "Who doesn't love to hunt snakes in a thunderstorm?"

Luci set her headset on the ground with the coil of black cable, then walked away. Tom followed.

200 yards from her yacht, Luci pulled out her sidearm, dropped the mag, and ejected the round. She slid it back into her holster, then laid her gunbelt on the ground beside the aluminum case. They walked back, and the two of them stood beside her yacht as the storm approached. Luci picked up her headset. "We need to talk."

"When a women says those four words, it means I already said too much."

288

Luci produced a flat plastic box, smaller than a credit card but thicker. She rubbed her thumb across and slid out a sheet of pink paper. She held it up to Tom's face, and he saw it was stenciled with her neat handwriting.

We are eavesdropped

Luci popped the pink paper into her mouth. Then she stepped forward into Tom's personal space. Her breath smelled of cinnamon.

Tom backed away. "I live by a simple rule, which I call, the *Intimate Rule*. The intimate rule is, d*on't poop where you eat."*

Luci stepped closer, back into his personal space. She grinned. "You want this?"

Tom retreated again, then noticed she was holding up another hand-lettered paper.

Engine pulse
Then privacy

Luci glanced meaningfully at her engines, aimed straight up over their heads.

Tom looked up at the looming engine pods. "Don't you think we're a bit close?"

"Open your mouth."

Tom sighed and opened up. Luci slid in the pink paper. It burned on his tongue, and Tom realized it was a paper-shaped breath mint.

"Wasps think I'm pretty." Luci stepped forward, crowding Tom. "We've worked together for months, but you've never touched me, not so much as shaken my hand."

Tom stepped back. "Why are you pushing me?"

"With our men, I could never do this." Luci stepped forward. "It's kind of fun."

"God dammit." Tom stepped back. "The *Intimate Rule* is important. We live in a fucking dark age."

Luci held out another paper mint.

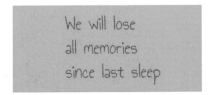

We will lose
all memories
since last sleep

Tom stared at the writing. He felt the first droplets of rain.

Luci popped the pink paper into her mouth. "Are you carrying any metal?"

Tom absently pulled out his keys, then walked to the open hatch and tossed them onto his seat.

Lucy walked away, paying out 40 feet of black cable. She jacked it into her headset and waved Tom closer.

Tom approached and noticed her headset had two sockets: one for the audio connection, and another for the black cable. He unjacked the black cable and looked at it.

The central conductor was black, not metal. *Could it be an infrared optical fiber?*

Luci held up the headset, and raised her eyebrows to send an unspoken, *do you consent?*

Do I consent? Would I erase today's memories in return for a chance to speak privately?

Wind gusted, and the temperature dropped.

Luci wants to make an EMP that will destroy any listening devices.

The storm was on them, rain falling harder. Thunder rumbled.

She wants it to look like we were struck by lightning. Her yacht probably will be, if her engines ionize a path up into that thundercloud.

Do I consent?

Our satellites can detect an EMP. Does she know?

Luci jiggled the black cable and looked enquiring.

Tom grabbed her bra through her shirt.

Luci squawked as her torso thumped into Tom, while his other hand laced into her hair. Luci's headset fell onto the dirt as she squealed and twisted to escape. Tom used his control of her head to direct her momentum, and after a quick spin, she ended up with her back pressed against him. He yanked her hair back, baring her throat as his other hand shoved her bra upward.

Her stretchy shirt was easy, but her bra was going to take more work. It seemed to be made of Kevlar.

Luci shifted, her intention transparent to anyone with 1,000 hours of judo. Tom faded left, and her driving elbow merely scraped his side. She shifted to take her weight off her left leg, so he kicked the inside of her ankle, spreading her legs as he clenched his fist in her black hair, holding her ear close to his mouth. "The Intimate Rule is not to protect *me*," he hissed. "It's to protect you *from* me."

She grunted, and Tom sidestepped as her left heel drove backward into empty space. "You're strong for such a tiny girl," he murmured, sliding his hand over her contoured abdomen. "But I am stronger. Hasn't anyone told you, given the chance, every man is a rapist?"

Then Tom found himself rotating through empty air. Fortunately, he had been in this situation hundreds of times. In his brain, the somatic spider calmly tucked his legs and tightened his grip on Luci, sharing his angular momentum with her.

He rolled smoothly onto the dirt and Luci rolled over him like a slinky walking down the stairs. Tom fetched up on top, looking down at her. "Where did you grk."

The improbably flexible little minx had hooked her ankle around his neck. Tom rolled into a back somersault and up onto his feet.

She was already standing. The two of them faced off.

Luci smiled triumphantly. "You fraud. I *knew* you could dance."

Tom brushed dirt out of his hair. "Where did you learn to do this?"

"That question is rude." Luci spun and bolted for her yacht.

Tom ran her down easily.

In Tom's mind, the sex monkey cackled with glee. *She could run faster. She let us catch her.*

Miss Manners sniffed. *You can't know that. Maybe the poor thing hasn't adjusted to our gravity.*

Tom dove onto Luci's back and rode her to the ground. She twisted in his grip, turning to face him before he took the impact on his forearms. She woofed and Tom used the moment to pin her elbows, twining his fingers into her hair.

"This won't work," she panted. "You didn't bring sashes to tie me. You can't make me hold still, unless you threaten to hurt me."

Tom considered that option.

"No," he decided. "Maybe when I know you better, I'll trust you."

"Bastard!" She grunted, trying to pry her elbows out from under Tom's forearms.

Tom gripped her hair tighter, holding her head still while her body wriggled. He descended onto her, slowly, rainwater running off his face onto hers, until their lips brushed, barely touching.

She stopped struggling.

When Tom came up for air, she sighed. "You pervert. We won't remember any of this."

"No, this moment is all we have." Tom yanked up her shirt.

Lightning flashed, and the rain pounded down.

Ten minutes later, Tom said, "I want it all," and rolled Luci over onto her stomach.

She gasped, her face pressed into the mud. "If you're about to do what I think you will, I'm pretty sure I'll notice, later."

"Dammit!" Tom rolled her onto her back.

Ten minutes later, Luci lay in the mud, panting. "You didn't have to pull out. We're all on birth control until we get our colony."

Tom splashed down on his back beside her. "That might have made an awkward question later. *What is this running down my leg?*"

Luci snorted a laugh. "You know, we could do this every week. Before we erase our memories, we could leave ourselves detailed notes, describing what we did to each other."

"Reading them would be interesting," Tom allowed, "except every time would feel like that first time with a girl I've never banged before. Who'd want that?"

Luci poked him, but not too hard.

"It's a fun idea," Tom admitted. "But we'll lose all of our short-term memories, and wake up disoriented. Would you really want to do that more than once?"

Luci laughed again, but not in the happy way.

Tom looked uncertain. "What?"

"You silk-tongued devil. We'd better hurry. The storm is peaking."

They stood up while the rain sluiced off the mud, then they pulled on their wet clothes. The clouds flickered with lightning.

Luci picked up the black cable. She held the jack in her hand, staring at it. "I should use my head."

"What?"

"The head, the bathroom in my yacht. You can do it outside. The world is your bathroom, and the rain will inspire you."

After a pause, Tom said, "Sure."

Five second after she entered her yacht, Tom peaked through the glistening raindrops on the rear window, and saw Luci leaning over her pilot seat.

Three minutes later, she emerged. "Ready?"

Tom patted his pockets. "I should put my wallet inside."

Inside the yacht, he looked at Luci's seat.

The cloth was wet. Tucked beside her joystick, he saw a flash of pink. Tom picked up the tiny sheet and read her neat handwriting.

Tom took me hard

Sorry, Luci, but this is where I eat, and I just don't trust you to behave reasonably. Tom slid the little snitch into his mouth. It dissolved on his tongue with a rush of cold heat.

Outside, Luci was lying on the ground holding her headset.

Tom looked down at her, trying to prolong the moment. Then he lay beside her, not quite touching.

"You're the first man who's had me in 90 years."

"I've always thought older women are nicer."

She poked him, but not too hard. "That's only *eighty* Earth years. Now tell me the story."

"What story?"

"You obviously made a promise, and didn't keep it. Was it your marriage vows?"

Tom did not respond.

"Now is the time," Luci added. "Neither of us will remember. You've never told anyone, have you?"

"It was my tenth birthday. My mother asked me to put oil in her car."

"And you didn't?"

"No, I didn't," Tom said quietly. "But I told her I did. Then we went for a long drive to get my birthday present, and the engine seized up."

Luci winced. "You must have felt terrible."

"We were way out in the country, so she had to leave me and walk 15 miles. I was alone in the car for hours, long past dark, thinking about my sin. I missed my birthday party."

Luci shuddered.

Tom noticed. "What's wrong?"

"I can't tell you."

Tom poked her, but not too hard. "I thought we were being honest."

"I just…" Luci hesitated. "That must have been brutal, and I feel your pain a little too much." She pointed to her tattooed cheek. "It's a side effect. Did you ever tell your mother?"

"No. To this day, I've never admitted what I did. My mother trusted me to keep my word, and I couldn't bring myself to disappoint her. I still can't."

"So now, it's a fetish. That's why your sentries work so much better than you claimed. You're afraid to break a promise."

"Now it's your turn to be honest. Why did you say you feel my pain too much?"

"I feel your pain because I think you are my son."

"What?" Tom blinked, but that might have been the rain in his eyes.

Luci sighed. "It feels so good to finally tell you."

Tom tried to process the revelation. "This must be important, but all I can think about is that scene in *Taboo 2."*

"Oh, my human brain knows the truth, of course. Only my animal brain recognizes you as my offspring. That's what this means." Luci tapped her hexagon tattoo.

"Wow. That puts a different spin on what we just did."

"More than you know. I don't want to forget this day."

Tom stiffened.

"Relax." Luci pulled on her headset. "I know you don't want drama, and I want you to get what you want. I always will, even if you learn to hate me."

Tom looked at her curiously. "You're a mass of contradictions."

"No, Tom, I'm not. It just looks that way, because you haven't had time to connect the clues." Luci scooted closer and kissed him.

100 years passed in five seconds, then Luci leaned away. "Good-bye, lover."

The Thinking Side

By Prof Charles Chow, Science Enforcer

The cherub sword –that marvelous device that propels the Worm spacecraft– has spawned the best popular theories since Elvis exhausted his life on the commode.

The theory I love most, because it made me laugh most, holds that the cherub sword accelerates iron *magnetically*. "Why else fuel it with iron," say the wits who spend weeks rearranging the magnets on their perpetual-motion machines.

I *could* believe the cherub sword accelerates iron magnetically, but only if I ignore its best trick, which is dialing up velocity *all the way,* converting iron atoms into gamma photons. This trick can't be performed by any known force of nature, of which magnetism is one-half of one of four.

We've found *four* of this universe's fundamental forces. Magnetism and gravity were known to the ancient Greeks, but the strong and weak nuclear forces were discovered only in the last century. A tad presumptuous, don't you think, to believe we've found them all?

Yes, I know it's *electro-magnetism*. I also know life isn't fair and dolphins aren't fish, so you can stop telling me.

Even the Greeks knew this universe contains at least one more force. The existence of a mysterious fifth force is, paradoxically, the *only* fact we know for certain.

As any smug sophomore can tell you, and will, the only thing we're really sure of is our *thoughts*. Our consciousness exists, so it's made of something, and it ain't the weak nuclear force. Amusingly, thinking about the fifth force proves its existence. We don't know much about it, except that it can move normal matter, as we prove by acting on our urge to feel up Susie, after asking her permission.

So stop rearranging the magnets, and stop trying to explain the cherub sword in familiar terms. Heaven and Earth contain more than is dreamt of in a consciousness that cannot explain its own existence.

Ten minutes later
In the mud

Tom realized he was awake. He must be, because he was looking up at falling rain. Eventually, his eyes focused. He yawned, turned his head and "YOW!"

Luci was lying next to him, close enough to touch, wearing her aviation headset. As he watched, her eyes fluttered open. Tom jumped to his feet, swayed, and sat back down in the mud. Forty feet away, he saw her yacht, parked with its engines pointed straight up. "What the fuck?"

Luci sat up quietly. A black cable trailed from her headset into the mud, then on to the yacht's open hatch. Overhead, the remnants of a thunderstorm washed out.

Tom staggered upright again. "How did I get here? Where *is* here? We're in a fucking *desert*." He wobbled over and peered into Luci's yacht. "That black cable is jacked into your instrument panel. Is anyone else here? Why the fuck are *we* here?"

Luci took off her headset and sniffed it. "This smells burned. What's the last thing you remember?"

"I was in my bed, and now ..." Tom rubbed his head, then sniffed his finger. "My *hair* is burned."

Luci stood up and looked at her muddy clothes in dismay. "The last thing I remember is crawling into my bunk on the *Finger*."

Tom rubbed his burned scalp. "I wonder how much time we lost?"

"Just a few minutes," said Luci, "plus all our memories since the last time we slept. Let's take a walk. Maybe we can find a snake."

Tom stared at her. Then he turned a slow circle, gazing out at the desert, empty save for a trail of footprints heading away from the parked yacht. "Great idea."

Luci was already striding away, following the trail of footprints.

Tom hastened to catch up. "All right, spew. What the hell happened?"

"I'm sure I did this. I planned to do this. We need to talk."

"If a woman says those four words, it means I already said too much." Tom probed his burned scalp. "What's going on?"

"I fired my engines at max exhaust velocity in atmosphere. It scrambled every electric device in this area, including our brains and all the listening devices hiding in our clothes. Apparently, some of what you thought was your hair was actually an antenna."

That shut Tom up.

"Some devices might have survived inside my yacht," Luci added. "Let's get some distance."

Tom looked back at her lipstick-red spaceship, now 100 yards distant. "You actually fired your engines as gamma-ray lasers, like the *Unexpected Finger?*"

"Not what you expected?"

"If you fire a gamma-ray laser in the atmosphere, doesn't it ionize the air molecules and blow away their electrons?"

"If you say so." Luci kicked a stone, sending it skittering away. "We call it a *brain hammer.*"

"Can *all* your engines do that?"

"Well, duh, did you think we invented *two* fantastic energy sources? Cranking a cherub sword up all the way is not really popular while we're flying in atmosphere, because the pilot will pass out and plummet to his doom. When I did it to us, I must have been laying on a rock." Luci rubbed her backside. "My butt is bruised."

Tom considered. "I don't think an EMP would scramble our brains and erase our short-term memories, at least not reliably. What did your engine *really* do?"

"Don't ask. If your queens learn the awful secret of the cherub sword, all is lost."

"Miss Dark, why are we here?"

"We are here because your queens hear everything we say. Tiny listeners were planted in our clothes, but they should be dead now."

"I believe some fairies crept down my chimney one dark night and drugged me, then gave me free hair extensions." Tom rubbed his burned scalp. "Isn't this a bit extreme? Couldn't we just change clothes and comb our hair?"

"Yes," said Luci, "or we could microwave our clothes. We've been doing that for a while, so your queens might have found a countermeasure."

"What countermeasure?"

"The wasps already put a microphone in your hair. I assure you, they are willing to put one under your skin. An occasional delousing seems prudent."

302

Tom looked at the empty desert. "This far out, a micro-bug couldn't transmit in real time, not even to a satellite, because it can't store enough power in such a small space, though maybe it could record, and transmit later."

"That's what we heard."

"You *heard?* From who?"

Luci chuckled. "It turns out, you can purchase excellent technical advice in exchange for a family vacation on the moon."

Tom thought about the technical geeks he knew. *Yes,* he decided. *A trip to the moon might tempt a geek to violate his non-disclosure agreement.* "Why are we here? What do you want to know?"

"Can we trust Frank Drummer?"

"Yes."

"Can we trust Sophie Flint?"

That one, Tom had to think about. "I've known Sophie since diapers. She's just what she appears."

"So, if I paid Sophie to store a bag of gold..."

"She wouldn't steal it, until she convinced herself you deserved to lose it."

Luci winced. "Why do you keep her around?"

"I keep Sophie around because she's smart. I lead so well, I can dance with a wasp."

"A wasp can be useful," Luci allowed. "But no sane man invites it into his bed."

"Unless he was raised by one. Miss Dark, you could have asked me these questions anywhere. Why are we here?"

"And he's smart too," Luci said wistfully. "We are here so I can ask you what I should be asking you."

"What should you be asking me?"

"That's the question. What should I be asking you?"

Tom didn't have to think. "You should ask me if your sentries carry only the software you wanted."

"Okay," said Luci. "Did you put software in our sentries that we didn't ask for?"

"No. And our government put a microphone in my hair."

After a pause, Luci said, "Fuck."

200 yards from the yacht, they found Luci's gunbelt lying in the mud beside an aluminum case that turned out to contain her stereo, GPS navigator, and both their phones.

They returned to Luci's yacht. Inside, she looked around her seat as if searching for something. Then she connected the stereo to a cable dangling from her instrument panel. The white Molex connector clicked shut. She tugged it to be sure, then slid the stereo back into its slot and tightened the screws. "I probably blew out my speakers."

Tom snapped his harness shut.

Luci searched around her seat again, then shaded her eyes to peer into the space beside her joystick.

"Did you lose something?"

"I guess not." Luci felt under her seat, and seemed disappointed. "You are always such a *gentleman*."

In Tom's brain, Miss Manners said, *that was a compliment.*

Sure it was, the sex monkey snarled.

The trip home was uneventful. Back at the Pine Shack, they headed to the lunchroom for a snack.

"Would that taste good?" Luci pointed to an abandoned fruitcake.

"Not really," said Tom. "Store-bought fruitcakes always skimp on the Portland cement."

Luci perused her many choices in the snack machine. "Why are you still single?"

"I was married for a while."

Luci carefully pressed *D*, then *6*. She waited, jaw clenching, while the screw rotated. When her Ding Dong dropped, she sighed in relief. "That doesn't answer my question."

"No, it doesn't." Tom pulled out a chair for her.

Luci settled into it, then winced and rubbed her butt. "I got a nasty bruise. You manage women easily, and you obviously need one."

"Why are *you* single?" Tom stabbed the fruitcake. "You handle men easily."

Luci froze into unnatural stillness, her Ding Dong held out, swaying.

Tom chiseled off a fruitcake shard with a grinding sound. "Sorry."

Luci blinked. "Ancient history. I haven't been laid for 90 years. Now quit changing the subject."

Tom nibbled the fruitcake chip experimentally. "You're wounded, and it's not ancient history." He looked at the chip, which seemed undamaged, then flicked it into the corner, bouncing it off the wall with a wooden *plock* and into the trash. "Confess. It will help."

Luci exhaled loudly. "I said you were good with women. Now stop picking my scab, and quit dodging my question."

Tom inspected the vending machine, and selected a sack of nuts. "My romantic demands are unreasonable, so I'm not dating until I have a pile of money."

Luci tugged at her Ding-Dong wrapper. Tom handed her the knife, and she sliced open the bag. "Shouldn't you choose the woman first, then build your success together?"

"That fantasy ended in divorce court." Tom presented his cash to the machine, which sucked it in efficiently.

Faintly audible through the walls, they heard protesters chanting, *Hey hey, ho ho, testosterone has got to go.*

Luci pulled out her Ding Dong. "What are your unreasonable romantic demands?"

Tom shrugged. "I want the normal things all men want from women: High standards, infallible memory, keen ear for verbal nuance, healthy appetite."

Luci wadded up her Ding-Dong wrapper and threw it at him. "What romantic demands?"

Tom ripped open his sack of nuts. "That information goes only to women who need to know."

Luci made a sour face, but relaxed as she gazed lovingly at the Ding Dong. She held it to her nose and inhaled deeply. "You should tell me your demands. I'm not like the other women you know." She tore out a chunk with her perfect, white teeth.

"I'm not like other women." Tom murmured. "How many times have I heard those words on last dates." He settled in across the table, taking the most distant chair. "So, Miss Dark, I'm keeping our relationship professional, because—"

Luci joined in, and they chanted in unison: "This is where we eat."

"Seriously, Tom, you can trust me. You shouldn't be so bitter, and you might be surprised what I would do for you." Luci sucked out the Ding-Dong cream and swallowed.

Tom crunched a nut. "No."

Luci sucked the Ding Dong dry and bit into the husk. "I'm sorry for you. I see you're lonely."

Tom closed his eyes. "I said you were good with men. I hate being alone."

"Me too."

"What?" Tom's eyes flew open. "How can you *possibly* be lonely? You're so beautiful, it hurts to look at you, or to look away."

"Do you think so?"

"How can you ask that?"

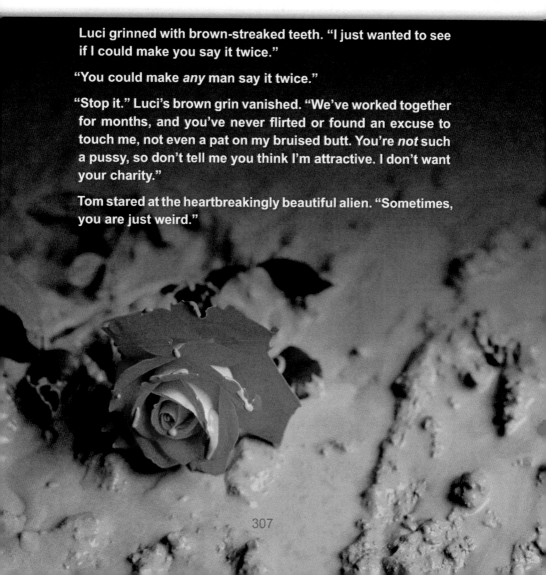

Luci grinned with brown-streaked teeth. "I just wanted to see if I could make you say it twice."

"You could make *any* man say it twice."

"Stop it." Luci's brown grin vanished. "We've worked together for months, and you've never flirted or found an excuse to touch me, not even a pat on my bruised butt. You're *not* such a pussy, so don't tell me you think I'm attractive. I don't want your charity."

Tom stared at the heartbreakingly beautiful alien. "Sometimes, you are just weird."

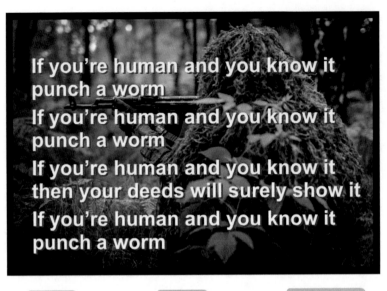

If you're human and you know it
punch a worm

If you're human and you know it
punch a worm

If you're human and you know it
then your deeds will surely show it

If you're human and you know it
punch a worm

Like   **Share**   **Comment**

COMMENTS Please respect the forum rules.

SoccerForLife Three days ago
This is obvious incitement to racial violence. How have we fallen so far so fast? Today, I actually heard a SCHOOL BUS FULL OF CHILDREN singing this song! I couldn't believe it! What if, instead of *worm,* they had said, *black?*

Pokemom Three days ago
SoccerForLife I can't believe you just compared the Worms to the struggle that African Americans must endure in this country.

LawFareForU Three days ago
SoccerForLife you are seriously out of touch. I'm surprised you are willing to post something so insensitive. If you don't care about the consequences for you personally, think about your children.

S. Quiblee Three days ago
YOU WHORE YOU FUCKING BITCH. Cunts like you should be hounded from public life..

SoccerForLife Three days ago
WTF is wrong with you people?

Moby Duck Three days ago
SoccerForLife is banned. I'll leave this thread up as an example.

Dinnertime
Mom's house

"You've worked with the aliens for *months,"* Scarlet called from the kitchen. "Have you had sex with Lucifa yet?"

"No, and I won't." Tom untied the big umbrella on the back deck. "I can't figure her out, so I'm afraid to touch her. My business doesn't need a freaked-out alien who thinks I did her wrong."

Scarlet arrived carrying a plate of red peppers. "Are we talking about the same Lucifa, the hot one?"

"Yes, that's Luci, and she's behaving weirdly."

"What constitutes *weirdly*, for an alien?"

Tom hoisted up the umbrella until it latched, casting the table into shade. "I told her every man wants her, and she didn't believe me."

"We must be talking about different aliens." Scarlet set the plate of hot peppers on the shaded table. "I thought you meant the devil woman, the one who pranked us in their First Contact, the one every man thinks about when he tries to get it up for his wife."

"Yes, that would be Luci."

"The famously beautiful Lucifa doesn't *know* men want her? Was she faking it?"

"She convinced me."

Scarlet walked back into the kitchen. "If she doesn't know she's beautiful, the alien men must be amazingly disciplined. Have you considered the best-case scenario? Maybe the alien women are just alien, in a nice way."

Tom opened the propane grill. "She looks beautiful, but she doesn't *act* beautiful."

Scarlet returned with a slab of bacon. "Sounds promising."

"Beautiful girls have this air. It's hard to describe... You know how your mother always makes it clear she loves you, no matter what?"

"Yes," said Scarlet. "I know."

"Beautiful girls radiate the opposite, but not Luci. Somehow, she seems... I almost want to say, for all her physical beauty, Luci acts like a fat girl, all hopeful and easy. But that's not right either." Tom shook his head. "Do you remember their first broadcast? It was *First Contact,* a huge event, and Luci used it to mock the Christians. When I asked her why, she said, quote, *because Christians are so polite."*

"Eew." Scarlet's nose wrinkled. "Yuck."

"Christians are like Frank Drummer; they don't retaliate for insults, though for different reasons." Tom lifted his grill scraper off its hook. "That makes them safe targets, just like Frank."

Scarlet sliced open the bacon. "Poor Frank. I don't think he's ever *tried* to hurt anyone, but he tells the truth, so he can't have friends. Do the aliens get along with him?"

"They did, until last week. You know I encourage my employees to talk about the elephant, so it's okay to tell me I'm short and ugly."

"You are *not* ugly. You're a handsome man."

"Thanks, Mom. Anyway, the Worms have always teased Frank, like they tease everyone, but it was just good-natured banter, obviously affectionate. Then, overnight, they started insulting him for real."

"Did Frank piss them off?"

"No more than usual."

"*Insult* covers a lot of territory," Scarlet observed. "How serious are we talking?"

Tom flipped the scraper over to the blade and hacked at the meaty charcoal. "Yesterday, Luci told Frank no woman will ever be attracted to him, because he's so fat. She actually *said it.*"

"Ouch. Did she add something nice to take the sting out?"

"No, she said women *should* reject him, because obesity showed he couldn't discipline himself. Though I guess, technically, she might have been trying to help."

Scarlet tugged out a slice of bacon and wrapped it around a hot pepper. "Lucifa tried to help Frank Drummer *by telling him he is unattractive?*"

Tom's mouth watered. He knew Mom's bacon-wrapped extra-hot jalapenos were stuffed with sweet cream cheese. "Apparently, the Worms fat-shame each other mercilessly. They say that's why they're all so thin. They think our eating decisions are actually made by the monkey parts of our brain, not our conscious minds, and the monkeys hate to be shamed. They say fat-shaming frightens the monkeys and makes it *easy* to eat less, no struggle at all."

311

Scarlet snorted. "Monkeys in their heads."

Tom set down the scraper. "Mom, *you* used to see monkeys in your head."

Scarlet stared at him blankly.

"You told me you lost your internal censor, so you could see how your mind worked. That's why you used to have seizures. Then your censor came back, so now you can't see the monkeys."

"That never happened." Scarlet turned away. "You must have dreamt it. Do you think the aliens are fat-shaming Frank to help him lose weight?"

"No, they attack everything about him. Last week, it was his porn."

"Every man likes porn. These days, that's hardly an insult."

"No, Mom, every man does *not* like to hear his porn preferences trumpeted around the office by laughing women who found his search history, especially if it includes *cuckold* and *pegging.* The girls are so relentless, they are obviously *not* just trying to help Frank lose weight." Tom switched to the wire brush and worried the crusted-on fat until it lost its grip and flaked off into the coals. "Besides, I don't think fat-shaming could ever work on Frank. He has no internal censor, so he already knows all his own flaws."

"Then why do the aliens torment him?" Scarlet wrapped bacon around a hot pepper and poked in a toothpick.

"I think they realized he won't retaliate." Tom turned on the gas and punched the red button. Nothing happened.

"Oh, no." Scarlet dropped the pepper and looked tired.

"I'm afraid so. Frank doesn't bother to retaliate, because he isn't hurt." Tom slammed his palm into the red button. The grill burst into flame. "But the Worms can't know that, even if Frank told them. They have to assume their insults are wounding him, even if he denies it."

"Are you sure? Could they just be teasing him because they know he doesn't care?"

"Luci laughed in Frank's face and said he has no Human friends, and probably never will."

Scarlet winced.

"Until last week, I never saw an alien *try* to hurt someone's feelings. Probably that's just a habit, because they're too dangerous to be rude. Then they realized Frank is a soft target, like the Christians, so they tore into him." Tom grabbed a cream-cheese-stuffed hot pepper and angrily jammed in a toothpick. "I really thought Luci Dark might be something special, but it turned out she's only sweet on the outside."

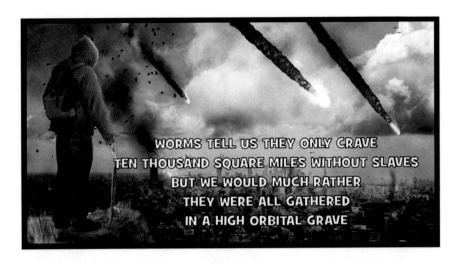

WORMS TELL US THEY ONLY CRAVE
TEN THOUSAND SQUARE MILES WITHOUT SLAVES
BUT WE WOULD MUCH RATHER
THEY WERE ALL GATHERED
IN A HIGH ORBITAL GRAVE

Like   Share   Comment

Comments. Please respect the <u>forum rules</u>.

Pokemom Yesterday
> The worms love to talk about ransom and slavery, but it's all bullshit. They just don't want to pay taxes.

LawFareForU Yesterday
> It's worse than that. They pretend they can't obey building codes or zoning laws or safety rules. They are like children who cry when we tell them they can't eat ALL the candy.

Moby Duck Yesterday
> Can you imagine a city without zoning and building codes? People would build whatever crap they wanted.

GooberGoodness Yesterday
> Actually, Houston grew up without zoning, and we didn't have building codes for most of history, so Paris was built without them.

Moby Duck Yesterday
> STFU Goober. Nobody believes your propaganda.

GooberGoodness Six hours ago
> What are you talking about?

S. Quiblee Six hours ago
> Goober obviously wants to live somewhere without an age-of-consent law, so he's looking for excuses to join a Worm colony.

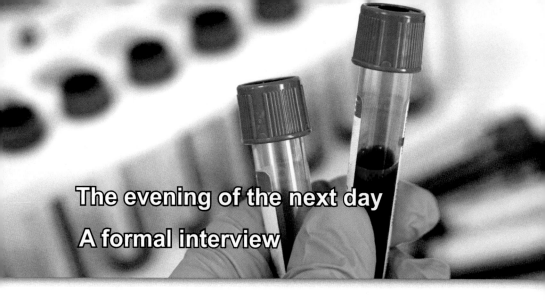

The evening of the next day
A formal interview

Luci walked into the tiny office she shared with Frank Drummer and closed the door. "How would you feel if you had a girlfriend, but she was smarter than you? I mean, *really* smarter."

"I'd feel sorry for her," Frank replied. "She probably won't find an acceptable husband."

Luci took awhile to process that. Eventually, she said, "What's your most painful memory from childhood?"

"None of your business."

"Will you give me a hint? Just generalities."

"Luci, what are we doing?"

"We are doing something I've been prepping for all day, so indulge me. When you die, what do you think will happen to you?"

"How should I know?"

"Does that worry you?"

"Death worries me a little," Frank admitted. "Is this going to take a long time?"

"Do you have seizures?"

"Like, dropping to the floor and frothing?"

"Maybe something less dramatic," said Luci. "Do you ever lose time, or realize you can't remember how you got here?"

"I've had no seizures since I was five and figured out how to stop them," said Frank. "What are we doing?"

"Are you…. Wait. You *learned* how to stop your seizures?"

"I already told you, my censor is defective, but eventually, I figured out how to control it." Frank folded his arms. "What are we doing?"

"We are calibrating. Relax and enjoy it."

"What are we calibrating?"

"I won't tell you yet." Luci lifted her briefcase onto Frank's desk. "What are you good at?"

"Logic, math and spatial reasoning." Frank tapped the briefcase. "Even *I* know nobody carries these anymore."

"I think briefcases are fabulous." Luci unsnapped the spring-loaded latches, then pushed them shut, then unsnapped them again. "I love doing that. What are you bad at?"

"Fashion."

Luci glanced at Frank's clothes. "You seem reasonably perceptive."

She opened her briefcase and withdrew a picture of six complex geometric shapes rotated to different angles. "Which of these is different from the others?"

Frank studied the picture for five seconds, then he pointed to the lower left corner.

Luci looked at the back of the card, then dropped it back into the briefcase. "Has your intellect been formally tested?"

"I took the GRE. That's an entrance exam for grad school."

"How did you rank?" Luci seemed genuinely interested.

"Among the people who take the GRE, I scored 90th percentile in math, and 40th in English. In the general population, I probably rank in the top one percent of math ability, though my verbal skills are mediocre."

Luci nodded thoughtfully. "What's the hardest thing you've done?"

"Grad school."

"Was it worth it?"

"I'm glad I did it, but I wouldn't do it again."

"Was anything unusual about your family?"

"Yes. At home, Dad seems like an alien, but out here in the world, he seems like the normal one."

"Would you let me inject you with a drug?"

"That question was not like the others."

Luci did not elaborate.

Frank considered. "Is it a work drug, or a fun drug?"

"I won't tell you." Luci reached into her briefcase and pulled out a silver case wound with a soft white cord.

Nine hundred miles away, in his high-ceiling corner office six blocks from the White House, Dominick Tork looked away from his bank of surveillance monitors long enough to press a blue button.

Frank's brow wrinkled. "Why would I let you drug me?"

"Because you know what this means." Luci tapped the blue square tattooed on her cheek.

Frank touched her cheek. "I also know about this triangle. It means your recently bit the forbidden fruit, and faced reality without a censor." He traced his finger down the row of tattoos. "But I don't know about this pentagon, or this hexagon, or this circle, or why Buff doesn't have a circle, or why *your* circle is crossed out when Natalie's isn't."

Luci flinched.

Frank looked at her curiously. "Okay, you can inject me. What will it do to me?"

"That's the right question." Luci unwound the soft cord. "So you trust me now?"

"Yes," said Frank. "You only flinched when I asked why your circle tattoo has a slash through it."

Luci opened the silver case. It held a glass vial, a syringe, and a white needle. "Congratulations; you finally found a way to upset me."

"No, I mean you didn't flinch *until* I asked about the slash. When I touched your face, right below your eye, you only blinked." Frank touched her cheek tattoos again. "Suddenly, these seem real. You had to remind yourself to be afraid of me."

Luci pulled the plunger out of the syringe, then screwed on the white needle and poked it into the vial through the rubber cap. She shoved the plunger back in, then sucked out the clear liquid. "If I spend enough time around Humans, I suppose I will acquire a flinch reflex."

"Yes," Frank agreed. "I believe you will."

Luci started to drop the empty vial back into the silver case. Then she reconsidered, and tossed it into the trash.

900 miles away, Dominick Tork keyed his radio. "Abort. You can't get there in time for the big sample, but she just tossed the residue into a trash can in the shared office. Echo Team, you get the trash. Charlie Team, set up for the, uh...." Dominick leafed through a 3-ring binder. "Charlie Team, set up for *Bumper Car.*"

Luci shook out the soft cord and wrapped it around Frank's arm, just above the elbow. As she pulled it tight, she grimaced disapprovingly. Frank's arm looked like jello wrapped by a rubber band. She laid the syringe against his skin, then paused. "Frank, if you've been lying to me, this could hurt you badly."

"Okay. How long until it takes effect?"

Luci pushed in the needle. "It's not fresh, so five to ten minutes." She dropped the empty syringe into the trash, then tucked the white needle back into the silver case and snapped it shut.

Frank turned back to his work.

Ten minutes later, when he still hadn't spoken, Luci prodded. "What are you thinking?"

Frank looked annoyed. "This stupid drug turned off my censor, so I can't shut out the distractions. Every idea is shouting for my attention. This hasn't happened since I was five."

Luci looked interested.

Frank stood up. "No point in trying to work. I'm going to the vending machine."

Luci walked beside him. "Think of a painful memory, something that hurt you."

Frank growled.

"Tell me about the painful memory."

"No."

"Are you thinking of it now?"

"Yes," said Frank. "Thanks for that."

"Does the memory seem different now?"

"No, it hurts just like it always does."

"Was grad school worth the effort?"

The empty wall caught Frank's eye, and he stopped to slide his hands over the paneling. "Deja vu."

"Deja who?"

Frank gazed intently at the dark wood, running his finger down a seam. "Didn't you already ask me about grad school?"

"Yes. Indulge me."

The fluorescent lights flickered, startling Frank from his reverie. "Grad school was harder than I expected. It cost more than it was worth, but the cost is behind me, while the benefit is mostly still ahead." He smiled dreamily at the overhead lights. "I'm glad my past self got suckered, since I care mainly about my future self."

"Have you considered suicide?"

"Why?"

"You tell me." Luci watched him.

"Killing myself would be stupid. Life is fun." Frank wandered into the lunchroom. He spotted the vending machine and pressed his nose against the glass. "So loud, all the voices and choices."

"Wouldn't oblivion be easier? You've been rejected so often."

"How would you know?"

"What if you screwed up and permanently blinded your friends?"

Frank slid a dollar into the machine. "So far, all of my regrets are useful, but if they start hurting me, I will censor them."

"Think," Luci commanded. "Of the questions I asked, which did you answer wrong?"

"Oh, we all agree, my big mistake was not asking you to pay me for this." Frank noticed something interesting about the garbage can. He dashed over and reached in.

"Frank! Try to pay attention."

"If you wanted me to pay attention, you shouldn't have drugged me." He rooted in the trash. "Why did you?"

"You're something I've never seen. I'm trying to figure out what you are, so I gave you a drug that will make you admit the truth."

"I think I know what this drug is, and it *won't* be popular."

Luci snorted.

Frank abandoned the trash and returned to the vending machine, "Are we up to the part where you offer me a reward?"

"Sorry; this is not foreplay."

Luci didn't really sound sorry.

Frank seemed disappointed, but not really surprised. He braced himself with one hand on the glass, and bit his lip in concentration as he punched in the code for a dark chocolate bar. "I'd like to know *your* true nature. You're obviously hiding it."

"I'm not like anything you've met before," said Luci. "Think of the last girl you dated. Are you glad you met her?"

"That which does not kill me."

"What does that mean?

Frank pushed open the tray and strained to reach his chocolate. *"That which does not kill me* is an idiom. It means she was worth the effort, but she really *was* an effort." He jammed his hand in deeper and claimed his bittersweet treat.

"Did you think of her that way an hour ago?"

"We did not think of Susan an hour ago." Frank unwrapped the dark chocolate and bit off a square. "She seems about as sweet and bitter as she did before you drugged me."

"Did she want you to be happy?"

"On our third date, I got drunk and told her what makes me happy." Frank's gaze wandered back to the trash. "When I realized what I'd admitted, I was afraid. But she just...the alcohol saved me from the worst of it. After that, she was always too busy to go out with me."

"What makes you happy?"

"The same things that make *all* men happy."

Luci chuckled. "Did you feel that way an hour ago?"

"We feel no new revelations."

"Really? *No* new revelations?" Luci grabbed Frank's hand, the one holding the dark chocolate, and held it steady as she bit off a chunk. "Have you ever known a woman who *wanted* you to have your heart's desire?"

Frank chewed thoughtfully. "Luci, what are we doing?"

Luci closed her eyes, savoring the bittersweet flavor. "We are asking you questions that make Humans lie to themselves."

"Why are we doing that?"

"So I can judge whether you have deceived me."

"About what, exactly?"

Luci stepped close. She pressed against Frank, close enough to share his breath. Her voice was soft, and hard, and chocolate flavored. "Frank, have you betrayed us?"

"Nope."

"Do you intend to?"

"Luci, I will not betray you, unless I think it's the right thing to do. Right now, I don't think it's the right thing to do."

Luci grabbed another bite of his chocolate. "There. That was not so hard. Sorry, I have to rush off now. I'll send Sophie in to keep you company."

On her way out, Luci poked her head into Sophie's office. "Frank needs someone to keep him out of trouble for an hour. Don't ask him any questions, unless you want an honest answer."

Sophie found Frank wandering around the prototype shop, and briefly considered asking him what he really thought of her. Very briefly. She heard the roar of Luci's departure.

Eventually, Frank's mind settled back to the state he called, *normal,* as the clamoring mental voices allowed themselves to be muffled. He thanked Sophie, picked up his laptop and his jacket, and locked the door behind him.

On his way home, Frank stopped for groceries like always. He parked his new car, grabbed a shopping cart from the lot, and never saw the minivan that swerved into him.

Washington, D.C.

Dominick Tork surveyed the crowded briefing theater. "Before I reveal this information, I will remind you of your security commitments."

Every face lost its expression. The 49 distinguished scholars, statesmen and executives of the Alien Regulatory Authority had not forgotten their security briefings, which had included their complete medical histories with everything related to anus and genitalia highlighted in red, dating back to the passage of the electronic health records mandate in the Affordable Healthcare Act. Each page was labeled,

PERSONAL AND CONFIDENTIAL
DO NOT DISTRIBUTE
EXCEPT IN EMERGENCY

"We have obtained blood samples from a Human who was recently injected with an alien drug. The drug was represented as a truth serum, but we believe it was even more dangerous. We believe the Human was injected with the *forbidden fruit,* an alien drug that forces you to look into your own mind and see what's hiding there."

The commissioners stiffened. They understood the threat.

At first glance, the Alien Regulatory Authority seemed a haphazard mix of politicians, businessmen, academics and civic leaders, with a generous sprinkling of psychologists. In reality, the mix was anything but haphazard. The 49 surviving commissioners had all been selected from a narrow, albeit deep pool.

Across the United States, every major telco nexus sprouted a welter of cables. Lost among the tangle was always one nondescript, armored tube that wended its way to the closest government server farm. Inside the government server farm, acres of racked processors swam upstream in endless rivers of ice-cold mineral oil spewed out by megawatt chillers, washing away the heat from reading text messages, listening to voice conversations, and looking at pictures from the unwary who left their phones uncovered, thinking they were safe because the phone was turned "off."

The real trophies, the congressman, the governors, even the biggest prize of all, the Supreme Court justices, knew their phones were monitored. Many went so far as to tape over the camera and physically destroy the GPS receiver chip, precautions suggested by the intelligence community so high-value targets would feel safe to leave the battery inserted. Then they could be snared by the bluetooth and near-field RF sensors that revealed who approached whom, and how close, and with what rhythm.

The A.I. who directed the program was called, *Randy.* All day, every day, Randy monitored smart-phone sensors, guided by the insights of very human Humans. Minute by minute, Randy streamed out the only data more valuable than nuclear weapon design.

Randy's output was stored in a heavily-encrypted SQL archive (pronounced, *"Sequel"*) that detailed who had sex with whom. Every record in Randy's archive included names, addresses, dates of birth, video if available, a rating of 1-5 stars, and a link into a short list of each state's age of consent.

Smirking eunuchs enjoyed pointing out that Randy's archive was a *relational* database.

Randy's archive included a 5-star entry for every one of the 49 scholars, executives and statesman of the Alien Regulatory Authority, because if it didn't, they wouldn't have been nominated. The Alien Regulatory Authority was to be autonomous, but that did not mean it would be out of control.

Of course, a secret sexual impropriety was not the only requirement. The second requirement was more subtle, and more important. To be eligible for a seat on the Alien Regulatory Authority, one must not produce anything of value, or even know how. Three of the commissioners were medical ethicists, but none were doctors. Two candidates had been disqualified for building their own back-yard decks.

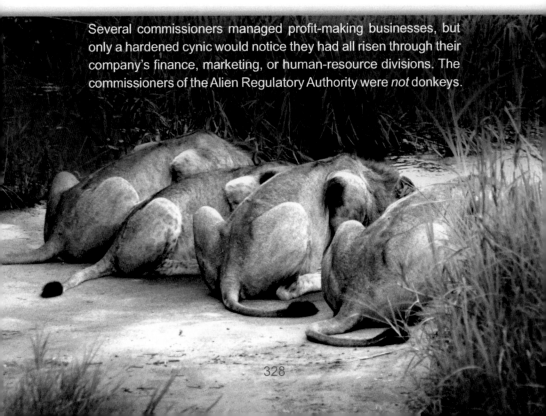

Several commissioners managed profit-making businesses, but only a hardened cynic would notice they had all risen through their company's finance, marketing, or human-resource divisions. The commissioners of the Alien Regulatory Authority were *not* donkeys.

The unfortunate Commissioner Simper had been singled out for death by exploding groundhog because he had carelessly mentioned he repaired his own car. The 49 surviving commissioners were utterly unable to create *any* material good. They would understand the threat of the forbidden fruit.

"The forbidden fruit is the only drug more destructive than a truth serum," Dominick continued. "Should it ever be widely distributed, our civilization will collapse."

Around the briefing theater, heads swiveled restlessly as 49 commissioners tried to avoid each other's gaze. Dominick noticed this subconscious evasion and understood it. In his previous career as a policeman, he had witnessed this discomfort dozens of times from semi-willing drug informants.

And he knew what to do. "Your job requires courage." Dominick's clarion voice echoed through the theater. "I thank you. Your culture thanks you, because it is *sorely* threatened."

Around the theater, commissioners grimaced and looked even less comfortable.

Let not your heart be troubled, thought Dominick, *for I bring glad tidings and an alibi.* "Any Human with a modicum of compassion would be horrified to think of what our citizens would do if they were exposed to the forbidden fruit."

Around the theater, some looked doubtful. Others looked interested. Dominick gave them what they craved. "For their own good, our citizens must sacrifice a few of their personal, short-term concerns, so you might lead them to a brighter future. Ironically, the most obvious sacrifices are your own careers, the years you have devoted to public service. You are living proof that democracy demands some sacrifice of the individual for the greater good."

Some of them bought it, and they all loved the word, *sacrifice.*

"Another example, small yet vital, is the trip to the voting booth. Each individual's vote is pure self-sacrifice, because a single vote has never changed the outcome of a national election, but each trip to the poll costs time and gasoline."

Now all of the commissioners looked interested.

Dominick gave them a taste of something they *really* wanted. "Our citizens are busy, and not all are mentally gifted."

That brought approving nods.

"They cannot understand their own long-term interests. Fortunately, evolution has solved this problem, at least partially, by creating a virtuous blind spot, an internal editor who saves them from wasting their mental resources." Dominick gazed about somberly. "What can it benefit a man to obsess over the short-term sacrifice you must demand of him? The virtuous blind spot makes his life bearable, and will be lost if our society is poisoned by that foul drug."

Dominick knew they didn't believe him, but that didn't matter. He had given them enough to *pretend* they believed. All around the theater, the relieved exhalations were clearly audible. Smiles broke out.

"Human happiness must be your highest priority. To that end, you should take... No. Not just take." Dominick straightened his jacket and stood taller. "You must *embrace* your compassion. *Celebrate* your desire to protect the vulnerable, especially the women and disadvantaged minorities at greatest risk. We *must* obtain a pure sample of the forbidden fruit, so we might devise a countermeasure, or at the very least, a means to identify users."

The one who spoiled the moment was, of course, the tall patrician, still trying to take charge. "We already procured a blood sample," he pronounced with authority. "You will have it analyzed immediately and isolate the drug."

Behind Dominick's hazel eyes, the gorilla stirred, awakened by the patrician's tone and his posture, by his *challenge.* When the gorilla was challenged, he knew what to do. "You demand I have the blood *analyzed?"* Dominick looked amused. "Do you know the number of distinct chemical compounds in blood?"

The tall patrician looked uncertain. "Not the exact number."

"Do you know the approximate number?"

The tall patrician regained his balance with a patronizing smile. "I am not a biologist."

"Nor am I," said Dominick. "But I took the time to inform myself, before I made suggestions."

Around the theater, commissioners smirked or winced, depending on their connection to the tall patrician.

"The number of known, distinct chemical compounds in human blood exceeds six *thousand.* Most can be detected only by a specific, yes-or-no test, which consumes a non-trivial fraction of our precious sample." Dominick gazed steadily at the tall patrician. "Each of the 6,000 blood components has, presumably, a function. Would you care to guess how many are known?"

331

The tall patrician squirmed. "As I said, I'm not a biologist."

Dominick turned away, paying no more heed to the tall patrician's challenge. "Of the 6,000 known blood components, we understand the functions of a few hundred. If we are to identify the forbidden fruit and devise a countermeasure, we must obtain a pure sample." Dominick grimaced. "And apparently, we need a *large* sample. We recovered 40 microliters from an empty vial and syringe thrown in the trash, but our scientists could identify only the saline carrier, not the active ingredient."

The commissioners looked disappointed, except the tall patrician looked angry.

"We need a large, pure sample of the forbidden fruit, and we need it quickly, well before that foul drug is released into our unsuspecting population. If you fail, everything you cherish is threatened."

Around the theater, the commissioners pointedly did not look at the tall patrician, whose gray suit now clashed with his red face.

"We have one clue," Dominick offered. "The drug was administered by syringe. Surveillance video indicates the needle was made of plastic, or possibly an advanced ceramic, but definitely *not* the stainless steel one might expect."

Now the commissioners looked bored.

"We believe the Worms discovered stainless steel only shortly before they left their world," Dominick explained. "Nonetheless, even if they had not mastered stainless steel, they could have made syringes from plain steel, as we once did. They did not, which suggests they don't want the drug to interact with iron. A possible interpretation, according to our chemists, is the drug binds to hemoglobin. If so, it would simplify the task of isolation."

The commissioners began to murmur among themselves.

"As you know," Dominick said louder, "several aliens have been injured in accidents."

The murmur ceased.

"Their blood and tissue have been sampled and subjected to a battery of laboratory tests."

The murmur resumed.

"The samples confirm what we learned from trace DNA. The aliens are, biologically, very nearly Human, augmented with genes from insects, sea lions, and radiation-resistant bacteria."

The murmur was so loud now, the commissioners couldn't hear him. Dominick stopped talking and reached around to scratch his back, incidentally sweeping aside his jacket to reveal his sidearm.

Commissioners elbowed each other, and the murmur faded.

"We found something surprising when a stored alien kidney was thawed. It turns out the alien tissue and plasma share a trait with some cold-weather insects; when frozen, they do not crystallize. Instead, they congeal into an amorphous, glass-like solid."

Amid the sea of boredom, two commissioners mouthed profanities. Dominick offered another clue. "We have managed to propagate cells from multiple Worm organs, 57 separate cell lines, which we have challenged with adverse conditions. When chilled or starved of oxygen, the alien cells secrete shock proteins and enter a dormant state of virtually zero metabolism. Even their neural cells can survive nearly a day of hypothermic hypoxia. They are effectively immune to frostbite."

Dominick saw more mouths opening as people connected the dots. The tall patrician, who was apparently a slow learner, spoke up again. "So, you were wrong to dismiss my suggestion they might hibernate?"

In Dominick's mind, the gorilla opened one eye, snorted derisively, and went back to sleep.

"Worm cells can support themselves for *hours.*" Dominick made eye contact with the tall patrician just long enough to communicate disdain. "This is too brief for useful hibernation, but is quite adequate to survive the thawing process, after the entire body is frozen to glass."

When the murmur subsided, a few people still looked bored, so Dominick spelled it out. "As you should remember, based on the *Unexpected Finger's* 8000-cubic-meter volume, we estimated the Worms' number at no more than a few hundred, perhaps only the 189 who have visited us. That is too few, we may hope, to overthrow our civilization."

Around the theater, Dominick saw more swearing as the implication sank in. "Since Worms can be stored as frozen cargo, you should now consider the possibility they number in the thousands."

The Thinking Side

By Prof Charles Chow, Science Enforcer

The *Forbidden Fruit,* the drug the aliens claim will "Dispel our delusions," may be the greatest threat we have faced since young Adolph hit on the idea of spicing up socialism with a little nationalism.

If any phrase ever deserved scorn quotes, surely it is, *"Dispel your delusions.* Delusion according to whom? You don't need to be a Doctor of Philosophy – and I am one – to know that when a man says, *Dispel your delusions,* he really means, *Make you think like me.*

Let's try that on for size: *The forbidden fruit will make you think like the aliens who are raping and killing us on the street.*

Here on Earth, shortly after World War II, a chemist named Victor Maddox managed to synthesize Phencyclidine. Since Maddox worked for America's (at the time) oldest and largest drug maker, Parke Davis, his discovery was quickly offered for sale under the trade name, *Sernyl.*

You may not have heard of Sernyl, since it was found unfit for human use and taken off the market. But it can still be purchased under different names. The names are: *PCP* and *Angel Dust.*

If you take PCP, you will think differently.

The parallels are instructive. PCP makes its users fearlessly homicidal. A PCP user might shoot a bank teller in the face in full view of an armed bank guard. Ring any bells?

A PCP user might think himself justified in sexually assaulting a woman because she flirted. Sound familiar?

Shortly after World War II, when PCP was discovered, we missed our chance to snuff an emerging menace before it spread. Let's not make that mistake again.

The Drummer's home
Two days after Frank's accident

Across the street from Tom Pine's boyhood home, in a house made of bricks, Frank Drummer's mother Melony ate breakfast with her husband, Collin. Outside, their fenced back yard sported an ancient swing set, a rusted monument to Frank's childhood.

Collin looked up from his newspaper. "Did you hear something?"

Melony cocked her head.

"Maybe traffic."

They didn't get much traffic here in their neighborhood of cul-de-sacs.

Melony looked up. "I hear it."

Five seconds later, the roar deafened both of them. Plates vibrated, then the back yard filled with orange smoke.

The noise cut off abruptly. Out the back windows, the smoke cleared to reveal the rusted swing set upended beside a spaceship. A small, middle aged redhead climbed out onto the grass and pulled her shirt over her head.

Collin watched, open mouthed, as the Worm tossed her elaborately engineered bra on the grass, then unbuckled her gun belt. She was old and skinny with spectacular muscle definition and a Frankenstein zipper on her cheek, just below her tattoos. As she pushed her pants down past her knees, she turned slightly toward the window, giving them a better view. Collin goggled.

Melony swatted him. "Show some respect. Turn your back."

Collin blushed and turned away from the window.

Eventually, the tiny, naked Worm tapped on the back door and held up a hand-lettered sign.

CLOTHES

PLEASE

Melony dug out an old sweatsuit, which the Worm wore with the legs and sleeves rolled up. Her name was Natalie.

"Would you like some coffee?"

"Thank you. Cream and sugar, please."

Collin sat quietly, watching the women interact. He seemed relieved not to participate.

Melony bustled about the kitchen. "I assume you came to talk about Frank?"

"Yes. Your son was struck by an automobile."

The teapot clanged off the floor.

"The car didn't seriously injure him," Natalie added hastily. "Just some bruises. He got an ambulance ride he didn't need."

Melony picked up the teapot. "You flew here to tell us in person, naked?"

"We are trusting Frank with quite a lot. We would like to know more about him."

Melony stared at the Worm for a long moment. "You've gotten to know my Frank. What do you think of him?"

Instead of answering, the alien said, "Do you own a gun?"

Collin's mouth dropped open. Then he shut it with an audible click. He winced and held his jaw. "I bit my tongue."

"We have no guns," Melony answered.

The Worm touched Collin's hand. "I'd like to speak privately with your wife, but I'm afraid your house may be bugged, because of your connection to us. And I suspect microphones in my clothes, maybe even in my gun. Would you be willing to carry my gun and walk behind us, out of earshot, to keep guard?"

Collin sat up straighter. "Certainly." Behind him, Melony smiled.

They left by the back door, and Natalie picked up her gunbelt. She presented it to Collin, then seemed to reconsider. She looked at Collin's ample waist, then at the belt, then back to Collin's waist. She slid a small, dense pistol out of the holster and handed it to him, butt first. "This is a nine-round autoloader. It's ready to fire, it has no safety, and the trigger pull is short. Don't worry about exact shot placement. Arteries conduct shock waves, so a hit anywhere on the torso will achieve your purpose."

Collin nodded seriously, holding the gun as if it were a snake. Then he noticed the women watching him. He pulled his shoulders back and gripped the gun firmly. "No problem." He stuffed the gun into the front of his pants. Then his eyes widened, and he hastily tugged it out. He looked lost for a moment, then put the gun in his front pocket. It sagged heavily.

A crowd had gathered in the front yard to peer over the fence. Melony suggested they go out the back gate and through the neighbor's yard. When they reached the next street, they set off down the sidewalk, away from the house.

Melony repeated her question. "What do you think of my Frank?"

"Your Frank is the most extraordinary Human we've ever met."

Melony chuckled. "Have you discovered how hard it is to insult him? Even *I* can barely manage it."

"We noticed." Natalie turned and saw Collin trailing well back. His posture was straighter than usual, but his gate was awkward because he was clutching his pocket. "We have no tame men. What is it like to be married to Colin?"

"Colin is just what you'd expect," Melony replied. "He is exactly what you expect, all the time."

Natalie winced. "Do you still take men on the side?"

"Why don't we skip this bullshit. You've discovered what Frank is, and you want him in your colony. You undressed in front of us to put me at ease."

"Bullshit doesn't work on your son either," Natalie said approvingly. "Okay, we'll skip it. Will you tell me about Frank's real father?"

They walked in silence for 30 paces before Melony spoke again. "Collin wants to believe he is Frank's father."

"Of course."

Melony walked faster. "You want to take my Frank, my only child, but I won't let you. I can report you to the government. They hate you, and they will stop you from taking my son."

Natalie smiled gently. "Melony, would you like to know *why* your son was injured?"

Melony's pace faltered. "What?"

"Frank was struck by a car, just after he was injected with a drug your queens fear. Now he can't remember what happened, and he can barely stand without fainting."

"What..." Melony's voice quavered. "What did they do to him?"

Natalie looked unhappy. "Frank is short about three pints of blood. We think *all* of his blood was taken, and partially replaced. His headache is so severe, they seem to have taken more of his spinal fluid than was good for him."

Melony weaved drunkenly.

"On Frank's back, we found four stitched-up incisions. We showed them to an Earth physician, who said they look like large-bore biopsies of the liver and pancreas. Frank won't be doing sit-ups for a while."

They stopped walking while Melony worked on controlling her breathing. "In this country," she gasped, "government is not allowed to do this. We have recourse."

"Oh, yes, you have *democracy,*" said Natalie, not unkindly. "That explains the 17-page consent form with Frank's signature in 30 places. He woke up clutching it."

340

"Okay, I'll tell you." Melony sounded dead. "Frank's father had what Frank has. We were a match made in hell."

"Will you tell me the real father's name?"

"It will do you no good. His father's name was Steven Jones. I don't know where he was born, or even his middle name. I tried to find him once, when I was thinking about divorce. Steven was a musician, diagnosed as autistic, which was laughably wrong. Maybe you could find him, with your resources, but i don't think he wants to be found. In our culture, men are not anxious to admit paternity. If you *do* find him, please..." Melony's voice faded to a whisper. "Please ask him to call."

"Drat," said Natalie. "Any chance you are still fertile?"

Melony managed a wry smile. "No one has asked about my eggs since they went to the medical waste incinerator."

"Siblings?"

"My sister died last year, but she didn't have what you want. I have aunts and uncles and cousins, but none of them can see into their own minds. Only me and Frank and Steven."

Natalie pushed up her drooping sleeves. "This gift of self-insight, do you know how many Earthborn have it?"

"I was young when I met him," Melony said quietly. "I was too stupid to recognize the treasure. Now, I have a few test questions I try on strangers, but so far... so far, no luck. I'm afraid we might be the only Humans who can look inside."

They walked awhile. A minivan drove past, packed with children who peered out the window at the two women.

"I know someone who could look inside for a while," Melony offered. "But she lost it, and I doubt it would breed true."

"Who?"

"She was my only real friend, and you already know about her: Scarlet Pine, Tom's mother."

Natalie missed a step and stumbled.

"Scarlet's husband killed himself," Melony explained. "She blamed herself, and I did too. In the aftermath, her censor made her forget to feed Tom. When she realized she had starved her child, she felt so guilty, she nearly killed herself. Instead, she killed her censor, to be sure she never did it again. I saw the change, and for a few years, I had a real friend. But then one day, when Tom was a teenager, Scarlet's censor grew back overnight, strong as ever. Now, she denies it ever happened, and I don't think she can remember."

Natalie looked disappointed. "What you describe is rare, but it's not unknown for the censor to vanish temporarily after a trauma."

"Could Frank visit me, or at least phone?"

"We will not restrain him, but your queens probably will."

"Could I go with him?" Melony was pleading now. "You keep saying everyone is welcome to join you."

"You'd be welcome, but in your heart, you know Frank no longer needs his mother." The alien turned to look at Melony's husband, trailing the women dutifully. "You can join us, if you want to, but when you learn the price, I fear you will judge it too high."

Melony sagged. "Have you nothing to offer me?"

"Yes, Melony, I do have something to offer you. We will give your son what every man wants, and if your talent breeds true, you can reasonably expect 1,000 grandchildren."

Four days later

Springfield, MO

When Frank recovered enough to work, he came in to help Tom assemble the prototype polymer extruder.

The extruder was a Worm invention, their payment for Tom's robotic sentries.

While they worked, Luci strode coltishly about the shop in 3-inch heels with a 3-inch binder of OSHA regulations balanced on her head, learning to walk gracefully in Earth gravity. She glanced disapprovingly at Frank, who was struggling to bend an aluminum bracket. "Frank, have you ever considered physical exercise? Some people enjoy it."

Frank didn't seem to hear her.

Tom dropped his wrench and stood up. "Miss Dark, my office, now."

Two minutes later, in Tom's office, Luci said, "What?"

"Miss Dark, I have to ask you to stop insulting Frank."

"Why? You told us we should talk about the elephant."

"Not *every day.*" Tom looked exasperated. "Frank won't let you bully him forever. When he finally snaps, he will make drama, and you *know* how I feel about drama where I eat."

Luci smiled.

Tom scowled. "This is not funny. Frank is important to this business, and I should *not* have to explain common courtesy."

"How about you loan me a couple of your armed guards, so Frank and I can take a walk?"

Tom pressed a palm to his forehead. "Why do you want to do that?"

Luci's smile broadened. "Do you trust me?"

Tom walked around behind his desk and sat heavily. "That did not answer my question."

"Why, I believe you're right."

"Of course you can borrow the guards, whenever you want. Will you promise to stop insulting Frank?"

"No. Please order your guards to stay well back, so they can't eavesdrop."

"Miss Dark, please. Throw me a bone."

Luci gazed at him soulfully. "Don't you trust me?"

Tom slapped the intercom and summoned two guards.

"One more thing," Luci added. "May I use one of your pencils? The simple kind that writes with Six?"

Ten minutes later, Luci strode through the prototyping shop. As she passed Frank, she grabbed his arm and dragged him out the door.

The usual gaggle of picketers milled about the handicap parking spot in front of the building, so Luci led Frank out the back door and through the weeds. Two guards trailed.

Luci opened her holster, withdrew her pistol, and handed it to Frank. "So you can guard me properly. Also, I thought you might like to know what it feels like to be male, with a dick."

Frank gazed at her intently, then loosed a noisy fart. "Ahh," he sighed contentedly. "You were right. That felt like coming home."

Luci tried to look disapproving. "Do you know which end to point at the enemy?"

"Good point," said Frank. "I forgot the guards are behind us, but I imagine the wind will save them."

"I meant the pistol. The main thing to remember is: never point it at *me.*"

"Relax, Luci, I do hardware. Why are we out here?"

"We're out here so I can offer something to you, and *only* to you. If your coworkers find out, it might cause strife." As Luci talked, she produced a flat plastic box, smaller than a credit card but thicker. She rubbed her thumb across and slid out a tiny sheet of pink paper, penciled with her neat handwriting. She held it where Frank could see.

She was trying to communicate privately, under cover of their conversation. Frank focused on the pink paper, wondering what she wanted to tell him.

> You will eat less
> and exercise more.

Frank's eyes narrowed. "You're doing this wrong."

"Open your mouth."

"No."

Luci poked him, but not too hard. "Open up. You trust me."

Reluctantly, Frank opened his mouth. Luci popped in the little paper. It dissolved instantly and actually tasted pretty good, like cinnamon. Frank realized it was a paper-shaped breath mint. His tongue tingled. For a moment, he worried about the ink, but then he remembered pencils write with carbon.

"Human telescopes are better than ours." As Luci spoke, she slid out the next message.

> Drug I gave you
> was Forbidden Fruit.
> It stifles the censor

Frank glanced back at the trailing guards. "I'm not surprised."

Luci fed him the paper and slid out the next one.

> You did not cry.
> The censor is your bitch

Now Frank was more confused, but in an interesting way. "Do you know where we're going? Because I don't."

Luci poked the paper at his mouth, and Frank dutifully opened up. The cinnamon was intense. His tongue was getting warm.

"After we finish the sentries, we want to build a big telescope. We may not finish it in time, before we move to our colony, but you could finish it for us. We only want *you,* because of your special skills, and we don't want you to tell the others. It might cause drama." As Luci spoke, she slid out the next paper.

"I'm willing," said Frank. "Let's talk about compensation."

"I think we can meet your needs." This time, Luci ate the paper, then she slid out the last one.

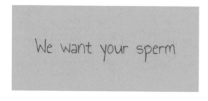

Frank stopped walking, and focused on his breathing for a while.

Luci popped the cinnamon paper into his gaping mouth, then tugged his arm to get him moving.

Frank recovered and sucked air over his burning tongue. "I look forward to you meeting my needs."

"Do you like turkey?"

"Turkey is not on my list of urgent needs."

"We decided to try it, though to us, turkeys appear grotesque. We would never breed something so oversized." She looked at Frank pointedly. "I bought a turkey baster. That's a big syringe, made for squirting turkey juice in the oven. Do you think we will need it?"

They walked in quiet contemplation awhile, as Frank reflected. "You know," he said thoughtfully, "it might be time to get back into shape. I think I'll start exercising."

Tom arrived at 7 AM and checked Sophie's whiteboard.

Don't forget Wednesday
is Natl. Secretary's Day

OSHA rules are for you.
Coffee does <u>NOT</u> count
as a fire extinguisher.

Sophie

He found Sophie manning the phone. "Where is Alice?"

"She quit." Sophie didn't seem upset.

"Crap!" Tom threw his coat on the floor. "Alice was the only one who knew most of the NLRB and FTC and CPSC and FMLA and ITAR and ROHS and REACH and FCC and ERISA and FLSA and OSHA and ACA and ADA and EEOC and EPA rules. Why did she quit?"

Sophie shrugged. "She left a two-word resignation letter."

"It will take *months* just to learn which rules apply to us!"

"Relying on Alice was never a good plan."

"Fuck!" Tom slammed his office door, pulled out a business card that was blank except for a phone number, and dialed it.

The phone was answered by the familiar voice of Dominick Tork. "Good morning, Mr. Pine. How are the sentries progressing?"

"What happened to Alice?"

"Ah, Alice, your foul-tempered receptionist. Regrettably, she decided to sue you."

Tom remained calm. "What happened to Alice?"

"She constructed a new legal theory," Dominick chortled. "The presence of a Worm male constitutes a *hostile workplace.*"

With effort, Tom kept his voice even. "What happened to Alice?"

"She claimed ambitious damages. In addition to the usual sum for hearing sexual comments, she demanded five percent of any future profits you might gain from dealing with the Worms, plus an additional penalty for calling her a *receptionist*. The penalty was rather large." Dominick seemed impressed.

"What happened to Alice?"

"Not to worry; Alice just checked into a hotel under a different name. I visited her to explain why suing you was inappropriate, and she decided to move to France. I'll be surprised if you have any future contact with her."

One day later
Springfield, MO
Equipment test

Tom arrived at 7 AM and found his chief administrator, Sophie, still manning the phones. He checked her whiteboard.

Leaving me presents
for Secretary's Day was
Not Appropriate

listening to Frank will
get you Fired

Your Boss

Tom closed his office door and stared longingly at his sealed bottles of precursor samples. Then he settled in and resumed his research into industrial chemical registration rules.

Two hours later, Luci knocked on his door. "We're ready to start."

"Go ahead without me." Tom waved helplessly at his computer. "These disclosures have to be certified by the CEO before the end of the quarter, and the website is slow."

Luci looked sympathetic. "Do you ever miss your dick?"

"That reminds me, I noticed you stopped teasing Frank. Thank you."

Luci closed the door.

Tom moved on to Page 347: *Rainfall drainage of secondary enclosing structures.*

Two hours later, as he waited for Page 419 to load, his office door slammed open.

"Help!" Luci squealed. "The catalyst tank is foaming!"

"Fuck!" Tom's chair fell over as he ran for the prototype shop.

The prototype extruder was fed by a prototype reactor, a 100-gallon stainless-steel cask where precursor chemicals reacted with a nickel-platinum mesh. The reactor was cooled by chilled-water tubes and equipped with a quartz window, which should have been blue, but instead showed ominous, swirling white and gray. Tom glanced at the pressure gauge. The needle was rising through 120 PSI. The vessel was rated for 200 PSI, and would burst at 300 PSI. He checked the thermometer. "Only 80 Fahrenheit, so it must be outgassing ethylene." He cracked the vent valve and sniffed. "Yep. The third-stage catalyst is poisoned."

Luci stared at the tank in dismay. "How could that happen?"

"Dunno, but new machines always find a way to surprise you." Tom cranked the reactor's chiller up to maximum. "In hindsight, skipping the Silicon test was not really that clever."

"No, not really," Luci agreed. "Will it explode?"

"No, it can't explode. When the pressure hits 200 PSI, the safety valve will open and vent ethylene. That's the gas you call, *4-2-A.*"

"4-2-A? Is that all?" Luci looked relieved. "We should open the windows and turn off anything that might spark."

Tom stared at the ominously brightening quartz window. "If we vent this much ethylene, we'll never dig out from under the paper."

Luci waved dismissively. "4-2-A is made by every tree. We use it to ripen fruit. Nothing in this room is more dangerous than lye."

Tom chuckled darkly. "I love that you think that matters. Where is everyone?"

"After the first hour, Frank and Sophie left to watch an EEOC compliance software demo. Buff is on the *Finger,* flushing our auxiliary heat sinks."

"Damn. So it's just..."

"You and me," Luci confirmed, "plus some hourly employees who could probably be helpful after only a few hours of instruction. How about we let it vent and don't tell anyone?"

"Crap." Tom stared at the rising pressure valve. "I wish we'd put in that dump tray."

"Tom, venting 4-2-A is a nuisance, but it's hardly a hazard."

"Yes, it *is* a hazard, because our security guards are retired soldiers with chemical warfare sensors."

"So what? 4-2-A is everywhere. It won't trigger a poison sensor."

"Yes, it will, if the sensor is a soldier's nose. Ethylene smells sweet." Tom paced around the tank, searching for options. "Civilians might think it's just flowers, but those old veterans will suspect a war gas and storm in here. Then they will file a report, which someone will read and see his big chance. Worm chemical plants will become an environmental cause, and within six months, the government will be funding conferences."

"Dammit!" Luci kicked the concrete floor. "Does *every* mishap rally a looting mob in your foul culture?"

"We're also an *old* culture," Tom said absently, watching the gauges. "Parasites have filled every niche." The temperature held steady at 80 Fahrenheit, but pressure was accelerating through 140 PSI. "We have to open the drain tap to get the precursors off the catalyst before it hits 200 PSI. It should be about 50 gallons."

Luci looked at the floor. "Fifty gallons will run down the hall and out the front door onto the protesters' feet. They will love that."

Tom glanced at the stack of empty five-gallon buckets that pile up wherever bulk liquids are used. "Can you hide from the people who... who we are hiding from, without triggering yourself?"

"I can't hide from your EPA." Luci dashed to the buckets. "But I can help *you* hide."

Tom started yanking open cupboards. "Don't forget, the precursor mix is alkali enough to clear a stopped drain. If it touches your skin, it will burn." He found the rubber gloves and pulled on a pair.

Luci was already under the tank. "The tap is too close to the floor. I have to tilt the bucket and hold it while you work the valve."

"Miss Dark, stand up. Neither of us wants to look back on this day and reminisce about *you* hauling 60-pound buckets of caustic liquid while I turned a valve." Tom tossed her a pair of rubber gloves. "Where are the emergency masks?"

"The masks are right where your queens say they should be, down the hall in the clearly-labeled safety closet with their filter elements stored in sealed bags."

"Well, the mask wouldn't keep it off my hair anyway." Tom looked around and picked up a clipboard. "Hold this in front of my face while you work the valve. Please try not to spray me."

Five seconds later, as the pressure gauge rose through 180 PSI, she said, "Ready?"

Tom tilted the bucket to fit under the tap, then turned his face away. "Go!"

The bucket thrummed as caustic liquid sprayed in under pressure. Tom heard it splatter onto the clipboard beside his ear.

"Full!" she barked, and the spray subsided.

Tom lugged the bucket into the corner, then tilted in a new one. "Ready!"

The spray gushed in with an acrid smell, splattering against the clipboard. Tom wondered which government agency's compliance form was protecting him, but it was too close to his face for him to focus.

"Full!"

By the fourth bucket, they had the rhythm.

At the 13th bucket, the stream petered out. Luci dropped the clipboard and bolted for the safety shower.

"What are you..." Tom began.

Luci yanked off her shirt and turned the spray on herself, soaking her intricately-engineered bra.

"Holy shit!" Tom stared at her left arm. Starting just above the glove, her skin had turned bright red. "Why didn't you tell me?"

Luci winced as she pulled off the glove. "We hit 190 PSI. It was not the time to be delicate."

Tom stared at the clipboard and Luci's blue shirt, both lying on the concrete, splattered with caustic chemicals. "That's the hand you used to hold the clipboard. Why didn't any splash on me?"

Luci didn't answer, just sprayed cool water on her angry welts.

20 minutes later, Tom and Luci sat on the capped buckets, sharing a can of cashews and watching the pressure gauge, now falling through 40 PSI.

Luci looked at her arm, shiny pink under a film of cortisone cream. "I hope this doesn't scar."

Tom seemed pensive. "Why did you stop teasing Frank?"

Luci grabbed a handful of nuts. "He convinced me he really doesn't feel insults. After that, teasing him seemed pointless."

"That's not the answer I was hoping for." For three minutes, Tom munched and pondered. "Do Worms have clear rules for what constitutes a good woman?"

"She builds good children."

"Is that all? Is motherhood your only standard for a good woman?"

Luci chuckled. "My dad said he knew Mom was a good woman when he misjudged his whiskey. He got stupid drunk with her, while she stayed sober, but the next day, he didn't feel like an idiot."

"He got drunk while she stayed sober," Tom mused. "But afterward, he didn't feel stupid. That's a rare woman."

"Yep. It's a high bar."

356

Tom stared at the splattered mess under the catalyst tank. "You're a mass of contradictions."

"No, Tom, I'm not. It just looks that way." Luci leaned back against the wall, careful not to touch her burned arm, and her mouth opened into her famous, heartbreak smile. "I did it again. I held open the jaws and took the pain."

"What jaws?"

"It's just an idiom." Luci gazed at her angry red welts. "It means I did the right thing."

"Do you still have those paper breath mints?"

Luci rooted through her silk pouch, then handed them over.

"My stomach hurts." Tom hunched over his knees.

30 seconds later, when he hadn't spoken, Luci looked concerned. "Did you try to eat the fruitcake?"

Tom straightened, hands in his lap. Luci looked down and saw he held a pink paper breath mint with a pencil-scrawled message.

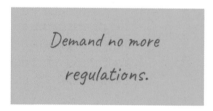

Luci shook her head.

Tom slipped the pink paper into his mouth, and revealed the next message.

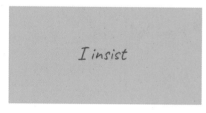

Luci sighed.

Tom tucked the second paper into his mouth and puckered.

"This is just too dangerous," Luci said reluctantly. "I thought we could tolerate your queen's interference, so long as it didn't target us directly, but I'm nearly triggered. If we can't get total exemption from *all* regulation, we're taking the sentry project to China."

"I understand. Production has slowed to a crawl, because only Alice knew most of the NLRB and FTC and CPSC and FMLA and ITAR and ROHS and REACH and FCC and ERISA and FLSA and OSHA and ACA and ADA and EEOC and EPA rules."

"Pfft. Your queens don't *want* you to follow those ridiculous rules. They want you to break them, so they can hold you for ransom, but that's over. They have to stop."

"I understand," Tom repeated. "I just can't agree. Eventually, you will get your colony and leave. After you're gone, the regulators will take vengeance on *me*. I need a lasting relationship with you, to protect me after you leave. How about you buy a lifetime warranty?"

"It won't work," said Luci. "If I buy a warranty, I buy your labor, but I don't buy *you*. You're not *my thing*, so I won't be triggered if your queens hold you for ransom. Sorry."

"I was afraid of that. We couldn't do business, if every long-term contract obliged you to defend me." Tom brushed the cashew dust off his fingers and stood up. "Well, if you won't defend something unless you recognize it as, *your thing*, then I guess we'll just have to make me *your thing*."

Two days later, Tom's employees jammed into the lunch room. In front, technicians hunched over their pads, playing *Sorority House Massacre 3* with the wood-chipper bonus pack. Behind them, the assemblers huddled over a single screen, watching *White Body-builders Get Run Down By Hybrid Cars.* In back, the salesmen chatted.

Up in the corner, the television showed a still photo of a grinning Oriental girl with a missing front tooth. She looked about eight, wearing a cheerleader uniform. Her picture was captioned, *ANOTHER ONE VANISHED.*

Tom counted heads, then looked around for a gavel. He couldn't find one, so he chaired the meeting to order with a folding chair.

The murmur subsided. The technicians paused their game and looked attentive.

"We work with violent aliens," Tom began. "They don't respect our laws. Does anyone wish to pretend they are outraged?"

Apparently, no one wished to pretend.

"The aliens are negotiating to buy 10,000 square miles of government-owned land for their colony, which will have a security system built by *us*, to guard the violent aliens from our government. Does anyone wish to pretend they didn't know?"

Around the lunchroom, Tom's employees glanced at each other.

"As most of you heard, Alice tried to sue me. She filed the papers, then changed her mind and moved to France. Since then, has she contacted any of you?"

Nobody moved.

"Her mother calls me every day," Tom added softly. "She asks if I've heard from her daughter. Sometimes, she cries."

Around the quiet lunchroom, expressions turned nauseous.

"Alice tried to sue me, so she was murdered. Does anyone wish to pretend they don't understand?"

If anyone wished to pretend, they didn't wish to admit it.

Five days later
Springfield, MO
An old friend visits

Sophie walked into Tom's office, plunked herself into his guest chair, and grinned.

"What?"

Sophie waved at the 7-foot painting that dominated Tom's small office, *Fluffer* alone on her park bench, waiting. "I never liked that painting, but now I do, because she's wearing clothes."

Tom's male employees hadn't needed much time to adapt to the *Pinup Girls are Allowed* rule.

"That's not why you're grinning," Tom observed. "Spill it."

Sophie's grin widened. "With all the police and protesters, this slum is now safe enough for your ex-girlfriend."

"You mean…"

360

"Yep. Donna Damper will arrive tomorrow at 9 AM to inspect us and verify our OSHA compliance." Sophie stood up, leaned across her boss's desk, and smacked him a high five.

Tom settled back into his chair. "Does she know?"

"Nope. Can I tell her?"

"Hell no; I want to tell her myself, but I'll let you watch, if you're nice to me all day today."

"Oh, all right," Sophie grumped. "I'll be nice for one day."

"Ah, life is good." Tom stretched, and scratched his chest. "You can start by getting me coffee. You know how I like it."

"Get your own coffee. I'm not your servant."

"I didn't think you could do it." Tom leaned back, rested his feet on his desk, and sighed contentedly. "Tomorrow will be a good day. I want you at Halliburton at 9 AM to help them with their Mark 2 loggers. I expect it will take you all day."

"Not tomorrow. You told me I could watch you with your ex."

"Shoo." Tom waved her away. "You're ugly when you pretend to be stupid."

Sophie reddened. "Oh, all right. I'll get your damn coffee."

"Too late. If I see you here tomorrow morning, I'll put you on audit duty for a month."

"Damn you! Why do you have to be such a cast-iron prick?"

Tom leafed through a pile of structural test reports.

Sophie sat in his guest chair, fuming.

Tom glanced up at her. "Why are you still here? Close the door behind you."

The next morning, Donna Damper arrived 40 minutes late. She was met at the door by Frank Drummer, carrying a rolled-up poster.

"Hello, Frank." Donna surveyed Frank's obese body.

"Hi, Donna. Remember that time we made out in front of everybody?" Frank leered. "I know you were just trying to make Tom jealous, but I really enjoyed it, because none of the other girls would touch me. Thank you again."

Donna's nose wrinkled.

Frank unrolled the poster. "You always find things we're doing wrong, so we've been looking forward to your visit. In fact, I wrote you a poem." He taped the poster to the wall.

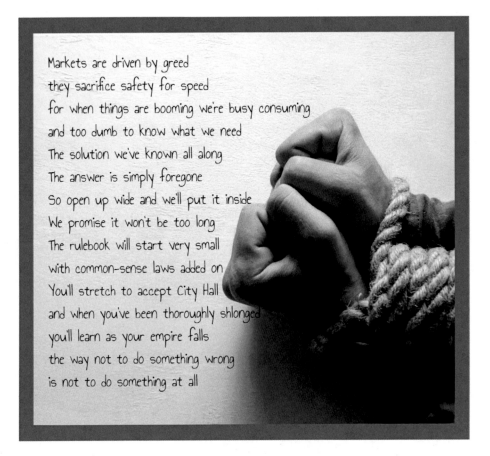

Markets are driven by greed
they sacrifice safety for speed
for when things are booming we're busy consuming
and too dumb to know what we need
The solution we've known all along
The answer is simply foregone
So open up wide and we'll put it inside
We promise it won't be too long
The rulebook will start very small
with common-sense laws added on
You'll stretch to accept City Hall
and when you've been thoroughly shlonged
you'll learn as your empire falls
the way not to do something wrong
is not to do something at all

Tom walked in. "Hi, Donna. How's life?"

"Quite good, without you in it."

Tom laughed. "Are you *still* mad I dumped you? Didn't you get some relief from taking my money? My personal favorite was the $300 you dinged me for the missing silicosis warning on a bag of sand."

"I'd love to reminisce," said Donna, "but not really. Why don't you just hand me off to your girlfriend Sophie, like last time?"

"Oh, no. This time, I'm handling your inspection myself."

Donna looked suspicious.

Tom looked happy. "Of course you know, we work with the Worms."

"Yes," said Donna. "Spaceships landing on the roof was a big clue."

"We're building their security system."

"Very nice. Shall we start with your machine shop? I'm anxious to see the changes you've made to comply with this year's revisions."

Tom stepped forward into Donna's personal space.

She stepped back. "Don't you dare."

Tom dared.

Donna retreated until her back struck Frank's poster. "What do you think you're doing?"

Tom pinned her against the poster, flattening her breasts as he leaned forward to whisper into her ear. "Things have changed between us," he breathed. "Now, if you interfere with my business, the aliens will kill you."

"You monster! You've got an erection."

"Oh, yes." Tom exhaled onto Donna's neck.

"Aren't you cocky," Donna hissed. "Well, Mister Pine, when you've finished building their sentries, your Worms will *leave,* and I will still be here. Don't think I'm not keeping score."

"I know you'll keep score." Tom pressed into her, and rubbed up and down. "So I offered the aliens a lifetime warranty."

"Nice try, but we already thought of that. Worms are not triggered by enforcement action against their trading partners, so you are bluffing."

"You didn't let me finish. I want to finish." Tom breathed harder as he pressed her into the wall.

She growled. "You will pay for this."

"No, I don't think I will. The aliens didn't buy a lifetime warranty. Instead, they bought 20 percent of my stock."

Donna stiffened.

"Now, my company is partly *their* company." Tom nuzzled her neck. "When you hold it for ransom, do you think they will just kill you, or will they knock down the OSHA building?"

"So you think you can ignore the safety rules? Just throw me out?"

"Oh, no, I've set aside three hours for your inspection, because I want to hear your *suggestions.* I might even agree with them." Tom reached around and cupped Donna's butt cheek. "Welcome to the consensual sector."

"Fuck you." Donna shoved him away and ran out the door.

"Damn," said Frank. "That was *hot.* Let's phone in some more anonymous tips, and see if we can get her to come back."

One week later
The White House Theater

President Mirror and Secretary Siphon munched popcorn and sipped expensive whisky while they watched the Australian Foreign Minister's last minutes on Earth.

The video was less than a day old, but had already gone viral on the Blue Star *Worm Stomp* channel at YouTube. The Blue Star Program had been negotiated by Kitty Siphon to address the problem of politically-motivated deplatforming, and it had been a smashing success. A Blue Star account could be created by any federal employee of level GS-15 or higher, and could only be deplatformed by the Blue Star Panel. The Blue Star Panel contained 11 members: one representative from each of the six major races and five main genders. The panel made all its decisions by majority vote, so the problem of political deplatforming was solved.

On the screen, the middle-aged Foreign Minister's skin looked gray. He sat behind his desk, eyes downcast. "I should tell the story," he mumbled. "Maybe someone will learn from my mistake."

Kitty relaxed in her custom-fitted doeskin seat and munched organic saffron truffle popcorn. "I can't believe this guy actually tried the forbidden fruit. I don't know if he was brave or stupid."

The president sipped his thousand-dollar bourbon. "Turned out he was stupid."

On the screen, the foreign minister smiled wanly. "The Worms offered to take me up into orbit to try the forbidden fruit. Honestly, I was mostly interested in the ride, but I tried the drug, God help me."

Kitty shuddered. "This is creepy."

"They picked me up in the Outback in one of their medium-sized spaceships, a six-seater. We were escorted by a smaller spaceship, a two-seater that never landed, just circled us keeping overwatch. I was strapped into the right front seat, then we took off vertically. We just flew straight up, then South over Antarctica, 200 miles high. The view was spectacular, and the pilot said this orbit would bring us back around to Australia by the time the drug wore off. It was my last chance to change my mind, and I should have taken it."

Kitty and Mirror watched, rapt.

"The forbidden fruit is not a fruit," the foreign minister explained. "It's a clear liquid in a glass vial. The alien drew it into a syringe and shot it into my arm. The intelligence briefing was correct; the needle didn't look like steel. I think it was some kind of white plastic. Supposedly, that means the drug would react with iron, but I don't know. I just know what it made me see."

Kitty grabbed the president's hand. She knew what was coming.

"Angie, I love you. Tell the kids I moved to America." The Australian foreign minister opened his desk drawer and pulled out a black pistol. He looked at the camera. "Don't try the forbidden fruit." Then he jammed the muzzle into his mouth and blew his mind.

The president seemed excited. "Didn't you notice?"

"Notice what?"

"What he didn't say!" President Mirror bounced in his seat. "He didn't say anything about a rendezvous! The Worm must have had the forbidden fruit *on board* at takeoff!"

"Ooh!"

"I'll tell the secret squirrels! The next time some idiot volunteers to try the forbidden fruit, we will get our sample."

"This is so exciting," Kitty breathed. "Do the eunuchs really think they can make a vaccine?"

"No, but they can probably make a blood test, maybe even urine."

"Then we should start training people to accept monthly screening."

"Say it's to protect our little girls," President Mirror commanded. "Pretty soon, that will be credible."

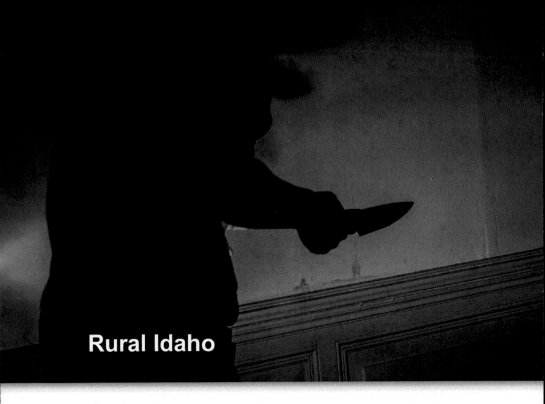

Rural Idaho

"Make sure Private Pure drinks enough water, or he might have another heat stroke."

The whole platoon guffawed. They'd spent all night prepping this ambush, and they'd been hiding in their holes since before dawn, passing the time by chatting on the common channel.

"That was not a heat stroke," Pure insisted. "I had an epiphany."

They were reminiscing about their search for the forbidden fruit in a patch of empty desert that had been visited by a Worm. Pure had interrupted the search by speaking gibberish for five minutes, then collapsing in a petit mal seizure.

"It was a sacred moment," Private Parts intoned. "The Apostle Paul had his epiphany on the road to Damascus, and Private Pure had his on the road to Reno. When you talked to God, did He command you to stop jacking off?"

Everyone laughed.

"Seriously," Parts added. "If you had an epiphany, what did you learn?"

368

"I dunno," said Pure. "By the next day, the details had faded like a dream. But for a while, my eyes were opened, and I could see clearly for the first time."

"Sounds like you just nutted," Private Parts offered. "When men get that moment of clarity, I try to be in the bathroom."

"Pure's heat stroke wasn't funny," said Canny. "He badmouthed the Native Americans, and said we only criticize the white settlers because they make us feel like pussies in comparison. If he hadn't been delirious, it would have been a serious diversity offense."

Which is why I'm going along with your retarded heat-stroke theory, Canny did not add. *Pure obviously found the forbidden fruit.*

Corporal Credulous sniggered. "Sounds like Pure found some peyote."

More laughing.

"Ha ha," said Pure. "What does peyote even look like?"

"Dunno," said Credulous. "Some kind of cactus."

"Just before my epiphany, I got poked by a cactus spine. Could that have been peyote? Would that, like, inject it straight into my blood and give me a super high?"

"Sounds plausible," said Credulous. "Hey, that must be the target."

They all watched as a black SUV pulled off the country road. The driver's door opened, and a man in a black suit emerged.

Sargent Stentorian pulled out his pad and ran the license plate. "That's a state government car."

"I recognize him," said Pure. "That's the governor of Idaho."

"The *governor?* Are you sure?" Corporal Canny dialed his scope up to its maximum 9X zoom.

"I recognize him," Pure insisted. "My parents voted for him."

"Quiet," Sargent Stentorian growled. "The Worms offered to let that asshole try the forbidden fruit, and he *accepted.*"

"L.T., did the secret squirrels mention the target was the governor?"

"Negative, but it doesn't change the mission."

"Jesus Christ," said Canny. "We can't mug the fucking *governor.*"

"Follow the plan," the L.T. snapped. "Don't forget this mission is *vital.* The forbidden fruit is like PCP juiced with meth, only worse, and the Worms want to give it to our kids. Maybe the doctors can make a vaccine, if they get a pure sample, which only *we* can obtain. It's a proud moment for me, unless you fuck it up."

Canny frowned.

"Radar contact," the L.T. murmured. "Two bogeys incoming, ETA six minutes. Get the truck rolling, and everyone check your pigeons."

The pigeons were pocket-sized homing drones. Each pigeon was programmed with its home coordinates, and when released, would fly home with its two-ounce payload. The homing pigeons were designed to return tissue samples to a field lab for fast genetic identification of targets who were dead, or should be.

Now, everyone in the platoon carried one. Canny pulled his out and pushed its *TEST* button. The LED flashed green, which meant it was charged up enough to reach its programmed home.

"I see the bogey!" Corporal Credulous sounded excited. "It's a six-seater, green, coming in from four o'clock."

"Calm down," said Stentorian. "Watch for the wingman."

"There's the wingman," Canny called. "Two o'clock, it looks smaller."

"Stay in your holes," Stentorian growled. "If you pop out before the countdown, you might see what your mama does with me. You'll never be the same."

In the distance, a brown UPS truck approached.

The six-seat spacecraft was painted green. The governor shaded his eyes as he watched it descend. He hadn't noticed the approaching UPS truck.

The green spaceship landed in a cloud of dust. The governor walked toward it as a green hatch opened and a brown-haired Worm male climbed out.

Stentorian: "Three, two…"

The brown-haired Worm extended his hand, then he sprayed red blood in three directions and collapsed among the echoes of simultaneous 6.5-mm *kabooms*.

"GO GO GO!"

Everyone jumped out of their holes and raced forward wearing brown UPS uniforms. Canny felt slightly ridiculous charging into battle wearing shorts.

The governor looked at the dead Worm in disbelief, then the UPS truck screeched to a halt beside him. Lieutenant Leaden jumped out with Corporal Credulous and wrestled the governer to the ground.

Canny was the first to reach the spacecraft, followed by Pure. They fairly dove through the open hatch and ransacked the interior, throwing out cushions and coffee cups.

"Got it!" Pure raised a silver case in triumph.

"The pigeon," Canny barked. "Hurry up!"

"The package is too big for the pigeon." Pure popped open the silver case. "It's got a vial and an empty syringe with a white needle, just like they said." He tucked the syringe into his pocket, then held up the vial of clear liquid. "Wow. The actual forbidden fruit."

"Get the fuck out," Stentorian bellowed. "The wingman is diving!"

The platoon scattered, leaving the governor on the asphalt road with his wrists and ankles zip-tied.

"Go!" Pure slid the vial into the homing pigeon. "You can't help."

Canny hesitated, then bolted.

Later, the drone footage showed what happened. Corporal Canny was 100 feet away, running flat out when the homing pigeon flew from the Worm spacecraft's open hatch, tumbling end over end. The clever little drone righted itself in midair, wobbled, then raced away north as the Worm wingman passed overhead at 200 knots and 50 feet altitude.

Private Pure was actually in the spacecraft hatchway at the moment the Worm wingman aligned his exhaust nozzle to do what the technical eunuchs thought he would, and the military analysts thought he wouldn't.

Based on the depth of exhaust implantation, plus the craft's estimated 900-kilogram mass and its brief, three-gravity forward acceleration, the airborne wingman must have exhausted approximately 40 grams of iron vapor over 0.3 seconds with a velocity of roughly 200 kilometers per second, carrying an estimated 1.6 gigajoules of kinetic energy.

373

The stream of hypervelocity iron vapor transected the grounded alien craft and triggered a secondary explosion of roughly two gigajoules, obliterating the target vehicle and incidentally killing the governor of Idaho plus three members of the assault team.

Fortunately, the homing pigeon survived the blast and reached the recovery area intact, carrying 4.3 cc of clear liquid presumed to be the forbidden fruit.

The secondary explosion damaged the wingman craft. By the time its pilot regained control, the surviving members of the assault team had reached cover in nearby civilian homes, and the Worm was unable to distinguish them from the local populace.

Thus, the mission succeeded, validating the command decision to eschew anti-aircraft weapons and preserve the appearance of civilian vigilante action.

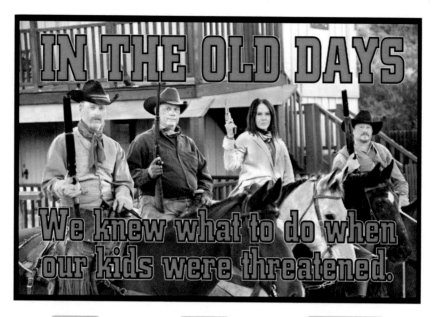

Comments. Please respect the <u>forum rules</u>.

Pokemom Four hours ago
We can deal with the Worm problem easily. They aren't actually tough at all, when they are confronted. We just need a little more testosterone.

LawFareForU Four hours ago
Testosterone is what CAUSED the Worm problem.

Pokemom Four hours ago
Testosterone is like lawyers. The enemy has it, so we need it.

LawFareForU Four hours ago
Please stop with the lawyer jokes. They are offensive.

Moby Duck Three hours ago
Heh. What do you call 50 dead Worms on the bottom of the ocean?

S. Quiblee Three hours ago
A GOOD START!

Page 1 2

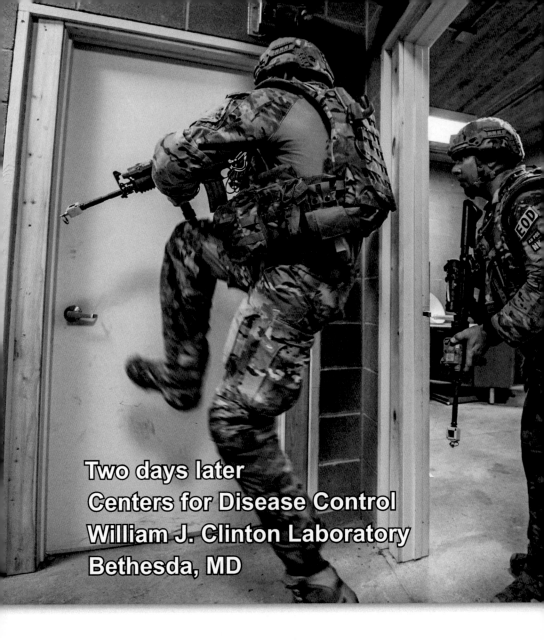

**Two days later
Centers for Disease Control
William J. Clinton Laboratory
Bethesda, MD**

Lola walked down a row of SPIFE-Touch electrophoresis machines until she found the source of the beeping, a stainer sensor alarm. She was just calling up the diagnostic menu when the exit door burst open and the lab was stormed by a dozen armed soldiers.

Lola was not as surprised as you might think, because this was the only lab considered secure enough to perform congressional STD tests.

An angry young man in camo fatigues stuck his rifle in Lola's face. "We paid *four lives* for that sample. Where the fuck do you get off telling us it was just *salt water?*"

The angry young soldier's breast pocket said, *CANNY.* He hadn't specified *which* sample, but Lola hypothesized he meant the one that arrived in an armored truck and was carried in by six athletic men in black suits with submachine guns who hung around awhile to flirt with the lab techs.

Ten older men in civilian clothes followed the soldiers into the room and fanned out among the machines, glancing over the status displays.

Lola picked up a blank mass-spec report and offered it to the angry soldier. "Here. Make your sample be whatever you want."

He lifted his rifle higher. "I lost my *best friend.* Do you want to join him right now?"

Lola checked her watch. "It's almost 10 AM, so I've already told 40 people they have cancer, and my estrogen patch fell off." She tapped the end of his barrel. *"This* doesn't frighten me."

The angry soldier grimaced. Then he lowered his rifle and squeezed his eyes shut. "Fuck! It was for *nothing.* Fucking salt water."

"Not quite," said Lola. "It also had some buffers. I knew you guys were excited, so I sent a lab tech out to some local drug stores. I thought it might be contact-lens solution, but it turned out your sample matched CVS-brand wound wash. It comes in a spray can, so it stays sterile."

"Four people died for *wound wash?*"

"Pfft." Lola waved dismissively. "Nobody uses sterile wound wash for wounds. It's used to reconstitute freeze-dried drugs for injection."

A female soldier walked up behind the angry one and rested a hand on his shoulder. "Are you *sure* the syringe was empty?"

"Pure knew the mission," the angry soldier snapped. "If the syringe had something in it, *he would have fucking said so.*"

Tom's office door opened to admit Sophie's head. "There's a man here to see you. I think he's a code inspector."

"Ooh!" Tom brightened.

The city code inspector was a dapper man in a blue tie. He was measuring the height of the lobby door handle when Tom and Sophie walked in.

"I think you're confused," said Sophie. "We don't oomph."

Tom held his hand over Sophie's mouth. "Don't spoil my fun."

She looked cross.

"I'm Tom Pine, the owner. I'm pleased to see you." Tom extended his hand.

The code inspector looked doubtful, but he shook the offered hand. "I understand you're installing a water fountain."

Sophie scowled: "How did you know?"

"We received an anonymous tip," the code inspector said mildly. "You should have applied for a permit."

"I improved my building without your permission," Tom admitted. "Will you punish me harshly?"

The code inspector smiled. "We don't like to say, *punish.*"

"That's very gracious, but if you don't threaten to punish me, why would I pay attention to your suggestions?"

The code inspector's smile never wavered, though his eyes narrowed. "We like to think you're a law-abiding citizen who *wants* to be in compliance."

"Ah, is that what you like to think? Let's go have a look." Tom walked away.

The inspector followed Tom and Sophie down a narrow hallway lined with seventies-era wood paneling. When they turned a corner, the code inspector's jaw malfunctioned and fell open.

Someone had hung a framed picture of a ballerina, posed with all the grace and beauty you expect from a ballerina, provided you expect her to be showing her boobs.

The code inspector pointed to the topless ballerina, and his jaw came back to life, working like a fish. "You can't…. This is a *workplace!*" He glared at Sophie. "You *permit* this?"

Sophie looked annoyed. "Tom doesn't want my permission."

"I have it on good authority that God intended ballet to be topless," said Tom. "Does she violate a code?"

"Well, no," the code inspector admitted. "I mean, I'll have to check to be sure. She is… she is *inappropriate.*"

"Yes, that makes her hotter." Tom pointed to the new water fountain, already installed in the hall outside the lunchroom. "There it is."

The inspector tore his eyes off the ballerina and took a moment to compose himself. Then he gazed somberly at the water fountain. "This connects to your drain, so I'm afraid you'll have to perform a drainage impact study."

Tom looked amused. "A *drainage impact study?* How much do you think that might cost?"

"Typically, a drainage impact study can be performed for a few thousand dollars, and takes about three months." The inspector glanced at the ballerina again, then peeked behind the fountain. "Since you didn't get a permit or an interim inspection, I'm afraid you'll have to remove this paneling to verify the compliance of your plumbing. Also, any other plumbing and wiring inside this wall will have to be brought up to the current code."

"No," said Tom, "I think I'll leave it."

"Mister Pine, it was not a suggestion. If you don't bring yourself into compliance, we will be forced to take further action."

"Bring myself into compliance." Tom enunciated the words slowly, tasting each one. "I'm going to enjoy not doing that.*"*

"Ah, you're one of those." The code inspector sighed. "I feel I must warn you; this process ends with you bankrupt."

"Actually," said Tom, "this process ends with you dead, and me pissing on your grave, if anyone can find it."

The code inspector blinked.

"Damn." Tom punched the wall. "I wanted to make this last longer. But when I get that close, I can't stop."

The inspector looked to Sophie. "Can you talk some sense into him?"

Sophie laughed. "Probably not. This company is 20-percent owned by the aliens."

The inspector blanched.

"You really should have asked around," Sophie added. "You're lucky the aliens aren't here now." She looked at the ceiling. "Did you hear something? Maybe one just landed."

The code inspector hurried for the exit, glancing at the ballerina as he passed. "I'll be in touch."

"No, you won't," Tom called after him.

"That was fun," Sophie admitted. "Someone tipped him off, though, which means we have a saboteur."

"Relax," said Tom. "The anonymous tipster was me."

Join the Worms
Cry all the time

Lunchtime

Sophie drove the older alien, Natalie, to the zoo.

On the way, they passed a billboard-sized highway sign flashing something about a 10-year-old girl and a white Honda Accord. Natalie watched the sign sweep past. "What was that?"

"Amber Alert. That's what those signs were built for, but it turned out men don't kidnap as many kids as we thought, so the Amber Alert signs mostly gave us driving advice, until lately. Now, we get kidnapped-girl alerts every week. Something changed." Sophie eyed the alien.

Natalie looked troubled, and they drove the rest of the way in silence.

At the zoo, their two bodyguards were joined by three local uniforms. All five followed the two women to the otter pool.

Wet weasels wrestled. Dry children stared at Natalie, until they were picked up by their nervous parents. The children seemed fascinated by Natalie's mysterious cheek tattoos. Their parents seemed more interested in her holster.

Sophie was glad the holster's threat was credible, because Natalie was barely five feet tall and couldn't weigh 90 pounds.

The day was cool, but Natalie was not. Sophie laid a palm on the little alien's sweating forehead. "Do you feel sick?"

"No," said the alien. "I just feel what you would feel, if you expected to be murdered."

"Yeah, well, blame yourself, and try to enjoy this place, because if you don't improve your image, you probably can't come back."

Ten minutes of every news hour was devoted to Worm atrocities. In the latest example, a woman with alien tattoos had tripped over a skateboard, then she beat the skateboard's 12-year-old owner into a coma. The Worm then fled, the newsreader intoned, as the television showed old footage of Natalie's boat lifting off.

"I *am* improving my image," Natalie replied. "I'm coming here, so these people can see me with their own eyes."

"You have to do more. You have to show us what you really are."

"No, child. The more virtuous we appear, the more you despise us." Natalie watched the otters squabble over a dead fish. "You don't hate us because we look bad. You hate us because we make *you* look bad. That is the only sin you cannot forgive."

"Very insightful," Sophie allowed. "Do you understand our nukes have enough range to reach your moral high ground?"

"I understand we cannot wake a man who feigns sleep. Our only hope is to stick with what we do well."

"You aren't so helpless," Sophie argued. "Plenty of people are saying the Worm atrocities are fake. It's pretty obvious, since the bad guys don't have spaceships, but you have to help. You have to support the people who defend you."

"Pfft. Everyone knows those attacks are fake. Your queens are doing what you hired them to do, lying just plausibly enough to let you feign belief and hide your real motive."

"Dammit, you–"

"Save your breath, child. In a contest of lies, we are hopelessly out-classed. The kids spent *weeks* planning their First-Contact prank, and hours carving Buffalo's fake penis. Then they half spoiled it by giggling. Oh, wow, that's clever." Natalie pointed up at a billboard.

Buffalo offered his grace
Promised his sheep his embrace
Then dangled a cock
that panicked the flock
and punked the whole
damned human race

Sophie looked up to see a billboard towering over the zoo, big enough to be seen from the Interstate. "That is not *clever;* it is *sophisticated*, and a year ago, it would have been public obscenity."

"I like it." Natalie produced a small camera and snapped a picture.

"I suppose you want to show that to Buff?"

"Oh, yes. He will love it."

"Well, we *certainly* wouldn't want to deny Buff whatever he wants," Sophie growled. "But that billboard wasn't put there to be cute; it was put there to inflame Christians. I can't believe you traveled all the way to Earth, then when you finally arrived, the *first* thing you did was mock the only Humans who won't admit they want you dead. Sometimes, you are staggeringly obtuse."

"Yes, Christians are certainly polite. That's why we taunted them. Let's go to Borneo and see a tiger." Natalie unfolded her map and rotated it, then rotated it again.

Eventually, they chose the path through Africa, beside the Snake House. "Ooh, look." Natalie nodded toward a short man with an ugly face.

"Do you think he's up to something?" Sophie glanced back at the guards.

"No, but isn't he pretty?"

Sophie's brow furrowed. "How can you ask that?"

Natalie turned to follow the short, ugly man's progress. "Don't you think he's well proportioned? And he has such a strong bearing, the way he carries himself."

"Oh my God." Sophie halted. "You adjusted your brain. You *changed* what you're attracted to! How did you do it? Wait, don't tell me; I already know. You killed the mental monkey that recognizes *ugly.*"

"Not quite." Natalie showed her palm to the guards, who reluctantly held their place while the women retreated beyond earshot. "It's the hexagon," Natalie whispered, pointing to her tattooed cheek.

Sophie's frown deepened into a scowl.

Natalie grinned. "I love feeding you clues. It reminds me of New Orleans. I took a swamp tour and threw dead chickens to an alligator."

"You did nothing," Sophie snapped. "It's just another stupid side effect. You recognize everyone as your own child, and what mother doesn't think her son is handsome?"

Natalie blew a raspberry. "I hoped this one would take you longer."

Sophie watched the short, homely man turn a corner, out of sight. "Beauty is inherently relative. If *everyone* is beautiful, then *no one* is beautiful."

"That is surely true, but beauty need not be defined by trivia. To me, faces seem no more different than brands of beer. I can distinguish between beers, and even have a preference, but mostly I just love beer. Hey!" Natalie pointed. "That monkey has a blue butt."

"So to you, the world is ankle deep in beer?"

"Our world, yes," the alien said sourly. "Yours, not so much."

Sophie didn't have to ask. "You like beer, but not beer bellies?"

"Correct. Beauty is sound structure, and I should not have told you this." Natalie sighed. "It's just so hard to be careful all the time, and you would probably puzzle it out anyway."

"Oh my God," said Sophie. "You don't see Luci like we do. No wonder she... *Oh my God.* Luci thinks her looks are nothing special!"

"To us, Luci appears beautiful in the way *any* healthy daughter appears beautiful. She is popular with children, but once they come of age and face the burning bush, they see her appearance as nothing more than average."

"Luci looks *average*," Sophie marveled. "But not even you could say that about Buff."

"No, child, I could not." The old Worm touched Sophie's hand. "Poor Buffalo was raised in the swarm by neglectful parents who let him grow tall. To us, he appears unsound. No woman would have him."

"That is ridiculous."

"Child, would you bind yourself to a man whose knees and hips will surely fail, reducing him to a crawling beggar before your children come of age?"

Sophie's jaw dropped.

"Buffalo chose his profession wisely, building spacecraft. If he had spent his life on the ground, he would already be trapped in a chair. Our world pulled us down so hard. We try to replace our joints with metal hinges, but they all fail at their attachment to the bone."

Sophie's mouth moved, but no sound emerged.

"Knees crumble first, then the stiff gate destroys the hips. To walk among the swarm, we had to step around the prostrate men who grew tall. Their begging cups frightened away the women who might be tempted by Buffalo's intellect."

Sophie couldn't decide whether to laugh or cry.

"Child, when Buffalo met you, he fretted for weeks before he let himself believe it was true, that you were actually *attracted* to his weakness." Natalie's eyes crinkled into a smile. "When he finally accepted that you enjoy the way he looms over you... Well, the change in him lightened all our hearts. You were his first fink, and better for him than you knew."

"My trophy, the man I thought every woman wanted, all this time, Buff was a charity case." Sophie moved a few steps away and gazed upward, toward the heavens. "Good one."

"Child, your *charity* was the reason Buffalo used his hands on you instead of his gun, and why he screamed to summon help."

Sophie's anger flared hot.

Natalie looked like winter. "Your survival disgraced him. Buffalo was barred from the *Finger* until he was retested to confirm he is ungovernable."

"Did he pass? Or did you hold him back for remedial murder school?"

"Buffalo tested better than *I* do. But even *ungovernable* has a limit, which we hoped you would not discover."

That shut Sophie up for a while. Eventually she said, "First fink?"

"You probably have a different word for it," said Natalie. "What do you call the bond a man feels to the first woman who reveals she wants him?"

Sophie considered. "We don't call it anything."

"Really?" Natalie seemed surprised. "Men are constantly rejected by women, so the first woman who reveals her attraction is such a relief, she will always hold his heart like no other. Finding your way back to your first fink is our most popular love story."

Finding your way back to your first. Sophie found herself thinking about Tom Pine. "We have *first love,* and the girl next door."

"Those are sweet, but not like a man's first... oh good grief." Natalie pointed. "How can that thing exist?"

"That's a giraffe. It eats treetops. I thought I'd bagged a trophy," Sophie said ruefully. "But Buff was just a pity fuck. No wonder Luci always smiled when she saw us together."

"Child, Buffalo doesn't need your pity. In a few years, I'm sure my monkeys will adjust to low gravity, and even *he* will attract me." But the old Worm seemed doubtful. "On Earth, a properly-sized man can actually perform a standing *backflip.*"

The giraffe lumbered over to the pond and awkwardly opened its legs for a drink.

Natalie watched it with distaste. "Could it *really* be so important to reach the top shelf? Humans must keep something very valuable up there, because I see you fink for the tall ones, which means Buffalo's future is bright. Already, the women are competing."

Sophie frowned. "Competing?"

"Oh, yes. I counseled him to hold out for his fantasy mate, but he is too hungry. Buffalo won't last three months before he is claimed by a far-sighted woman."

"He actually thinks I'm as beautiful as Luci?"

"Child, you radiate intelligence and fertility, more trophy than Luci ever could be. If Buffalo could still parade you on his arm, he would have to beat women off with a carrot."

Sophie shook her head. "No way could he prefer me over her. When Luci smiles, even I feel a stir, and I don't go that way."

"Oh, child, Luci is not a woman to be envied."

"Oh, no, of course not. Who'd want to be *her?*"

"Haven't you puzzled out why she represents us, when we negotiate with your queens?"

"Of course. You chose Luci as your ambassador because men have all the power, and she reduces them to drooling idiots."

"No, child. We see how your men react to Luci, but we chose her for her character. She understands you."

Baboons screamed.

"In our culture," Natalie explained, "when we come of age, we must be tested to prove we are Worm and not wasp. The test is a brutal kindness, because if a wasp is forced to behave as a Worm, the poor thing will eventually kill itself. But between Worm and wasp there is a gray zone, where suicide is possible but not certain. We call this gray zone the *borderline,* and it's where Luci lives."

"You mean..."

"Yes, child. Luci is a borderline, only barely one of us. She is so close to wasp, she can actually wish you harm. When her first four children all inherited her worst urges, Luci lost her mate, and she is not likely to attract a fit replacement. In a sense, she and Buffalo are kindred souls. If only she could desire him."

Sophie held her reply because a gaggle of children approached, trailed by a cheerfully exhausted mom. The oldest child, a girl of 13, earnestly explained they were home-schooled, here to study zoology, but xenology would also be acceptable. Natalie delivered an impromptu lecture on the relation between body size and gravity.

When the autographs were all signed, and the children had dashed off to the next attraction, the Worm touched Sophie's arm. "Child, I will tell my friends you discovered our secret, that a man you deem homely might be coveted by hungry Worm women. Your insight will be noticed, and I hope our respect will buy your silence."

"Silence? Why are you keeping this secret?"

Natalie strayed too close to the border. A baboon hurtled onto the chain-link fence, baring its fangs as it jerked the woven metal. Natalie grimaced. "We want immigrants, but only if you come for the right reason. Most of you are wasps. Each one we reject will be affronted, and seek to harm us."

The baboon dropped to the ground and turned around to show Natalie its ass. Then it leapt onto the fence again, pumping its body against the supple barrier. The chain mesh rippled and the baboon snarled.

Sophie understood. "You turn short, ugly men into trophies. You would be swarmed with hopeful wasps."

"If only we could be swarmed with *our* kind. The skills they restored to us would change everything."

"Oh my God. You think Tom Pine is *handsome.*"

"Oh, he is more than handsome," Natalie breathed. "He's the perfect height, he's fit, and he built your company. Tom Pine is *smoking.*"

Sophie was incredulous. "Tom has no chin! He looks like a ferret, and he is *five foot three.*"

"Exactly! His face reminds me of a cute animal, and 5'3" is a perfect balance of strength and quickness. Luci can barely keep her hands off him. But you're changing the subject. Will you respect our secret?"

Sophie considered the request. *Worm women crave short, ugly men* was a ripe secret. She could think of several people she would enjoy telling, but then it would surely get back to Tom. Could that be stopped? "How long can you hide this secret?"

"On our world, we hid the hexagon's meaning for five generations."

"You kept a secret for *five generations?*"

"Yes, child. Thousands of wasps knew the truth, but their testimony was lost among the millions who cited false rumors as facts. Their queens were happy to help us bury the truth in a blizzard of lies." The old Worm took Sophie's hand. "But I think you could expose us. The Humans know you work directly with us, so if you revealed the truth, you might be believed. Will you keep our secret?"

Will I keep the secret? On reflection, and considering all relevant factors, Sophie decided the Worm women's opinion of short, homely men was a secret that Tom Pine, her beloved boy next door and Plan B, should be shielded from, to help him enjoy his realistic options.

The same moment
Shenandoah National Park

Luci faced the U.S. government's clown. "I enjoy offering to liberate your slaves," she began. "It's fun to watch you contort yourself trying to evade the truth. But now, I wish to discuss emigration in the other direction."

The clown looked surprised. He said, "I am surprised. Can you forsake your culture and embrace ours? That seems unsafe."

"You needn't worry; our emigrants would not be dangerous like me, not even as dangerous as you."

The clown looked bland.

Luci looked weary. "But you wouldn't fret over a few dead slaves. Rest easy; our outcasts won't proselytize for us. Quite the contrary, so you'll probably want to televise their pathetic weeping. They will cry and say we brutalized them. Most will be skilled thespians who will recite any script you give them, provided it slanders us."

In the *Lens*, Kitty Siphon relaxed.

Luci tensed. "You know our nature. If we misunderstand a word, we could be triggered to murder. Nonetheless, we live in peace, because we can give each other the benefit of the doubt." She pointed to her cheek. "If someone with these tattoos *seems* to demand ransom, I know I'm mistaken. We argue it out, or in the worst case, we both bite the forbidden fruit, to learn which of us is being an ass. This is possible only because I can give him the benefit of the doubt."

Kitty felt a premonition.

"All children are wasps," Luci continued. *"Nobody* could give them the benefit of the doubt, yet we never harm children, because our monkey minds can't see kids as a threat. Unfortunately, they lose that protection when they come of age. When a girl matures into a woman, she must become a Worm. Otherwise, she could not long survive among us."

The clown and the Worm stared at each other through the clear Lexan barrier that separated them, and kept them safe.

"Even now, after five generations, your genes linger in our blood." Luci said, *your genes* in the tone normally reserved for the words, *cheesy discharge*. "When children come of age, they must face the burning bush and become Worm, so we can give them the benefit of the doubt. This rule has ruthlessly enforced itself for five generations, purifying our race. Yet still, we lose one child in four. The unlucky fourth is born wasp."

Luci had averted her eyes, turning away from the clown and his cameras. In the distant *Lens*, staffers began whispering. A secondary screen had zoomed in to Luci's hands. She was twisting them together in a constant, restless hand-washing, as if trying to wipe off a sticky slime.

"The bitch is actually *nervous*," Kitty observed. "I wonder why."

In the sheet-metal shed, Luci interrupted her hand washing to wipe her eyes. "No wasp can face the burning bush. It would frustrate her main drive, make her hate the pursuit she was built for. It would be kinder to cut her throat, rather than set her on the path to death by her own hand, but we can't kill our babies, even in mercy."

They lose one child in four? Luci's voice was fading, barely audible. Kitty waved for the audio eunuch to boost the gain.

"We cast them out," Luci mumbled to the floor. "We drive our babies away. It's the worst moment of motherhood, short of a child's death. In fact, it hurts worse, because we see it coming, not to mention the shame."

The clown said, "Am I to gather..."

"YES, YOU FAT, SMIRKING WASP!"

In the *Lens*, staffers murmured in surprise. Luci hadn't shouted before, except that one time she tried to kill the previous clown.

She was standing now. "I will probably lose my daughter. I want her to live with you proudly, with some status, instead of sneaking around your foul culture like a fugitive. And we are done here." Luci slapped her spaceship. "Open the hatch."

Nothing happened.

"I SAID, *OPEN THE FUCKING HATCH!*"

The fucking hatch did not respond. Luci closed her eyes, inhaled, and spoke calmly. "I won't hurt him. Please open the hatch."

The hatch clicked. Luci kicked it open and slammed it behind her.

If only a payment would cover my shame
in a pile of gold
where you would remain
Under my money, you'd laugh at the rain
and I could unsee what my darling became
if Mommy could forge
what a beast cannot feign

Just because a man wants to be a Wyrm

doesn't mean he's a child molester.
Americans are presumed innocent.

Like   Share   Comment

Comments. Please respect the <u>forum rules</u>.

Pokemom Two hours ago
Sure. He probably just loves the Wyrm cuisine.

LawFareForU Two hours ago
The U.S. Constitution guarantees the right to be considered innocent until proven guilty in a court of law.

Moby Duck Two hours ago
There is Wyrm cuisine?

Pokemom Two hours ago
Of course there is Wyrm cuisine. What do you think happened to all those little white girls? No bodies have ever been found.

Moby Duck About an hour ago
ROFL Pokemom. I guess they think the white girls are more tender.

S. Quiblee About an hour ago
Yes, white girls have better marbling

LawFareForU About an hour ago
You guys are disgusting

Moby Duck About an hour ago
Yeah, well, it's a war. We have to toughen up.

Page 1 2 3

The next day
A bad day

The Pine Shack work day had trudged on long past dark. Finally, Natalie said her goodbyes and headed wearily up to the roof.

As she walked toward her boat, she waved to the pair of guards. They waved back.

That was when she noticed someone had wrapped her boat with black webbing. *What the hell?* Her boat's tail even looked wrong, and its nose was too short. Natalie blinked, then with horror, she realized her tail engine had been removed and replaced with something else. The aft engine capsule was sitting on the deck, beside a metallic cylinder she now recognized as her nose engine cluster, fringed with serrated metal where it had been sawed off.

She started to draw her pistol, but something struck the back of her head, the rooftop deck rushed up to meet her, and everything went black.

Natalie had not noticed a pair of taut Kevlar cords knotted to the rooftop air conditioner. Two black cords rose up into the darkness, one slanting northward and the other southward. Six feet up, each cord passed through a football-sized black cylinder.

Inside each football-sized cylinder, unseen, a piezo load cell measured the Kevlar line's tension, beaming its findings via radio to a helicopter hovering 8,000 feet above. A computer monitored the line tension and adjusted the helicopter's lift, conscientiously allowing for droop and delays in turbine response.

Within ten seconds, Natalie was strapped into a nylon harness. The first guard clipped the harness to the northern rope, and pulled a release pin. The Kevlar twanged free of the air conditioner and the black cylinder shot upward, trailing Natalie's small body.

They hustled to attach the second rope to the webbing wrapped around the half-gutted runabout. Then they pulled the second release pin. The Kevlar twanged. Natalie's boat rose up onto its tail, then lifted off the roof. As the boat was hoisted into the air, the second guard yanked a lanyard to ignite a conventional rocket motor that had replaced the boat's tail engine. The little rocket roared and lit up the rooftop but didn't actually thrust, because its nozzle had been sawed off.

As Natalie's boat ascended through 1,000 feet, the rocket burned down to its base and ignited a block of magnesium.

From the ground, the spitting magnesium resembled the glare of a Worm tail engine. If someone had been watching, he might have said the alien craft rose more slowly than normal, and its engines lacked their usual flare. That would have been okay. Engine malfunction is tragic but familiar.

Natalie's boat continued to rise as it was winched upward toward the hovering CH-53J. All three of the helicopter's turbines screamed at full military power, lifting the load, until the burning magnesium reached a detonator.

Inside the Pine Shack, Luci and Sophie leaned over the conference table, checking production numbers when the window blew in. Sophie screamed and covered her face, far too late, but thankfully the glass was tempered. Both women turned toward the gaping hole and up to the sky, where a shower of glowing debris rained slowly down toward a cacophony of car alarms.

"Oh no!" Luci clutched at her glass-sprinkled hair and wailed. She sounded so desolate, so lost, Sophie was more upset by Luci's reaction than by Natalie's death.

Luci turned and buried her face in Sophie's chest, sobbing. Sophie stiffened, then tried to offer some comfort.

YOUR ACTIONS ALONE
WILL NOT BRING VICTORY

YOUR ACTIONS ALONE
BRING SELF RESPECT

Punch a Worm
You'll like yourself better

Like   Share   Comment

Comments. Please respect the <u>forum rules</u>.

LawFareForU Four hours ago

This is so insightful. In the past, I failed to act, because the alien problem seemed too big for any individual. But now I see, *that doesn't matter.* I will do what all Humans should do, and if other Humans don't, so much the better for me.

In the West Wing, President Mirror prowled.

41 feet away, his aide pack slumped sullenly, carrying stacks of paper filled with boring stuff they wanted to tell him. Three aides huddled over a pad, and one said, a little too loud, "The entire Dallas Cowboy cheerleader squad went through the body scanner at DFW airport. This is the raw data, and you can see *everything.*"

President Mirror wouldn't fall for that trick again. When he walked over to look at the pictures, they would try to show him some stupid foreign policy brief.

A blonde in her twenties pushed through the aide pack. She crossed the imaginary line into the 40-foot zone of aide exclusion, obviously determined to approach the president. Then she saw Mirror's dark expression, and stopped six feet away. "Sir, it's time for your meeting with Harold Hob."

Mirror looked blank.

"He's the head of the FDRA."

Still blank.

"The Footwear Distributors and Retailers Association."

"Ooh!" Mirror brightened.

They met in the Oval Office and chatted about sports for 20 minutes. Or rather, President Mirror chatted, and Hob listened.

"This has been so nice," Hob interrupted eventually. "Though I can't help wondering, was there a specific reason you summoned me?"

The president sobered. "Yes, in fact, there was, and I'm afraid it's rather serious. Am I correct in my understanding, you get 40 percent of your profits from your Western Footwear division?"

"That's about right," Hob said cautiously. "Why?"

"We have been approached by concerned activists. You see, the cowboy boot symbolizes the repression and even the genocide of Native Americans."

Hob laughed. "That's ridiculous. The average cowboy-boot buyer hasn't thought about Indians once in the last month."

Mirror stiffened. "Mister Hob, I'll thank you not to utter that offensive term in my office."

"What offensive....Oh." Hob's smile faded. He sagged in his chair. "How much do you want?"

"This is not about money," Mirror said sternly. "Some feel it is time to raise the American people's consciousness of this issue. I understand a public-relations firm has been retained to help restore the indigenous peoples' dignity."

"Yeah, whatever. Just tell me how much."

"Mister Hob, I don't think you're taking this seriously. The suffering of this land's native people beneath the boot of white oppression is not something to be slyly celebrated with footwear. I think we can anticipate congressional hearings. Within six months, wearing cowboy boots will be rightly considered a firing offense."

Hob pulled out his checkbook. "Do you think 300 grand would assuage the Native Americans' grief?"

"Perhaps," the president allowed. "For this year."

Hob filled in the amount. "Have you set up a foundation, or should I just make this out to the party?"

When Hob had left, Mirror returned to pacing the West Wing. He glanced at his watch.

Damn. 30 minutes until the Distilled Spirits Council. Their rep had squirmed when Mirror suggested a million dollar donation to his presidential library fund, until Mirror mentioned he was reconsidering the question of federal marijuana enforcement. Now, the distilled-spirits reps were setting up a presidential tasting with an assortment of museum-quality whiskies delivered by armored truck. Mirror wandered toward the Mess to watch the uncorkings.

Before the president had taken two steps, a scrum of Secret Service agents charged around the corner and picked him up by his arms and legs.

"What the hell?" Mirror hated it when they did this.

The Secret Service emergency hustle varied with the circumstance. In public, where the president might be watched by snipers or, worse, cameras, they hustled him along upright to shield him with their bodies and preserve his presidential image.

401

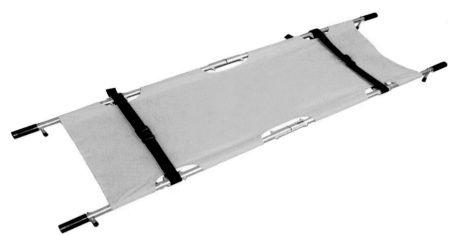

Here in the White House, with nobody watching, they just picked him up and carried him horizontally. This shaved 6-10 seconds off the time to move Mirror from the staff offices to the elevator, depending on how many people they passed who might like to chat.

The hidden elevator opened as they approached. Once inside, the agents levered Mirror upright and pushed him into the back wall, one burly agent on his left and another on his right. Each wrapped a meaty hand around a gilded steel handle, then clapped his other hand on Mirror's shoulder. "Gravity One!"

"Gravity Two!"

Mirror looked curiously at the hands on his shoulders. "Why are you *OW!*"

Agent Oak pressed the red button that unlatched the massive spring, and Mirror's phone left his shirt pocket, whacking his nose on its way to the ceiling. The two burly agents pressed hard on Mirror's shoulders as the elevator sprang downward.

The downward acceleration lasted three seconds, then positive gravity returned. Mirror settled onto his feet and held his injured nose. "What is going *HOOF!*"

One burly agent had reached around and, in a smooth judo move, rotated Mirror onto his back, not quite hard enough to knock the wind out of him. Six agents crouched around him, poised like sprinters at the starting blocks, each using one free hand to hold him down.

Mirror, lying on his back, heard a whine like tires on a highway. "What is that *WOOF!*"

He exhaled as the four-gravity deceleration pressed him into the floor. The crouching agents grunted. Then the weight lifted, the elevator door slammed open and the six agents sprinted out, carrying Mirror with them. He rolled his eyes in frustration.

They had descended to the 93-Mile Tunnel, the rail line to the *Lens* and the Deep Bunker. The sleek, 30-foot Presidential Fast Train waited with hatches open.

Mirror was unceremoniously dumped into the middle hatch. He found himself sprawled in his form-fitted chair. An agent reached in, pulled the chest harness over Mirror's head, snapped it to the waist buckle, then retreated. The hatches slammed shut and Mirror's ears popped. Outside, someone thumped the train three times.

Through his window, Mirror saw everyone diving behind the blast shields. Then the second elevator opened, revealing the commerce secretary on her back, surrounded by crouching Secret Service agents. One of the crouching agents was Sheila Bear, who took in the scene and hastily slapped the control panel. The elevator slammed shut.

403

"Oh no," Mirror moaned. "You aren't really going to *YOW!*"

The president was slammed back into the doeskin seat. The train windows darkened as the tails of the rocket exhaust billowed forward.

The five-gravity acceleration lasted three seconds, then cut off abruptly and Mirror lurched forward into his harness. "All right, God dammit, what's going on?" He was getting angry.

"Sir, the capitol may be under attack."

"What? How?"

Agent Oak sat stiffly in the next seat, scanning his console. "An alien object is descending toward the Mall. They gave no notice."

"Object? What kind of object?"

"We don't know yet." Oak's voice was calm.

The train hummed, preserving its six-ton battery by sucking power from the electrified rails. The colored walls flashed by, and the wheels pinged like a chorus of blacksmiths as they flew over the gap for the second blast door.

"Are you closing the blast doors?"

"Not yet, Mr. President. Most of the Cabinet and Congress are following us. The bogey's trajectory gives us at least five more minutes."

"We still have *five minutes?* Then why did you slam me around?"

"Standard procedure, Mister President, for an approaching missile." Agent Oak was his usual deadpan self, but Mirror was sure the man's mouth twitched.

Five minutes later and 16 miles down the track, everyone admitted the capitol was not being attacked by aliens.

"Mister President, a two-seat alien craft has landed on the White House lawn." For an instant, Agent Oak's calm facade slipped, and he looked troubled. "It's Gabriel Tide, the owner of the Worm mothership. He's demanding you come out to meet him."

20 minutes later
The White House lawn

Gabriel stood stiffly before his 2-seat runabout, the *First Knuckle*.

Eventually, he was approached by a man wearing a green tie. "Mr. Tide, my name is Dale Drover. I apologize, but there is no way you'll be allowed near the president carrying a weapon."

Gabriel's voice was cold. "It's not safe to ignore my demand."

"Mr. Tide, I understand, and I may have a solution. I have contacted the commerce secretary, and she has agreed to meet you. She is our highest commercial negotiator and regulator."

Gabriel spat on the scorched grass. "I would sooner speak to your highest underwear thief."

Drover pulled off his headset and stepped closer. "She is president Mirror's best friend," he murmured. "She has his ear like no other." Drover replaced his headset and stepped back.

Gabriel grimaced. "Very well." His tone fell between anguish and exasperation. "I will speak to the Queen of Lies."

Drover retreated.

Kitty Siphon was grateful when the elevator lifted her back to the surface at a reasonable pace. The instant the metal door slid aside, her secure phone beeped.

It was Dale Drover. "The Worm king agreed to meet you. I told him you were the president's best friend."

"Are you sure that was wise?"

"No."

That was Drover's most amazing trait, his astonishing failure to excuse his actions, a failure virtually unknown in public servants. "Madam Secretary, the Worm looks angry, but I think he's frightened."

Kitty let out her breath. "Finally, some good news."

"Not really. He has a gun."

When Kitty emerged, blinking, onto the White House lawn, she found a circle of burnt grass surrounding a parked spacecraft and a rigid Worm. She hesitated only a moment before she strode forward.

Agent Bear fell into step beside her. "Madam Secretary, our intel suggests the Worms carry implanted suicide bombs, so I have declared suicide-vest protocol. My options are limited."

Kitty shivered. "Can you handle it?"

"Yes, Ma'am. This is the job I was built for."

"I love it when you say that. I'm so nervous, I'm likely to piss myself. Tell me your mission again."

"Madame Secretary, my mission is to watch over those who have been entrusted to my care. It is literally the job I was made for."

"Thank you, Sheila." Kitty's pounding heart slowed a little, and she smiled warmly as she approached the Worm who carried 60 pounds of TNT-equivalent in his skull. "Good morning, Mr. Tide." She extended a steady hand.

Gabriel reached around her head and grabbed a handful of hair. She felt the cold touch of metal under her chin.

"GUN!"

Kitty dimly sensed her encircling security detail pointing weapons. Agent Bear smiled and aimed her submachine gun at Gabriel's balls.

The Worm's voice was gravel in Kitty's ear. "Bring me Natalie."

Kitty had never been physically threatened, and she knew she had leaked some urine. She hoped it didn't show. "I'm sorry," she quavered. "Who is Natalie?" She could imagine only the image of the *DayChat* hostess on her last cover of People Magazine, with her head engulfed by Gabriel's muzzle flash.

"You know perfectly well," Gabriel hissed, pressing the gun into her jaw. "You took her in a fake accident."

Kitty fought her panic. All she could think to do was play dumb. "I don't know who you mean."

Drover stepped up and earned his pay for the year. "Madam Secretary, the Worm ship that exploded yesterday, the pilot's name was Natalie Clover." He turned to Gabriel. "Was she your woman?"

Gabriel's eyes closed, but his grip didn't waver.

"I am truly sorry," said Kitty, regaining some composure. "It was an accident, some sort of engine failure."

Gabriel opened his eyes and snarled, spraying spit. "I *built* that fucking boat! Tell me where she is, or the next thing out of your mouth will be your brain."

Kitty raised one hand to rest lightly on Gabriel's arm, the one that gripped her hair. "I am sorry," she said softly, gazing into the Worm's wet eyes. "We found almost 20 pounds of body parts."

Gabriel stared at her for long seconds. Then he released her hair and lowered his gun. His shoulders sagged.

Kitty smiled triumphantly and glanced to Drover. He gave her a quick thumbs up.

Agent Bear lowered her weapon and stood aside. Gabriel limped slowly toward his runabout, then stopped and reached to his belt, tugging open a silk bag. Agent Bear raised her gun.

The Worm tossed a coin onto the scorched lawn. "For the grass I burned." He levered himself heavily into his cockpit. As he drew his canopy shut, he looked back at Kitty. "I swear I will piss on your grave, after it cools."

Everyone stepped back and covered their ears as the Worm spacecraft roared skyward. Within a minute, it was merely a daylight star, then it was gone.

When the Secret Service agents had returned to their holes, Kitty turned to Drover. "Did we get a good shot?"

Drover nodded optimistically. "I think so. When he wrapped his arm around you, it blocked my view of his gun, and I think it will look affectionate. I managed to get his spaceship and the White House into the frame."

"Thank God," Kitty breathed. "He scared the piss out of me. I wish we could just fake a picture."

Drover shook his head vigorously. "It would be detected within a week. The internet is crawling with PhotoShop junkies."

"Yes, yes, and they aren't *all* on our side. Let's go in, so I can change clothes."

They walked toward the White House. "That was risky to mention his woman's body parts," Drover murmured. "What would you have done, if he'd asked to see them?"

"Not a chance. He was begging me to admit we were lying about her being dead. So I reminded him what would happen, if he made us prove we weren't."

"Nicely played. Do you really want to leak a picture of you *hugging* Gabriel? He's supposed to be a monster."

Kitty chuckled. "I so enjoy your naiveté. I wasn't hugging him; he was hugging *me*."

Drover stared at her blankly, and she touched his hand to silence him as they passed the White House threshold and its guards.

When the soundproof door clicked shut behind them, she explained. "We'll leak the picture of him hugging me, because the Worms are not just monsters. They are also *Daddy,* with all of Daddy's authority. That's why everyone hates them. The Worms are jammed so full of moral authority, it sprays out of their butts."

Drover looked thoughtful.

Kitty grinned happily. "And Daddy just sprayed his moral authority on *me.*"

Sophie faced the workshop door and steeled herself, willing her hammering heart to slow down.

It didn't. She pushed through the door, and found Buff in his usual spot at the workbench. She had been surprised when he showed up for work the day after Natalie's death. "How are you holding up?"

Buff straightened, but he didn't turn to face her. "My animal mind recognizes her memory as my daughter. Funerals are hard for us."

Outside, faintly audible through the walls, a crowd of protesters chanted, *Karma's a bitch! Blow up your ship!* until Frank Drummer's bullhorn-amplified voice broke in to lead them in a cheerful chorus of, *Hey Hey! Ho Ho! Indoor plumbing's got to go!*

Sophie hesitated, then she approached and stood behind Buff. "You could take some time off."

Buff waved at the half-built extruder prototype. "This is... it's something to do."

"Accidents happen. We have to accept that."

Buff glanced at her sharply, but did not reply.

Tentatively, Sophie rested a hand on his shoulder.

Buff laid his hand over hers, just long enough to lift it off. "You should leave."

Sophie's anger flared, but she dared not speak as she granted Buff's wish, and slammed the door behind her.

Worms were pariahs alone
Hated by everyone known
So they came to our planet
Critiqued how we ran it
And now it feels just like home

The next morning

Kitty Siphon's bedroom

The Eastern sky lightened with the first hint of dawn. Kitty sprawled across her bed, half awake, her mental monkeys unchained and wandering beyond the bounds of logic. She let them roam, because sometimes they found something.

The Worm technology promised so much, yet their culture threatened even more, and somehow, the pieces didn't fit. Kitty sensed she had missed something crucial, but what? If only she could investigate properly, with her best agents. Unfortunately, her best agents *knew* they were her agents, so they must not meet a Worm who might read their minds and identify Kitty Siphon behind the curtain.

In a rite of passage, half of us are trained to perceive hidden thoughts. Maybe there was some way to identify *which* aliens could mindread. It was only half of them, the bitch had said, because...

Kitty sat bolt upright. She hastened to her computer and called up the surveillance video of the old, redheaded female Worm reminiscing about a rite of passage, where men were trained to recognize women's sexual interest. The old Worm called it, *Sunrise.* To teach the young men, older women volunteered to be drugged into a horny, almost-mindless animal state and repeatedly raped. Apparently, it was a rough six weeks for homely men, condemned to learn by watching, not by doing.

Kitty remembered the first meeting with the Worm ambassador.

SHIT

125 cm³

From behind her Lexan barrier, Luci had claimed she couldn't play word games. *I can't deceive you with clever wording,* she had mentioned several times. Too many times, Kitty now realized, because the Worm had also declined to explain her hexagon tattoo. Explaining the hexagon would *violate a cultural taboo,* Luci had claimed. That might have been technically accurate, but it was a deception, because the taboo was *ours,* not theirs, as revealed later by the Pine surveillance.

Perhaps the Worms couldn't lie outright, but that hardly mattered, because Luci had deceived the clown with a cleverly-worded truth.

And Luci's most crippling revelation, the threat that hobbled Kitty's ambitions, was her claim to read minds. *Long and humiliating training to perceive hidden thoughts,* she had said, *with drugs you have not yet discovered and physical invasions you would deem criminal.*

Luci's clever words had described *Sunrise.*

Kitty smiled appreciatively. "You sly bitch."

Dominick Tork turned up his speaker volume and attended his largest video display.

The image was clear and well-lighted. An old, redheaded Worm female was strapped to a gurney, naked except for the bulky helmet of the hammerhead, comical on her tiny body. Dominick knew her well, from many hours of surveillance video.

The interrogator continued his narration. "The chemical anesthesia is waning. The subject will regain consciousness gradually over several minutes. We do not require the subject's vision, so I will disable the occipital cortex."

The hammerhead clicked, but the small body did not move.

"I am disabling the right frontal lobe, the right parietal lobe, and portions of the left frontal lobe and cerebellum."

The hammerhead rattled and the body twitched.

"The remainder of the left frontal lobe should resume function soon. As you ordered, I have spared the region surrounding the implant in the left parietal lobe. This is the verbal area, so the subject should speak and understand speech. However, we could not map precise functional areas with the subject unconscious."

413

Minutes passed in silence. Then the little Worm stirred, struggling weakly against her bonds.

"The subject's visual field is entirely blank. She knows she is physically restrained, but with her limited brain function, she cannot deduce why."

Eventually, the Worm stilled.

"She should be receptive to interrogation. Her willpower centers are not mapped, but we may hope they lie in her brain's non-functioning zones. The sedatives should keep her calm and passive."

Dominick spoke into his mic. "Commence the interrogation."

"When I question her, she will eventually deduce she is captive."

"Please confine your observations to the non-obvious."

The interrogator seemed unperturbed. In fact, he seemed to have no emotions whatsoever. "Very well. Are you sure you can't tell me more? I am handicapped by ignorance."

This is such an interesting contest, Dominick mused. *Our technical knowledge versus their telepathy.* "Your ignorance protects us both," he spoke into his microphone. "Your delay does not."

Bitter experience had shown that every minute might be the subject's last, so this time, Dominick had decided to begin with the crucial questions, relying on simple misdirection and direct brain stimulus rather than time-consuming theater.

When the interrogator spoke into his mic, the voice that emerged from the speaker was Gabriel Tide, the Worm leader who had foolishly revealed he was this subject's romantic partner. "Natalie, it's me, Gabriel. Your kids are in danger. To save them, we need the burning bush. Quickly, remind me where we stowed it."

A moment passed. Then the small body flailed, flopping against the gurney. "NO! NO!" She strained against her bonds, and her back arched.

In his distant office, Dominick was startled by the distinct cracks of breaking bones.

The interrogator seemed bored. "Something about that question tipped her off. I have to damp her motor controls."

The hammerhead rattled, and the small body went slack.

"The subject has broken her left and right humerus, her left tibia, and probably some vertebrae. Hopefully, she can still speak."

The small alien's mouth moved. Her voice was clumsy now, her consonants softened as if she were mentally retarded. "Ife ih mah asss giff to ooh, ah ih wah mah firsss."

Dominick turned up his volume. "What was that?"

"I damped her motor controls. Mongoloid speech is a common side effect," explained the interrogator. "The subject said, *life is my last gift to you, as it was my first.*"

Dominick slumped back into his chair, frowning. His frown deepened when his phone chirped. It was the special phone, the quantum-encrypted one. He pushed the button. "Yes, Madam Secretary?"

"The bitch played us! They read minds about as well as my ass! We can ask them whatever we want!"

Oblivious to the interruption, the interrogator moved on to his next question, delivered in Gabriel's soothing voice. "Quickly, Natalie, what is the first step to adjust our recognition of children?"

Natalie's broken body hung slack, the restraining straps redundant. Dominick noticed a faint sparkle on the subject's cheek. "That is good news, Madame Secretary. May I ask how you know?" As he spoke, he moved the mouse to the subject's face and zoomed in to her cheek.

A gleaming trace had crossed the alien's tattoos. The tears were probably just physiological reaction to the hammerhead.

With visible effort, the old Worm said, "Wheh ah oo?"

Gabriel's soothing voice said, "I am with you."

"NO!" Dominick lurched forward, but his display had already gone blank. He sighed and switched to the video from the overhead drone, in time to watch the hot debris rain down on the desert.

Kitty Siphon strolled the West Wing with a spring in her step. When she spotted the president, she dragged him into the empty Cabinet room for a private conference.

Mirror glanced at his aide pack hovering 41 feet away, then he closed the door. "What?"

"No mind reading!" Kitty bounced. "It was a bluff!"

Mirror's face fell. "No telepathy? Are you sure?"

Kitty patted the presidential arm. "There's still a chance they communicate through their brain implants, but they can't perceive *our* hidden thoughts."

Mirror looked hopeful. "So there's still a chance for a national telepathic network?"

Kitty smiled sympathetically. "Now we know our clowns are safe. Would *you* like to give them the good news?"

"Yes!" Mirror brightened. "I'll summon Congress in groups of 20, and personally explain how the Worms can't retaliate, because they won't know who voted to fuck them. We can do *anything* to the Wyrms, so long as we pretend we don't want to. Each briefing should take about an hour."

"Have fun. I'm so relieved, and the polls look good."

"Ooh!" The president liked good polls. "How good?"

"Our campaign finally worked," Kitty gushed. "Three months ago, if we nuked the Worms, one person in ten would admit they were happy. Now, it's *two out of three.*"

Mirror's eyes widened. "Two out of three would support us?"

"Yes! And four out of five would support *threatening* to nuke them, to make them pay their fair share."

"Wow. And we haven't even released the video of the little girls."

"It's a happy day." Kitty opened the door and skipped down the hall like a schoolgirl. "I'm off to the *Lens* for this week's negotiation, and this time, I know the bitch can't read my mind."

One hour later
Shenandoah National Park
Human-Worm colony talks

The clown completed the gold-weighing ritual, then he thanked the little girl at her little wooden desk.

Watching from the distant *Lens*, Secretary Siphon looked forward to today's session. Negotiating with the Worms would be fun again, freed from the vile threat of mind reading.

Inside the shed, Luci Dark looked even stiffer than usual. She was standing, clutching a metallic cylinder the size of a thermos, marked with a yellow Post-it. What might it contain?

"Today's meeting will be brief," Luci announced, "as will all subsequent meetings. If you feel short-changed, you may demand a refund of the day's fee, and our negotiation will be ended permanently."

"Something's up." Kitty pointed to the ranking war pig. She didn't know his rank, but his shirt had the most trinkets. "Be ready."

The war pig pulled his keyboard one inch closer.

In the shed, behind her Lexan barrier, Luci set the metal cylinder on the floor and peeled off the Post-it. "Please write down this web address and password."

The clown nodded and produced his notepad.

"God dammit!" Kitty snarled as the Big Screen bobbed nauseously. "I have to watch this for *hours*. How many times do I have to tell you to stop nodding?"

418

Luci slapped the Post-it against the Lexan. "On this web site, we will detail our planned visits, should you wish to provide armed escorts."

Kitty froze.

"Since we arrived, 40 of my friends have vanished without explanation or in unlikely accidents." Luci looked even more disapproving than usual. "Forty is more than enough. You're just being pigheaded. The next time one of us is harmed, you will lose your capitol."

The video image shifted as the clown straightened. "Did you just threaten to attack Washington?"

"Yes. I understand this is a bitter pill, because you cannot abandon your heart's desire while any hope remains. Therefore, I offer to destroy your hope. If you wish, I can–"

"Before we discuss hope," the clown interrupted. "I must ask you to clarify your threat."

"Very well," said Luci. "Here is my threat: If one more Worm is harmed anywhere on Earth, the *Unexpected Finger* will flatten Washington, D.C."

The *Lens* buzzed. In the shed, the clown seemed to relax. "Thank you. How do you propose to set our minds at ease?"

"After 40 victims, the *human* portion of your mind knows you cannot learn our secrets by kidnapping us. Yet still you try, because you can have no peace while any hope remains. Therefore, to ease your minds, I offer to destroy your hope. I offer to make a new lunar crater, plainly visible from Earth. You must look at the glowing crater, see it with your own eyes to frighten the *animal* parts of your mind. Then, you will find you can relax and enjoy safer pursuits."

"She is offering to *demonstrate* their weapon?" Kitty snorted. "She thinks I would *give up* my option to claim ignorance later? What kind of idiot does she think I am?"

Around Kitty, the *Lens* staffers looked uncomfortable.

"I will pass your offer to my superiors," said the clown. "However, I don't expect they will request a public demonstration."

"Your queens *don't* want a demonstration? Why not?" The Worm seemed confused. "The show would be... oh you're *kidding*. They don't want to admit they knew the risk?" Luci paused, and rubbed her face. "This is just embarrassing. You will confess your sins against us. You will detail your crimes to every queen on Earth, and you will commit to destroy any queen who fails to protect us."

"Excuse me," said the clown. "I did not hear you correctly."

"You heard me perfectly," Luci snapped. "We don't wish to repeat this ordeal. If any queen, *any queen* attempts what you attempted, I will gleefully destroy *your* capitol. To save yourselves, you will restrain the other queens. You will convince them they cannot steal our beautiful secret. You will convince them it is death to try, because it would be *your* death."

"I will pass on your demand," said the clown. "In the meantime, our capitol contains many innocent civilians. We believed you were unwilling to harm them."

"Oh, please." Luci rolled her eyes. "When you learned our nature, did it take you five minutes to pinpoint our weakness? Did you think you were *clever* to masquerade as your victims?"

Uh oh. Kitty felt a prickle of premonition.

"Did you think you were the first to notice our Achilles' heal? Did you imagine you were the *only* wasps who realized you could escape our wrath by hiding inside a committee? How did you imagine we survived?"

Kitty's prickle of premonition blossomed into an itch.

Luci glared. "We are ungovernable, not suicidal. Wasps *always* dress in the skin of your prey, so we must be able to defend ourselves. I bear the mark of that dishonor as a warning."

Kitty glanced at the war pig. The snipers were ready, but no, killing Luci wouldn't help, probably.

Luci pointed to her cheek, singling out the square tattoo with its distinctively thick top line. "You noticed the token of my parasite immunity is asymmetric: the heavy roof."

Kitty's itch of premonition matured into a foreboding.

The clown seemed intrigued. "You assured us the heavy roof merely warns of an allergy."

"You mistook my meaning. You thought of an allergy in my body, when you should have thought of my mind."

An allergy in her mind? Were the aliens phobic?

Luci stood stiffly. "Do you know the nature of allergy?"

Oh, yes. We know the nature of allergy.

"As we understand it," said the clown, "allergy results when our immune defense overreacts and attacks healthy cells."

In a flash of insight, Kitty Siphon saw what was coming. In her mind, monkeys howled, then attacked each other. The compassionate censor struck, and Kitty relaxed as half of her consciousness vanished.

Luci clenched her small hand into a fist and punched the Lexan. The clear plastic barrier rattled in its brackets. "You thought you had hidden among your prey," she spat. "You thought you were safe from my wrath, because I can't discern *which* of you wants to sting me. Now, I confess: I don't *need* to know which, because I believe your capitol contains four wasps for every innocent. To kill four wasps, I can..." She trailed off.

Kitty Siphon paled as her mental monkeys began to wake.

"My shackles are *open,*" Luci gritted, "To destroy four wasps, I can kill one innocent, you bastards."

Kitty staggered as the alien upended the game board. No, Luci had not upended the board, she had *revealed* it. The Worms' infuriating arrogance, their unapologetic sexual violence, their wanton disregard of Human sensibilities had been *intentional.*

Luci kicked her folding chair. It clattered off the shed wall. "Your slander campaign achieved its purpose and freed you from shame. You have so tarnished our name that you feel safe *openly admitting* your bestial lust to plunder us. *You* convinced your subjects to display their depravity. Now, at last, *I* am convinced your capitol contains four wasps for every innocent. You found my emergency key and released the shackles from *my* bestial lust."

Kitty struggled to conceal her rising horror and fascination as the Worm assumed an odd, sideways posture, one muscular arm stretched toward the clown and the other drawn back.

The clown saw it coming, but did not flinch as Luci struck the Lexan, this time rattling the whole shed. If not for the transparent barrier, Luci's palm would have struck the underside of the clown's nose. It did not seem the kind of palm strike that leads to nosebleed and swearing. It seemed more the kind of palm strike that leads to men in white coats barking orders as they jog alongside a gurney.

"You foul animals," Luci snarled. "You force me to allow this hunger in my very soul."

Kitty swayed. Staffers stared, open mouthed.

The Big Screen showed only clown shoes. He was gazing at his feet, oddly calm. "From the beginning," he murmured, "your first communication, the momentous *First Contact* was an offensive prank, which you spoiled by laughing too soon." The Big Screen slewed as the clown looked up at Luci. "It was not a prank; it was a *taunt.* You spoiled it intentionally, so you would seem poor liars. And all this." He waved at the utility shed and the Lexan barrier. "This ridiculous venue, insisting on a single representative instead of a proper diplomatic team, it was all a charade. You staged this show to convince us we had found your weakness. You *wanted* us to feel safely hidden among our swarm, so we would feel safe to turn the swarm against you."

Kitty felt she should act, give the clown an order, but *what* order? She saw no exit.

Absent orders, the clown straightened his jacket. "I congratulate you for your discipline in not defending your honor for all these long months, in the face of your casualties. Please relay my admiration to your leader, Gabriel Tide, for his *DayChat* television performance. To flaunt our most precious taboos, then show weakness by deeming himself a worm, he taunted us masterfully."

Luci glared. Her face reddened, and her breathing deepened. Finally, she could contain it no longer and snorted a laugh.

"I am sorry," said the clown. "I do not see the humor."

Luci wiped her eyes. "This is rich. Gabriel's job was to taunt your Human shield, the rank-and-file swarm you thought yourself safely hidden among, and goad them into revealing their wasp nature, so we could fire through them to kill your queens. Instead, he had to be his noble stupid self and try to *warn* you. We were so angry at him, I think every woman on the *Finger* slapped his face. It was just blind luck that you interpreted his warning backwards."

"His *warning?*" The clown sounded doubtful. "I watched Gabriel's *DayChat* performance 20 times. He systematically savaged our most sacred beliefs regarding race, religion, and sexuality, even *child* sexuality. Then he admitted you consider us to be wasps, and you consider yourselves worms, the natural prey of wasps. What better way to provoke us, short of shooting an unarmed woman, which *he then proceeded to do?*" The clown lifted one skeptical eyebrow. "That was a *warning?*"

From the distant *Lens*, Kitty watched Luci lift her folding chair back onto its legs. "You know our world was plagued by literal wasps?"

The Big Screen slewed as the clown sat down. "So I surmised."

The Big Screen was abruptly obscured by two enormous pink blurs, which resolved into the soles of Luci's bare feet planted on the Lexan. "An adult wasp is the size of a horse, and is armed with a pneumatic weapon that throws poison darts 100 yards. The darts contain a calming poison that renders the prey passive, unwilling to defend itself as it is dismembered and eaten. The anguished howls are heart wrenching."

The Big Screen tilted as the clown leaned to see around the alien's feet. "Am I to gather these fearsome wasps eat worms?"

Luci grinned. "You are such a moron. We don't spell our name with an *O*, we spell it with a *Y*. The wyrms were our world's most powerful animals, the only creature that could crush a wasp. You would call them, *dinosaurs*. When that idiot Gabriel called himself a wyrm, he was trying to warn you."

In the *Lens*, Kitty Siphon felt nauseated.

"Now you know." Luci sighed contentedly. "Confession is so good for the soul." She picked up the metal cylinder and unscrewed its cap.

"Gaa! Shit!" Kitty lurched to her feet. The war pig was half out of his chair, one hand pointing to Kitty and the other hovering over his keyboard.

"Hold." Kitty raised a shaky palm. "Wrong body language. That's not a weapon."

"Finally, our weapon is loaded." Luci upended the cylinder and slid out a can of Bud Light Lime, followed by a two-inch ball of something brown. "The date we burn you to death will be named a joyous holiday."

The clown straightened. "If we are to descend to threatening insults, you won't find me unarmed."

Luci smiled thinly. "I tried to buy grain alcohol."

The clown stared.

"When I tried to buy pure alcohol, I learned you force the distiller to poison his product. The poor man couldn't bring himself to say the word, *poison.* He called it, *denature,* to evade his shame."

"An unfortunate necessity," said the clown. "If you wish to spend a few hours, I could educate you as to the need."

Luci pulled her feet off the Lexan and leaned forward. "You force him to *poison his customers*," she hissed. "The poison blinds any slave who dares drink without paying you for permission. You actually *do it.*"

"Do you wish to spend the day discussing our tax system, so you might understand what you are talking about?"

Luci waved the brown sphere. It was the size of a tennis ball and looked like dried clay. "You've opened our shackles, so we can give you these."

In the *Lens*, Kitty Siphon glanced at the war pig. "Tell the snipers to stand ready, but for God's sake, don't shoot that brown ball."

The war pig looked annoyed.

The clown remained calm. "Is that a weapon?"

Luci chuckled. "You could say that. It's an assortment of seeds from our world. This ball can survive reentry from orbit, then will dissolve on contact with water."

A murmur spread around the *Lens*. A eunuch said, "Oh, fuck."

"We brought *lots* of seeds," Luci added. "We weren't sure what we'd find here. Would you like to know something interesting about our ecosystem?"

In the *Lens*, a gray-haired botany eunuch said, "Yes!"

"Here on Earth," Luci explained, "plant growth is limited by Fifteen, because most of it is bound to Twenty."

Kitty stood up and shouted. "Does anyone know what she just said?"

The gray-haired botanist volunteered. "Madam Secretary, she just said our plant growth is limited by the availability of Phosphorus, because it is bound to Calcium. She is correct."

Kitty: "Uh oh."

"On our world," the Wyrm continued, "plant growth is *not* limited by Fifteen, because our plants can separate it from Twenty."

"Madam Secretary, if that's true, then their plants don't need phosphorus fertilizer. They might make kudzu look like a potted fern." The gray-haired botanist seemed excited.

Kitty rubbed her temples.

In the shed, Luci set the brown ball on the floor and nudged it toward the clown. "Check for yourself. If you break it open, I suggest you do it indoors."

The ball rolled under the barrier, wobbling erratically as if it were extremely lightweight, like Styrofoam.

The wobbling brown ball fetched up against the clown's Wingtip shoe. He picked it up, and found it was ice cold. "Do you intend this as a threat?"

"I sure do. That ball is cheap, and we've got thousands. It would be a shame if something released them into an unstable orbit."

"Find out what we're up against," Kitty growled. "How many Wyrms did they bring? Hundreds? Thousands?"

The Wyrm leaned back and planted her feet on the Lexan. "At first, you killed us to drive us away. Then, you killed us to show your subjects it was possible. Now, you kill us to learn our secrets. The day we burn you all to death will be named a joyous holiday."

"A civilization of millions must make hard choices," the clown retorted. "Hard choices you are spared, living in small towns and enjoying your condescension."

Luci popped her beer. "Each target we destroy will create ten more, so we need not hesitate to flatten your capital."

In the *Lens*, Kitty clutched her stomach. This was her realm of mastery, and she had already realized the Wyrms need not hesitate to fire, because destroying the capitol would provoke massive anger. Every decent Human would yearn to retaliate. The Human's hatred would trigger the Wyrms' emergency defense mode, freeing them to repeat the cycle of hate and violence until no Human cities remained.

"Or perhaps you will sting us again, and release our *last* strategic defense." Luci sucked a deep slug of beer. "If you attack us, you will see for yourselves why we had to leave our world."

In the *Lens*, Kitty forced herself to stay calm. Professional.

"That tale brings us no pride, but we've decided to reveal it, to help your queens judge wisely."

"Thank you," was apparently all the clown could think to say.

"On our world," Luci began, "the swarm was poor and we were rich. What little the wasps possessed, they gained mainly by trading with us. Naturally, they wished us dead. Wasp men plotted to destroy the rivals who shamed them, and their mothers helped. Only their maidens camped outside our walls, seeking opportunity and driving their men into jealous frenzy. I know jealousy is well understood by your queens, as the source of their power."

The clown withheld comment.

"For five generations, the swarm plotted our destruction but had no means to achieve it."

The *Lens* fell silent. Staffers had stopped typing, and just watched the Big Screen.

"Then at last," said the Wyrm, "at last, they found the means. Our survivors barely escaped in time, and at least 19 did not."

"Pardon me," the clown interrupted. "Nineteen casualties was considered a major loss?"

Dammit, how many of you are there?

"The 19 weren't lost; they were *released.* Nineteen of us saw wasps openly looting our havens, and decided our civilization faced extinction. This is our last safety, which you are about to trigger. If we decide our civilization is about to be destroyed, we are released. Once that happens, we cannot stop ourselves from killing *all of you,* even if our grown children stand among our targets. That is the cautionary tale."

"Only 19 released, out of how many total of you?"

"We knew the 19 were just the first, so we chose to leave before we were *all* released. We froze ourselves into that miserable *Finger* to give our wayward children a chance, albeit a slim one."

The *Lens* staffers murmured.

"We couldn't bring the 19," Luci said quietly. "So we left them behind to face 600,000 wasps, including my sons."

Dammit, how many of you came here, thought Kitty. 600,000 was not the relevant number, though it worried her. *Wait, who had the slim chance?*

Luci looked into the camera. "At last, you understand. This whole wretched adventure, abandoning our homes and everything we had built, was probably for nothing. We didn't get out in time. Against 19 of us, the swarm had little hope. Our world is probably empty."

"If your world is empty," said the clown, "you could return to it."

"Gaia is *probably* empty, though in a sense, you are correct. We *wanted* to go back home, when we realized how far you had fallen." Luci shook her head. "I see it with my own eyes, but I just can't *believe* you pay your queens for permission to work. How could any man perform after he has been so humiliated?"

In the *Lens*, staffers looked at each other uncomfortably.

"But we *can't* go back," said the alien. "Not so long as we still lose one child in four."

Kitty's mouth opened in sudden comprehension.

The clown waved noncommittally, his blurred fingers flicking across the Big Screen. "I don't see the relevance."

Luci contemplated her beer. "If only we hadn't built that damned *Finger.* If our exiled children were going to die anyway, we might as well have stayed and killed them ourselves. Then, when my daughter came of age, she might have survived outside our walls. The swarm would be dead, but she could forage in their ruins, harvest their abandoned crops, even start to rebuild their society. But that was 90 years ago, and our ecosystem was robust. By now, our farmland has been smothered by forest. If we returned to our world, then when I must cast Delilah out, she would not survive her first summer."

The distant *Lens* hushed. The image of Luci shifted as the clown instinctively leaned away from what he knew was coming.

"Ironic, isn't it," Luci murmured. "We *need* your foul culture as our chamber pot. Quite the joke on us."

The next morning, on her way to work, Sophie turned the radio to the news.

> *In a coordinated crackdown on dangerous incitement, the nine largest social-media platforms announced today they will no longer permit content that advocates violence against Worms.*

Sophie arrived at the Pine Shack to find it surrounded by soldiers. Men in desert-tan camo tended desert-tan cement trucks pouring footings for something substantial. Out back, the weedy lot overflowed with desert-tan amored personnel carriers. Down the block, protesters milled resentfully behind concertina wire.

Sophie was greeted by a desert-tan soldier. His stern face peered out from the gap between his helmet, abdominal casing, and inch-thick Elvis collars. Sophie rolled down her window and pointed at the cement mixers. "I want to see your building permit."

"Good morning, Ms. Flint," the unsmiling soldier intoned from behind his carapace. "How is your day going?"

"If we'd been introduced, I'm sure I would remember."

The armor leaned forward to peer into Sophie's car. "Ms. Flint, how often do you use the word, *frenetic?*"

Sophie opened her purse, withdrew a lipstick, and looked in her mirror. "This is not how I imagined our conversation."

"The word, ma'am. How often do you use it?"

Sophie carefully applied her lipstick, then returned it to her purse. She glanced at the armor's name patch. "Lieutenant Leaden, tomorrow morning, when you ask how my day is going, what will

happen if I say, *frenetic?*"

432

Lieutenant Leaden gazed at her soberly. "Ms. Flint, I was warned you would be difficult."

"Who told you that?"

"Ma'am, that information is deeply classified."

"What will happen if I use the panic word?"

"Ma'am, it will be best for you, and for me, if you never learn what happens when you use the duress code."

Sophie looked annoyed. "Shall I use the duress code if I *suspect* trouble, or only if I'm certain?"

"Use it when you suspect, ma'am, but be prepared for a certain amount of inconvenience. All of your close relatives will have to buy new front doors and back doors and probably some windows. Also, you will need a new car."

"I understand." Sophie waved at the busy workmen. "Why are you here, interfering with my parking?"

"Ma'am, I am interfering with your parking because the Wyrms have been threatened. We are here to protect them." Lieutenant Leaden stepped back and waved her forward. "Thank you, ma'am. You may proceed."

"I don't think so. We've been threatening the Wyrms for months. What changed?"

The armor rotated and lifted a conspicuously naked right hand toward a row of similar armor, bristling with gun barrels. "Ma'am, do you see the female at the end of the rank of warriors?"

"The one with the rocket is female?"

"Yes, that is Private Parts. She provides our air defense. In her heart, I believe she perceives us as her family, which she is defending."

Sophie nodded approvingly. "That sounds sensible."

"Yes, ma'am, and if I were to tell you the nature of the new threat, Private Parts there would jam half of her anti-aircraft missile up my ass for not telling her first."

**Later that day
Washington, D.C.**

President Mirror teed off. He swung smoothly through the ball, and with a metallic *ping,* it sailed down the fairway.

Secretary Siphon teed off. Her shot hooked left, and she winced at the clank.

"Don't worry, Madame Secretary; the limo is armored."

As usual, the entire golf course had been closed and sprinkled with Secret Service. When Kitty Siphon and President Mirror set off down the fairway, agents Oak and Bear remained at the tee.

"This part annoys me."

"Me too," said Agent Oak. "But they want privacy."

"Privacy." Agent Bear snorted. "You know, I think Cougar actually believes her secure phone is secure from *me.*"

"Has she said anything suspicious?"

"Nothing that threatens Tiger."

Two hundred feet down the fairway, Kitty Siphon glanced back to be sure their Secret Service bodyguards were beyond earshot. Then she turned to Mirror. "Any news on our forbidden fruit sample?"

"No, the labs still insist it's just salt water, and it did nothing to three volunteers, except one got diarrhea, probably from a burrito."

"Do the eunuchs have any theories?"

"Of course the eunuchs have theories," said Mirror. "The eunuchs *always* have theories. Their least-wacky idea is the salt water contains undetectable nano-machines, waiting to be activated by a signal from a Wyrm skull implant."

"Undetectable nano-machines?" Kitty seemed doubtful.

"The eunuchs say it's plausible. Apparently, seawater is packed full of viruses that nobody noticed until about fifteen minutes ago."

They reached the pond, where a Canada goose was paddling to shore. The big bird waddled up onto the grass and took four steps before its head flew off, tumbling end-over-end through the air. Kitty ducked as a supersonic rifle crack echoed down the fairway. The goose fell over as its head splashed into the pond with a quiet *plop.*

Down the fairway, the blonde amazon Agent Bear whooped and waved her scoped rifle.

Kitty sighed. "Now we have to worry about explosive drones disguised as *geese?*"

"No," said the president. "But I told the Secret Service we do. They shit on the green. If the forbidden fruit gets loose, it won't matter if the aliens number only 200, because a million of our donkeys will join them." Mirror thumped his club into the turf. "If they steal a million of our donkeys, their culture would be viable. Worse, it would be an *example.* It could wake up *all* the donkeys and throw us into the mass-starvation scenario."

Kitty nodded grimly. "On another unhappy note, we've tried the hammerhead 20 different ways, and it just doesn't work around their skull implant. The implant is made of iron, so it screws up the hammerhead's magnetic field. I think it's time to face reality. We probably won't get the human remote control."

"Is there *no* hope for a nationwide telepathic network?"

Kitty shrugged. "The alien skull implants are obviously made to monitor *something,* but what? It's not electrical. My alpha eunuch thinks the Wyrms know what self-awareness is made of, and that's what their brain implants monitor. He thinks the implant is like a toaster; it's simple and easy to understand, unless you've never heard of electricity."

The two heads of their security details had drifted too close, but they retreated when Mirror waved angrily.

Kitty watched Agents Oak and Bear back away. "At least we can stop worrying about Wyrms reading our minds."

Mirror sagged.

Kitty touched his shoulder. "I know how badly you wanted it, but mind reading was a hoax. The bitch bluffed me with it to slow us down and limit their casualties while they provoked us."

Mirror released their shared golf bag. It toppled over as he sank to the ground, seeming to shrivel as he hugged his knees. "Alone in my head, forever. This nightmare will never end."

Kitty sat on the bag. "You won't get your telepathy; I won't get my human remote control, and we won't turn everyone into our doting parents. Our dreams are burning to ashes, and I think it's time for the Wyrms to burn too. Every moment we delay, we risk a mass release of the forbidden fruit. I don't know why they are waiting. If they release it before we have a screening test, how could we stop people from experimenting with it? We'll lose the donkeys."

Mirror rested his chin on his knees. "We still have hope. Let the Wyrms build their colony, and we can blanket the place with micro-bugs. There's still a chance they have telepathy."

"That's what they are maneuvering us into." Kitty stood up. "*While* they are stealing our donkeys."

"Yes, I suppose that changes our priorities." Mirror rose heavily to his feet. "I got a request from the bioweapon eunuchs. We had hundreds of them searching for the Wyrm allergy, but that supposed allergy was obviously a hoax. The eunuchs need a new project, so I told them to figure out the Wyrm birth control. They want a dozen female Wyrms for test subjects."

"You want to neutralize their birth control? Why? Do you think we could breed soldiers we can store in the freezer?"

"I guess we could." Mirror took a smooth backswing and chipped his ball onto the green.

"Do you think we could birth some little hostages?"

Mirror slid his club into the bag. "You're full of good ideas, but think bigger. A fetus in the womb is half foreign, so it must be shielded from its mother's immune system."

"Ooh! Their vault has a back door!"

"If the eunuchs could experiment on pregnant Wyrms, they might figure out *how* the fetus protects itself from Mommy. Then, maybe they can do the same for a war virus." Mirror handed Kitty a five iron, then waited while she drove her ball into a tree. They ducked as the ricochet hummed over their heads. The ball rolled back up the fairway, where it was retrieved by a junior Secret Service agent.

As they walked toward the green, Kitty thoughtfully tapped her chin. "It's so dangerous to detain them, now that they are willing to attack Washington. I wonder if we could talk them into patenting their birth control? A patent application has to explain the invention clearly, so anyone can understand it."

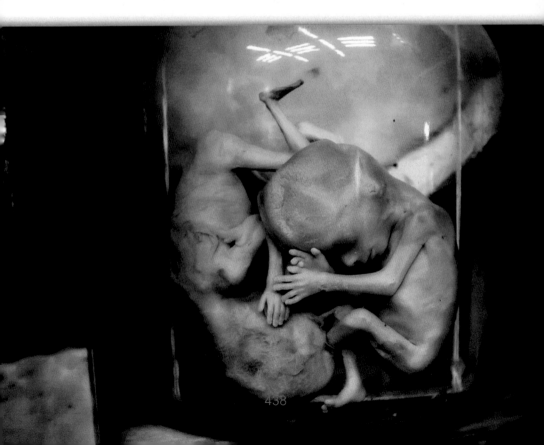

438

Six days later
Shenandoah National Park
Human-Wyrm colony talks

The U.S. government's clown strolled through the forest to Luci's yacht, parked beside the utility shed.

As always, the 9-year-old girl waited for him outside, but this time, her little wooden desk was bare, no brass scale or notepad, just a single gold coin, the size of a quarter. "You're not supposed to give me any gold," she explained. "However, you may give me some candy."

"I'm so sorry; I have no candy, but I do have this." The clown produced a pack of Camels and shook one out. "Would you like a cigarette?"

In the distant *Lens*, staffers laughed nervously. Kitty Siphon snorted. "Nice, but something is wrong."

The little girl accepted the cigarette, sniffed it cautiously, and tucked it into her shirt pocket. Then she tapped the gold coin. "You are supposed to take this, to pay for your time."

The clown put on a frowny face. "Is our meeting canceled?"

"No, Mom is here. You can go in."

Watching from the *Lens*, Kitty Siphon didn't know whether to be pleased or alarmed. She settled on, *alarmed* as the clown hesitantly entered the shed.

Inside the shed, he found Luci behind her Lexan barrier, wearing loose, long sleeves instead of the snug athletic shirt she usually wore to show she was unarmed. Ominously, she was standing. The usual folding chairs were absent. The clown faced her and said nothing. Plainly, his adversary had planned today's program.

"I have good news and bad news," she began. "It is good news for me, and bad news for you."

The clown remained still.

"I hereby invite you to represent your queens at the ground-breaking ceremony for our colony. It is 9,900 square miles of land formerly known as, *Western Australia.*"

In the *Lens*, Kitty's heart sank.

Luci slapped a yellow Post-it on the Lexan. "Here are the precise boundaries and the date, should you care to attend."

"Thank you for inviting me," the clown said calmly. "On behalf of the United States, I congratulate you and wish you success."

"You are welcome," Luci replied. "May the success you wish for us be returned to you tenfold."

"It appears our negotiation has ended." Ambassador Peter Slip, the U.S. government's clown, pulled the tiny speaker from his ear and unjacked it from his belt transceiver. He tugged the wires out from under his shirt and wound them around his hand. "Before we adjourn, I would like to ask a personal question."

In the *Lens,* a eunuch tapped his screen. "Switching to secondary audio."

Kitty growled dangerously. "Slip, what are you up to? I want her to patent their birth control, and this might be our last chance."

Slip tossed his earpiece on the floor and stepped on it. "Some time ago, you warned me, obliquely, against kidnapping your friends. You claimed a capacity to read minds, and hence trace your captor's chain of command to retaliate against the actual decision maker. We were killing you, so you took the battle to our queens."

Lens staffers flinched as Kitty slammed her fist on her console.

Slip ground his earpiece under his sole. "Your mind-reading misdirection was magnificent. I wanted you to know I noticed."

Luci nodded graciously.

Slip removed his glasses, with their breathtakingly expensive cameras. "At first, I dared not believe." He dropped the video glasses on the floor and crushed them beneath his heel. "I dared not believe, yet it is true." He kicked the debris into the corner and stepped up to the Lexan wall. He raised his empty palms to rest on the transparent barrier. "You are *ungovernable,* yet you live in peace, because you can give each other the benefit of the doubt."

Luci stood, impassive.

"Nonetheless, with blood and treasure at stake, you *lied,* and your timing was vicious. You knew what our queens had done, that they must fear dire retaliation if you learned their thoughts. Your mind-reading fraud threatened them with personal violence, which forced us to do what *you* desired." Slip leaned forward until his nose almost touched the Lexan. His face twisted. "Luci, *you held us for ransom by lying and threatening us.*"

Lucifa Dark smiled cheerfully, wrinkling her cheek tattoos. "You know I got this job because I'm borderline."

Slip hesitated.

"Relax," Luci added. "I know you listen to our private conversations. Do you remember what *borderline* means?"

"Yes," said Slip. *"Borderline* means your personality falls close to the border between wasp and Wyrm. You are barely a Wyrm, but you *are* a Wyrm. How could you act as a wasp?"

"Would you like to know the great thing about being borderline?" As she turned to leave for the last time, Luci waved vaguely at her cheek tattoos. "The great thing about being borderline is: *I can always give myself the benefit of the doubt."*

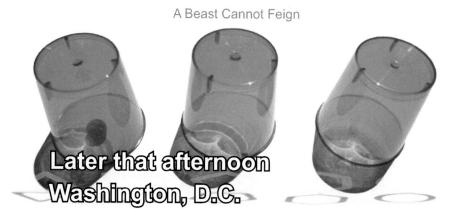

Later that afternoon
Washington, D.C.

President Mirror teed off. He swung smoothly through the ball, and with a metallic *ping*, it sailed down the fairway.

Secretary Siphon shook hands with her club. She hooked her right pinky firmly around her left index finger, and flexed her other fingers to establish her grip. She spread her feet to shoulder width at right angles to the fairway, and took two smooth practice strokes. Her head remained perfectly motionless as her shoulders rotated through her swing. Then she stepped forward and laid her clubhead behind the ball. She held her posture as she swiveled her eyes toward her target, then back down at the ball. She took a deep breath, let out half, then tossed her club on the turf. "Fuck golf. Bring me a Mai Tai."

Ten minutes later, she strolled down the fairway with the president. "They got their colony."

"Yes, they did." Mirror glanced back to be sure their Secret Service protectors were beyond earshot. "Any day now, they will release the forbidden fruit, so it's probably too late for a vaccine. Did we ever get another sample?"

"No, just the dose for the governor of Idaho, plus some residue when Luci got careless and threw an empty vial in the trash. The eunuchs tested both samples every way they can think of, and they can't find anything but salt water. The forbidden fruit must be an undetectable nano-machine, and it's probably activated by the alien brain implant."

An aide hustled toward them, waving a sheet of paper.

Mirror glowered. "This better be good."

The aide handed over the paper. "Mr. President, an A.I. found this in peer review at *Nature.*"

Mirror glanced at it. "And?"

"Sir, do you remember the Wyrm doomsday weapon, the seeds that can thrive without phosphorus fertilizer?"

"Uh oh." Kitty looked over the president's shoulder. The paper was a scholarly journal abstract, titled, *Novel Phosphorus Fixation Mechanism In Recently Identified Succulent.*

The aide looked nervous. "Sir, one of their doomsday plants must have escaped. It's a cactus, and it's spreading all over the world."

Down the fairway, a girl in a blue skirt ran toward them shouting until she was tackled by Agent Bear.

Everyone stopped to watch. Agent Bear and the blue-skirted woman lay on the grass awhile, apparently chatting. Agent Oak stood over them aiming his gun. Then they stood up, and Bear pointed to the president. The blue-skirted girl resumed running.

She puffed up to President Mirror, gasping, and handed over her phone. "This just showed up on the internet. We're spamming an alternative version that says it's a 4-chan prank, and the cactus is actually a poison that causes permanent palsy, but the A.I. has found 90 copies of the original, and predicts it will spread."

Mirror looked at her phone. It showed a picture of a gnarled cactus with 2-inch spines, and a caption:

THIS IS THE TREE OF KNOWLEDGE
IT BEARS THE FORBIDDEN FRUIT
IT IS DANGEROUS

"Fuck me!" Kitty kicked the grass.

Mirror looked annoyed. "Invisible nano-machines in a *cactus?*"

"No," Kitty snarled. "There are no fucking invisible nano-machines. All this time, the drug is in the *needle.* That's why the bitch left the vial in the trash for us, so we would grab *it* instead of grabbing *her.*"

Mirror pointed to the aides. "Scram."

When they regained their privacy, Kitty sipped her drink. "Our time is up. The Choice is on us."

Mirror didn't need to ask. The two of them went back a long way, and they had discussed the Choice many times. They stopped while Mirror chipped his ball onto the green. They walked on.

Kitty took the president's hand.

200 feet up the fairway, Agents Oak and Bear smiled. Cougar and Tiger hadn't walked hand in hand for months. It must be the Mai Tai.

"Now that the Choice is real, do you feel any differently?"

"No," said the president. "The Choice is easy."

Most people thought the Choice was hard. Most people had no chance of becoming president.

"I agree," Kitty replied. "It's better to rule in Hell."

They stopped while the caddy refilled Kitty's drink. The caddy bowed and retreated. They walked on.

"How are the opinion polls?"

Kitty bit off the cherry from her Mai Tai and tossed the stem onto the fairway, "The polls are excellent. Seventy percent will support us, and the other 30 percent would never vote for you anyway. Do you think we need a Gulf of Tonkin?"

"Gaa! When the war pigs realized *I* would be president, they reworked the nuclear code system specifically to prevent false-flag attacks." With an effort, Mirror calmed himself. "We don't need more provocation. If you can't give me five Casus Belli before breakfast, I need a new best friend."

The secretary of commerce poked the president, but not too hard. "How much time do you need?"

Mirror considered. "A week."

"That works for me. Tuesday morning, I'll give the Authority a firm shove, and we can move to the Deep Bunker."

70 busy hours later
Washington, D.C.

A secure telephone flashed in Dominick Tork's high-ceiling office, six blocks from the White House. Only one caller had this number, or the quantum-entangled circuitry to use it.

Dominick pushed the button. "Good afternoon, Madam Secretary."

As usual, Kitty skipped the preliminaries. "We're finally ready to take out the *Unexpected Finger.* Tuesday morning, after I brief the Alien Regulatory Authority, the president and I are heading down to the Deep Bunker. I want you to join us."

"Thank you, Madam Secretary."

"Plan on remaining in the bunker for two years."

A silence followed.

"Madam Secretary, could you repeat that last part?"

"The war pigs want to hit the *Finger* over Antarctica with a series of 60 stealth nukes that will push its perihelion into the atmosphere. If it works, the initial blasts will only sunburn a few penguins, then the debris will reenter the atmosphere over the Pacific. We tested the Wyrm doomsday seeds, and they can't survive in salt water."

"If it works?"

"The war pigs seem confident." Kitty sighed. "But nobody has ever done this before, and that damn *Finger* weighs 3,000 tons. Pieces might break off into stable orbits, and if one of the pieces does something dramatic, most of the Earth's population will enjoy a direct line of sight to the excitement at least once per day. Or, some chunks might make it over the North Pole and reenter in Asia, where the doomsday seeds could get a foothold. But don't worry; we built the bunker with an unlimited budget. It's packed with 100 years of food, and state-of-the-art labs. I'm sure we'll suppress the alien weeds and restore our agriculture."

Silence.

"Oh, Dominick, we aren't monsters. Eighty percent of the population was going to starve anyway, when the Wyrms steal our donkeys. We have to risk it."

"Very well, Madam Secretary. Thank you for your confidence."

"Tuesday."

The secure telephone beeped and went silent. Dominick leaned back into his leather chair and looked troubled.

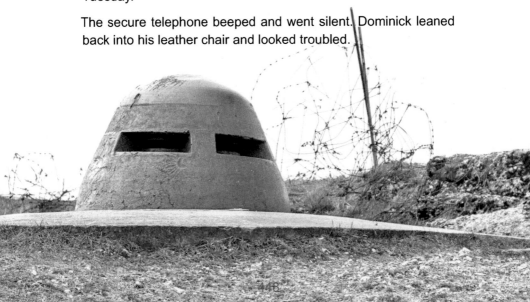

Tom Pine was composing a spill report when his phone rang.

The spill was minor, a quart of harmless Zincate solution, and Tom was exempt from EPA regulation because nobody dared punish him. But now, Tom found he enjoyed filling out EPA forms. In the section titled, *Root Cause of Accident,* he wrote, *Affirmative action.* In the section titled, *Proposed Corrective Action,* he had written, *Plug my drain with your...* when his phone beeped. He pressed the flashing button. "This is Pine."

"Good morning," said Dominick Tork. "How is progress?"

"I started a new project, a metal vapor deposition tank."

"Really? What does that have in common with your other products?"

After a pause, Tom said, "Nothing."

"You should not divide your efforts. And we shall have to chat about the technical details, but now we must discuss another matter."

Tom's tone became guarded. "Yes?"

"From time to time, I report to a committee. They have some policy responsibilities concerning the Wyrms, so I will need you to brief them on your experiences."

"Why me? You know everything that goes on here."

"You should not underestimate yourself. The Wyrms have launched many joint projects with Humans, but they don't supervise them personally. Few Humans have met Worms more than two or three times, so your prolonged interaction offers a unique perspective. Plus, the committee is influenced by other, less rational considerations."

"Let me guess," Tom guessed. "They hate you."

Dominick considered. *"Hate* is too strong a word. It is more that they perceive me as a stern father."

"And a committee can be trusted to act with all the wisdom we expect from teenage girls."

Dominick chuckled. "Dealing with you is such a pleasure. Please clear your calendar for Tuesday "

Monday
Aboard Luci's yacht

Tom sat beside Luci, watching the Earth recede. This was his favorite part of the trip. When the g-forces subsided, he unstrapped.

Luci watched curiously as Tom pulled off his jacket. When he unbuttoned his shirt, revealing crisply defined pectorals, she looked surprised. "Mr. Pine, you've been hiding your lamp under a bushel."

Tom held a finger to his lips and turned on her music player, cranking up the volume to fill the cabin with, inevitably, *Don't Fear the Reaper.* He winced at her choice of music, and unzipped his pants. Luci rotated her seat for a more relaxed view.

Finally, when Tom was as undressed as any man could be, he waved a hand at Luci, inviting her to join him.

Without actually speaking, Luci managed to convey a stern, *"I beg your pardon?"*

Tom grinned and unrolled a tiny note.

Do you trust me?

Luci's next expression translated as, *are you serious?*

Tom continued to grin.

Luci rolled her eyes. Then she twirled her finger, indicating he should turn his back.

Tom shook his head, and his grin widened.

Luci glared at him while she pulled her shirt over her head.

When all of her clothes had joined Tom's on the floor, they crowded into her tiny bathroom. Luci faced the mirror with Tom pressed against her back. She had trouble closing the door. As soon as it clicked shut, she whispered, "This better be good."

"I just wondered if I could get you to do it."

She used her uninjured right arm to elbow him, but not too hard. "Lucky I don't believe you."

"Admit it," Tom commanded. "You're enjoying this."

She elbowed him again, but not too hard. "At least this time, we won't wake up lying in the mud."

"Miss Dark, I just want information."

"What you want is obvious. Pressing, even."

"We need to talk." Tom switched off the light. "Just you and me, with no third parties. I've checked my hair, but I'm afraid bugs might have been planted in our clothes."

"You've certainly solved *that* problem, so nothing will stop us from transferring information, and possibly some DNA."

"Miss Dark, what do you really want?"

"Right this moment?"

"Be serious," said Tom. "I may have a chance to help you, with the government I mean, so what should I ask for?"

Luci tensed. "Truly?"

Tom painted on his sincere smile. In the dark, it was wasted.

I want you, Luci thought. Aloud, she said, "I just want to be ignored, so I can find a husband and a home. I hate living alone in a frozen can, and I hate fearing every passerby might murder me or force me to murder him."

"I thought so."

Luci relaxed against his chest. "You could have asked Buff. I might have paid to watch."

Tom resisted his urge to poke her, then realized he was doing it anyway. "One more question. Why do you take the risk, coming down and hanging out with us? So many of you have been killed, and you could have gotten rich over the phone."

Luci's shoulder-length hair tickled Tom's cheek, snagging in his afternoon stubble. "Partly, we come down because we need immigrants. We want you to see us with your own eyes. Then, later, some of you won't believe the lies."

"And the larger reason?"

"The larger reason is, we have a treasure. We found the beautiful secret, the burning bush your queens crave above all other fantasies. It would transform you all into their willing slaves."

After a pause, Tom said, "Did you answer my question?"

"Your queens are desperate to steal our burning bush. So long as they had any hope, *no* queen would sell us a colony. And even if they did, we would have no peace. Eventually, you would make war on us, hoping to gain prisoners to interrogate."

When Tom comprehended, the vertigo struck. He braced his arms against the swaying walls. "You can't mean..."

"We had to let your queens choose their own targets. If they decided for themselves which of us they would torture and kill, your queens could convince themselves with fewer victims. More of us would survive to see them give up hope and sell us a colony, so they can send in spies."

"You lined up in front of the machine gun *so the gunner could choose his own targets?*"

"That was our strategy."

"That's not a *strategy,*" Tom hissed. "It's a *buffet.*"

453

"Oh, we were strategic," said Luci. "We even timed our big reveal, when we admitted the burning bush's real potential, how it could enslave you utterly, so your queens would give their final, utmost effort to steal it, just before we made them stop. Now, they *know* we can't be coerced, so instead of making war, they will send in spies."

Tom's gorge rose. "You must be kidding. There has to be a strategy better than offering yourself for sacrifice."

"If you concoct a plan that ends in fewer deaths, please share it. We found none I could believe. At least, none I could believe when I bit the forbidden fruit and faced the question without my censor."

"No," Tom insisted. "This is ridiculous. There must be a better way."

"There would be many better ways, if *you* were queen. But you will never be a queen, because you don't *want* to, not badly enough to do what it takes. The competition is so vicious, no man even *tries* to become queen, unless he is tormented by his need to dominate other men. If such a man promised to leave us unmolested, he would be lying. Nobody abandons his deepest yearning while any hope remains."

No man abandons his deepest yearning while any hope remains. Tom thought of *Fluffer,* the dream he had never surrendered. "There, at least, I have to agree with you. Did you really risk all this voluntarily? You *personally* agreed to walk among us, and risk being captured and tortured?"

"I volunteered years ago, when I took Gabriel's gold in return for my best effort to bring us to a safe haven. My best effort is now *his thing,* so I can't withhold it."

Another wave of nausea.

"Cheer up," Luci added. "I think your queens are convinced, so I may live to hold this over my friends, if I can find some friends. Plus, Gabriel paid me a *big* pile of gold. I can buy a fabulous house."

Tom stopped asking questions. "Thank you. Let's get dressed."

Luci's head turned, her hair stranding through Tom's unshaved whiskers. "You won't try to ravish me?"

"Unfortunately, I asked you to trust me," said Tom. "So now I'm obliged to behave stupidly."

In truth, his interest had faltered. Despite rumors to the contrary, sex and death did not go well together, at least not for Tom. "And besides..." he began.

Luci joined in, and they chanted in unison: "This is where we eat."

"We're in a bathroom," Luci observed. "The *Don't poop where you eat* rule doesn't really work here."

"Miss Dark, open the door."

"Not yet. I want to brag. If I don't get to tell you how clever I was, I'll explode." Luci wiggled, and Tom's interest reawakened so abruptly he expected a boinging noise. Luci wiggled again. "I think you might explode too."

Tom waited patiently.

"I bluffed your queens," Luci chortled. "You know I can't really read minds, but I pretended I could, so your queens would have to be careful while they tortured us. I wanted to slow them down, because we couldn't defend ourselves yet, and I didn't know for how long."

"Clever girl."

"That wasn't the clever part." Luci leaned back into Tom and turned her head so she could murmur into his ear. "Your ambassador complained that mind reading gave me an unfair advantage. So I told him not to worry, because I promised to ignore any thoughts he didn't reveal by word or deed."

Tom snorted. "You *promised to ignore?*"

"Bitchy, wasn't it? The clever part was, right after I did it, I realized he would test me. The ambassador was probably thinking something outrageous, to see if I would respond. So I looked him in the eye, and reminded him I promised to ignore his thoughts, and would he please be more polite." Luci giggled. "The poor guy thought he was controlling his expression, but he wasn't."

"Miss Dark, you always find a way to surprise me."

With some effort, Luci turned in Tom's lap to face him.

He was surprised.

Luci pressed against him and whispered into his ear. "I wish I could tell you our story, why we had to leave our home. The story is bitterly sad, too harsh for children, but we will tell them, and they will tell their children. It is the epic tale that will define our culture."

Tom closed his eyes, hoping the story had a happy ending.

"At the story's end, a hero appears, the man who stops the tragedy from repeating. His name will be known by every schoolchild." Luci rested her hands on Tom's hips. Her breath warmed his neck, right beneath his ear. "That hero is *you.*"

She pulled back and flipped on the light. "Let's get out of here before you give me a bruise."

"Jesus Christ." Tom sounded like he was strangling. "Wait a second."

A minute passed before Tom could breathe normally. "Okay, I'm ready to be the hero."

"What do you mean? You already did it."

"I did?" Tom looked confused. "You mean my sentries?"

Luci leaned her forehead against Tom's chest. "To you, the sentries are just business, but to us, they are salvation. If only..." Her voice broke."If only *we* had known how to make them."

Tom waited quietly.

In time, Luci recovered and mustered a weak smile. "To show our gratitude, we left a gift in geosynchronous orbit above your capitol."

"Oh, good," said Tom. "I'll pick it up, next time I pass by."

"That might be a bad idea. I was being ironic when I called it a *gift,* but I think you'll be pleased."

"Miss Dark, what did you do leave in orbit?"

"We bought a comm satellite, and programmed it to point its dish antenna at your capitol. Then we replaced the dish antenna with a cherub sword big enough to turn Washington into a volcano. Any Wyrm who reaches the satellite can fire it."

The little bathroom fell silent.

"Eventually, your queens will realize they cannot steal our secret," Luci murmured into Tom's ear. "That is when they will attack us. If a single Wyrm pilot survives long enough to reach geosynch orbit, your Washington queens will *not* inherit the Earth."

Tom waited nervously with Frank and Sophie in a rosewood-paneled corridor outside a briefing theater. The double door was guarded by a squad of blue suits with stern expressions and wires dangling from their ears. Above the door, a red-let display said, *IN SESSION.*

"I've enjoyed chatting with you," Frank Drummer said into his phone. "I wanted to say that now, before we meet face-to-face and I find out you've been lying about your appearance." He hung up and peeled out of his overcoat.

Tom whistled. "Damn, Frank, you're getting into shape *fast.* Two months ago, you looked like mashed potatoes, but now you look like a raw potato. What happened?"

Frank tossed his overcoat onto a hand-carved, leather-upholstered bench. "I decided exercise and starvation was worth the grief."

"Really? What changed?"

Before Frank could answer, the red *IN SESSION* sign was replaced by, *ENTRY AUTHORIZED,* in green. The engraved hardwood doors swung open and a blonde amazon emerged, followed by a petite, 40-ish woman. Tom was startled to recognize Kitty Siphon, the secretary of commerce and famously the president's best friend. She swept past, eyes forward, leading a phalanx of charcoal suits.

Tom was next. He stepped past the two remaining door guards and peered between the cracked doors into the briefing theater.

458

Every seat was full, every suit perfectly tailored, every tie on the current color list, and every face tight with fear.

"They look like politicians," Tom observed, "except more nervous."

"What?" Sophie shouldered Tom aside and peeked through the gap. Then she pulled back. "I thought they would be analysts."

Tom shrugged. "That's what I expected."

"Oh fuck."

Tom couldn't tell whether to be amused or frightened. Frank looked amused.

Sophie looked frightened. "We have to do something. That's the *Alien Regulatory Authority.*"

"I know a tap dance routine," Frank offered. "It makes people treat me better, because I do it poorly, so they look good in comparison."

"The commissioners are *panicking,*" Sophie hissed. "Tom, that is the ARA, and *they are panicking.*"

"Maybe I could–"

"Shut up, Frank."

Everyone froze as a pack of patricians strode past.

"Uh oh." Tom pressed his eye against the gap. "*That's* why the commissioners are upset. They lost everything."

Frank's brow furrowed. He obviously didn't understand.

"Our government –every government– wants only *four* things from the aliens." Tom ticked them off on his fingers. "The burning bush; the cherub sword; immunity to infection; and for all the aliens to die so they won't recruit any Humans. Now the government won't get any of those things. Instead, the alien colony will be a haven for *us.* Our best men will bolt to it, followed by our best women. If our productive class breaks free, our *influence* class can't survive." He pointed at the double doors. "Now those perfectly-groomed influencers must choose between war and starvation."

Frank waved dismissively. "Don't be melodramatic. The Wyrms just offered to take people who don't fit in with normal Humans. Your economy won't collapse."

Tom: "Your life must be a series of rude surprises."

Sophie: *"Your* economy?"

The conversation paused while a brood of old ladies gabbled down the hall, led by an elderly male tour guide who pointed to the double doors. "In that very room, I personally witnessed the greatest event of the Reagan presidency. I remember it like yesterday."

An old lady raised her hand. "Is that where they held the Iran-Contra hearings?"

"No." The elderly tour guide looked wistful. "That's where I saw Linda Lovelace testify before the Meese Commission."

"You have to stop them," Sophie continued when the hallway cleared again. "Tom, the ARA will nuke the aliens, so *you have to stop them*. You *can* stop them!"

Tom glanced at the two door guards, then he led Frank and Sophie down the hall out of earshot. "The ARA *wants* to kill the Wyrms. What makes you think I could stop them?"

"They do want to get rid of the aliens," Sophie admitted. "But attacking the *Finger* is hardly safe."

"Actually, attacking the Wyrms *would be* pretty safe," said Frank. "The top U.S. officials can flee to an excellent deep bunker system. I know, because I helped design it."

Tom groaned. "You *helped* our politicians build bunkers to protect *them* but not *us?*"

"You can stop the attack," Sophie hissed. "You are the world's expert on alien security, so just say they are careless. The burning bush has to be sited somewhere Human immigrants can visit, so we can send in spies to steal the secret."

Frank seemed confused. "Why are you so focused on the burning bush? Wouldn't our government be more interested in their disease immunity? The burning bush would just turn humans into slaves. Who wants that?"

Tom chuckled. "Don't you just love Frank?"

"No," said Sophie. "Do you understand what you have to do?"

"Why are you so determined to save the Wyrms? I didn't think you liked them all that much."

"I *don't* like them," Sophie growled. "But attacking them is *not safe*, not for anyone outside of Frank's stupid bunker. If even *one* alien fires his engine in cherub-sword mode above the U.S., we get an EMP on steroids. If we lose our electronics, who do you imagine will feed us? France?"

Tom considered the question. "Our situation might actually be more dangerous than you think."

We left a gift in geosynchronous orbit above your capitol.

Everyone froze as a flock of schoolchildren chattered down the hall. Their harried chaperon looked desperate.

Sophie dragged Tom back to the briefing room. "Throw in some anecdotes, all the times when aliens were careless and blurted out things they shouldn't. Say they don't appreciate the threat of computer hacking, since their world had no computers, so they actually *asked us* to network their sentries together with no real safeguards. Tell them the aliens will need to move people through the burning bush by the *millions*. Convince them spying will be *easy.*"

"Don't worry," said Tom, "I know what to do."

When Tom opened the double doors to the briefing theater, he bumped into Dominick Tork coming out.

Dominick took Tom's elbow and led him back down the hall, away from the door guards. He glared at Frank and Sophie when they tried to follow.

"Tell me our situation, as you understand it," Dominick said quietly when they were alone.

"The ARA commissioners control nuclear weapons," Tom replied. "They are panicking because the Wryms got their colony. In the short term, the commissioners fear they will lose their personal status. In the long term, mass starvation, though that is less important. The commissioners will probably order an all-out surprise attack on the Wyrms, including a nuclear strike on the *Unexpected Finger*. Any Wyrm survivors will retaliate however they can."

We left a gift in geosynchronous orbit above your capitol.

"Dealing with you is always a pleasure," said Dominick. "Do you know how to save your friends?"

"Sure. I can stop the attack by telling the commissioners how to get the burning bush. All they have to do is allow the Wyrms to build their colony, then send in spies."

Dominick looked relieved.

Tom looked surprised. "Are you nervous? *You?*"

Dominick smiled thinly. "The last time we spoke, I said your experience with Wyrms gives you a uniquely valuable perspective. Do you understand now what I meant?"

"Yes. I designed the Wyrm security system, and I've hung around with them for months while we tweaked it. Who but me could say they're an easy target for espionage?"

Dominick patted Tom's shoulder. "Now do it."

Three minutes later, in the briefing theater, Dominick walked to the podium first. "The next material is particularly sensitive. Before I present it, I wish to remind you of your security commitments."

For some reason, the commissioners looked sour.

"Our next guest is Mr. Tom Pine, the designer of the Pine robotic sentries. As you will recall from my earlier briefings, the Wryms must rely on Mr. Pine's robotic sentries to safeguard their colony, by identifying imposters masquerading as Wyrms. Mr. Pine has extensive personal experience with Wyrms, working closely with them for months while he constructed their security system to their specifications. He understands the Wyrm security hardware, and more importantly, their security *attitude,* better than anyone."

Tom walked to the podium. The mic was set for a man of normal stature, so he tugged it down to his level, then he surveyed the 49 commissioners, plus Dominick, Frank, and Sophie standing in the back. "First the bad news," he began. "You know the Wryms' cherub sword could kill us all, but you might be surprised to learn their burning bush is *worse.* It could enslave Humans utterly."

The commissioners didn't look surprised but did look interested. Sophie looked nervous.

"So let me set your minds at ease," Tom continued. "There is no way *any* Human will steal those terrible secrets. You don't need to worry about the cherub sword or the burning bush falling into the wrong hands."

In the back row, Sophie gasped audibly. Beside her, Dominick remained deadpan, and there was no telling what might be happening inside Frank Drummer's head.

"The Wyrms have protected those two secrets for *five generations* against a desperate enemy who outnumbered them 20 to 1, including many of their own *children.*"

The commissioners looked sick. In the back row, Sophie looked astonished.

"In my opinion, the Wyrms will never bring a burning bush to the Earth's surface where it might be observed by Humans. Likewise, all cherub swords will be manufactured off-planet, perhaps on Mars. They already put a picnic table there, with a view of Valles Marineris."

In the back row, Dominick cocked his head and looked puzzled. Beside him, Sophie silently mouthed, *What the fuck are you doing?*

Frank seemed calm, as always.

"So you can relax," Tom continued. "The awful secret of the cherub sword is safe, and so is the beautiful secret of the burning bush, even if my robotic sentries are somehow compromised.

The commissioners did not seem to be relaxing.

464

"You've seen them keep another secret," Tom continued. "You know a Wyrm man can't actually rape a woman, not if she asks him to stop, but she *must say the words*. We've all seen the videos of women getting raped because they didn't *know* they could just ask him to stop." Tom pointed to the commissioners. "You guys kept that secret, because it made the Wyrms look bad, but they could have stopped you. The Wyrms could have announced it to the world, and made themselves look good. But they didn't, because keeping it secret served a higher moral purpose."

The tall patrician jumped to his feet. "There is *no* moral purpose higher than preventing sexual assault!"

The other commissioners dutifully applauded.

"Actually, there is," said Tom. "You guys were hiring people to masquerade as Wyrms and murder innocent Humans on camera. The Wyrms knew, if they didn't rape a few women, *you would,* disguised as them, and afterward, you would mutilate the girls to make it look worse. The Wyrms decided it was better to do it themselves, even though it made them look bad, which really makes *us* look bad. Well, it makes *you* look bad."

The tall patrician sputtered. "We would not do that!"

The other commissioners looked uncomfortable.

"Why not," Tom asked curiously. "You murdered Wyrms to steal their secrets, and you're *still* murdering Humans to discredit Wyrms. Why would you be squeamish about a few rape-mutilations?"

"We aren't doing *any of those things,"* the tall patrician snarled.

Now the other commissioners were avoiding each others' gaze.

"That's weird," said Tom. "I just assumed you were carefully not pushing the Wyrms too far, since you're still alive. If you *aren't* giving the orders, you might not live much longer, because the Wyrms *believe* you are. Whoever is really in charge might be willing to push too hard, since the Wyrms will blame *you*. Wow." Tom shook his head. "You guys are *brave."*

In the back row, Sophie groaned.

"You're getting *screwed,*" Tom added. "We all see the Wyrms attacking us, and you doing nothing about it, even though you supposedly have the power, so everyone thinks you are just cowards. People have no idea of the risk you are taking, because you're not really in charge, but the Wyrms believe you are."

Sophie clutched her head. Dominick looked thunderous.

"But at least their dangerous secrets are safe." Tom relaxed, leaning casually against the podium. "By custom, the Wyrms bite the forbidden fruit every month. It shuts down their mental censor, and forces them to see the world clearly. Most people know this. What most people *don't* know is how it affects them. You see, normal people, Humans like us, we can protect a valuable secret, for a while. But over time, we get careless. As the years pass, and nothing happens, we slack off and let our guard down. The Wyrms can't do that; they can't slack off. Somehow, the forbidden fruit keeps the threat fresh in their mind. They will *never* get careless with the two secrets that matter: the forbidden fruit and the burning bush."

Dominick stood up. "Ladies and gentlemen, I've been informed this facility has been threatened. Please evacuate now, in a calm and discrete manner that does not alarm the civilians in the hallways. They will be apprised of the risk, once you have reached safety."

The 49 distinguished scholars, executives and statesmen bolted for the exit and filed out in order of physical strength.

"There wasn't really a bomb threat," Tom remarked when the double doors thumped shut behind the slowest commissioner, a small woman in her sixties.

"No," said Dominick. "But you had done enough damage. I thought I made my intentions clear to you."

"You did," Tom said equably. "I just didn't make mine clear to you."

Dominick lunged forward, fists clenched, his flaring nostrils inches from Tom's forehead. "You *dare* to..." Then, with visible effort, he calmed himself. "Please explain what you hope to achieve by provoking me."

Tom snorted. "Provoking you is its own reward. Every time we meet, you threaten me with a stick. You should try a carrot sometime."

Dominick stepped back and smoothed his suit coat. "Mr. Pine, dealing with you is always a pleasure. And now, I believe the die is cast, so I have matters to attend." He walked out.

Sophie strode forward, grabbed Tom's lapels, and jerked his face close to hers. "What the fuck was that! Now the ARA will attack the Wyrms! You could have stopped them! Why didn't you?"

We left you a gift in geosynch orbit above your capitol.

Tom's arms rose between Sophie's and moved outward, tearing her hands off his lapels without apparent effort. "What happened to me, the first time I tried to hire someone?"

"Ow!" Sophie clutched her forearm. "What are you talking about?"

"What happened to me?"

"You were stupid enough to test a job applicant's I.Q., so you got sued for racial discrimination. *Get over it.* We're about to attack the aliens, and *you* could have prevented it. You still could!"

"Yes, I could. I just don't want to."

Sophie goggled. "How can you want us to attack them?"

"Because they will retaliate," Tom hissed. "And *I had to sell my house.*"

"God dammit," Sophie snarled. "We might nuke the *Finger!*"

"That's a real risk," Tom agreed. "You know, I just realized, for my whole life, whenever a movie character said, *If you want to make an omelette, you have to break a few eggs*, that identified him as the villain, the guy we were supposed to hate. A generation of Western children grew up on those movies, so now they think we shouldn't have freedom unless it's free."

Sophie tapped on her phone. "You think a holocaust counts as *breaking a few eggs?*" She held the phone to her ear. "Luci? Listen to me, and don't ask questions. Tell the *Finger* to change its orbit. Do it *now.*"

The phone emitted chattering noises. "Just *do it.*" Luci hung up.

"Ah, Sophie, you are so smart, but you never were good at math. There are 200 aliens and 8 billion humans." Tom glanced at the ceiling. "We probably don't want to hang around this city. Let's head home."

"You guys go ahead," said Frank. "I have to run some errands here."

"Don't take too long," Tom suggested.

"My fellow Americans, I have grim news."

"Bitter news," Kitty interrupted. She and the president were alone in the West Wing's TV studio, so she operated the camera.

"I bring bitter news. In all my time as president, and before that as senator, and before that as father, this is my most strenuous hour, my hardest choice." Mirror wobbled, but caught himself. "I had to make a *hard* call," he grated, "yet it was not not a *close* call. Since the Wyrms arrived, we have all hoped, despite what they have done, one day they would prove to be our friends, or at least, neighbors we could tolerate."

"Our donkeys' *tolerance* keeps us out of tar and feathers," Kitty snapped. "Don't piss on that word. Instead of, *tolerate,* say, *coexist.*"

"Someone with whom we could coexist. The Wyrms are hiding a secret I have not revealed, a secret I *could not* reveal. Since they arrived, we have seen indications, troubling indications." Mirror produced a white handkerchief and wiped his brow.

"Good." Kitty nodded approvingly. "Don't forget to do that."

Mirror tucked his handkerchief into his pocket. "In recent months, alarming numbers of children, young girls, have disappeared."

Kitty zoomed out a little.

469

"At first, we couldn't believe it. *I* could not believe it, but we can no longer doubt. My fellow Americans, my fellow *Humans,* it is my sad duty to inform you... to confirm the dark rumors about the forbidden fruit. That foul alien drug dis-inhibits men. A man who uses it may be seized by an uncontrollable urge to..." Mirror paused, and shuddered. "The effects of the forbidden fruit are unspeakable, but as your president, I must inform you that your children have been kidnapped by forbidden-fruit addicts, for use in sexual practices which resulted in death."

"Hold on." Kitty adjusted the camera's color filter, pushing the slider from red to green to heighten Mirror's pallor. "Okay, go ahead."

"In recent weeks, when we detect a Wyrm entering our airspace, they have been continuously supervised by members of our armed forces. This was done on my order, with the approval of the Alien Regulatory Authority, when we began to suspect the awful truth. But the Wyrms descend on us so quickly, we cannot always reach them in time to save our precious babies. I am sorry, I am so sorry I could not do more, but we didn't know for sure, and sometimes our little girls get sick, horribly sick, and we hoped... I hoped our sick little girls might be saved by the Wyrm immune system, if only we waited. Now, that hope will haunt me as long as I live."

Kitty watched Mirror's image. "We were right to focus on the little girls. Nobody cares about boys."

Mirror began panting like an overheated dog. "Earlier this week, we received information, conclusive information, that our hope was a cruel hoax. We now know the Wyrm's disease immunity was given to them by their alien rescuer. Immunity is built into them, but they don't understand it, and they *cannot* give it to us, even if they wished to, which they do not, as their leader made plain. And in the last two days, 17 more little girls have vanished. So this morning, the Alien Regulatory Authority instructed our armed forces to take action." Mirror appeared to be hyperventilating. "The heroic United States soldiers *will protect our girls,* whatever the cost."

Kitty purred. "Give me the success version."

"As of this moment, the Wyrm mothership, the cruelly named *Unexpected Finger*, has been disabled by the U.S. Space Force. On its current trajectory, we expect the hulk to enter our atmosphere over the Northern Pacific."

"God," Kitty breathed. "I want this to be real."

"We have succeeded," Mirror continued. "We struck our enemy a mortal blow, yet many Wyrm stragglers still lurk in our atmosphere, *our* territory, and each has been surgically implanted with a suicide bomb, lethal out to 100 feet. The bomb is detonated by remote control, if the Wyrm is apprehended. Be vigilant, and if you see a Wyrm, immediately alert the authorities."

Kitty zoomed in.

Mirror's haunted face hardened into anger. "Better yet, if you own a rifle, you know what to do. Kill the bastards from 100 yards, every foul one, and our justice system will treat you fairly. We are provoked beyond all endurance, and this time, we shall leave due process to the almighty."

Kitty clapped. "That will steal half the redneck vote, but don't just promise to treat them fairly. Declare a general amnesty for anyone who kills a Wyrm."

"No," Mirror said firmly. "Blanket amnesty would let the shooters ignore me. If a redneck wants to kill a Wyrm and be a hero, he must *ask me* for a pardon."

"Oh, all right." Kitty smiled tolerantly. "Are you ready?"

Mirror considered. "Yes."

Five seconds after the president pressed the concealed elevator button, a scrum of Secret Service agents raced around the corner. Mirror raised a palm. "Chill. We are traveling to the Deep Bunker, in a calm and leisurely manner. Congress will be joining us, along with the Alien Regulatory Authority and some key staffers and family members."

And his top 15 donors, he did not say.

Agent Oak frowned. "Why?"

"Just a little drill."

"Mister President, you should have informed me."

Mirror patted Agent Oak's shoulder. "Surprise reveals more, don't you think?"

Oak's face relaxed into blank neutrality, except his eyes.

Six agents followed them into the elevator, which descended gently.

When they reached the Presidential Fast Train, Agent Oak moved to take his normal seat, but Mirror touched his shoulder. "Max, I have some classified matters to talk over with Cougar."

Agent Oak raised an eyebrow.

Cougar raised a warning finger.

Agent Oak sighed. "The next presidential fast train must be an *actual* train, with a second car for us."

"Good man." Mirror ducked into the open hatch, and Kitty climbed in behind him. They accelerated smoothly, and soon the alternating red, white and blue wall segments flashed by at a dizzying 200 MPH. Every two minutes, the train wheels chimed as they flew over the gaps for the blast doors. At this pace, they would reach the Deep Bunker in 20 minutes.

Kitty settled into her comm station. "Let's hope we don't actually end up hiding down here for two years."

They heard a chirp. Kitty looked surprised and pulled a phone from her breast pocket.

Mirror relaxed in his custom-fitted seat and cracked open a bottle. "That phone really works down here?"

Kitty put the phone to her ear. "Speak." She listened in silence for five seconds, then she slapped the console. "Shit!"

Mirror sipped his certified organic silica-free mineral water. "What?"

"The A.I. found blueprints of our bunker system on the internet. They were just uploaded in the last hour, but they've already dispersed to Chinese and Russian chat boards, so whoever posted them has enough tech savvy to...oh." Kitty groaned. "Frank *Drummer.* He helped *design* the bunkers."

Then you fired him and I sent him to Antarctica, she did not add. *I guess he didn't forget.*

"Shit!"

Kitty held up a hand for silence as she listened to her phone. "The commissioners found out about the blueprints and panicked. Now they say we aren't safe, so we have to call off the attack."

"Shit!"

"Let me think." Kitty covered the phone, looking away from the windows and the flickering wall stripes. "The Wyrms probably haven't seen the blueprints yet, so time is critical. Can you make the war pigs push the button themselves, today?"

"Easy." Mirror twisted open a second bottle. "If we show the kiddy snuff porn to the Joint Chiefs, they will compete to be most outraged. We don't need the Alien Regulatory *Authority.*"

Kitty pressed the phone to her ear. "Still there? We have to attack *today,* so hustle down to the Deep Bunker. The bunks will fill up fast, but I'll clear one for you."

The phone emitted panicky noises, and Kitty rolled her eyes. "Dominick, try to relax. The bunker is just a precaution. Probably the worst that will happen is a few penguins get sunburned." She snapped her secure phone shut and leaned back into her doeskin seat. The train wheels *clanged* over the gap for a blast door.

Mirror sipped his mineral water and closed his eyes to block out the vertiginous flashing walls.

They rode on awhile.

"The next time we see the surface," Mirror mused, "the world might have changed."

"And we will still own it."

That brought out Mirror's famous, easy smile.

Kitty lurched forward. "Oh my God!"

"What?" Mirror was startled out of his reverie. He had never heard Kitty sound terrified. Red lights flashed across his console, and a shrill buzzer drowned out all other thoughts. He reflexively clapped his hands over his ears and looked out the forward window.

200 yards ahead, two seconds away at their hurtling speed, a blast door was sliding briskly shut.

475

Back at the elevators, a two-inch-thick steel door sported two keyholes, one keypad, and a placard that read, *Secondary Security.*

Behind the steel door, a steel chamber had been paneled with 60-inch monitors. The monitors looked expensive, and they were, but they were filmed with dust and showed little of interest. The lone exception, midway along the left wall, showed the ninth blast door and the Presidential Fast Train.

Frank Drummer knelt on the floor before an access panel. The open hatch dangled a white cable, six twisted pairs neatly labeled with the numbers *7-12,* all wrapped with white tape to form a single, pencil-thick signal buss that ran through his fingers on its way to a white, 12-pin Molex connector that was not connected to anything. The connector was labeled, *Doors 7-12 Command Loss Failsafe,* written in Frank's handwriting.

Frank had helped wire this room, before he had been fired by President Mirror. He pushed the Molex back into its mate. The paired connectors clicked together. He tucked them up into the tangle of wires and closed the access panel, turning its handle 90 degrees. He heard distant shouting, mingled with the clamor of alarms. He rose easily to his feet, tugged off his rubber gloves, and patted Agent Bear's butt. "You were made for this job."

"Yes," said Agent Sheila Bear, the head of Kitty Siphon's security detail. "I was built to protect the people entrusted to my care."

They both looked at the dusty image of the Presidential Fast Train, parked against the ninth blast door. The sleek, 30-foot car was now only 18 feet long and not really sleek anymore. What remained of Kitty Siphon oozed out into a growing puddle on the concrete floor.

Agent Bear smiled toothily. "Bitch, when you plan a holocaust, don't leave my daughter on the surface."

Four weeks later
Springfield, MO

Tom reached the Pine Shack at 7 AM and checked Sophie's whiteboard.

All food on desks is now Prohibited because I am tired of arguing my candy dish is different from Frank's crock Pot.

Sophie

Tom closed his office door and paused, his eye caught by Fluffer. Her 7-foot picture dominated his office wall, a slender girl sitting alone on a bench made for two, waiting.

She was waiting for Tom to make his fortune, then find her.

Some timeless period later, Tom was startled by Sophie's knock. "Roust!" she barked. "We're all here."

All of Tom's employees had jammed into the lunchroom. In front, technicians hunched over their pads playing *Sim Orgy* with the *Mormon Tabernacle Choir* DLC. Behind them, the assemblers huddled over one screen, watching *Nice People Burned Alive Six: Christians in Africa.* In back, the salesmen chatted.

High up in the corner, the silent television showed a talking head, captioned, *NEW PRESIDENT SHUFFLES CABINET.* Then the talking head was replaced by broccoli, captioned, *NEW SURGEON GENERAL SAYS RAW VEGETABLES TOO RISKY.*

Tom looked around. Finding no gavel, he fruit-caked the meeting to order, startling his employees. "Some of you have called this a goodbye party. It is not."

The room quieted. On the television, the broccoli was replaced by cascading snapshots of little blonde girls, captioned, *Gone?*

"This is not a goodbye party; it is a goodbye *meeting,* and hence a deductible expense. Oh, wait, I forgot." Tom slapped his forehead. "I don't *need* a deduction, because I decided not to pay taxes."

This brought a weak chuckle.

"For such a festive meeting, you are no doubt puzzled by the absence of exotic dancers." Tom pointed to Buff. "I was afraid our guest of honor could not restrain himself, and I would have to pay the girls extra."

Good-natured booing ensued. Sophie did not smile. Neither did Tom. Eventually, his employees noticed and quieted. Tom spoke softly, but his words filled the silent lunchroom. "Does anyone not understand, the Wyrms are the best thing that ever happened to us?"

Nobody did not understand.

"Does anyone doubt that, because of them, we are now bigger than sliced baloney? If you doubt it, please speak up now, so I can push your head into the toilet."

Apparently, no one doubted.

Tom's gaze drifted to the floor, which he seemed to be addressing, his voice barely audible when he said, "Goodbye."

In the silence, Luci and Buffalo seemed made of wax. Lifelike.

Tom inhaled, and let it go. He looked up at his hushed employees. "What are you waiting for? Start drinking."

After the goodbye meeting, Frank Drummer walked out to the parking lot.

He waved to the soldiers at the concertina wire, and had just opened his car door when a voice behind him said, "Good evening, Mr. Drummer."

Frank turned around. "Oh, hi, Dominick. What's up?"

Dominick Tork was dressed in a gray business suit, as usual. "I stopped by to congratulate you."

"Thanks." Frank rubbed his ample-but-shrinking belly. "I still have another 50 lbs to lose. It turns out the secret is to eat less."

"Dealing with you will be a real pleasure," said Dominick. "I *am* pleased to see you shaping up, at long last, but I came to congratulate you for being *here,* in this lovely parking lot, rather than a federal prison."

The bored soldiers guarding the parking lot watched curiously, but did not approach.

"Yeah, my dealer tags expired," Frank admitted, patting his semi-new sedan, which still had a paper license plate. "I've been meaning to put the new plates on. Was it *you* that stopped the DMV from throwing me in prison? Thanks for that."

"I'm sorry I could not congratulate you sooner," Dominick continued as if Frank had not spoken. "I have recently changed employers, and things have been a bit hectic in Washington, since the president was assassinated."

Frank looked surprised. "President Mirror was *assassinated?* I thought he was killed by a sliding door. Do you suspect the Wyrms did it? That's what people say on the internet, but I thought it was just a conspiracy theory."

Dominick wrapped a friendly arm around Frank's shoulders. "It was unfortunate that *you*, a technical architect of the bunker system and a disgruntled ex-employee, happened to be visiting D.C. at the exact moment of the fatal malfunction. The coincidence could hardly fail to be noticed by the investigators, who I assure you were quite diligent."

"That *was* inconvenient. I didn't get out of D.C. before they threw up all the roadblocks, so I ended up missing my flight. Am I a suspect? Nobody has even asked me about it, but maybe they will, eventually."

"I think not," said Dominick. "As it happened, I was in a position to show the detectives your exact whereabouts throughout the relevant time period. When I demonstrated you had said or done nothing suspicious, they focused their investigation elsewhere."

The soldiers turned away, apparently deciding Frank and Dominick weren't going to do anything interesting.

Frank said, "Thank you for that."

"I felt it was the least I could do, given the risk you took. Speaking of risk, you might be interested to know the Alien Regulatory Authority has ordered a crash program to construct a *new* deep bunker. It seems they no longer feel safe in the old one, since someone posted its blueprints on the internet."

"That *is* interesting," said Frank. "I learned so much from working on the first bunker, do you think they might hire me to design the new one?"

"That would amuse me," said Dominick "The commissioners are frustrated by the lack of progress in identifying the traitor who made a new bunker necessary. They actually *shouted at me.* They are angry because they lost their safe refuge, and hence their preferred strategy. I wonder if your Wyrm friends will ever know how much they owe you?"

"Maybe you could tell them," Frank suggested.

"That would not be appropriate." Dominick tucked a business card into Frank's shirt pocket. "Good luck with your work on the Wyrm sentries. If you see anything interesting, please call me, day or night. Perhaps I will call you, from time to time, so we can chat."

After the goodbye meeting, Sophie found the alien Luci alone in the lunchroom, microwaving a last bag of popcorn.

Sophie sat and nervously fiddled with the salt shaker. "If I joined you, and made myself *maternal,* do you think I could have Buff?"

Luci shrugged. "That's not for me to say."

Sophie stared at her.

"Yes," Luci added.

Sophie fiddled with the salt shaker. "I think so too."

Luci stuck a popcorn bag into the microwave and pushed the *potato* button. "You were his first fink. Of course you could have him."

They listened to the popping kernels awhile, and Sophie brooded. Eventually, she stood up and paced. "How can I want to change what I want?"

The microwave dinged. Luci opened the door and gingerly plucked out the bag.

Sophie paced restlessly, back and forth. "When you bite the forbidden fruit, what's it like?"

Luci tore open the bag. "Ow!" She dropped the steaming bag on the counter and shook her scorched hands. "Biting the forbidden fruit is like pulling back the shower curtain to find an angry moose."

"You say the forbidden fruit stifles your mental censor, but are you absolutely *sure?* I don't think my brain is censored."

"What does a clever censor conceal *first?"*

"Himself, of course. The idea is to extinguish bad ideas, not call attention to them with a big, red..." Sophie stopped talking and looked chastened.

"When your censor is stifled, you will see him, and you'll finally see the difference between what you *believe* and what you *want*." Luci poured the popcorn into a bowl.

"You can't see your own desires without a drug?"

Luci snorted. "Wouldn't *that* upend the world."

Sophie opened the refrigerator, then closed it. She resumed her pacing. "This would tell me if I belong with Buff?"

"Don't expect a miracle. The forbidden fruit reveals your motive, but it won't plot your strategy."

"What if it turns out I like to hurt people?"

"Then you will know."

Sophie paced restlessly.

"Sophie, you're a woman. When your censor is stifled, you will realize you feel happy when you do what your culture expects." Luci offered her bowl of popcorn.

"Because I'm a *woman?*"

"Yes, because you are a woman."

"Oh, nice. The forbidden fruit will be loved as much as you are."

Luci laughed bitterly. "On our world, the fruit was forbidden by every queen. Anyone caught with it was punished harshly, as they will be here on Earth."

Sophie stopped pacing. "Why?"

"Compassion, mostly. Have some of my popcorn."

"Compassion? Does it hurt to look inside? What do you see?"

483

"You see *yourself,*" said Luci, "but that's not why it will be banned. The forbidden fruit stifles your compassion. Without your mental censor, you are merciless."

"And you never thought to mention this until now?"

Luci shrugged. "It's not the main benefit."

"Only you would describe *merciless* as a benefit."

"When a wasp is caught thieving, and begs for mercy, the censor gives you compassion by hiding his future victims."

Sophie grabbed a handful of popcorn. "Compassion is not just for thieves. It's much more."

"True enough," Luci allowed. "When a child cries about schoolwork, the censor gives you compassion by hiding the child's future."

"You think we'll ban the forbidden fruit so we can pamper our kids?"

"I'm sure you're too wise for that. Do you believe women are just as strong as men, or should men be restrained when you're around, or do you enjoy believing *both?"* Luci looked enquiring. "If you had to choose only one belief or the other, which do you need more?"

Sophie scowled.

Luci popped a white puff into her mouth. "I love this stuff. No nutrition, yet so satisfying. And you can relax, because everyone knows a woman can do anything a man can do, only better. In fact, the next time a hurricane knocks down your power lines, I think I'll take my daughter to the blackout zone to watch the women bring back your electricity."

Sophie's scowl darkened.

"Damn." Luci looked thoughtful. "A shell is stuck in my teeth. Wasps also have a problem with infidelity. Best to dispel your delusions *before* you marry, or never."

Sophie's dark expression turned thunderous.

Luci stuck a finger into her mouth. "Do you understand yet, why the forbidden fruit will be banned?"

With some effort, Sophie produced an icy smile. "I guess there's no point in being offended by alien ideas."

"So I often remind myself." Luci spat out a hull.

Uncomfortable silence followed.

Eventually, Sophie relented. "The forbidden fruit will be banned because our society is built on compassion and equality and monogamy."

"Yes," Luci agreed. "It is."

"If the forbidden fruit shows me something shameful, could I forget it later, or would I be stuck with it?"

To Sophie's surprise, the alien flinched. Luci looked at her popcorn, then dropped it back into the bowl. "Over time, you'll forget the worst revelations. But like the wise man said: *A sober fool ignores his drunken self.*"

"When he said that, he was probably drunk." Sophie paced restlessly. "I wish I could know if I want to know the truth."

Luci stared at the popcorn. "Wouldn't that upend the world."

Sophie decided she'd had enough. On her way out, she passed Tom coming in with an oversized shoe box. Sophie glanced back at the alien, then at Tom.

Tom smiled amiably, holding the shoe box. Sophie hesitated. Finally, she left without speaking.

Tom closed the door behind her, then he set the oversized shoe box on the table. "Luci, I want to teach you to dance tonight."

"It's a bit late for first names," said Luci. "I know you don't mean *our* kind of dancing, and I'm not the type for disco."

"You were born to disco." Tom opened the shoe box to reveal red-trimmed black cowboy boots. "But not tonight."

"Tonight, Mr. Pine, I am leaving for good." Luci rinsed out her bowl. "Besides, you can't teach me to dance without violating your sacred *Intimate Rule;* Don't poop where you eat."

Tom took the dripping bowl from Luci's hand and tucked it into the cupboard. "You don't eat here anymore."

Two-step lessons began at 6 PM, a crash course for newbs. "No spins," Tom pronounced as a helicopter buzzed his pickup. He glanced in the rear-view mirror at the trailing caravan of desert-tan humvees. "You just focus on following my lead."

On the seat beside him, Luci folded her arms.

"Don't worry," Tom added. "I know how to lead. You'll have no trouble learning to do what I want." He took the ramp to the interstate, his military escort trailing obediently.

Though not for long. Luci watched three humvees switch lanes to pass Tom's truck, then they converged in front to take the lead. "Did you tell them where we are going?"

"No." Tom waited until the last moment, then he veered onto an off-ramp, forcing the leaders to continue on to the next exit. In his mirror, Tom saw the trailing humvees rocking as they swerved to follow him.

Yet follow they did, and two humvees roared past to take point. Tom immediately turned left. Behind him, tires squealed.

Luci turned to watch the scrum behind them, as their escorts tried to get out of each other's way so they could turn left. "Did I explain those soldiers are here to protect *me?*"

Tom glanced in his mirror. "Do you know the most annoying thing about marriage?"

"Divorce? Monogamy?"

Tom paused. "The third most annoying thing about marriage was having to change my plans when my wife made them a command. She liked to predict what I was about to do, then order me to do it. Once, on a road trip, she realized our freeway exit was the last one for six miles. Just for fun, she *demanded* I take it."

"Did you exit? Or did you drive 12 miles to show her who carries the dick?"

"Neither. I slammed on the brakes in the middle of the freeway, and we sat there with cars zooming past on either side until she apologized."

Luci waved at the military vehicles. "You'll never see them again. You're not training them to lead you around."

"I'm not worried about training *them*." Tom tapped his own head.

The escorts stopped trying to pass. Ten minutes later, the caravan reached Tom's destination.

Humvees streamed into sequential parking spaces, and by the time Tom and Luci reached the front door, armored soldiers waited to usher them into the Wild West Club.

Inside, the register girl glanced nervously at the ceiling covered with farm implements. They all heard the muffled thump of circling helicopters. Tom pulled out his wallet. "Two for beginner lessons."

Soldiers poured in and flowed across the hardwood.

"Make them pay the cover charge," Tom advised. "They buy hardly any drinks, and I know Lieutenant Leaden carries a wad of cash for just this situation."

Eventually, a dozen nervous dance students were surrounded by 40 armored warriors, half of them carrying heavy weapons.

The dance teacher was a wiry, 50-ish woman in cowboy boots, a frocked dress, and a Carolina accent. She gazed sourly at the soldiers, then turned to Luci. "Darlin, is this invasion your doin?"

"Not me," said Luci. "I thought *you* invited them."

"Well, bless your heart," said the instructor, hands on her hips.

Tom nudged Luci. "Stop it."

The instructor turned toward a female private whose breast patch said, *PARTS*. "I would be so grateful, Miss Private, if you could give us a second or two of warning before you launch that anti-aircraft missile in here."

Private Parts looked sheepish and leaned her MANPAD against the bar.

"Welcome, everyone. My name is Mary May. And yes, before you ask, she is *that* alien." The instructor singled out a man in a gray suit. "Sweetheart, would you do me a kindness?"

"Me?" The gray-suited man looked behind him.

Mary May smiled warmly. "Welcome to beginners' country dance. Before we begin, would you oblige me by asking Miss Lucifa here if the good people on her world danced the Texas two-step?"

The gray-suited man looked alarmed.

"Now, darlin, everyone is going to ask her. Let's get it over with, so the poor thing won't have to hear the same line from all of you."

The gray-suited man drew himself up and faced Luci. "So, did you?"

Luci glared at Tom, her expression conveying, *this is your fault.*

Tom smiled amiably.

"No," Luci snapped. "We only did a different kind of dancing." She waved at Tom. "Pretty soon, I will show him."

The gray-suited man looked uncertain.

Tom leaned close to whisper in Luci's ear. "Country dance people are surprisingly friendly, if you let them. Instead of, *fuck you,* they say, *bless your heart."*

Luci held out five more seconds. Then she gave up, and produced her famous, heartbreak smile.

The gray-suited man stepped back a pace.

"Call me Luci," she said lightly. "Our gravity was too heavy for dancing, so I will hardly notice when you step on my feet."

It didn't work. The students still looked tense. Soldiers watched intently, except Private Parts kept glancing at her missile. Luci breathed, and closed her eyes as she steeled herself. Then she unbuckled her gun belt and handed it to Private Parts.

The circle of dancers seemed to relax. Mary May touched Tom's arm. "Darlin, would you happen to know which of these noble warriors is in charge?"

"That would be Lieutenant Leaden." Tom pointed to a desert-tan lump by the bar. "I'm sure he'd love to meet you."

"Thank you so much." Mary May stepped back and raised her voice. "Lieutenant Leaden, would you kindly join us?"

Leaden dutifully approached, and Mary May sized him up. "Mister Lieutenant, are you decent under that shell?"

Leaden looked wary. "Why do you ask?"

"I ask because I am short two gentlemen." Mary May smiled sweetly. "And I blame you. Kindly remove your armor and ask the bartender to cover the soles of your combat boots with slick tape."

Lieutenant Leaden's entire body said, *no,* and his mouth had just opened to join the chorus when Mary May showed him her palm. "Before you speak, darlin, be aware I am sleeping with this club's owner, and I know what *Posse Comitatus* means. I will not hesitate to have the bouncer toss you all on the street."

By the door, the bouncer looked nervous. Leaden folded his arms.

Mary May stepped forward into Lieutenant Leaden's personal space. Soldiers hooted as she ran a long, red fingernail down the length of his M4 carbine. "Why, bless your heart, Mister Lieutenant. You don't believe a gracious belle like me would throw you out on your ass?"

Her voice had changed. In fact, it had changed a lot. Lieutenant Leaden stiffened as he recognized her accent.

"Yeah, that's right," Mary May twanged. "I'm from New Jersey. Do you still think I won't make a scene?"

Another armored soldier approached Leaden quietly from behind. The patch on his desert-tan breast said, CANNY.

"Shut up, Canny," Leaden growled without turning around. "I already know you volunteer. Strip down and show these ladies a good time."

Mary May stepped back in satisfaction.

Around the floor, male soldiers stepped forward.

"STAND YOUR POSTS!"

The soldiers stepped back and looked surly.

Lieutenant Leaden propped his weapon against a chair and cracked open his abdominal casing with a rip of Velcro. "Officers should lead from the front."

Mary May organized her students into two circles, men on the outside, and explained the basic step.

Luci gazed at Tom speculatively. "This is a partner dance, but you've never touched me."

"Except when I was sitting on your toilet with you in my lap and we were both naked."

"That never happened. And besides," Luci sniffed. "It was *me* that touched *you*. I noticed you were careful not to touch me back."

Tom grinned and grabbed Luci by the back of her neck.

She gasped.

"Not by the neck, darlin." Mary May strolled past. "We don't do it redneck style. Kindly rest your palm on her shoulder blade."

Tom looked Luci in the eye and twined his fingers in her hair, just tightly enough to hold her head in place while his left fingertip traced the row of tattoos beneath her wide, blue eye. Then he released her hair, and shifted his hand to her back.

"Not how I imagined," Luci muttered.

Mary May waved to the D.J., and the speakers boomed out Ty England's, *Should have asked her faster*. "On my count," Mary May trilled. "Men lead forward with their left foot, ladies back with your right. Ready, set, *Slow, slow, quick-quick.*"

Tom stepped forward and bumped into Luci. "Was that more what you were expecting?"

Luci looked down at her feet, trying to get out of his way. "I am never going to learn this."

Four frustrating minutes later, Mary May called a halt. "For you first-timers, we live by an ironclad rule: Every five minutes, we change partners."

Luci rolled her eyes. "I should have known."

Mary May cued up Drake Milligan's *Dance of a Lifetime*. "When I say, *switch,* gentlemen rotate clockwise to the next lady."

Luci looked around nervously.

Mary May noticed. "Ladies, you go home with the man who brung you. In the meantime, any man you dance with will get the courtesy of your full attention. Switch!"

Tom abandoned Luci to the uncertain mercy of the next stranger. His new partner was a plump, cheerful little woman. He took her hand and drew her in. "Hello. My name is Tom."

"Betty," the plump little woman replied cheerfully. "So, what's she like in bed?"

"Dunno," Tom admitted.

Betty looked disappointed. "Well, you shouldn't wait too long. I'm surprised we aren't at war with them already."

Tom's next partner was an attractive woman, about ten years younger than him and four inches taller. He checked her left hand for a ring, not trying to hide his intention, then stepped confidently forward into close dance position. "Hi, my name is Tom."

She looked down at him, and straightened her arm to push him away. "Hi, Tom. How do you know Lucifa?"

"I make robotic sentries for the Wyrm colony."

"Interesting." She didn't sound interested. "Are you an engineer?"

"I own the company."

She relaxed her arm and stepped closer, smiling down at him warmly. "Is it a *big* company?"

Tom worked his way around the circle in 30 minutes. When he rejoined Luci, he found her flushed and grinning. "I'm actually getting the hang of it. This is so much fun. Why didn't we do it sooner?"

"Because you made me choose between reproduction and survival."

Luci poked him, but not too hard.

Ninety minutes later, when the club opened to the general public, Luci was following almost gracefully. "This is amazing. Do we keep switching partners?"

"Normally," Tom replied. "But I'm done sharing you. For the rest of the night, you're all mine."

Luci pulled back. "Don't I get a say?"

"No." Tom pulled her closer.

"I didn't think so," she said contentedly as they twirled through the gathering crowd, ignoring the gapes and stumbles as other couples noticed Luci's tattoos then recognized her face.

"I know why they're surprised to see me," Luci remarked. "Why do they seem startled when they look at *you?"*

Tom glanced at the mirror. A short, ferret-faced man with an implausibly beautiful partner glanced back. "They are trying to decide: Am I rich, or do I have an abnormally large dick?"

"I will never understand the swarm," Luci muttered. "I wish I could spin like that."

Two boobs under a cowboy hat spun into their path, then out again.

"I can lead spins." Tom accelerated to thread the gap between converging couples. "But spins are for the spectators. I come here for weightless turns."

"Weightless?"

"It comes with practice. Some women follow so well, they feel like part of my body."

Luci's hand moved across Tom's shoulder, exploring the layered muscle. "I want to feel weightless."

"If only you had access to some sort of space vehicle."

She poked him, but not too hard. "This is the easiest first date ever. Who taught you how to be so comfortable? I know it was a woman."

Tom didn't answer, just led her through a circle.

She turned with him, kicking his toes only once. "Tom, why are you single?"

Tom glanced at the mirror again. "You mean, besides the obvious reasons?"

"What are you talking about?"

Tom chuckled. "Charity from you, of all people."

"Tom, my question was serious."

"And your question is bigger than you know. Just enjoy tonight."

Luci pulled back to look at him, her blue eyes studying the weak-chinned face his mother said was handsome.

Whatever Luci found, she kept to herself and returned to his embrace. Soldiers watched through the gaps in their body armor as the clock ticked 8:15 PM, and Tom piloted the tiny Wyrm through the shifting couples.

After six songs in 15 seconds, they took a break.

Luci glistened and fanned herself. "This exercise is making me thirsty. What should I order?"

"At a country bar," Tom explained, "you may choose beer, whiskey, or Margarita."

"What is *Margarita?*"

Tom raised an eyebrow. "Luci Dark, are you offering me your lime?"

And suddenly, the DJ was announcing last call.

"Holy shit," Luci murmured. "Is it 2 AM?"

"You learned fast," Tom breathed into her ear.

Three slow songs played in five seconds, then the lights went up.

Tom and Luci crossed the parking lot reluctantly, surrounded by soldiers.

They drove in silence, absorbed in thoughts.

"What now?" Luci's voice was soft as the light from the sleeping city.

Tom glanced back at the ranks of high, trailing headlights. "Do your people use the expression, *unfinished business?*"

"No."

They drove awhile.

"But I understand," Luci added eventually.

"Unfinished business is the memory that does not fade."

Tom's pickup rumbled through the darkness, streaming humvees like a comet. Luci glowed in their headlights.

"On balance," Tom said quietly, "I want you and I to be unfinished business, so I'll take you back to the office."

In time, they reached the Pine Shack parking lot, and the desert-tan guards waved them in. Tom walked around to her door, but found she had already opened it. He strode to the barricade.

Luci's boots clip-clopped on the concrete as she stepped up beside him. They looked outward, beyond the soldiers and concertina wire, across the cracked and tilting street and upward toward the stars occulted by a massive hulk, a square of darkness outlined by the slow pulse of aircraft warning lamps. The Pine Tower.

Luci gazed up at the half-finished giant. "Our path is open to all who desire it. If you *can* desire it, we want you."

Tom took her hand. He didn't make a production of it, just picked it up like he owned it. "I'm staying here. Running my business is actually fun now, and by December, the road to your colony will be one-way."

It was true. Already, communication was allowed only through a new U.N. agency charged with intercepting objectionable material.

"Tom, this civilization will probably collapse. The men we recruit will not be chosen randomly."

If we don't nuke you first, Tom did not say.

Across the street, an old parking lot had been ripped up. Beside the heap of broken concrete, a massive tangle of twisted rebar was marked with a printed sign:

FOR SALE
#00000000 Steel Wool
6 Tons

Overhead, a motionless crane dangled a sagging bundle of new rebar. By December, this building would shelter 900 extruders and 200 employees. All would answer to Tom, as would the men who were building his mansion. This morning, Tom's concrete crew had laughed when they realized the city code enforcers had sneaked into the construction site at night to post unasked-for permits.

Finally, Tom would earn enough money to rejoin the mating game, this time on terms even a short, weak-chinned man could enjoy. With his new wealth, Tom could escape the shame of his short stature and bang 20 hot women in the next year. He would choose one to be his wife, and she would count herself lucky despite his appearance. The year after that, he expected to bang 20 more women, and each time would be a party with his best friend, sometimes with a crowd.

"Luci," he said as gently as he could, "anyone who joins you will have his assets confiscated, and no government will let you export *anything* to its citizens. You'll be lucky if they let you buy raw materials. Every enterprise in your colony will struggle, and mine would not survive. While out here..." He waved at his new building.

"Out here, you will thrive as your world crashes around you. It's so ironic; you will prosper because none dare rob *us*." Luci stood unnaturally still. "I lose you because I protect you, by threatening your queens."

"Yeah, I was hoping you'd do more than just threaten."

In the darkness, a siren wailed. Distant dogs barked in reply. Luci turned away, toward the tiny clapboard factory where they had worked the hours of the year together. "Tom, I..." Her voice broke.

Tom was not surprised by the lump in his throat. He dropped Luci's hand and swept her into an embrace, lifting her off the crumbling sidewalk. At first, she stiffened. Then she hugged him back fiercely.

They held it for a long moment. Tom clutched her a little tighter. Then he set her down and turned back toward his success. For the first time in years, he found himself remembering the last moment of his marriage, when he kissed his wife's forehead, then handed over his key.

Now, once again, familiar doors were sliding quietly but finally shut. New doors were opening, just out of sight. His eyes ached with the pressure of 20 years' uncried tears, but his face was dry when he dropped Luci's hand. "It was good."

Luci nodded woodenly. "Yes, it was."

Then she walked away.

Of all the Humans on Earth, Frank Drummer had been first to recognize the approaching Wyrm mothership, when his tiny gamma-ray telescope had been dazzled by the enormous double spike of the *Finger's* exhaust. But Frank hadn't done it alone; he'd had a colleague, Earnest.

Frank had parlayed his success into a brief gig as a presidential tech advisor, while Earnest's fame as co-discoverer had payed off with something more durable, an endowed chair at a university whose name was familiar to every girl he dated. His chair was only an associate professorship, but Earnest was willing to say, *Diversity is our strength* like he believed it, so everyone knew he would be promoted, after a decent interval.

Better yet, Earnest headed the scheduling committee for a massive new orbiting gamma-ray observatory. In fact, Earnest had been so much the obvious candidate, his only admitted competitor was a notorious free thinker whose job application had included a proof of his fetish theory. On Pages 3-6 of his job application, the free thinker showed conclusively that a cornerstone of physics, the Second Law of Thermodynamics, was a mere statistical tautology.

The proof almost went unread, which would have been a real loss to science, because at the proof's conclusion, where a hidebound traditionalist might have written, *Q.E.D.,* the free thinker had summed up with, *Thus, I am not a nincompoop.*

502

It was an instant classic. The free thinker was not seriously considered for the job, but his proof was saved and read aloud at parties. From that day after, in serious research workshops, serious astronomers often summed up their presentations with, *thus, I am not a nincompoop,* because astronomers aren't good at being serious.

At the moment, Earnest was doing what he loved best. Well, maybe not *best,* since that required a hot tub and a girls' gymnastics team, but definitely in the top ten. The gamma-ray observatory was online, beaming its data down to three server farms and Earnest's desktop. His computer showed the message,

COLLECTING

Earnest still used Frank Drummer's software, because it was a tight, elegant pleasure. Unfortunately, the pleasure ended early when Earnest's display flashed the dreaded warning:

DATA ABSURD

I THINK I AM BROKEN

Earnest jerked upright in a moment of guilty panic, until he remembered he couldn't really damage the orbiting edifice without entering his admin password, which he had forgotten. His fingers chattered over the keyboard. Within seconds, the alarm message was replaced with,

THINKING

Ten seconds later, the display blanked then filled with a graph, the fuzzy straight line of a gamma-ray spectrum, punctuated by an enormous, familiar double spike, with a caption Earnest had never seen outside of emergency drills.

TWINKLE DETECTED
PERIOD=0.85 SECONDS

Earnest lurched out of his chair and ran to his other computer, the one that tracked all the Wyrm spacecraft.

The computer confirmed what Earnest already knew: The *Unexpected Finger* was passing behind the Earth, out of sight. None of her daughter boats were accelerating, so none could be spouting gamma rays, and in any case, small spacecraft don't twinkle. Only one thing did, when viewed from orbit.

Earnest did not swear, and his hand shook only slightly as he opened his desk drawer, lifted a stainless steel safety catch, turned a brass key, and pressed an illuminated red button. Around the world, this resulted in considerable activity.

Earnest had often thought about this moment, and what he should do. He briefly considered calling his old colleague, Frank Drummer. Very briefly. Then he settled back into his chair while the orbiting telescope counted photons.

A battery of cherub swords is easy to recognize if it is rotating, because the multiple exhausts are not perfectly aligned. Each exhaust points slightly outward, to aim its thrust axis at the ship's center of mass. As the battery rotates, its exhausts will periodically seem to brighten. It *twinkles.*

Twinkles are detected by a statistical trick called, *autocorrelation.* For example, the *Unexpected Finger* rotated once every 5.1 seconds, so one of its six engines rotated past every 5.1/6 = 0.85 seconds, shown by a spike at 0.85 seconds in the *Finger's* autocorrelation.

Earnest's display blanked, then it graphed the estimated autocorrelation for the new object, showing a clear spike at 0.85 seconds, just like the *Unexpected Finger*. The "spike" was really a broad hump, covering the range from 0.81-0.89 seconds. The hump would narrow into a proper spike as the telescope collected more photons to tighten its estimate.

But the hump didn't narrow. Instead, as Earnest watched in fascination, the hump's smooth summit grew ragged, then split into nine separate spikes. Earnest picked up his phone, and with a shaking finger he called the contact labeled, *CRY HAVOC. DO NOT CALL.* His voice quavered a little, but he spoke clearly enough to add one detail to the message sent by the illuminated red button.

Around the world, this caused additional activity.

Ten hours later
The *Lens*

600 feet beneath a Maryland chicken farm, the Big Screen showed a telescopic view of the approaching fleet.

The display revealed nothing useful, just starry sky with nine crosshairs, each pinpointing a patch of darkness.

The darkness was a relief. At this distance, optical telescopes had easily spotted the sunlight reflecting off the *Unexpected Finger*. The approaching ships must be much smaller.

Upon President Mirror's death, Vice President Hairline had been promoted to the expensive chair, which he now swiveled toward his comm officer. "Try the boy again."

The boy was 12 now. He had been the first Wyrm to meet with an Earth leader, and he was still the only Wyrm who would take the president's calls, sometimes. The *Lens* echoed with the sound of a phone ringing, then a click. "Hello?"

"This is the President of the United States."

"Oh, hi," said the boy. "What's up?"

"Young man, nine cherub-sword-powered craft are approaching the Earth. They have already passed the orbit of Mars."

"Ah, you noticed. They actually launched first, but they took a longer route to hide their exhaust."

President Hairline waved angrily, and the *Lens* quieted. "What are those ships doing?"

"Well, duh, they're bringing people to our colony."

The president recovered quickly. "How many people? How big are they?"

"They are all Narwhals, like the *Unexpected Finger,* but better. The *Finger* was the prototype Narwhal."

The *Lens* fell silent.

"You won't actually see them, until they get closer," the boy added. "They are covered with soot. That's why we painted the *Finger* white."

The president remained admirably calm. "This is a bit of a surprise."

"I told you we've dealt with wasps before. Did you really think we'd let you nuke *all* of us?"

President Hairline refrained from swearing, with some difficulty.

"Look, I have to go," said the boy. "I'm expecting a call."

The speakerphone clicked, then fell silent.

Beside the president, his best friend and national security adviser clutched her perfect hair. The president turned toward her, his expression thunderous.

"All this time," she moaned, "the *Unexpected Finger* was their clown."

November
The Pine Shack

Tom arrived at 7 AM and checked Sophie's whiteboard.

Black Silicone out
use clear

When speaking to customers,
do **NOT** hint that our
competitors accept free
integrated circuits from
chinese intelligence. This
means you, Frank.
Sophie

When Tom reached his office, he found the door open and Dominick Tork waiting inside.

Dominick had changed. He had never been flabby, but now he looked like flabby's nemesis.

"You've been lifting weights," Tom observed. "At least."

Now Dominick looked as muscular as the average Wyrm male. He displayed an impressive arm and flexed. "I feel like I've returned to high school, complete with acne and constant anger." He grinned. "I also crave sex all the time, and my cock gets hard for no good reason. Did you know I captained our varsity wrestling team?"

"I remember," said Tom. "Do you still wrestle?"

"I suppose you could say that. But enough small talk; tell me about your new building."

Tom chuckled. "The city permit office sent a memo to all their employees, forbidding them to talk to me because I don't respect their authority. A concrete inspector came out anyway. He showed me the memo, and we had a good laugh, then he found a serious concrete problem early and saved me a pile of money. That got him fired, which I think he wanted. He said he had to atone for his sins, so he could feel worthy to join the Wyrms."

"Excellent," said Dominick. "I'm pleased to see you prosper."

Tom looked doubtful.

"I'm quite sincere," Dominick added. "When a man has nothing to lose but his health, he behaves erratically. Such men must be restrained with precautions I find tedious. But you, to your credit, now have a great deal to lose."

Tom took his seat behind his desk. "Dominick, the Wyrms own 20 percent of my company. You can't threaten me anymore."

"Oh, I'm not threatening *you*. In fact, I'm quite fond of you, so I came to give you a head-up." Dominick handed over a sheaf of papers.

Tom took the papers warily. "What?"

"We've researched Wyrm psychology extensively. It turns out, they don't recognize people as property. Hence, they do not recognize a customer as, *my thing.*"

Tom sighed. "You figured out they aren't triggered when their customers are coerced."

Dominick beamed. "Dealing with you is such a pleasure."

Tom glanced at the sheaf of papers. The first page began with, WE HAVE DETERMINED YOU MAY BE IN VIOLATION. "You're sending these to my customers?"

"As a courtesy, we plan to remind your customers that products derived from Wyrm technology are inherently dangerous. Thus, any use of your remarkable polymers must regrettably subject them to enhanced regulatory scrutiny." Dominick looked concerned. "You borrowed quite a lot of money to build your factory. I hope you sell enough Wyrm polymer to stave off bankruptcy."

"Okay, Dominick, what do you demand?"

"I demand nothing; this is entirely voluntary. I'm planning a little trip, and I would enjoy your company."

"Oh, good." Tom dropped the papers on his desk, then leaned back and rested his feet on them. "I've always wanted to see Paris."

"You and I will fly to Australia together, to visit the Wyrm colony."

"Why? We don't have Wyrm tattoos, so we won't be allowed into any sensitive areas."

"Let me worry about that."

"You *will* have tattoos?" Tom looked surprised. "You'll face the burning bush and become a Wyrm? I didn't think you were the type."

"Dealing with you is such a pleasure," said Dominick. "You might be interested to know, the Wyrms are more numerous than we suspected, perhaps as many as 20,000."

Tom whistled. "Twenty *thousand?*" Then he saw Dominick's point. "Ah. They don't expect to recognize each other, so they wouldn't be surprised to see a stranger."

"All the more so because they are receiving a flood of Human immigrants. Nonetheless, given their history, the Wyrms must distrust unfamiliar faces. Thankfully, *your* face is well known to them and will surely divert the conversation into safe topics."

Tom didn't bother asking about his telescopic sentries, mounted throughout the new colony watching for imposters. He thought about his security guards, whiling away the long watch of the night with nothing to contemplate but the half-built sentries and their hourly wage.

"Our visit will entail an amusing irony," Dominick continued. "I hope it won't be wasted on you."

"Officially, you will be my Wyrm guide," Tom predicted. "While in reality, I will vouch for *you* and help you avoid faux pas."

"A sweet irony, is it not? I should require your help only briefly. Once I establish myself, you may return home. Plan on 15 days, counting travel."

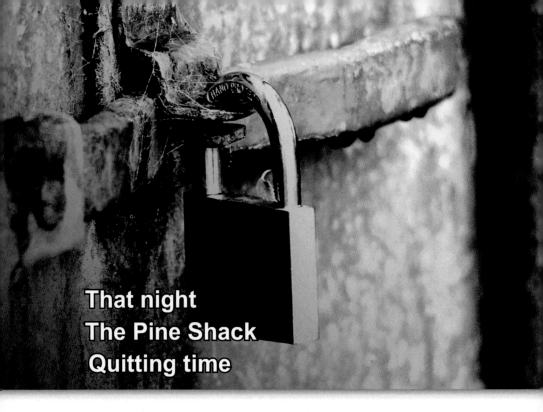

That night
The Pine Shack
Quitting time

Sophie finally finished auditing the production time cards at 8 PM. On her way out, she stopped to update her whiteboard.

<u>All Employees</u>

I understand a desire to kill Frank. However, this is not grounds for sick leave.

Sophie

Tom walked in. "I want to take you out for dinner, right now."

Sophie froze. "Okay," she replied in what she hoped was her normal voice. The last time Tom asked her to dinner had been before he had hired her. Since then, whenever she suggested it, he had always answered, *"Sorry, but this is where I eat."*

She would rather he had slapped her.

At the restaurant, their conversation was easy as always. Tom drank most of a bottle of wine, but as always, he kept his distance, never touching her. Then he ordered a double bourbon.

Sophie raised an eyebrow. "Tough day?"

"Not especially," Tom replied. "I just want to loosen up."

"*You* want to loosen up?"

"Does that surprise you?"

"Yes."

Tom tossed his drink and ordered another. "A thick skin is not something I have; it's just something I *do*. Maybe I need a break."

Sophie leaned forward and pressed the back of her hand to Tom's forehead. "You don't seem feverish. Are you feeling okay?"

"Cut it out." Tom pushed her hand away.

"Seriously," said Sophie. "What's up?"

"Seriously," said Tom, "I want to get drunk."

"Okay. I'll drive."

"I can afford an Uber now. You can get drunk with me."

"I don't think so," Sophie decided.

"You want to stay sober while I get drunk?" Tom gazed at his oldest friend. "This won't end well, but maybe that's what I need."

"I'll keep you company. Why are you getting drunk?"

"Because it's Karaoke night, and we're close enough to hear it." Tom downed his bourbon and ordered another.

Sophie shook her head. "We've known each other since diapers. You can't lie to me."

"So you think."

"So I know. And why would you bother? There's no point."

Tom stared into his drink. "What do you mean?"

"I mean, you don't *need* to lie to me." Sophie took a moment to build her courage, then she laid her hand over Tom's. "You and I are bound together as closely as two people can be."

"Halfsies on a Cleveland timeshare?" Tom pulled his hand away. "We never did that."

"You idiot."

"I know," said Tom. "You were my girl next door."

"No," said Sophie. "I mean we *created* something. We beat down obstacles and built real things, tangible things, and we are still doing it together. That binds a man and woman together more closely than *anything.* I know you feel it."

Tom considered. "No," he decided. "Family is closer."

"Family is more durable," Sophie allowed, "but not as tight. You don't seem to understand that, so you always hold me at a distance. You're terrified you won't live up to some masculine expectation, or some implied promise, so you are always so careful not to say anything personal. But you don't need to be careful with me."

"So, Sister Sophie, do you think I should admit I am afraid?"

"Sure," said Sophie. "Tell me you're afraid, or excited, worried, uncertain, even just horny. You *never* open up to me."

"No," Tom mused. "I don't. You're right."

"There was just that one time. You were tired and discouraged, so you let down your guard. You told me how you enjoyed hunting with your wife, but she hated it, so she sabotaged you."

"Oh, God." Tom held his head. "I told you about *hunting.*"

"And nothing bad happened," Sophie added. "You opened up to me, revealed something disgusting about yourself, and you thought I would hurt you. You were wrong."

Tom sighed.

Sophie pressed. "What's the point in getting drunk if you won't show your real self?"

Tom finished off his drink. "Maybe I want to."

Sophie waved at the waitress to bring another bourbon.

"I'm curious," Tom admitted. "What do you imagine I'm hiding?"

"Nothing nasty," she replied immediately. "When men open up, they all say the same stupid thing. But you have so much integrity, you'd never be one of those assholes who talks about how his wife is not enough for him, and he needs some on the side."

Tom contemplated his empty glass. "Sophie, take me home."

From any other man, that would have been a proposition. "Come on." Sophie hauled Tom to his feet.

Outside, as they walked through the darkened parking lot, Tom wobbled a bit, but didn't need help. "Have you gotten over Buff?"

Sophie's heart raced as she searched for the perfect answer. Finally, she settled on, "Ancient history."

"I'm sorry. I was hoping you two would find a way."

"You're just trying to distract me."

"Yep."

They reached Tom's well-used pickup truck, and he opened the driver's side door for her. Sophie started to climb in, then turned to face him instead. She stood rigid, willing her heart to beat slower as she humiliated herself for her first friend and now her only love. "Tom, I'm *over* Buffalo.*"

Tom didn't answer, only studied her face. Sophie stifled her urge to say more.

"Always open doors for whores," her old friend murmured, "but prim and proper, poke her pooper."

Before Sophie could decide if she was insulted, she was yanked forward at the waist. She arched awkwardly as her hips left her body behind, and she felt Tom's knuckles inside her jeans, dangerously far down her belly. Then his arm wrapped around her shoulders and drew her in against his surprisingly solid muscles. How had she not known he lifted weights? Then she forgot everything as he grabbed a handful of her hair and pressed his lips against hers. He drove her back, pinning her against his truck. She woofed with the impact, momentarily opening their kiss.

Sophie was shocked into immobility. She had known Tom his entire life, and this attack was inconceivable. Then he pressed his mouth against hers again, and she felt his hand run up under her blouse, pushing her bra roughly aside. She tried to resist, she tried to try, but her knees went weak and she melted into him.

When Tom finally paused to breathe, Sophie gasped. Tom let go of her breast. "Sophie, you're beautiful and smart." Then, to her astonishment, Tom grabbed her hand and pressed it to the front of his slacks. She jerked it away. He smiled faintly. "Just so you know I'm sincere."

Tom's physical attraction was obviously sincere. Nonetheless, Sophie foresaw a big *but.*

Tom pressed closer, until she smelled his whisky breath. "You were my girl next door, and my first kiss, and 30 years later, here we still are. What you *don't* know is, I have a sexual demand you would not accommodate, and it's not negotiable."

Sophie tried to take offense. She failed, and tried again. Fail again. Tom was obviously telling the simple truth, even though he omitted the crucial detail. "What sexual demand," she asked, genuinely curious.

"Do you trust me?"

"Yes."

"Then you should believe me. You *don't* want to learn the details." Tom did not actually move, but somehow he seemed to withdraw, retreating into the hazy distance while his meaningless parts pressed against her.

"No! This is too important!" Sophie wanted to clutch at him frantically, but they were already embraced, weren't they? "You have to trust me," she pleaded. "I'm not like other women."

Tom released her and dropped his keys on the hood. "I won't need the truck. Just leave it at the office."

He turned and strode back into the restaurant, and that was that.

Much later, Sophie realized it was actually *she* who had rejected *him.* He just wouldn't tell her why.

That comforted her a little.

Everyone was surprised when Tom missed a day of work. He spent the day running errands, then went to Mom's for dinner.

Scarlet was slicing the fixings, so Tom picked the wine. "Remember when you taught me the Combover Rule? You told me I couldn't lie worth a damn, but I could keep my mouth shut."

Scarlet ripped open a bag of onions. "You were so serious."

"Was that true? Was I actually good at keeping secrets?"

"Not really. But when I said you were, I could see your little gears turning as you decided to live up to it. After that, I was pretty sure you wouldn't blab and get me thrown in jail."

"Do you remember my first kiss?" Tom drove in the corkscrew.

"Of course I remember. It was your first kiss, so I let you choose the target. You picked the girl next door, Sophie Flint."

"When I kissed her, she kicked me and called me an asshole."

"A harbinger of her future affections." Scarlet dropped an onion onto her cutting board.

"It was *her* first time too. I didn't realize it at the time, but she only kicked me because I ruined it. I was terrified, so I hesitated, and half-assed her first kiss."

"Of course you were terrified. She was your first kiss."

"You never let on that I had failed," said Tom. "In fact, you made me believe getting kicked was part of the plan. That was merciful. Thank you."

"I couldn't build your confidence by pointing out you got kicked for lacking it, and besides, the plan *did* work, to both our sorrow." Scarlet slammed her knife into the onion. "That cold-hearted bitch *still* hasn't gotten over you."

"Ah, happy memories." Tom popped out the cork. "Sophie hit on me again. She came on to me in classic Sophie style, by complaining about what I wasn't giving her."

"I hope you let her down easy. Her parents still live next door, so please don't poop where I eat."

"I tried." Tom poured out two glasses of wine. "I took her to dinner. Afterward, outside in the parking lot, she screwed up her courage and threw herself at me. I didn't want to hurt her feelings, so I fly-pulled her and felt her up."

"You fly-pulled *Sophie Flint?*" Scarlet threw the onion at him. "Just when you're finally about to make some money? Have you lost your mind?"

Tom dodged the onion, and held up a placating hand. "Mom, I can't be sued, and can you imagine working with a Sophie scorned? I had to convince her *she* was rejecting *me.*"

"Hmm." Scarlet sniffed. "After all these years, the dragon finally shows the ice princess his teeth. I wish I could have watched."

"Sophie is actually my closest friend." Tom gazed at the onion rolling around the old linoleum floor of his childhood. "How pathetic is that."

"Thomas, you can make *any* woman want you, if she hangs around you long enough to realize what you are."

"Thank you, Mom." Tom recovered the onion, and handed it to her with a glass of wine. Then he turned on the television, muted the sound, and selected a news channel. "Sorry for the distraction, but I'm about to start making real money, so I have a bullseye on my chest. I have to watch for mobs gathering."

The television showed a promo picture of a Pine robotic sentry. It was captioned, *WYRM COLONY USES HUMAN-MANUFAC-TURED ROBOT TO IDENTIFY, EXCLUDE HUMANS.*

Scarlet winced. "So, what about Internet dating? Why not try it?"

"I did. Attractive women are flooded with offers, so they have to screen their prospects."

Scarlet sipped her wine in silence.

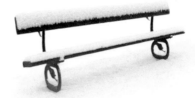

"Relax," said Tom. "I'll say it for you. Women screen for height, then they look at the face pic. For a man like me, internet dating is not much fun. My only hope is one of those rich-guy-only dating sites. What kind of girls do you think I'll find there?"

"You'll find actresses, just not the ones who will stay in character for 40 years. Thomas, you are a handsome man."

Tom smiled. "I think you actually believe that. Unfortunately, other women can't see me through a mother's eyes, so I have to be rich."

Scarlet changed the subject. "Speaking of actresses, what's up with Luci Dark? Is she still tormenting Frank?"

"Luci left for their colony, but she'd already stopped insulting Frank. She said it was pointless, once she was convinced it didn't hurt him. Those were pretty much her exact words."

"Wow. She is a serious bitch."

"I was impressed." said Tom."What do you think of Wyrm culture?

"If a woman flirts, a Wyrm man will take her by *force.*" Scarlet grinned. "What's not to love?"

"Other than the sex, have you thought about their philosophy?"

Scarlet's grin vanished. "As far as I can tell, their philosophy is, *keep your fucking hands off me.* It's the opposite of their sex life."

"That about sums it up," said Tom. "*Keep your fucking hands off me, except for sex.* Do you think that's a good philosophy?"

"No, I do not."

"I didn't think so." Tom contemplated his unfinished wine. "I have to go."

At the door, Tom hugged his mother a little longer and tighter than usual. "I wrote a little speech, and here it is. I intend to spend most of my new money on girls and mansions, but I owe you a big debt for your courage. You defied your culture and even risked arrest to teach me the truth, which is not easy for a woman." He offered her a set of keys. "So I'm giving you my car."

She refused the keys. "Thank you, my ungrateful son, but I don't want your pickup truck. No offense, but it's a piece of shit." She opened the door, looked at the driveway, and said, "Oh."

"I would never give you my *truck.* You weren't that good a mom." Tom jingled the car keys. "I don't have all day. Do you want a Miata, or not?"

After a 28-hour flight and a three-hour jeep drive, Frank and Earnest stood at the railing of an observation platform, looking down into the nascent Wyrm colony.

The valley echoed with the yammer of construction. From here, Frank could see three of the walled havens: *Dying Mudhole, Moldy Cellar,* and *Mistake.* He knew twelve more havens were growing beyond the horizon. Dark clouds loomed overhead.

Earnest looked away, so he missed the initial strike, but he noticed his second shadow and turned to see a white beam lancing down through the overcast to spear an angry squid on the ground, each thrusting tentacle a smoke trail of what must be car-sized flying debris. Earnest stumbled back. "Holy Fuck!"

Frank chuckled. "That jet is *rising* from the ground. Someone lit off a cherub-sword tunneler."

The low clouds retreated from the beam's intolerable touch, and Earnest's visual monkeys reconsidered. Now, they saw an incandescent column of iron atoms spouting *upward* from a fountain of destruction. He whistled.

"That visible beam is just the placeholder. Cherub-sword tunnelers dig so fast, the blowback throws them off the hole, even with 300 tons of armor. They need that second sword firing backward to hold them down." Frank frowned. "The placeholder is shooting almost straight up, so the cutting jet must be pointed straight down. How deep does he want to dig?"

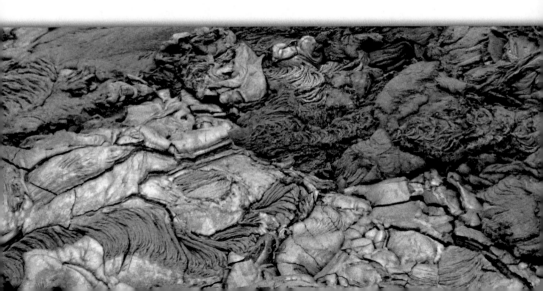

Earnest shaded his eyes. "Maybe he's fusing the dirt into a stone wall foundation, and he wants it *deep* to keep out the evil wasps. Why do all the Wyrm havens have awful names?"

"They're afraid to promise more than they can deliver," said Frank. "How are things going for you? Are you enjoying life?"

"My life is *sweet.* I'm a lock for tenure, and my vita is so long, smart chicks are giving it up easy."

"Good for you. What do you think of the Wyrm philosophy?"

"Their *philosophy?"* Earnest snorted. "You seriously think a normal Human could believe that crap?"

Frank gazed at the beacon of white flame rising into a perfect circle of blue sky. "How would I know?"

Earnest nodded absently, and they watched the show awhile.

"Earnest," Frank said eventually, "I want to tell you, collaborating with you was easy. I know I never said it, but you're a good partner."

"Aw, how sweet," said Earnest. "So you're finally admitting you're gay? I knew it, when I saw you got back into shape."

Sophie approached a gate in a Wyrm haven's 25-foot wall of fused stone.

The 15-foot steel door was guarded by two Pine robotic sentries and two humans, a man and a woman sitting at a folding table. The woman ran out to hug Sophie. "Welcome home!"

Sophie did not hug her back.

The greeter disengaged and offered a bottle of water. "My name is Tina. I'm so glad you came."

"Thanks," said Sophie. "My name is Sophie Flint."

"Oh, hello, Sophie. Luci is expecting you." The greeter waved to her companion. "Open up."

The steel gate began to swing ponderously open.

Fifteen minutes later, Sophie settled into a reclining camp chair in a small, white tent with Luci and a potted cactus.

Luci tore the wrapper off a plastic mouth guard, the type boxers wear to protect their teeth. "Are you ready?"

"Ask me in an hour." Sophie tucked the guard into her mouth.

"It is my honor to be doyen for your crowbar," Luci recited. "When you look into your own mind for the first time, you should not care what *I* expect you to see, so I will leave before the fruit strikes you."

Sophie didn't really want to be alone, but Luci must know what was coming.

Luci produced a pair of pliers and twisted a needle off the potted cactus. "When your censor retreats and you see yourself, you might wish to reflect on your most painful memories, especially from childhood. Your new perspective might bring you comfort."

Sophie nodded absently.

"You will walk your own path, as you should." Luci wrapped a cord around Sophie's arm, just above the elbow. She found the vein easily. Then she tossed the needle onto the ground, untied the soft cord, and took Sophie's wrist.

"Your pulse is strong," she said three minutes later, and departed.

Sophie sat nervously, and wondered what she would think.

An hour later, Sophie emerged from the tent. Luci was there, waiting alone on a bench made for two.

Sophie sat beside the Wyrm, sightless eyes glistening. "It was the last thing I expected."

Luci waited quietly.

"I see every child I could have birthed, laughing and playing and *living*, and my grandchildren, *lifetimes* of joy and pain and discovery I could have created." Sophie doubled over, gripping her head with both hands. "Their lives would have been terrible and wonderful and *long*, if I hadn't casually smothered them, every time I said *no* to sex. How can I have been so selfish?"

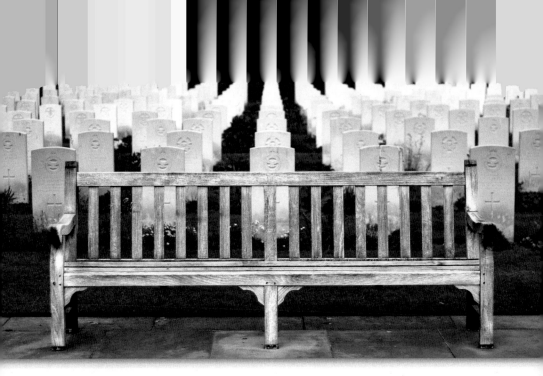

Luci patted the Human's leg.

Sophie raised her face, wet with tears. "But how can I want children, when they ruin everything? My career, my friendships, my marriage, even my body. How can I... I don't want this choice."

Luci offered a box of Kleenex. "Any moment now, the serpent will be released to comfort you. Tomorrow, this memory will feel like a dream."

Something rumbled and the ground shook. Sophie looked up and saw the looming clouds brighten. A tear dripped, unnoticed, down her cheek. "I want Buff, but I could never really own him."

"No, you cannot own a Wyrm man, not in the way you want."

"I know you could change me." Sophie spoke slowly, feeling her way. "You could rearrange my brain to turn me into Buff's willing partner. I would be his cheerleader, and I would be settling for less than the dominance I was built for. I don't want to be a Wyrm."

Luci seemed sad, but not surprised. Somewhere, a dog barked.

"Oh, God." Sophie sat up straighter and wiped her eyes. "All these years, how did I not notice I'm a bitch?"

Tom and Dominick finally huffed up to the crest of the last ridge, and gratefully shrugged off their backpacks.

Dominick cracked open a bottle of warm water and drank greedily as they looked down into *Putrid Cesspit,* an embryonic Wyrm haven.

Both men were fit, but their clandestine approach had required a grueling, three-day hump through arid brush, racing to thread the last gap in the 196-mile land border before it was closed by Australian fence teams. Tom leaned on his walking stick and breathed. "We should have come by boat, or bought a Land Rover."

Tom's stick was too heavy, and in truth, it was a nuisance, but a walking stick seemed proper when hiking through the Outback.

Down below, Putrid Cesspit was completely encircled by a 25-foot wall of fused stone, but the structures inside were only skeletons surrounded by tents.

The wind carried sounds of construction. Overhead, dark clouds loomed. A few men queued up outside the wall before a massive steel gate. Two Pine sentries loomed over them, searching for imposters wearing tattoos they hadn't earned.

Dominick was dressed like the men below, in soft canvas pants, a heavy holster, and a bag of gold coins. His jacket looked like a well-tailored martial artist's outfit, tied with four sashes. His cheek bore the five Wyrm tokens, in green to complement his hazel eyes.

"Are you *sure* you want to do this," Tom asked. "You can't threaten the Wyrms with an EPA audit."

Dominick smiled. "Working with you is such a pleasure."

"Uh oh." Tom pointed toward the gate. "They know you're coming."

"What?" Dominick stepped forward, "How can you tell?"

Tom's walking stick was a steel-tipped shovel handle. It was too thick, it was too heavy, and it was halfway through its humming arc. Tom held it in a baseball batter's grip, and grunted with the effort.

A good baseball player can whip the tip of his 30-inch bat to nearly 100 MPH. Tom could swing the first 30 inches of his stick about as well as he could swing a baseball bat, but he was tired and stressed and only managed 70 MPH, a decent bat speed for a 15-year-old boy.

The stick's 30-inch mark lay midway down its length. At the 60-inch point, the 14-ounce steel tip levered up to 130 MPH before commencing its 2,000-gravity deceleration, traveling another four inches while it matched velocity with Dominick Tork's head.

Dominick's ear intersected Tom's walking stick at what turned out to be the sweet spot, 11 inches behind the weighted steel. The impact made a cracking sound, but the ashwood did not crack.

In a quirk of physics, fast-moving objects do more damage when they survive the collision.

Dominick Tork dropped silently to the rocky ground. His mouth yawned open and his body twitched.

Tom stood over him and raised the stick, but not like a bat. This time, he held it like a post-hole digger. His heart raced, but his voice was calm. "Every time we met, you led with the stick. Maybe you should have tried the carrot."

From the haven below, a spear of white light burst skyward to pierce the clouds. The gray overhang recoiled from its incandescent touch, clearing a path to blue sky.

"And you *really* should not have shoved me onto the ground and stolen my lunch in second grade," Tom added as he drove his steel-tipped stick downward to pierce all of Dominick Tork's future ambitions. "Did you think I would forget?"

Somewhere amid the sounds of construction, a dog began to bark.

Tom closed his eyes and leaned on the stick. It wiggled in his grip as Dominick's body thrashed.

By the time the wiggling stopped, Tom felt almost normal, though perhaps a few years younger. He opened his eyes and pulled out his pocketknife.

Three minutes later, in the 43rd year of his life, early in the Northern Hemisphere's Autumn, Tom Pine considered dropping Dominick's tattooed head into his pack. The head still dripped blood, so he decided to leave it on his walking stick like a popsicle. He shrugged into his backpack, hoisted the head-on-a-stick over his shoulder, and started down the trail to something different.

The Series

Gaia's Wasp

Dandelion Slap

Sainthood in Sixty Seconds

A Beast Cannot Feign

If God says, Pull My Finger...

Image Credits

All images used with permission, but the models and photographers do not endorse this book and most would be horrified. To make it worse, some images have been modified by me.